THE UNSPEAKABLE
A N D   O T H E R S

THE UNSPEAKABLE
A N D   O T H E R S

Dan Clore

Afterword by

S.T. Joshi

WILDSIDE PRESS
NEW JERSEY • CALIFORNIA • OHIO • NEW YORK

*This book is dedicated to all those who
lack the courage to look in the mirror.*

THE UNSPEAKABLE AND OTHERS

Texts in this volume have previously appeared in *The Urbanite,
Deathrealm, Terminal Fright, Lore, Epitaph, Black October Magazine,
Cyber-Psychos AOD, Cosmic Visions, The NetherReal, Creatio ex
Nihilo, Cthulhu Sex, Mythos Online, Dragon et Microchips: Le Seul
Fanzine Qui Rêve, Necrofile: The Review of Horror Fiction, Weird
Times,* and *The Last Continent: New Tales of Zothique.*

An original publication of Wildside Press. For more information,
contact:

Wildside Press
PO Box 45
Gillette, NJ 07933. For
www.wildsidepress.com

Contents

Oddments and Oddities

Introduction

S.T. Joshi

The tradition of prose-poetry—or, more generally, what might be called the Asianic style, or the style that features lush, dense description, elaborate sentence-structure, and an atmosphere of poetic incantation—is not strong in English literature. John Lyly (*Euphues*), Sir Thomas Browne, Samuel Johnson, Edward Gibbon, Thomas Babington Macaulay, Oscar Wilde, Walter Pater, H. P. Lovecraft, Clark Ashton Smith (probably the best prose-poet in English)—after these writers are named, one searches with difficulty for others to join their ranks.

It is to the work of these writers that Dan Clore's own tales and sketches bear closest analogies. It should come as no surprise that Clore, one of the most perspicacious of modern critics of supernatural fiction, draws heavily upon Lovecraft and Smith. The echoes of Lovecraft's "The Outsider" in "The Unspeakable" and "Skull of Ghoul;" the nod to "The Dunwich Horror" in "Beneath the Abyss;" the borrowing of the title of "The Abomination of Desolation" from a prose-poem of Smith's; the utilization of Smith's invented realms of Atlantis, Zothique, and Hyperborea in "The Emperor Ausso," "The Connoisseur of Corpses," and "Mouth of the Gaw"—all these and many other tips of the hat to the twentieth century's chief exponents of the Asianic style are scattered throughout this volume. Was it not Lovecraft himself who scorned the "machine-gun fire" of Hemingway, and who recognized the value of a well-placed adjective? Now that writers like Thomas Pynchon and Gore Vidal have shown what can be done with adjectives, adverbs, and conjunctions, we may perhaps be less intolerant of prose that fails to adhere to the barebones aridity of Hemingway and Sherwood Anderson.

What is also refreshing in Clore's work is a misanthropy as rare in literature as the Asianic style itself. Here one can only look to some of the darkest satirists of the past two millennia—Juvenal, Jonathan Swift, Arthur Schopenhauer, Ambrose Bierce, and Shirley Jackson almost exhaust the catalogue. The idea that we are required to extend benevolence to human beings merely because they are human beings is one of the deepest and most irrational prejudices in human thought. Let us recall Lovecraft: "may not all mankind be a mistake—an abnormal growth—a disease in the system of Nature—an excrescence on the body of infinite progression like a wart on the human hand? Might not the total destruction of humanity, as well as of all animate creation, be a positive *boon* to Nature as a whole?" Whether Clore agrees with this remark is only for him to say; but that misanthropy is at the heart of all the tales of Lord Weÿrdgliffe can hardly be gainsaid.

Clore's work might seem intolerably forbidding were it not leavened with a rich dose of parody, including self-parody. He himself becomes a character in his own work in "Rejection Letter." The parodies of science fiction ("A Cavern in the Sky"), fairy tales ("The Eunuchorn"), and, most delightful of all, Lovecraft's Cthulhu Mythos ("The Dying God," "Twilight of the Elder Gods," and many items in "Oddments and Oddities")—or, shall we say, the self-parody the Mythos has already become in the hands of Lovecraft's self-styled disciples and imitators—are among the most delightful items in this volume.

Work of this density and texture had best be read in small doses. The incantatory prose of, say, *"Mare Tenebrarum"* must be savored to be appreciated. Our attention-deficit-disorder culture is not conductive to slow absorption; but it is the only way to gain the fullest measure of satisfaction from the tales and vignettes of Dan Clore. With this volume we encounter that rarest of literary experiences: work that makes us unsure whether to question the author's sanity or our own.

Tales from the Unspeakable

The Unspeakable

"Since everyone else has perished under the moth-fluttered beams of your all-penetrative gaze—And only I remain, living now, here in this castle—Allow me to accept your noxious and pestilential presence as my sole companion. The only one that I've ever known, aside from the creeping worm of unsolaceable solitude and the crawling vermin of ineluctable loneliness—Your sere face—From somewhere, from someworld, a sunken memory of your visage arises within my asphyxiating consciousness—Your etiolate frame—Everyone else dead now—Hunched-over thinness—Withered skin and hyaena-like incisors—Thin as a skeleton's etiolate emaciation—Those glassy eyes—Like pallid pools in gleaming phosphorescent glooms—Yellowed by no jaundice—Yes, I remember your visage from—But I can't place it. Yes, I accept you as my sole companion—The only one that I've ever known—That visage—Yes, the hideous exhalations of your eyeballs have slain everything, even the cachinnating chorus of echo—" ("Ohhh—") "has now utterly perished. That visage—Yes, I accept its presence as my sole companion—But I remember—That image of utter despair, the dripping eidolon of everything unholy and unhoped-for—Yes, I accept, as my sole companion, that unspeakable epiphany of everything unclean, uncanny, and unkempt!—

"Allow me, then, to introduce myself, since you keep your eyes (those eyes!–) fixated upon my own, as keenly poignant as the pallid heat of grinding tongs in some divine tormenter's grasp–I have no memories of Others after the very first, when the face of Maternity's (*was* it Maternity's?–) mocking voice stooped over me and muttered the single word *Câchemaur*, which, so I take it, represents my name. That name has sounded and re-sounded, ever since that primordial era, through the caverns of my insomnia's sibilant, sibylline, whispering voice. The place had no light, save for the glimmerings of luminescent fungi and phosphor. That, and the torches and candlesticks that I found ly-ing about the place, and sometimes chose to make use of–when I felt I could stomach the vision of my surroundings. The place, the castle, had endless, winding labyrinths of corridors and stair-ways, of dungeons and iron gratings, of rotting armor and de-cay-inhabited storerooms, of bloodstained walls and decrepit tapestries. Outside, the place resembled a swamp, with shifting mists and stunted trees jutting out of the waist-deep and greyish brack of the waters. That visage–Yes, I accept–That face–I hate–

"Sometimes, nauseated by the vaporous miasmata that slowly suffused the castle like worms in a cadaver, I tried to find some way beyond the marshy vault. Above, no sun or moon's orb shone down through the wall of faintly-glowing haze and misty cloudwisps, nor did any rain drip down from those hanging, groaning clouds. Nightwind and eternal crepuscule moaned and slowly swept through the green-litten vault. But the marsh merely ended against some sheer cliff's face, that rose unclimbably above, into the mists. Those glassy eyes–I remem-ber–But no, I don't–

"I nourished my body on the squealing of rats, and the creeping of soft white things that squirmed through the layer of sediment that covered the castle's flagstones, and the many-legged crawling hairy things, and the blackwinged fliers that seemed to appear as from the mists above. I nourished my mind (if I dare call it such!) on the mould-encrusted, hidden manuscripts and tomes I found stacked on shelves in various rooms of the château. Reading these (and who taught me how to read?), I imagined the people described therein and their actions, and imagined myself like them, as one of them. Now, I know the truth all too well to imagine such!—(Or do I?—) I acted as a knight, and even smashed in the skull—using a bar from a rust-encrusted, broken gate's grill, since I had no other sword—of one of the unmoving persons that I found under the mud a few paces from the gates (they call these persons *dead*, or so I understand—) I found myself wishing that I too had a nice wooden box to sleep in, lined with soft silken cushions, like the ones they had, although the boards had started to rot, or more than started—Pretending to defend, thus, an Other, which I believed to have recognized as a woman, by certain differences from myself—(there wasn't much left to go by!—)

It didn't work!—No, she (if indeed I identified it as a *she* correctly—) showed no signs of gratitude for that gallant and valiant deed!—

"But I digress—I found no way past the swamp, nor did the passageways and daedal corridors in the castle allow of egress to any other place—But once, outside the gate, in the swamp, I noticed a tower—a tower which, it seemed, I must never have ascended, or discovered, in all of my searches and peregrinations through the structure's labyrinthine windings—a tower, that rose up through the mists into the cloudy haze of the vaulting sky. Well did I mark the location of that new and alien feature. My imagination depicted to me scenes in which, from the tower's height, I discovered a way to go beyond the swamp and beheld the shining lights from above described in several of the many books I'd just read through, for the hundredth time—And some companion for me—Some displacement or dislocation from my

ghastly isolation—Some *Other*—That visage—Those glassy eyes—
Worm of unsolaceable solitude of ineluctable corridors and stair-
ways of loneliness—

"Inside, I looked at the site in which I thought some stairway
or ladder must allow of ascension to the tower. I searched. I
couldn't find it!—I despaired—I screamed—No one heard—I came
to the room in which I'd read so many volumes—To kill the consciousness of my own existence—I screamed—I tore the books
from their shelves—I struck the wall with the iron bar—It broke
through!—Beyond—A room filled with broken bricks and débris.
They must have been hiding some stairwell. I began to empty the
room of the bricks. I had to take care not to let the pile fall onto
me. Beneath the bricks I found more of the unmoving persons—More of the *dead*—I dug faster—I cleared the chamber.
Some companion—

"The chamber stood empty. I perceived, I noticed, the wood
of a trapdoor in the ceilingstone above. Stubs of wood stuck out
of the ceiling and flooring where once a ladder must have stood. I
brought in a table to stand on so that I could reach the trapdoor.
It creaked and dropped a pile of rubbish and unmoving persons—Nearly crushed me—I leapt down and aside—Found the going, more difficult, from then on—Cleared, several stories of the
tower—That tower, didn't have any windows—Moth-filled beams—
Asphyxiating consciousness—That face I hate— Nightwind—Castle—The cobweb-patterned corridors and stairwells of loneliness—

"At last, I reached the final level of the tower. Climbed up
through a trapdoor. I looked around. Light struck up against my
eyes with resplendent blindingness. I shielded my two burning
pupils and looked around—I looked down at the ground—It was-
n't more than three or four feet away!—I jumped down to
it—Stones stood jutting up from the dirt. I read names on them—I
wondered where the persons bearing those names might have

gone—If I could find them—Maybe one of the women named—(I could recognize that they were women by the illuminatory and significative power of the blazoning beacon of grammar—a much more reliable guide than the phantasm of physiognomy's faint and flickering will-o'-the-wisp—) But oblivion has eternally effaced their names from the silent cenotaphs of my memory—If one of them, might happen to offer me, the companionship, that the unmoving one below—Had failed to offer—Trees waved their branches fantastically about me—Shadows against the unveiled sky—No, I don't—I cannot—

"In the distance I discerned the shape of a castle's outline—Headed towards it, across the ground I'd never known before. Half-blind I dragged my body inside. I indistinctly discerned the forms of moving persons. It seemed to me that I recognized them as, as, as *happy*—I knew the characteristics of that quality by the laughter and other cheerful noises I recalled from the crumbling books I'd read—The unmoving persons never made those sounds—Not with me near them—I sometimes thought I could hear them making them amongst themselves, when the nightwind's complaints left me in doubt of whether I lived amidst the ruins of nightmare or insomnia—I went towards them—I had finally found an Other—

"I don't know what happened next—The stinking sting—The stunning stench of putrefaction stung and stank in my nostrils—I shielded my eyes with one hand and held out the other to the moving ones—Their gaiety had disappeared—Costumes and masks—I recall—I went towards a woman—She fell back—Her eyes turned into sunken craters—She fell—Smouldering carrion—Her flesh crept and her skin crawled away in horror—I knew not the cause—I saw more of them—The man with her also fell—He clutched his forehead—His skull cracked open and something red spilled out onto the flagstones—Smoking and choking—Bubbles—Froth—Never knew the unmoving ones to act that way—

"All, everyone I found, with my dimmed sight, collapsed thus into the dilapidation of the human frame—The stench—Intoxicated me, drowned me, inebriated me, transported me above the reeking vaults of loneliness up to the corrosive moons of despair—I couldn't count the people dropping and squirming—putrescent—splitting apart in desiccation—No memory of that visage arises—Nothing in the books resembled this, I thought—Everyone fell in ecstasies of miasmatic convulsions—Gargoyles' sneering grins crumbled into dust—A hunchbacked dwarf, whom I took for a freak, present for the entertainment of the moving ones—(Read something like that in the books once—) Fell laughing—Vomited black, atrabilarious merriment and splenetic mirth—Then he slashed his throat—With a knife—And his wrists—And fell—Something red flowed—And stopped moving—

"The place lies strewn with the skeletons of some phantasmagorical orgy—The chastising purification of all-chastening putrefaction—A primaeval chaos of elementary eradication—That visage—Yes—The whirling vortex of—The dripping eidolon of—I hate—Worm of unsolaceable light in the universe—Utterly annihilate—Solitude of ineluctable glass—

"Finally I saw you here at the end of this hall—The mystery of their annihilation became apparent—The double hells of your infernal eyes—I don't know whether or not to call the former inhabitants of this castle *dead*, even though they don't move any more—Not after their seething agonies and contortions of esoteric revelation—But I rather incline—That face—I rather incline—To the view that you alone—I rather incline—That you alone—That you alone truly deserve the vermiculate blazon of that eldritch and darksome epithet—That you—That you, alone, are truly *dead*—

"Since I need some Other, and you too, perhaps, need some Other—And no one else could stand up under the horrific beams of your sulphureous eyeballs—Those monstrous eyes that exhale moth-filled cones of gaseous, mephitic vapors like twin beacons of solitude—That face I hate—Yes, I accept—My sole companion—But, some memory arises, of those twin pools, of those abyssal onyx pupils—That visage—Glassy eyes of moon-staring hatred—But some memory arises—Those ebony suns of everkilling rays—The slain ghosts of faded phantoms disintegrate—

"Yes, now I have placed that memory. I recognize that visage now—That face I hate—Yes, I recall it now—When I wanted water to drink—I took a torch with me—Looked down into the pool in the courtyard—(Can't drink from the swampy morasses outside—Too many leeches!—) That deathlike face rose up to meet me—I shuddered and ran—Fear of the corpse—Came back—Again—That deathlike face—I never drank, except in the dark, since then—(I thought that if I couldn't see it, then it couldn't see me—) Reading I found a story—Someone looked into a pool—And he fell in love with the one he saw—He saw his—Reflection!—His—Reflection!—The mystery—solved!—resolved!—Now the same—That same face—

"I wish that the twin coffinlids of my eyeballs were nailed shut over those double optical graves—Eternally occulting them from everything external and exterior—Or that I could extinguish every source of light in the universe—Utterly annihilate the suns and stars of everywhere—Of everyworld—Of all the inverted, idiotic abysses—Since, without one, or the other, of these conditions being fulfilled, I might yet, again, someday, come across this mirror, again—See that face, I hate—Nothing left now, but to smash this, looking-glass—

"The mere image of an appearance's semblance doesn't always convey the most accurate and meaningful formulation of the corresponding reality's mordant bite—And its mocking, ironic, spasmodic, lugubrious, precipitous interment and inhumation of all abstraction and intellect—

"So that the cobweb-patterned fragments of my image might more accurately reflect the fractured hatred and horror that gnaw wastingly away at my despair and my solitude—

"Yes, nothing left now—The iron bar acquits itself of its duty, well enough—Just as on the *dead* man's skull—Cobweb-patterned—

"*That—Face!—*"

—Lord Weÿrdgliffe, the Waughters.

The Unknown Elixir

Take a Coëtanean dog and an Armenian bitch, join them together, and those two will beget for you a male puppy of celestial hue: and that puppy will guard you in your house from the beginning, in this World and in the Other.

What the hell was that supposed to mean? Elssinore had discovered many cryptic statements in the Bibliothèque de l'Abbaye de Saint-Crapauld, but the words of Hali, Philosopher and King of Arabia, as set forth in his Secret, tended to exceed the others in the obscurity of the symbolism of their Qabalahistic ciphers. He felt exceedingly inclined to put the volume in with those which he had finished studying, but that grouping now included all save the one he now held in his hand, which he had set aside more than once, to read later on, when he should have the background knowledge required to sound its mysteries more fully. But at this point, he realized that nothing lay in the study of the subject of the philosopher's stone but futility.

It did not correspond to the truth, then:—the rumor which had circulated through the village of Ximes for a century, that whoever had the daring to explore the secret recesses of the library of the ruinous Abbaye de Saint-Crapauld should find out the mystery. But after reading every tome that resided in that monastery, he had not discovered that, the dream of which, had excited his brain from the earliest days of his life. Must he then give up, a failure?

As these thoughts traversed the corridors of his consciousness, he heard a rumbling sound as of an enormous belching. Again, the eructation re-echoed. And again, for a third time. It seemed to have come from directly beneath him. But nothing, he knew, lay beneath that chamber, at the bottom of the abbey. He crouched, and began to dig at the edges of the flagstone beneath him, which soon came loose. Once some seven or eight flags had been removed, a great hole gaped in the floor. He gazed down, holding his lantern to see into that sunless abyss, deeper than the well of Democritus (as his scholar's mind put it), and he discerned within the dark recesses the formless bulk of a couchant mass. The mass stirred a little, and put forth a huge and toad-shaped head. A nauseating foetor rose up to greet him. The abomination's eyelids fluttered as it glanced up with lambent coals inside two narrow slits, and then it spread seraphic wings and slowly arose, not moving its wings. A nimble and iridescent aureole surrounded the warts and wrinkles of its greenish and glistening skin.

The obvious realization occurred to the young man: this creature, whatever its nature, must know the secret. He inquired of it whether that were the case or no.

The thing, pot-bellied and crouching in the posture of a statue of the Buddha, replied that, from its appearance, one might better judge it an anti-Midas than an alchemist; that changing gold into lead might better match its talents than the converse; and that it might, through its mere touch and not through any expertise in the spagyric arts, mutate the known universe into a shapeless dungheap relieved only by rivulets of bilious slime and oceans of foetid ochre. It clutched its écru underbelly, turned a little bit to its left, and launched a jet of acrid vomit filled with still-living slugs, worms, and woodlice which soiled the several piles of books that lay scattered thereabouts as they crept away in a daze.

But the youth knew the sort of ruse to expect from such a one. For all of the authorities avow that the philosopher's stone (which some, in their ignorance, have foolishly mislabeled the sorcerer's stone), the elixir, does not make vulgar gold, but rather, what they picturesquely term philosopher's gold. This constitutes not a means to gain gaudy trinkets, unworthy of a superior mind, not wholly confined to the material, but rather, it confers enlightenment and immortality upon the one who drinks it, finely powdered and mixed with liquor. Furthermore, an unsightly appearance could not rule out the being's knowledge: for do not the Holy Scriptures describe the Omnipotent in even more fearsome, if not outright uncanny and eldritch, terms? And do not the more redoubtable Elder Ones exceed even that depiction, in terms both of dreadfulness and arcane knowledge?

Yes, but how did the youth know that he did not find himself face to face with a demon?

And if he did? Does not the word demon reflect its own proper etymology and meaning, from the Greek daimon or daemon, such as the universally admired Daimon of Socrates, as set forth by Apuleius, in his work of that title? And does not this in turn correspond with the Augoeides of Pythagoras, (consult his Life, by Iamblichus, perhaps in a less-bestained copy than the one over there), and the Holy Guardian Angel of Abramelin, portrayed in the book of his Sacred Magick, given by Abraham the Jew unto his son Lamech? Which demonstrates well enough its inability to tell its client a falsehood, does it not?—

The entity conceded the argument, and admitted that it had the much sought-after récipé. But it could only reveal it on a certain condition. The recipient must know that: while, truly enough, his brain would never cease functioning, nor his heart pumping blood, the elixir carries, as well—a terrible burden. For the youth, once he had partaken of it, would "become as a sign unto the generations of men, of what human life means, and what it can become, if it were only to reach its ultimate fulfillment."

The youth readily consented, finding the latter condition not at all unwelcome. He could hardly do any less, after all, for his fellows. The thing described the process, which for good reason we will not detail in this place—not wishing to compromise the reader—and departed on motionless wings, leaving a trail of unctuous and ebullient slime in its wake.

* * * * *

The deserted abbey became a series of laboratories for the next nine months. Flashes of lightning illuminated the building's ruins, and innumerable alembics and retorts filled the rooms where monks had formerly slept. Finally, the pregnant pot gave forth with the stone, and the young man's project had succeeded. He ground the stone, which had the size and shape of the ball of dung impelled by the radiant scarab-beetle, not a well-known species in those latitudes, in a mortar. He mixed the powder with a bottle of red wine, which he had purchased in Ximes, at the onset of his researches, sparing no expense, so as to celebrate his victory at the same time as he should consummate it. He swallowed the bottle in a single draught.

There appeared to Elssinore's vision the creature which had previously given him the récipé, as it alighted from a flight on its hesitant wings; and as he felt the potion take effect, his vision blurred, and when he cleared his eyes, instead of the unknown monstrosity he beheld waves of greyed hair and the billows of a wrinkled forehead. The identity of the human before him had been plainly revealed to his consciousness by the defaced features of the man's defeatured face. For, while travelling from the

Faroe Islands on their way to France, he and his parents had stopped over in England, and there they had heard the frightful Legend of Lord Weÿrdgliffe, who from his earliest years had never laughed like others did. The Legend continued, whispered by the lips of persons over-given to the reading of Gothick Romances and Shilling Shockers, that one day he had finally resolved to do it, and that he left off writing his objectionable Tales of Terror, and that as he stood before a mirror in the mansionhouse on his ancestral estates, the Waughters, he took a penknife with a steel edge, and split the flesh at the places where the lips meet. After a few minutes of comparison, after he had cleared the blood that flowed abundantly from the twin wounds, he saw full well that this wasn't the laughter of others!—But a strange pride consumed him, and he denied that this meant that he wasn't laughing, and claimed, that, in fact, only he truly knew how to laugh, and he resolved that he had in fact succeeded—only too well—and that others would see the point of the jest that could produce such a grimace, even if he would have to topple the entire universe, overthrow God, Satan, and the more dreadful Outside Things, to make them do it—(Having succeeded in something as difficult as laughing, he didn't acknowledge any limits to his powers—) At this unwelcome recognition, Elssinore began to fear that he had only prepared himself to become the butt of some incomprehensible practical joke—

The Master of Unwarrantable Metamorphoses spoke: "I believe that you have somewhat misjudged the character of my words, which in some cases carry a certain burden of ambiguity, which can have a dolorous significance for their misinterpreter." He seized an anvil—at first he wanted to use a hammer, but decided that such a light instrument would not produce the desired effect—and hurled it at the forehead of the unfortunate, who fell insensate beneath the blow. Lord Weÿrdgliffe knew well enough that the effect would not outlast the moment, and he immediately stripped the young man of clothing and sliced off his eyelids with a penknife. Then he took up a razor-sharp axe, and whacked off the youth's arms, legs, and genitalia, which he threw to a pair of hedgehogs, who didn't turn down that generous offer. From each of the novel apertures formulated by that mutilation, blood spurted as though from bottomless and unfathomable fountains. The Baron grabbed the beautiful youth by his hair of gold and carried him to the top of the highest tower in the ruinous abbey. He swung him around like a sling, soaking the abbey's surroundings in gushing jets of blood, until, at a precisely calculated moment, correlated with the swiftness of movement to create a certain well-specified angle, he instantly arrested the motion of his arm of ironical iron, which had as its effect: the youth's hair ripped loose from his head, sending the torso—launched by the centrifugal force—flying towards the stars (he did not smash into an oak-tree), and leaving the Baron with a beautiful, blond mane in his hand.

They say that, when Lord Weÿrdgliffe runs through the fields, steeped in some fit of mental alienation and lunacy, as though surfeited with an incommensurable pride by the ultimate fulfillment of his anterior designs mingled with the poignant pangs of an implacable conscience, chased by the little children and old women, who throw rocks at him, as if he were a blackbird, clutching a blood-soaked mane in his hand, holding it to his breast, nobody connects it with the eldritch, crimson comet, which, according to the credulous beliefs of superstitious peasants, priests, and kings, returns periodically (even though no one has yet determined the exact law governing its occulted orbit) to the earth, to appear in the heavens, dripping a drizzling scarlet rain of misty blood onto the farms, castles, churches, and everything, and foretelling disaster and calamity to come for all who behold it. Even the peasants disbelieve the testimony of the most keen-sighted among seers, who aver that once they had wiped their far-focused lenses of the ruddy liquid which had besmeared them, they would behold, concentrating their gaze upon the spot in the sky where the heavenly body should have appeared, a limbless trunk, attached to a hairless head. The most far-seeing of them all froze in terror, muttering only, *"Jambebleu!– Jarnicotondieu!–*That expression–on its face–horror–" No further revelations were forthcoming from the astounded gazer, who immediately entered a monastery and took an irretractable vow of eternal silence. They say that those few of good conscience wish that an enormous black cloud would swallow up the sun, the moon, the stars, and the will-o'-the-wisps of the swampy morasses–If only its omnipotent darkness might efface the unwelcome awareness brought on by that sanguinary meteor.

–Lord Weÿrdgliffe, the Waughters.

Ole Skin-'n'-Bones

Not everyone has had the good fortune to see through another's eyes. But before you've misunderstood me, and taken for a cliché what in the author's mind had been conceived with a true originality, await attentively that part of the story in which the opening line finds its immaculate consummation, and above all patiently, for it seems to me certain as a matter of fact, that in fact—not everyone has had the good fortune to see through another's eyes. In the meantime, don't overestimate the importance of this preliminary foreshadowing, but place the matter in its appropriate light once you've seen its true relationship to the other sections of the tale, and know its proper function.

When I first achieved existence in this wretched world— wretched, because it didn't accept the abortion to which it had given birth, with an appropriate welcome—I underwent the dejection of rejection and fled screaming from the human hives. No need to retrace the tracks of so painful a course of quotidian torments now. So watch me as, yet in the primordial era of my youth, I enter into the grandest phase of my career, when, crouched within the caverns of my thought, instead of betraying the mindless Minotaur of my perverted drives and attempting to appease the disgust of others, I found that their pain might give me as great a consolation as my repulsiveness gave them an offence!—And I resolved to offer up the whole human tribe in expiatory holocausts on the altar of my insane invidiousness!—

In the darkness of the night I stalked the featherless, bipedal prey that served me as game animals. A remarkable thing!—an unexpected occurrence!—with each victim taken, my framework of bones saw an unprecedented decrease in the amount of flesh concealing it! The cowering peoples, telling stories (audacious lies!) around their fireplaces, their voices scarcely audible above the winds whipping in vortices inside and outside their chimneys, and the whimpering of guard-dogs outside, disliking the lurking nightfear even more than the sleet and cold, would say that the flabberghastly phantom—who would descend from his crumbling, spiraling tower, in the dead of night, to take his choice of victims among the mob sleeping to evade its own horror and find a sort of deceptive peace in that way—that this phantom, appeared as little more than a skeleton which had been soaked in acid to remove the least vestments of its carnal and charnel essence!

The result: the stultified mobs masked me beneath that unbecoming nickname, *Ole Skin-'n'-Bones*. If I hadn't had any reason to act as I had until that time, then surely that gave me sufficient cause—But I couldn't dispute the verisimilitude of their nickname for me. Whenever I would palpate my face with the hand with which the patricide had slaughtered his mother, it sunk into the two empty sockets wherein you would expect to find eyeballs—in less perfect beings. My next piece of prey, then, a beautiful sixteen-year-old boy, yielded up his eyeballs to me on his deathbed (metaphor: actually, while buried neck-deep in living cockroaches). I twisted those orbs around in my fingers: then—stuck them right into my evacuated orbits. I had them in backwards at first, but wheeled them around quickly enough. Those spheres worked!—I could see with the boy's eyes!—For some while I added this novel torment/appropriation to each one of my long string of victorious vengeances. I became a connoisseur of visions, of sights—each one unique, unmatched by any other.

(Mothers, lying to make their children behave, would tell their bastard brats that I would come and fetch out their eyes if they didn't go to sleep like good little kids and keep their eyes closed all night.—As if it would bother *me* to wake a victim up before indulging in its sorrows!—I even like to suavely caress their c***s in their dreams, so that the contrast between that pleasurable illusion and the reality will make them feel it all the more!—)

To feed my hunger for that unheard-of hobby, I constructed an ingenious device. The sullen mobs didn't fail to notice the three years I spent locked away in my laboratories, when they could venture out of doors in some slight safety (I still took off weekends and holidays for my recreational predation, of course). This creation (creature, if you understand the word properly) resembled nothing so much as a black, bat-winged octopus. It would fly through the air in the clouds and mist, then swoop down onto some unsuspecting person—often having, intermediately, hidden, on top of a roof, waiting for the numskull to open the shutters of his casement and then stick his ungainly head out for a breath of fresh air in the stuffy night, and find himself inextricably intertwined within the ropy tentacles of the magnificent Eyeball-Extractor!—

I soon accumulated an enormous array of eyes, which I carefully arranged on a set of shelves lining the dizzy stairwell up to the top of my zigzag tower. But I realized that eyeballs alone do not make an entirely satisfying collection. No, the entire fleshly envelope should become my clothing; I should assume their obscene identities more fully. One night, I lay beneath the canopy over my satin bed, with a beautiful, blue-eyed blonde's flesh wrapped tight around me!—It didn't give me quite as much voluptuous pleasure as you might not have had any right to expect!—

Anon, I excavated vast, vaulted caverns wherein to hold the entire reserves of the flesh of everyone soever.—The eyeballs I still kept in my tower, which opened (at the bottom, through a trapdoor) onto that daedal network of labyrinthine storage. (When I would ride about in those tatters of humanity, the foolish would mutter that my victims had come back to haunt the living, and that therefore I didn't have as much power as people had formerly supposed.—The idiots!)

A few decades in the laboratories and a creature made for each organ, each muscle, of the body, and the peoples, who hadn't dealt with their unexpected blindness with as much composure as souls as cold-blooded and indifferent as myself would prefer, not liking overt displays of emotion overmuch—save only laughter and orgasmic revelry at another's pain. They found themselves as bereft of corpulence as bereft of sight, and concluded, in their inexorable logic, that they must have died. Armies of skeletons marched in serried legions to graveyards and cemeteries, screaming in their madness as they digged into the dirt and swam down to the presumed resting-place. A few even took the precaution of hammering together coffins and carving tombstones for themselves before sinking into voluntary nullity—if you want to know the epoch in which this dénouement occurs, just read the most recent of the final dates in any cemetery soever.—I don't think any have gone without one of these fools, at the very least. Quite a few acted as the executors of their own wills, which didn't always hold up under probate—Many gave themselves memorial services—

Now, I serially clothe myself in these novel vestments, traversing the former citadels of men, playing an unwinnable game of hide-'n'-seek with the army of oddities who track me and rob me of my organs and everything. I cackle with glee when I go into some outhouse to take a piss (it's hard to hold water once the new-and-improved Bladder-Bandit has done its job) and the fabulous Penis-Pilferer suddenly pops out of the shapeless hole to rob me of the last shred of flesh I wear on my wearied bones; thrilled and shuddered with anticipation, I make my way straight back to the armory of human clothing and again begin my obscure manoeuvers within the next suit of second-hand flesh.

—Lord Weÿrdgliffe, the Waughters.

At the Waughters

And after their latest round of picaresque episodes, Konrad and Holtzer, companions in adventure, headed out on the road that leads through the forests of Averoigne, past the sullen peak of Mont Soânge, and onward into unrecognizable morasses. Night had begun to fall before they had fully crossed the unnameable swamplands into which they had strayed, and the many crossroads in those parts seemed to mislead them even further into the inextricable situation into which they had fallen. They had hoped to reach drier—and inhabited—lands before the bell of curfew tolled the departure of daylight, but that desire had long since vanished away into nothingness, as darkness now reigned over the environment with an adamantine hand.

A faint and flickering bluish light appeared at a great distance away from them, floating several feet above the ground. It came directly towards them and began to move away, hesitated, returned, and then it repeated the gesture. Feeling that they could scarcely become any more lost than they already had, the companion travellers resolved to follow it, whether it should prove a mere will-o'-the-wisp or no. It led them along a winding path, and they soon enough beheld before them, standing in the yellowish moonlight, an antique château, with a moated ditch and four turrets jutting into the ebony vault above. The pixie-light hesitated, then it led them further on, across the drawbridge and through the unlocked gates of the mouldering mansionhouse. They followed the glimmering illuminator through hallways ornamented with ancestral lines of armor sporting an elegant 𝕎 monogram over the left side of the chest, and through a doorway into a rather sizable room furnished with armchairs and beds, and a fireplace.

The light winked out in the blink of an eye.

The two found kindling-wood beside the fireplace, which still had a full provision of logs on top of its ashes and embers, and a tinderbox placed handily on the mantel. Konrad, who was wearing lighter clothing, in addition to having gotten a little wet, when he had stumbled in the swamps outside, and fell to his knees and hands in a pool, set the wood and lit the fire and sat down by it, holding his hands out to warm them up. Holtzer searched the apartment for a candle, a torch, a lamp, or any other object to provide light by which to see about one, but found nothing but sets of obscure and aged books and assorted kickshaws and bric-à-brac adorning the area.

While Konrad remained by the fire, gazing into it as if into the heart of a dream, Holtzer began to speak to him. The situation of their recent events reminded him of a Ghost Story, or so he said, and he asked Konrad if he would like to hear it, to help them to while away the time. The other asked him for the name of the story and its author, so that they should not duplicate his own reading, and he had—of course—read widely; and as for the genre of the Ghost Story, he declared, he always appreciated a good shudder, he viewed the form as one of his very favorites, and their current surroundings would prove most suitable, or so he thought, to put them into the mood appropriate to such a work.

Holtzer answered that he had in mind the tale entitled "At the Waughters," written by one Lord Weÿrdgliffe. His companion answered that he had not so much as heard of this Weird Tale, nor even of its author, and he requested some information on the latter. The former replied that the author was none other than Sir Robert Democritus Weerie Skythropos Asshton-Urquhart III, the Seventeenth Baron Weÿrdgliffe, who quite understandably wrote under his title alone as his *nom-de-plume*, his full name proving slightly unwieldy in casual conversation. He had named the mansion, referred to in the story's title, after his own, the Waughters; it half-seemed that some mysterious enigma had revolved about those ancient estates, but one which he couldn't quite recall to mind—What could it have been?—

Shrug;—

But it did not surprise him, he declared, that his friend should not have made his acquaintance, literarily speaking, for he lived in total obscurity on his estates in Scotland (or was it Wales?), and his works, published only in small editions, had become known only to the most avid connoisseurs of the horrid genres, who collected rare and often censored works. He rather thought, so he said, that the author had even cultivated his own obscurity, seeking to veil himself within a shroud of mystery, and actively courted the suppression of his volumes by a morality-inclined government that did not shrink from the use of violence to communicate its point. Indeed, only through a very few appearances in scattered anthologies and low-circulation journals did general readers even know of his existence. But howsoever that might be, on to the tale.

All of this time, Konrad did not look away from the hearth, and frequently stoked the fire with a poker to encourage its often sputtering health. Holtzer pulled an armchair up nearer, finding himself warm enough at some greater remove from the fireplace, and sat down, ready to speak.

Two picaresque and Teutonic rogues, (he began), very much like us, just like us had gotten lost while travelling through France, where the place-names lack a sufficient number of consonants to allow one to determine one's whereabouts with any degree of precision. So they had wandered into a swamp very much like the one in which we have so recently found ourselves. There, exactly as in the one which we have strayed into, a blue and gleaming light had come to them, and it led their winding way to a mansionhouse, which seemed to answer in every particular to the description of the one in which we ourselves now desire to rest ourselves for the morning, and perhaps to discover the inhabitants, to thank them for their hospitality in entertaining us as unexpected and uninvited guests on this night.

The two wandered through the hallways of that place until they discovered a room very close in appearance to this one, with crumbling books on the shelves, a fireplace, and furnishings like those scattered about in here. While one of them tended to the fire, the other began to retell a narrative which he had once read in an anthology of Ghost Stories, hoping to put a little bit of fright into the other's mind, and perhaps even to give him the inspiration for a nightmare that might provide the crumbling foundations for some immortal literary classic, unless forgotten before—or immediately upon—awakening. And what, after all, causes that lapsing into oblivion?—If it's not the ego's repulsion at the horrors which it has so recently undergone, which proves that those dreams *not* recalled would provide even more suitable material for a Tale of Terror than those remembered—But I hope that you will keep some parchment, a pen, and an inkpot handily beside you as you sleep, so that such a fate will not await you, for I have designs similar to those of that Horrid Story's character—

While that character recited this tale to his compeer, he suddenly paused, and the other, who had not, in all the time in which his friend had been telling the story, looked away from the fire, into which he gazed, as if into the heart of a dream, still did not look away from it. At this point, the one recounting a narrative, which he had read many years before, began to make a sound, which began like a stifled scream of horror and continued with a bizarre squishing and slurping noise, and then abruptly ended with a lapping and sucking sound, that sent shivers through the spine of his companion. (At this point Konrad felt shivers run down his own spine, tickling it like a pair of nimble-footed spiders, and admired the narrative skill with which Holtzer retold the Weird Tale he had memorized, upon a single reading—who knew how many years before the present occasion.) The other, having by that time felt sufficiently warmed by the flames which he had stoked up many times during the preceding recitation, got up and turned around to pull up a chair beside his companion and noticed that his friend, while still sitting in the chair, no longer made even the slightest motion, and had a strange look upon his face. He went over to him, and believed that he could not merely have fallen asleep at such a juncture. (Konrad, still too cold, stoked the logs burning in the fireplace.) He touched him gently and whispered his name. No response. He shook him, and noticed an odd property to his head. He felt his head, and perceived that it had become deflated like a balloon, as if the skull had gotten pulverized in some outrageous vice. The eyeballs rolled out of place onto the floor in front of the chair, and he looked into the emptied sockets and saw right from the front to the back of the annihilated skull. He let the body fall limp in the armchair.

At this point he heard a cacodaemoniacal cackling laughter, and looked back in the room, towards the door, which he had believed shut and had not heard open—and no other exit existed. (Konrad could not tell whether it was the remnants of the coldness that still penetrated his body or this last detail in the story that made him feel an invincible tremor pervade his frame. He again prodded the burning logs with the poker.) A glow seemed to form in the back of the chamber, and as he stared at it, paralyzed in fright, it appeared to alter its shape into a skeleton, but not the mere animated skeleton of the Horrid Story's cliché, but one some seven feet tall, with fingers perhaps seventeen inches in length, ending in talon-like nails, and a skeleton which appeared to have undergone a weird metamorphosis, as if it had taken sail on a vessel which had felt itself drawn by the silvery songs of the sirens of the stars and drifted upwards from the mist-shrouded oceans and through the atmosphere past the moon and on into the outer abysses, wrecking against some rocky reef of the aether, setting the bony framework afloat in the void like some piece of celestial flotsam, where it had undergone a *space-change*. It glowed, as if covered with encrustations of the grey-green lichens that grow on the arid and icy plains of Pluto, and with the mercury-freaked fungi that sprout in the cavernous grottoes of Saturn, and the polypous purple anemones revealed in the tidepools of Achernar's seventh planet's slow seas, and the phosphorescent mould that grows on the excremental shells of the loathsome semi-amphibian inhabitants of the third moon of the seventh planet that orbits Sirius C. It gleamed with a hazy cerulean glow, tinted with shades of magenta and ultramarine. Its eyesockets held diamond-shaped effulgencies of incandescent amber. Its jaw lowered, the uncreaking hinge-action clearly visible, and a lengthy, tapering tongue of sable extended as it raised its arms and made a beautiful gesture with its lengthy fingers. It approached—

Here Holtzer stopped speaking, and—after a pause during which Konrad knew for certain that he had become warm enough, and that only the narration to which he had been listening so intently created the effect of tremendous mystery which he felt overpowering his senses—he made a sound that began like a stifled scream of horror, continued with a bizarre squishing and slurping noise, then ended with an odd lapping and sucking sound. Konrad listened closely to this noise, admiring the skill of his friend in reproducing the sound described so carefully by

Lord Weÿrdgliffe, and then repeated by himself, in the story he was retelling. Silence. He now got up, as he wanted to pull up a chair beside his companion's, and continue the evening's entertainment—so delicious, when he saw that his friend was sitting in an unusual slump in the armchair. An odd suspicion overcame him, and he pulled his friend's head up by the hair, seeing that his skull no longer retained its solidity, and his eyeballs rolled out of their vacant sockets onto the floor, and he could see right through to the back of what now passed for his skull. A chuckle of immeasurable irony rose into the air in an ascending spiral—

He looked behind the chair, and a glow appeared in the room, which had no exits, save for the single door, which he had believed closed. There, the glow took on form more and more distinctly, and there appeared to him a skeleton, but not the mere animated skeleton of the Horrid Story's cliché, but one some seven feet tall, with fingers perhaps some seventeen inches in length, ending in talon-like nails, and a skeleton which—

It approached him, with its slender fingers outstretched as if to grab a hold of his head. He wanted with all of his force to scream and relieve the enormous pressure of the terror seizing complete hold of him, but he couldn't succeed in doing it. Seeing no possible means of escape, his entire life passed before his eyes inside an infinitesimal space of time, and as it neared the end, he realized that his companion had not finished the tale, which he was recounting at the moment of his decease. He knew that the Ghost Story has strict rules of composition, and that one of its elementary principles requires that the leading character not die at the hands of the apparition of the uncanny, of the epiphany of the eldritch, who makes his first on-stage appearance at the climax of the story, just after he has annihilated some lesser character, as a demonstration of his gruesome powers—of this precise structure he felt certain, guaranteeing his escape as the story's inevitable dénouement. So, he held his breath and closed his eyes and leapt headfirst into the story his friend had been telling.

That fall, that setting of himself into an abyss, produced an odd sensation. It felt like he had jumped into a lake of eyeball-shaped ice-cubes, made from his own blood, frozen solid by the agency of some unheard-of fear. Only someone who has had such an experience can know what it felt like, for Konrad, as he felt the very words and sentences of that Tale of Terror thickening into realities around him, brushing against his skin and finally wholly enveloping his entirety.

What he had failed to realize—was, that Lord Weÿrdgliffe, because of some strange and egotistical pride, did not always follow the narrative conventions laid down by other writers, and that, by the manœuver which he had hoped would save his life, he had merely delivered himself directly into the skeleton hands of the Textual Trickster. Lord Weÿrdgliffe grasped him firmly about the head with his grotesquely bony fingers, wrapping him thoroughly with their knotty knuckles, and as the unfortunate scoundrel clawed at his rib-cage—nearly pulling one of his ribs off, so much strength did he manage to apply, much unlike most of the victims the Baron had taken—he carefully applied pressure in a precisely calculated manner. Konrad's skull popped like a punctured balloon, and then it felt itself reduced to a fine, white, flour-like powder. The adventure-seeker started to bleed out through his nostrils, the only part of the surface of his face or scalp currently left exposed, and then his entire brain flowed out of his nose into a puddle of red and grey matter onto the floor in the corner of the room, in squishy and slurping spurts and jets. Lord Weÿrdgliffe placed the limp cadaver in the armchair which he had intended to pull up beside his companion, put the eyeballs back into their proper position—for they had fallen out during the posturing of the corpse, set his companion likewise back into his former place on his armchair, once again putting the eyeballs into their former homes—they slipped out twice, and only with some small difficulty did he manage to get them to stay in place, and left the two friends there to engage in further refined conversation.

He got down on his hands and kneecaps, extended his raspy black tongue, and started to lap up the brains lying in a liquefied puddle on the floor, sucking that exquisite sauce down his osseous gullet with an ineffable satisfaction like that of a strayed mongrel bitch avidly devouring the roadside regurgitations of a spermatophageous gastronome.

—Lord Weÿrdgliffe, the Waughters.

The Abomination of Desolation: A Hieroglyphic Tale

"Mene, mene, tekel, upharsin."

The one who, for the space of seven days, has fled from the tight pursuit of the whooping phantom of his unceasing Conscience, hasn't had time to eat or to shut his eyes, or so much as take a single drink from his carafe to humidify his desiccated palate, but he now perceives the Nemesis-Phantom fading from his consciousness as he falls asleep on the edge of a cliff, henceforth unable to resist that impulse towards oblivion any longer, even if it means precipitating himself onto the breakers below, or allowing the Universal Enemy to seize him by the base of his spine with her claws;—and if he's the one who's reading me, then he's capable of divining, with some rigor, what a degree of heaviness and gravity weighs me down into an immutable immobility greater than that of the paralytic venom of the spider-daemons who inhabit the hells beyond Rutilicus.

Any origin of myself lies outside of my knowledge. I drifted through the outer reaches of space for countless aeons in a state of unconsciousness until I entered the atmosphere of this planet and crashed onto the Muvian landmass. Here, I stood, an enormous shapeless chunk of crimson-red crystalline rock like a spurting geyser of blood frozen instantly in the depths of the intersidereal void. The peoples inhabiting that land came and gawked at me, staring in awe at the immense irregular monolith that suddenly stood motionless in their midst. That emotion touched me, made me aware; from that point on, I fed on their wonder and awe like a vampire.

At that time, I still felt merely an awareness of that act of feeding itself; my mental tentacles lashed out and their manifold suckers seized onto everyone's brain; this aroused the ire of many, who determined to destroy the new religion, which had committed the unforgivable sin of having arisen around the worship of a new object—unknown to tradition, besides feeling somewhat enervated and embarrassed by my forays into their innermost recesses. The party of conventional religion stormed the natural temple—I mean, the empty field in which I stood, alone and apart from other geographical features—and slaughtered the priests and adorants scattered about—when they performed that act of rigid morality and justice, I noticed, for the very first time, that I received an even greater ecstasy from the death-spasms of those souls than from their living worship, a fact worthy of note to one such as I—and then they rushed upon me, hammers and picks in hand. They smashed away at me for a long time; but, just as you sculpt an elephant by cutting off every piece of the rock which you have chosen as your material—that does not look like an elephant, they only managed to break off every part of the gigantic stone that did not look like—Myself; they had only succeeded in perfecting the idol which they despised, for then I had taken on my form fully, and that form proved indestructible, and furthermore, I had gained complete awareness of myself—and of all other things.

Now—I stand, the enormous unmoving dragon of Outermost Chaos, my slack-jawed serpentine head surmounting innumerable coils, my uncounted scales not flaking away from my rigid hide, my numerous talon-equipped limbs easily surpassed in size by my upright ithyphallic member. The Cult of Adjectives applied the following epithets to me:

The Indescribable.

The Ineffable.

The Rutilant.

The Incomparable.

The Colossal.

All of these fail to communicate the properties of the substantive to which they have been applied; in short, they lie shamelessly.

I organized the continent along a hierarchic plan, with myself as the head. You know full well that I cannot move, so you cannot fail to guess the method of communication I chose to transmit my thoughts to the minds of men: I would send them dreams. Now, as you might expect, I had a little difficulty in putting my own desires into terms that they could understand, and the apocalyptic symbolisms I bombarded their wearied brains with would outdo the apocryphal writings of more than one religion. But soon enough, the message got through, and an entire society organized itself around the propitious project of providing me with human sacrifices. The Lords of Mu went even further, and conquered Lemuria, to bring me its amber-breasted titan-women as further tidbits for my hallucinatory holocausts.

This arrangement seemed entirely satisfactory to everyone, including the former opponents of my worship, who conceded that by now the Cult of Me had endured long enough to fall under the heading of *Tradition*; until, one day, a prophet arose from amongst the people, a young man whom no one had hitherto ever heard of, from a small tribe of enslaved islanders, who claimed that he had divine visions revealing to him a god unlike myself, and who had no material form. Such heresy did not please the priests of my religion, and so they naturally determined to include this upstart in the next conflagration set to flame forth within my bowels. He welcomed the chance, so he said, to prove his faith in the invisible, intangible deity which he worshiped, and he called me a pathetic fake, and a pitiful fraud, and said that my power could hardly touch him, protected by his guardian angel, equally insubstantial as his god, even in the belly of the beast, and that furthermore, what seemed miracles—on my part, merely represented clever illusions—produced by my priests' mechanical contrivances. He learned all too well that he hadn't read the writing on the wall—after all, hadn't he simply misinterpreted a dream which I myself had sent to him one night, suffering from the indigestion induced by toasted headcheese?—and so I toasted him. A look of total surprise overtook him in the tenth of a second he took to transform utterly into ashes; he didn't seem to expect his immaterial ally to abandon him so quickly to the wickedness of idolatry.

But I had to think long and hard upon what he had said. I couldn't help but admire that noble dream of freedom which his non-existent god had represented. In my condition, you can't help but want to move around, at least a little bit, even if you don't care to soar above the world like a solar eagle. Then I started to pay attention to the debate between my worshipers and that group of skeptics (heretics!—) known as the Iconoclasts, which had arisen in the wake of that young prophet: the first, who called themselves my partisans, claimed that they didn't really commit idolatry by worshiping me, but that I merely gave a material form to a spiritual entity; the latter, who desired my destruction, made the contrary claim that nothing but my material form existed, and no spiritual entity lurked behind it. Consequently, they wanted to smash it, as a false claimant to divinity. I succeeded in synthesizing their views, and determined then that I must have some spiritual essence, which would exist in a state of perfect freedom, if it were not imprisoned within its material trappings, which immerse it in complete immobility.

So, I inspired the Iconoclasts, in their turn, to worship me unknowingly—by destroying me. They stormed the holy grounds, and set upon me in a fury unknown to a haggard pack of rabid dogs, but they failed to make the least dent or impression upon me, for I don't have feet of clay, or a brain of clay, or for that matter any other bodily part of clay, but all of an adamantine hardness. Soon enough, and long after I had seen the futility of their attempt, my partisans retook the area, and served them up to me as a between-meal snack.

I saw the right tack to take soon enough, for I continued to inspire more and more Iconoclasts likewise, partially through the inspiring dreams that the young prophet had so misinterpreted, and which, I found, I could count on any old idiot to misinterpret equally well to the same effect, and partially through increasing the number of victims that I would demand, which had as its effect not only the increase of the outrageous resentment against my depredations, but the satiating of some small portion of the wrathful spleen I felt when I thought of my radical impotence, which only increased my algolagniacal pleasures, and one always likes to meet two needs with one manner of fulfillment: this is known as *economy.* Each time, I noticed, that the two opposing camps came into conflict, the Lords of Mu seeking yet more unfortunates to roast in my guts, and the Lemurian armies fighting rebelliously against that tyrannical action, they invented greater and greater weapons of destruction. I assumed that once they had reached a certain level of effectiveness, even the hardness comprising my physical existence should fall beneath its power.

War succeeded war, in a sublime pageant of death. Eventually, entire cities lay in ruins at the touch of a single button, and still I stood, cramped in the unyielding confines of my stony body. Finally, an epochal apocalyptic battle began, and the two landmasses, Mu and Lemuria, utterly annihilated each other, falling beneath the waves in pyres of flame created by human artifice, while yet other, new, lands arose in a compensatory matter from the oceans, and I, I remained as if untouched by the unmitigated calamity that had completely blotted the human race from the shameful face of the earth.

There, beneath the ocean, I felt my situation even less savory than the one which I had put up with before that time. No fish brought sacrifices to me; neither octopus nor stingray would condescend to worship something, so they told me in response to the dreams I sent out to them, so ugly as a human being, which my actions, if not my appearance, indelibly and ineffaceably marked me as. I cannot tell the depth of my despair at that point in the current story. I couldn't even straighten myself out—for the calamitous collapse of that prior continent had left me leaning at an absurd angle;—I could just imagine the fish laughing at me as they swam overhead as I continued to watch the sea anemones grow.

But things didn't turn out quite so badly as you might have expected. For it seemed that some very few bands of men had survived, such as those out on fishing expeditions, who felt no small surprise to notice the ocean-floor rising up around them, their boats sinking into the slime in which fish flopped around, and these men rebuilt civilization from its last shredded tatters. It took countless millennia before those men had reached a stage of development great enough to prove a threat to their own continents, and thus a promise to restore my own. It would injure my ego too much, if I didn't take credit for their actions, and it would injure their own egos even more, if they felt that, on the contrary, they had the sole responsibility for the destruction which they wreaked on a planet that provided them with their lives, not to mention on their own fellows, whom they constantly preached to about the love of one's neighbor, and so this part of the tale must take a form determined by that ironic law of iron necessity, whether it represent the facts or no (for after all, when Truth and the Ego find themselves in conflict, which side wins that determined struggle—every time, as if its opponent had failed to fight with her full strength?): my dreams, transmitted to them *via* telepathy, inspired them to annihilate each other in an unprecedented apocalypse—don't blame them, oh no, not those benevolent mice, who could never perform a hurtful act without some outside force acting as provocation, enslaving them through some hypnotic power of cretinization.

That catastrophic event had as its inexorable result, the fall and demise of their civilizations and continents, and the rise of my own land, not exactly in its old configuration, but in a new one, never before seen. Once again, a few handfuls of men survived, who didn't seem to worry too much about historical precedents, even if they had such knowledge, by record or by inference—not something which human beings excel at in any case—and so they went ahead and again set up the Cult of Me which I ordained for the worship of Myself, and needless to say, the rival Cult of Iconoclasts as well. Humanity seemed even stupider and more brutish in its most recent incarnation, and it took until the sun had started to dim before they developed any weapons of power, to use in their eternal conflicts on the omnipotent subject of Me.

So, they succeeded in wholly exterminating their own tribe from the rocky crust of the cold orb which they had emerged from, like some sort of parasitic excrement. That final spectacle of annihilation brought me such a thrill that my immobility was nearly broken by a shudder of delight—impossibly. Now, still untouched by their weapons of unlimited destruction, I lay here, as immobile as ever, unprovided with sacrifices to feed my bleeding lusts, staring off into the receding distance like a sphinx of the icy fields, and I can only hope, that when this planet, on which I feel myself spinning around and around, and going in an inward spiral towards the dying sun—or at least, the sun, in critical condition (I don't yet know how to distinguish the medical crises of stars)—that when this planet, I say, already a heap of dead rock and dust, falls into the cooling ashes of an extinguished celestial ember, that will finally set me free from the apparently indestructible vestment of an adamantine body which I ceaselessly wear.

                                           —Lord Weÿrdgliffe, the Waughters.

The Mirror of My Self

"No one has my form but the *I*."
—Jean-Paul.

(Journal fragments.)

If I exist—then I'm not someone else. I don't admit that equiv-ocal plurality within myself. And yet, when I reflect on certain de-velopments of past times—These ambiguous events— which, certainly, practically everybody has experienced, and hence im-pose no need for an exploratory explication here, since everyone has at one point or another looked at some thought or deed and seen the exact image of *another* in it—excited my interest in the mirror offered to me for sale by the dealer, previously unknown to me, in antiquities and oddities, who contacted me through the mail, unsolicited by me, and whom I have still never seen face-to-face, for he sends his faceless hirelings to conduct his af-fairs. I didn't want a mummy's foot to use as a paperweight: that kind of a morbid relique doesn't appeal to me in the slightest. But a full-sized mirror, of unknown manufacture, and the glass still cov-ered with a cloth, leaving it virginal of the contact of any eyes so-ever—that seemed the exact item to suit my needs. I definitely didn't want a mirror tainted by the reflections of other people, however beautiful, but merely wanted it to accurately portray my own uniqueness as an individual. According to a vulgar superstition, windowpanes, once stared through daily for many years by the inhabitant of a house, will, for decades and perhaps even centuries afterwards, present the image of that eternally absent personage's face. If so—which I definitely do not admit to believing, not having fallen a prey to unreason, and even feeling the greatest possible contempt for those who have—then a mirror should work just as well for such an inexplicable and uncanny effect.

* * * * *

I installed the mirror in my bedroom, where not even my faithful servants can ever see it, for I keep my door locked whenever I use it, and cover it with a cloth whenever I am not using it, and have forbidden all my domestics to ever behold that pane of glass upon the direst penalties for transgression against my orders. Now, I look at myself for hours upon hours, every day, making that spectacular viewing into my principle occupation. Sometimes clothed, in many different and varied costumes, but most often buck naked, I cannot look away from the fascinating figure standing before me: Me. I'm not claiming that I'm any more agreeable in appearance than anyone else, even if I do deny that I rank any lower than mediocre on the score of physical beauty, but after all, in accordance with the opinions of political and economic philosophers, who have made the most thorough study of the rights of man, everyone has equal rights, and I, therefore, have as much right to admire myself as anyone else, even the most beautiful, even were that admiration to bring me the greatest disgust and horror at such an image possible.

* * * * *

In town today, the people seemed to look at me a little oddly—

The fools!—They understand nothing!—

* * * * *

More and more, I prefer the company of my own image to that of others and their images. So, I keep the company that I enjoy the best. And who could say that it doesn't also benefit me the most? For I've noticed that my reflection has slowly grown different from the one which I had for so long identified as myself. What else can this mean, but that I have finally found the method of coming into my full flowering, of truly becoming myself, and not what others have made me into? Once, it hurt me inside when I noticed that I differed from others, but now I've gotten over that childish emotion, and I revel in my unparalleled uniqueness!—And the most notable fact of all, the more I see my new image, the more familiar it seems—What could provide a more perfect proof that it represents precisely my very own identity, hidden for so long in the cellar of the unconscious, crammed into that cranny of oblivion by my preposterous awareness of other people?—

* * * * *

A hideous pain gnaws at my soul. I think of things—My thoughts rush through my head like a cataract—Despair—It has become intolerable for me to endure the company of others. I have discovered myself—

I suffer.

* * * * *

I just spent the entire night prowling about the countryside, plotting crimes against others—

The darkness and the mist veil too much from the sight of men. But nothing hides *them* from *me*—I overtook one, and quickly pounced onto the brute—While my arms held him in an immutable immobility I chewed his face off, tonguing in turn his nose, eyes, lips, cheeks—

Before long, he no longer wore the look of total surprise that he had assumed at my first appearance—

I felt unsatisfied with the cruelty inherent in that act—So, after having swallowed down his tongue, I extended my own tongue into his emptied eye-sockets and—

But some things one can hardly write, even with oneself as the sole readership. And if *someone else* were to read this journal, just imagine his censorious look of displeasure at my self-indulgence in such a whimsical subject!—

I cannot help but smile as I wonder: what tale would that fellow have told his friends and family members, to account for such a novel mutilation?—

* * * * *

I noticed a strange thing this afternoon. I moved the mirror out from the wall a little bit, so I could clean it—I won't let the maids near it, you understand—and I saw then that its back had a strange design on it. It juts out, about a quarter of an inch, much like a *bas-relief.* It shows a full-sized human figure—from the back. But this figure has some odd qualities. It reveals such a leanness of muscle and fat that the ribs stick out of its back. Added to this great thinness, a lankiness of form in its fantastically slender arms and fingers, its legs and feet. Not to mention its vestigial tail, or the odd incrustation upon the spine, as if a strange centipede-like creature were growing out of the vertebrae!—And the skin has such an inhuman texture!—I cannot find any words to describe it—

What might this novel feature portend?—

I put the mirror back into place against the wall.

* * * * *

My image changes more and more into my unrepeatable self. The Unique One. I see it in the mirror. My face has started to look like a skull, with a piece of leather drawn over it. My ribs stick out of my chest—my fingers have grown longer, my nails sharper and black as obsidian—my eyes have sunken back into my shriveled-up brain, and burn like smoldering embers, a crimson glow replacing their former incandescent amber—my teeth make me look like a hyaena—my hair hangs in greyed locks—and that unbearable grimace—

No doubt, even this image hardly gives the barest reflection of the enormous suffering that overtakes me—

I only know, that I've seen this image somewhere before—

* * * * *

I've reached the point of total disgust with all humanity. I made a pact with Hatred to eliminate the entire tribe. But since it would take far too long to annihilate the whole race, I have resolved instead to make them suffer, one by one, torments as great as my own—

And what inspired my suffering and my hatred of my fellows?—Nothing, unless it was themselves!—

* * * * *

I no longer allow my domestics and servants to view me. (I doubt that they mind that very much—they had started to show signs of repugnance at my appearance.—Perhaps, if they didn't consume so much from the winecellars, they wouldn't have stayed on here at all.) They leave my meals by the door—I don't need any other interference in my apartment, cleanliness not being the principal motivation of my determination; I could hardly live without their aid, in the estimation drawn from my former life; in the prediction drawn from my current existence, I consider that I might merely grow a little thinner, and perhaps even become wholly myself all the more quickly!—

* * * * *

To generate surprise, an essential element—when attempting to make a torture aesthetically pleasing, as well as an appealing sacrifice to the baser instincts—utilizing my inherent genius for invention, I transformed a cemetery into a field of unheard-of booby-traps. An aged gentlemen, on a visit to his wife, who had not replied to his entreaties for some forty years, found himself grasped tightly about the ankles by a pair of skeleton hands, which pulled him screaming into a second honeymoon bed with his beloved—a whole town, each idiot in his turn, fell for this simple trap. The next ones, a couple, whose infant had deceased from cholera, joined it, its tiny little fingers clamping onto their toes—The rest of that city soon followed, not suspecting what had overtaken the others—

I cannot help but admire my ingenuity in contriving such a mechanical device—

* * * * *

Insomnia—
Nightmare—
What's the difference?—

* * * * *

I have now realized from where I recognize the image that stands before me in the mirror. When yet a child I once read one of the many Penny Dreadfuls by the infamous Lord Weÿrdgliffe, entitled, rather pretentiously—or so *I* thought—*The Unspeakable; or, The Anatomy of Otherness: A Gothick Romance*. This volume, in a series of interrelated, but also frequently inconsistent, tales or poems-in-prose, described the most brutal acts of gratuitous sadism, in frenetic and spasmodic prose, in sentences of awkward construction, as if to mimic (or merely reflect!) the processes of a decaying mind, meditating on acts of violence, and a noteworthy feature of that booklet, was that it included Lord Weÿrdgliffe himself as one of its key characters, and always presented him in the most unflattering light, as the worst sort of human monster imaginable, from the viewpoint of another person, never specified, who acted out the part of the writer. He constantly attacked others with the most bizarre practical jokes imaginable, which often led to their deaths—or more usually, less pleasant results, for them—but as for him, *he* found their novel torments most amusing, in a sardonic sort of way. As you might guess, I found the book merely nauseating, and felt revolted by its senseless nihilism and juvenile rebelliousness—Not to mention such annoying stylistic excesses as the pointless and gratuitous mention, seemingly in every single story, of the centrifugal force—Although, years later, I chanced to read an essay by a Belgian critic, known mostly for his political pamphleteering, who remarked of the tome, that "Lord Weÿrdgliffe takes the disintegration of contemporary social organization to its logical conclusion: to the stage of its self-destruction. The individual's absolute rejection of society as a response to the society's absolute rejection of the individual." That speculation did intrigue me—somewhat.

Now, that book had illustrations—And the depiction that I now see, whenever I look into that mirror by my bedside, looks very much like a combination of one of them—a woodcut representing the spectral apparition of Lord Weÿrdgliffe—and the appearance of my former self!—

* * * * *

With my change into myself, has come, *pari passu*, a change in my view of others, who I now see in hues not quite as illusory as the imposed opinions—which held sway over my feverish brain for so long, imprisoning it into the pre-formed moulds of received ideas—those prejudicial viewpoints have dissolved, as if eaten away by acid, and now, when I look at a human being, I see a sort of absurd assemblage of sausages and slugs, of cubes and catafalques, of vowels, of eggs and infernal machines—an aquarium's phenomenon and a bearded lady. The ensemble simultaneously reveals an uncleanliness too great for a sewage-pump, and a delectable quality too fine for the most refined gourmet—

A young boy, like a slice of baloney—A young girl, like a rasher of bacon—Make me feel an insatiable hunger—

* * * * *

An astonishing event occurred last night. While on my customary foray of unmotivated destruction I entrapped an auburn-haired woman of perhaps twenty-eight. She struck me as of the greatest beauty, which naturally increased my own pitch of fury into an intense and rabid rage—I condescended to give her the taste of my tongue, as I have so many others—When I raised her skirts and my tongue touched her angelic cheek, that white and pink cheek became as black as a chunk of charcoal!—It exhaled putrescent miasmata—gangrene, and no doubt about it!—The evil rodent extended over her whole figure, and from there, exercised its furies on the lower and higher parts; quickly enough, her entire body was nothing but a vast, unclean sore. Myself, frightened (for I didn't believe that my tongue contained a poison of such virulence), I started back, but then I felt the mark of the most intense voluptuous pleasure in the deed, and, having lived through a moment of doubt, threw myself headlong right back homeward into the career of evil!—

I consumed the corpse on the spot, licking it up to the last drop from the ground it soaked, like water imbibing sugar—

That sumptuous banquet cost me a ferocious case of jaundice-yellow diarrhea.

* * * * *

Every experience abrades against my brain like a sandpaper scalpel—All of my nerves, ripped loose from their normal placement in my body, feel adamantine fingernails scratching across them as though on a blackboard in some training school for the education of infernal torturers—

I wish that I could withdraw myself into my ego *in toto*, like a turtle enarmoring itself inside its impenetrable shell, but with no need to stick my limbs out for any purpose—

* * * * *

When I look into the mirror now, I see a figure that exactly conforms to the woodcut in that obscure book, which I mentioned in a prior date's passage—I mean the book that I wrote—no, I mean the book that I *read*—in those halcyon days of my youth, the one about, the one by, Lord Weÿrdgliffe—

* * * * *

My mind is an open wound, and I have forbidden Sanity to scab it over with a scar—It drips ice-cold blood and a bubbling yellow pus, that flow down the stairs, and on out of the windows of awareness and out into the world—

* * * * *

I have now performed a most fascinating experiment with the marvelous mirror. I wanted to see if my back would match the back portrayed on the mirror's reverse, for it seemed to me, that judging it—solely by analogy, for I don't know of any other case precisely like my own uniqueness—from the appearance, presented to me in the mirror, of my face and front, that the back depicted there should fit fairly well with it, and thus that my own might well correspond to it, just as my front matches its own frontal image—

So I took another mirror in, to look at the reflection of my back in that one. But instead—*mirabile dictu*—it merely showed that the mirror still painted the portrait of my appearance from the front!—An unforeseen occurrence!—It would only show *that*, that image alone, and nothing else, no matter what arrangement of mirrors I made—

Using two wholly other mirrors, I demonstrated to myself that my back, far from identical to my obverse side, did in fact match that on the reverse of the strange mirror. It must produce that image itself!—

* * * * *

This morning, I just threw a casual glance onto a city standing on the side of the mountain that lies near the fens wherein my mansionhouse stands—Now, what do I see?—All of the inhabitants are dead!—Their flesh turned to liquid right on the spot, melting on the conical rays emanating from my ebony pupils like butter on a hot knife!—

A perpetual cloud of birds of carrion comes from the four corners of the horizon in order to feast on the remnants of the village, just now crushed like an anthill beneath an elephant's foot, but the stench from the aromatic atoms in the effluvium rising from those chalk-white bones in ascending spirals and helices, offends even their rapacious olfactory nerves with its monument to enormity and wickedness, and they fall, uncontrollably puking out their acidulous carrion guts (doesn't that last detail make your mouth water?—), onto the ground in unvanquishable disgust as they seem to begin to comprehend what takes place in a human mind, even if most do manage to keep it locked away beneath the cellar doors of the subconscious—

As for me, I feel the greatest intoxication imaginable as I breathe in the odor of putrefaction emanating from the fuming and fulminating city, ahhh—

Perhaps my gaze can kill even the planets rotating in outer space—

* * * * *

I tried to find a new copy of the book by Lord Weÿrdgliffe, that Penny Blood. I wanted to compare my own image in the mirror with the one in the book. But I failed to keep all of the books of my youth, and the dealer in antiquities has informed me, that all known copies of the volume have met their deaths in bonfires, at the hands of angry mobs, offended by its insurrectionary style and waves of theoretical wickedness, and that those few selections of it that have appeared in low-circulation journals and obscure anthologies often occur in a censored form—When they attempted to assassinate the man himself, believing, from taking him at his own word on the matter, that he had snatched countless victims from their midst, and inflicted the cruelest agonies upon them, they found that his mansionhouse, known as the Waughters, had disappeared from the swampy morasses of its estates, as if it had vanished away, dissolving into vapor, or into the world of unsought-for dreams and the purely fantastic—

The artist who carved the woodcut—from the life, the dealer informs me—cut his own throat before jumping into a well, from which his body was never recovered, and from which no one will now drink—

This information throws me into the deepest pit of despair—–
I feel myself swimming in the lake of sorrow—

* * * * *

I shot out of bed in a cold and glacial coating of sweat—

* * * * *

Despair has become omnipotent in the slaughterhouses of my brain. Not even the novel tortures I ceaselessly devise to execute on an unsuspecting populace can come close to reaching my goals of making others suffer the torments that besiege me—Those pranks just do not give the greatest possible measure of satisfaction—No, they would have to become me, to be me, to know the pain I feel—The pain itself, in fact, of *being me*—That torment, I cannot inflict by any method known, however extraordinary. I certainly don't belong among those who can imagine that the mere harm that can be inflicted upon the human body is the ultimate culmination of horror and weirdness. I know a torment too keen, too mordant, to lapse into such an error—

* * * * *

I have now found the means of wreaking my vengeance on humanity, even though I can only perform it on them one by one, but this method can surely find its extension to the entire race, given time—

It didn't take one of my bizarre inventions, relying on mechanical principles, but only a power, drawn purely from myself—

I stare at the mirror more and more, every day concentrating my forces on it—

I pour myself into the mirror, into the glass, and know that it will one day reflect my image back onto someone else, that it will impose my image upon his own, eventually obliterating all traces of his prior appearance—

* * * * *

I posed as a dealer in curiosities, working through the mail, and hirelings, who must never behold me, and managed to find a buyer for the mirror!—He thinks that no one else has ever used it, and that he alone will have ever beheld his visage in the pane!—

I bust a gut laughing when I think that now I have realized my plots against another, that the unsuspecting fool will endure the most distressing angst after he daily looks into *the mirror that makes the viewer resemble IT!*—The idiot will think that he has become me!—And that fact itself, will mean that he has, in point of sheer fact, become me!—

I triumph!—

* * * * *

Upon mature reflection, I only experience an inextinguishable regret at the irremediable situation, knowing, that I cannot reverse the process, and, just as my victim has become me, become, in my own turn, him, his ("my") victim—for, after all, for this sort of undeserved victimization to gain its greatest consummation, it should become reciprocal,—since cruelty gains its poignancy from the spectacle of the perception of the prey's agonies' effects upon your own mind, and that effect can reach its greatest pitch of intensity only when it becomes identity, complete and unabridged,—and I shall, therefore, never know the indescribable torments inflicted upon that one—by myself!—

    —Lord Weÿrdgliffe, the Waughters.

Beneath the Abyss

I'm disgusting. When coprophageous swine look at me—they puke. When flies approach too near me, attracted by the fragrance that makes carrion-flowers wilt—they fall dead. Worms refuse the putrid flesh of my corpse (I don't dare call it a body), at the price of their lives—cut one in half, and both halves squirm away in equal repulsion. Jackals and vultures spurn this cadaver, feeling their essential dignity soiled by its generous offer. Dung-beetles reject my excrement when I proffer it to them, repelled by such uncleanliness. The microorganisms of disease and decay decline to infest my mucosal members and slime-dripping trunk, feeling themselves polluted by their mere proximity. When pregnant women see me, squatting on my Cyclopean pedestal, they spontaneously abort out of the fear that their children should become my like, and the fetuses scuttle away in the scum like horseshoe crabs—even though they don't know what this sight portends.

My pulpy head resembles nothing so much as the shapeless form of the silken octopus. Impossible to tell whether its hue more closely matches the yellowish glamour of blennorrhoeal pus or the greenish nuance of sinusitis. A single eye, set vertically, all purplish pupil, reigns on my bulbous brow. Around what passes for my mouth—an adamantine beak that would serve for the mastication of nutriments, had I any need for such—a group of tentacles clutches a seraglio of four hundred suckers. A double row of dorsal tendrils twitches down my back, jutting out of my cartilaginous vertebral column. A leathery, reticulated hide covers my body down to my waist. From my shoulders sprout four flexible, cylindrical members, made of a ridgy, semi-elastic and extensible substance—two of them terminating in enormous claws or nippers, the other two in novel sensory organs of audition and olfaction. In place of nipples, a pair of short greenish-grey tentacles with red sucking mouths limply protrudes. An unspeakable orifice usurps the place of my navel, oozing a foetid yellowish-brown ichor from its dilated sphincter. Don't even mention what lies beneath my waist—for there all resemblance to the human form leaves off, and sheer phantasy begins.

I didn't always look this way. Once, everyone rejoiced at my presence. From my childhood others had noticed that my thoughts gave solace to the sorrowful. At the suggestion of my teachers, I studied philosophy and poetry, and as an adult, I filled ninety-three volumes with the sentiments and reasonings that make one glad to breathe the air and to see the light of day. No home in Thule, so they told me, lacked a nook devoted to the dog-eared tomes that I had penned with a quill plucked from the wing of a russet archaeopteryx; the alleys of cities and the chasms of mountains echoed with the hymns and chants which I had composed. Still, they asserted that a mere glance of my amber eyes conveyed more of my elevated ideas and emotions than four hundred and eighteen pages of crabbed script. Little can I judge of that, except by the multitudes of pilgrims who came—every day—to ponder my august visage, and who, as I lifted up my eyelids, retired in a trance to depart for the most distant wastelands, daring hurricanes and the desert's simoom, to tell the unbelieving foreigners what they had seen, and submit to seventy-eight years of torture in the dungeons of Hyperborea for promulgating unforgivable heresies against the vermiculate cult of the gods who (so they say) had filtered down from the starry spaces or emerged from the deepest bowels of the earth. Or, by the wild beasts, tamed by a single glimpse of my eyes, such as the saber-toothed tigers who forsook their ravagement of the countryside and its inhabitants to come and lick the dust from the soles of my feet.

And yet, it occurred to me—how little of one's mind even the eyes can translate into the body's sensible language. Once divulged, this thought inspired a noble project in the hearts of those who had consecrated their lives to the improvement of others' by means of the inventions of science. They studiously applied the insights revealed in my many volumes that treated of chemistry, biology, medicine, and the kindred sciences, adding the corrections of experiment to the precepts of intuition. Coils of tubing connected pear-shaped alembics, and prismatic fluids flowed incessantly from one vessel to another. They exhausted entire herb-gardens and metallic mines in the discovery of suitable materials for that unheard-of labor. After many decades spent in scientific strivings, they announced that they had arrived at the goal which eleven millennia had previously failed to attain. They had succeeded in creating the elixir that would render the body a perfect eidolon of the mind that so dimly shone through it, like that final glimmerings of a lightning-bug drowning in quicksand. So that the invention might benefit everyone as much as possible, they declared that the most beautiful soul should partake of the honor of initiating the elixir, of which they had succeeded in creating but a single dose, so great was the requisite labor.

They had an enormous amphitheater constructed so that everyone might benefit from the view of what dull and dense matter had always kept hidden. They erected this pedestal in the exact middle, and just go ahead and read the hieratic hieroglyphics carven on it for yourself, to see whether or not the label corresponds to the properties of its referent!—The thronging peoples gathered around to view that divine spectacle. All fell into hushed anticipation as I lifted that crystalline phial to my lips. What more do I need to say?—The experiment worked.

* * * * *

In the desolate solitude I remained. No mirror stood handily by the roadside to show me how I now appeared; and yet, from the somewhat remarkable reaction which that metamorphosis had engendered, I had conceived some idea of it. Again, I maintain that the experiment worked. Don't let yourself be fooled by a prejudiced viewpoint or a narrow morality, but think impartially and disinterestedly. Judge a unique being by the unique standards that pertain to it—I'm not asking for anything better than that. Immortal and alone, I dedicated every moment to meditation upon my aweful martyrdom-apotheosis, which I received as a supreme sanction. After a few centuries of the most intense concentration on my novel state, I orchestrated the members that serve me in the prehension and manipulation of objects. I palpated my carcass with those twin nippers, down to beneath my waist—(I have needs, just like anyone else)—the secret was discovered. I held and beheld that nameless organ—a semi-translucent whitish-pink, of a rubbery texture, and terminating in a polypous head with rings of luminous yellow eyeballs. In a frenzied ecstasy, I performed the appropriate operations—although discovering their exact nature required no small amount of experimentation. All the while I meditated upon my own beauty and what it meant.

The dam burst. There, on the ground, was a creamy and putrid mass, seething with corruption and hideous rottenness, neither liquid nor solid, but melting and changing before my eye, bubbling with unctuous oily bubbles like boiling pitch. In the midst of a congeries of iridescent globules I saw a writhing and stirring as of limbs or tails. That liquescent lump of solidified slime altered in consistency; and after about five minutes, it slowly seeped into the ground, leaving behind nothing but the mordant aroma of rancidity and contamination—That pungent incense inspired within me a hope which would not be disappointed.

The solitary foecundation, which had been nothing in other, similar cases, was accepted, that time, by fatality; and at the end of a few days, many thousands of monsters, bursting forth from the earth like a multitude of tiny spiders from a cyst in your armpit, were born into the light. No one can imagine my pleasure when I beheld the first of my children. One in particular caught my attention, larger and more ferocious than the rest. It slightly resembled a tadpole, with a lengthy tail attached to its almost globular torso-head, with seven long, sinuous limbs, terminating in crab-like claws, a triangle of three staring, fishy eyes, and a distended lateral system suggestive of gills. An obliquely-poised flexible proboscis did not reveal its true function as its four shapeless nostrils tested the ground, slurping like squishy, bloodsucking leeches. A dense growth of dark, slender tentacles or sucking filaments covered the monstrosity's body-head, each one of them tipped with a mouth suggestive of the head of a lamprey eel. I found it, if possible, even more beautiful than myself.

Almost immediately, the creature noticed the thousands of forms that flopped and fluttered around it on misshapen pseudo-pods and half-formed wings. What had formerly appeared as an organ of respiration now revealed its true character. It pounced upon a thing like an eye-covered starfish and sucked it into its proboscis-like member. Now it devoured something which combined the forms of the centipede, octopus, and vampire bat as it exuded a foetid green ichor. Next a cone-shaped being, partly squamous and partly rugose, which slowly meandered across the plain, leaving a steaming trail of yellowish ooze. One by one, the thing consumed each and every one of my lesser offspring.

Its body had distended to many hundreds of times its previous size. It lay down, a look as of contentment emanating from its eyes. Soon, however, it started to quiver like a mass of gelatin and all of the filaments covering its body-head stood on end. Its tail twitched fitfully and feverishly. A sort of hesitant snort or sneeze disturbed its proboscis' repose. A shiver shook through its entire body, it shuddered, and there explosively erupted from its erect proboscis' four nostrils all of the creatures which it had just devoured. They lay dazed across the landscape in their thousands, covered with a sticky gluten which I recognized as not intended for digestion. The warmth of the sun, which seemed to blush in shame at the very sight, soon revived them to their former state of liveliness. I recognized then that my offspring, like their father, would only perish with the universe.–If then.

I also divined the purpose of that creature's teratological conformation. I looked down at the horror, and its gaze met my own. Love shot back and forth in sparkling beams of glittering sparks between our four eyes, as three hundred and thirty-three eternities of infatuation compressed themselves into a few moments' space. We bruskly fell one against the other, like two lovers, and embraced with dignity and recognition, in a hug as tender as that of a brother or a sister. Carnal desires closely followed that demonstration of friendship. Our manifold suckers and oral orifices glued themselves tightly onto each other's viscous hide, like leeches; our tentacles interwove around the cherished objects which we were surrounding with love; my nameless organ rammed into the unnameable nostril on the entity's ambiguous proboscis; I then noticed (what an unexpected development!–) that I had three more of them, and attained complete union with the thing; in the midst of the raging tempest; in the glimmer of lightning flashes; breathing a glaucous mass of pussy exhalations from every pore; with the dilapidated amphitheater, covered with mud and the excremental effluvia of myself and my offspring, as our hymenaeal bed; rolling in a ball of devotion more cherished than a scarab-beetle's; we united, in a prolonged copulation, chaste and hideous!–

As we accomplished that ineffable union, the ground beneath us shook, and, caused by I have no idea what, our footing shifted ever downward, as the continent, which rocked us like a cradle, sank slowly down beneath the ocean's abysses. As the amphitheater crackled into ruins; as the storm abated into shifting currents of seaweed; as rivers of lava tongued the liquid enveloping them; watched by the guardful and uneasy eyes of sperm-whales, sharks, ichthyosaurs, octopi, coelacanths, scorpion-fish, sting-rays, plesiosaurs, jellyfish, anarnaks, plankton, and my immense, tenebrous spermatozoa, we sank, my child and I, to the ocean's briniest depth, and I quadruply impregnated my beloved progeny at precisely the moment when the thunderous regions of Thule became the unsounded unknown!–

* * * * *

My present position offers nothing offensive to me. If anything, I welcome the darkness—which shall not, however, outlast my ugliness. Here, for every second of every night (we have no day), I maintain my lugubrious meditations on the future state of the universe, when my innumerable offspring shall overrun the entire world and—Thule once again having risen above the waves—I shall reign as the supreme Lord of All, my beauty acknowledged by those prodigious gargoyles and grotesqueries, the sole inhabitants of the earthly globe and the sidereal spheres—all other lifeforms having perished utterly under their pestiferous presence. Meanwhile, with a constancy unknown to human procreation, I continue to engender the sublime oddities that sprout from my son's unnameable nostrils, deluged with entire floods of my steaming semen. Perhaps even before Thule once again arises they shall overflow the sea and spill over onto land, invaginate the rocky orb with their tenacious sliminess, spread throughout the aether, blot out the feeble sun, the stars, and the planets revolving in nullity, fill the void and fill the universe with their enormity unto the last curved rim of space, until they bloat against and strain at the bounds of existence with their acidulous viscosity and shatter through its limits as though through the perfumed linings of the dilated sphincter of some vast, celestial anus.

—Lord Weÿrdgliffe, the Waughters.

The Web of Lord Weÿrdgliffe

But these are mysteries which I evolve in the profound
Abysses of the Mind.
—*The Chaldaean Oracles of Zoroaster.*

Lord Weÿrdgliffe felt a great weariness weighing him down,
pulling him to the center of the earth, as if his limbs had altered
into the density of the leaden tears that would roll down his
cheeks at his reptilian remorse over some outré crime. The act of
writing imposes a heavy burden on the one who attempts it, but
when you feel an octopus writhing in your brain like a fixed idea,
goading you on to that act of virtuosity, you cannot let go of the
pen until the tale to be told finds itself in a state of completion—and Lord Weÿrdgliffe had that need to such a great degree,
that he had managed to achieve his purpose on this very day,
even though he had to write in a mirror-image on the page, because he had woken up that afternoon with his hands attached to
the wrong wrists.

Ever since he had begun the literary task which still occupies
his principal attention, he had noticed that each time he awoke,
his body felt strange, as if the joints and hinges holding it together had started to come loose—he could of course attribute
that to the mirroring of his mental by his physical state, but the

latest awakening's odd effect had erased that impression from his mind. It seemed a solid certainty, as he put together the pieces of the story into a form resembling his own disjointed image, that some trickery must nightly take place, and he had resolved that he would find out the nocturnal bandit, who took such liberties with one who didn't wish to recognize any power outside of himself. So, he planned on taking the sneakthief by surprise: he knew that he couldn't avoid sleeping, but it seemed tolerably certain that if he awakened early, he would overtake the culprit, and only one thing could prove strong enough to rouse him from his slumber: a nightmare. With great difficulty—because of his reversed hands—he drank an entire bottle of laudanum, scarfed down three platefuls of Welsh rabbit, and swallowed a further bottle of laudanum.

He lacked even the force to undress himself, and barely made it to his bed before his consciousness felt itself snuffed out like a stuttering candle. He dreamed of—I have no idea what, for Lord Weÿrdgliffe always conscientiously avoids making such unsuitable disclosures—but in any event the nightmare proved powerful enough to effect his awakening, and he beheld a tableau which, much like his recent nightmare, shocked him into a state of greater lucidity.

He looked at that spectacle from his pillows, on which his head lay, companionless, while a group of creatures, man-shaped, but whose bodies revealed the similitude of anatomical figures, the likeness of a diagram of the veins and arteries, their pores breathing blood and bile, sported with the other parts of his cadaverous body. One of them held his calves, which he halfheartedly juggled, while another frolicked similarly with his thighs; the two soon joined together in a dual performance. One played at walking with his feet; another enjoyed himself flipping his arms around on their springy elbow-joints; one pulled his organs out of his limbless torso one by one, and threw them about the room, bouncing them off of the walls at absurd angles, calculated to amuse the others, who laughed profusely at that comical scene. Three final members of this crew of chimaerical criminals, rounded out the spectacle, the one holding his two hands, using the right hand to suavely stroke his crimson-veined cock, and the left to titillate his anus with its index-finger, the other two employing, the first his prick, which he held at the level of his groin, as if it rightfully belonged there, the second likewise utilizing his anus to create for himself a novel vulva. Those rascals could hardly contain themselves at the virtuosity of that method of amusement—particularly upon the moment of penetration—and one of them, with the laugh of a hyaena, declared that each should play such a role in turn, and only regretted that it would make some of the other corporeal parts of Lord Weÿrdgliffe lack abuse for the want of time.

So much did this manner of enjoying themselves preoccupy those ghoulish scoundrels, that they only noticed that Lord Weÿrdgliffe had opened his eyes when his own laughter exceeded theirs in volume: he hadn't expected such a sight, which didn't entirely lack appeal to his sense of the fantastic and the grotesque, and he felt a little surprised that he hadn't thought to victimize others in just such a way.—For he always found a heady voluptuous ecstasy in such trifling pleasantries. But those skinless culprits screamed like someone being flayed alive when they perceived that his ivory-white lids had exposed his ebony eyeballs, and they precipitated themselves out of the room like an avalanche, leaping through the window—its panes and shutters unclosed by the first one to bash his way through—each of them carrying the bodily parts which, in their momentary inattention to detail, they bore away like trophies or mementos.

Lord Weÿrdgliffe's head rolled in laughter off of the pillows and onto the tapestried flooring, then hit the wall with a thud, and, on its return journey, saw the bed loom up above it, and knocked against the chamberpot with a resounding *ding!* At this

point Lord Weÿrdgliffe realized that his present situation involved a certain degree of seriousness; he couldn't expect to get
put back together, even with his appendages carelessly placed in
incorrect locations, and he could hardly compose the works
which he felt compelled to write, even if it should bring on a universal hatred—not an unexpectable result, in his case—without
his arms and the trembling fingers of his shaking hands. Using
his eyelids to gain purchase on the rug, he pulled himself several
feet away from beneath the bed, but the exertion proved too great
to maintain for any length of time. He could never catch up with
those ghouls in this way. Now, the Baron, as everyone admits—at
least those with a thorough knowledge of the subject at hand,
who don't bow down in obeisance before vulgar prejudices and
ignorant opinions—has a head of hair which expresses his will
more tellingly than that of others, and so, to give himself a more
useful power of motion, he bunched his green locks up at the top
of his scalp, and transformed them into eight willowy tentacles,
which reached up and then back down to the ground so that his
current totality resembled nothing so much as a daddy-longlegs.

    With great, loping strides, Lord Weÿrdgliffe scuttled to his
desk, clutched his armchair with two of his tentacles, and pushed
it over to underneath the window. He climbed up and out—

    Splash!—he landed in the mud. He hadn't even bothered to
look to see whether it was raining or not—such considerations
don't often occur, to one who lusts for the adventure of hunting
down his own body snatchers—and so their tracks had gotten difficult to discern, not an easy task in the darkness—infrequently
relieved by lightning-flashes, anyway, but he headed out in the
direction indicated by the few signs remaining. Those distorted
indices lead him on along a winding path, which eventually pe-
tered out, after he had rounded several clumps of trees, and he
had just determined that he should give up the chase, and find
someone else's body to replace his own former body, when the

rain, pouring down, flashed into a veritable flood, and swept him off and down the sloping declivity. His tentacles twitched wildly on that savage ride, and, to his great dismay, he found himself dumped into a river—he hadn't even known that one existed so close to the Waughters (and who hasn't heard the whispered legends of that shunned mansionhouse which the Baron Weÿrdgliffe holds as his ancestral estates?)—and which overflowed its banks in the storm.

An hour or so of experiment provided him with the ability, in some sort, of directing his movement through the water, although he could not escape the ranting and raging currents, increased by the momentary influx of crystalline liquid. Mentally, he attempted to calculate how soon he should reach human habitation, and figured that when he did, he could climb ashore—unseen, that goes without saying—and then appropriate to himself the body of some stranger. He hadn't yet succeeded in reckoning the distance—because he didn't know the river's path, he told himself—when he noticed a boat floating along beside him. His tentacles clamped onto the hull with improvised suckers, and he plopped up on board. A man stood guard, staring forward at the prow. Lord Weÿrdgliffe quickly climbed up to the very top of the mast, then hurled himself on an exact trajectory that succeeded in landing him precisely on the man's head. He grasped him solidly with his tentacles, then reached his head around, and bit through the man's throat, before he could so much as scream for help. With teeth like Lord Weÿrdgliffe's, it doesn't take too long to chew through someone's neck (he doesn't have rotten gums), and that man's head dropped off in an instant, departing to keep the fishes and crawdads company. Lord Weÿrdgliffe grabbed tightly in a circle around the neck area, and firmly planted his own head onto the other man's body. What he hadn't counted on, was that the dead body, slain just a moment before, would remain dead, and when it fell back onto the deck it knocked the back of his head against the boards. That smarting wound induced the Baron to infer an insult, and he launched the corpse over the side of the boat, even though positioning his current conformation for that act of revenge took no small effort of mental and physical exertion.

Obviously, he needed to take a different tack with his next prospective body. After scoping out the layout of the boat, he tapped a tattoo onto a cabin door, and sang out an invitation in a sweet and alluring voice. Out came a dupe. The Baron leapt down onto his neck from behind, and he extended a short stem from the lower side of his head, which tapped into the spinal column of the sailor, and his nerves took root in the hapless idiot's system. The poor fellow, not knowing what was happening, shouted in amazement, releasing an enormous scream of the most poignant agony, until Lord Weÿrdgliffe, dissatisfied with his new host, not liking arrangements of collective ownership very much, bit his nose off, tonguing the twin nostrils before spitting it overboard, and then stabbed him with four of his tentacles, two through that new-and-improved airhole, and two more through the pupils of his eyes, which dilated prodigiously to encompass and incorporate those tendrils, to grope his brains from the inside, doing no small amount of damage in the process.

The man's cries had roused another passenger, and she appeared on the deck, emerging from another cabin down below. When Lord Weÿrdgliffe saw her, with her feminine figure, as beautiful as an hourglass ticking away the grains of slow sand that must fall before the blade of the guillotine whacks off the head of a precocious criminal, creating a gestalt effect of a Classical beauty, well-suited to unite with a Romantic passion, he knew what he had to do—for how many times in the past hadn't he wanted to have just such a body, to do with exactly as he pleased?—

The male body fell dead behind him (its old head just couldn't find the force to retake its former empire, what with its current condition and all), as he uprooted himself and leapt towards the woman. That vision of loveliness, inspired by a cryptomnesic recall of a story by Lord Weÿrdgliffe (like most readers of that unwholesome author she had completely suppressed all conscious recall of his work after the perusal of but a single story, met with by chance in an obscure journal of no significant circulation), grabbed him by the tentacles, and swung his head around like a sling, the suckers clasping hold of her arm desperately, until, at a precisely calculated moment, she instantly arrested the motion of her arm, which had as its effect: the Baron's tentacular crown ripped loose from his scalp, sending the bodiless head—launched by the centrifugal force—flying towards the stars, and leaving the beautiful woman with an octet of twitching tentacles in her hand. After a few minutes of amazement, she tossed those loose-jointed limbs overboard—they floated out to sea, twitching the whole way, and may still remain twitching yet—for it seems that no one so far has searched the desert islands of the Hyperboreal seas for those unique treasures—perhaps they have established themselves as the immanent gods of some race lost from cartographical knowledge. —Neither you nor she would have expected that woman to possess a degree of strength so great, but just so strongly does the horror inspired by the Author of Inexplicable Iniquities take hold of one—

The Baron's head flew screaming past the moon, past the planets, and on into the spaces between the stars. After an indeterminate, and uneventful, length of time, it collided against an enormous webbing stretching from star to star, stuck fast to its gluey strands, rebounding back and forth in ever-decreasing oscillations, sending vibrations out along that constellation-covering cobweb to the infernal and eldritch spider-daemon who inhabited it. Lord Weÿrdgliffe couldn't help but wonder just what sort of prey that creature relied on for her normal nutritive functions—(how could he have known that she often trapped entire planetary systems within her complicated snares, to devour the bewildered populations of their worlds at her leisure?)—when she appeared to his sight, drawn by the vibrations which she had taken as those of a potential mate, for they lacked sufficient strength to indicate prey,—her arthropodal articulations glittered, as beautiful as the ceremonial vestments worn by a wizard lich twenty centuries after its nominal decease, for the performance of the rites which should prolong its existence for another millennium, and as she stared into his two eyes, with her seven multi-faceted orbs, she thought that she recognized a kindred being, in that the ferocity mirrored in those glassy globes seemed nearly equal to her own. That momentary hesitation proved decisive. For as she held him, staring into his pupils with the reflective lenses of her fascinated eyes, he extended a root from his throat, out between her mandibles, and into her abdomen, wherefrom he took total control of her body. With a feeling of sadness, he shriveled her now dried-up head and let the powdery ashes fall drifting into the void.

An enormous gossamer strand of spider-daemon-silk shot out across the emptiness, with a unique being trailing along behind it. Another one intersected and stuck fast to the planet known to the insignificant ants that inhabited it as *the earth*, and the entity crawled across it with an awkward nimbleness, then alighted on the puny pebble.

Still—something unaccountable, truly enough—the Baron desired the homely comforts of his former body. The spider-daemon's physique gave great benefits, no doubt, but he could scarcely write one of his Horrid Tales while having the use only of its agile legs;—although he could, if he had wanted to, have created a text, which would have stretched from star to star, but he felt that he could hardly find a sufficient audience to read such a production.—For he didn't consider the planet-sized worms of the aether worth communicating with, but only that most nauseating of all monstrosities, toad-faced Man—

With a lengthy process of hide-'n'-seek, he discovered the cemetery-abutting den of those grotesque pranksters who had robbed him of his everything save for his head, and found that each one had retained whatever part he had taken, for they all declared that they had too great a fear to return them to their prior possessor, but also cherished them too greatly to let them go un-owned. The Baron found the most of them in proper enough working order, with only insignificant defects in the others, and after having wrapped those wags in silken-stranded bonds, which resembled nothing so much as cocoons and held them in total immobility, hanging upside-down from a nearby gallows, but leaving their faces exposed, so as to enjoy their presence as an audience, he re-assembled his threadbare body, and placed his head back on top of it, and he couldn't help but feel two or three bitter pangs of crocodilian regret over the many victims he could have ensnared within its excellent silken surprises, as he saw the spider-daemon's cadaver crumble into dust beside him.

After a few instants of intense examination he discovered that he could recognize the faces in front of him. For unlike most authors, Lord Weÿrdgliffe had achieved such great prowess in that art, that he had actually managed—for only a few instants, true enough, but still a noteworthy accomplishment, unachiev-able by any lesser author—to effect an exchange of relationship with his readership, so that they found themselves trapped within the limits of the text, while he roamed freely in the material uni-verse, and the gruesome company currently disgracing his pres-ence he recognized exactly as the most devoted readers of his Penny Dreadful, *The Unspeakable; or, The Anatomy of Otherness: A Gothick Romance*, which had won him the vilification of the vast majority, including an older author of the weird and fantas-tic, widely considered a master of gratuitous sadism and unrea-soning atrocity, and who had called that volume: "The foulest toadstool that has sprung up from the reeking dunghill of the present times."

But these few, he suspected, had felt impelled to continue reading him despite themselves and their repulsion, and the corrosive effect of his wording had gradually turned them inside-out, so that they had assumed the appearance which they now took for granted as the token of their identity, and when this realization struck him on the forehead like a slingstone, he completely forgot the stinging roots on his scalp, and, encouraged by a degree of artistic success which could inspire his so-called fellows to truly become his fellows—in point of cleverness in cruelty, if not of ugliness in appearance—he cut each of them free with the obsidian fingernail of his middle finger, one by one, swinging them by the feet and hurling them a half-mile's distance—so that they would divine his intentions correctly, and headed back to the Waughters, where he sat down at his desk, took up a pen and some paper, and to further increase the probability of the materialization of his idealistic goals, for he desired nothing more than that others should become as monstrous as himself—eventually, he thought, this would create a Utopia populated entirely with such bizarreries, and he would hardly mind making his relationship with them reciprocal, in such a circumstance—he began to write a Horrid Tale, to mutate his readership's bewildered brains into festering wounds pullulating with a palpitating progeny of pestiferous vermin, beginning with the sentence: "Lord Weÿrdgliffe felt a great weariness weighing him down, pulling him to the center of the earth, as if his limbs had altered into the density of the leaden tears that would roll down his cheeks at his reptilian remorse over some outré crime."—And the text continued onwards to its inevitable conclusion, the trademark signature which makes its unwelcome appearance at the end of each and every one of his eldritch and unwholesome texts:

—Lord Weÿrdgliffe, the Waughters.

Insectoid Aeons

When the razorblade slit into my wrist—don't play the innocent fool with me, and pretend that you lack all awareness of the
grievous situation that necessitates suicide; for, after all, when it
comes to a tribe as nauseatingly unclean as humanity, it appears
clearly enough that any number larger than one must be one too
many—at the very least—and that the rest have to go. And since I
lacked the power to exterminate the entire race of vermin—for
even *my* vomit (*I*, who felt that disgust at my fellows more keenly
than any other) could hardly accumulate into a tsunami immense
enough to inundate the entire earth in a universal deluge, thus
producing the much-desired result—I found myself with no alternative to escaping through the one doorway left open by the
bolted padlocks of circumstance.

When the razorblade slit into my wrist, a great startlement
and surprise took hold of me, to see that instead of disburdening
myself of the cross called *life*, I had merely cut a seam into a suit
of skin which I had formerly considered an integral part of my
ego. But no sooner did I peel that layer off than I had it removed,
revealing my body in its pristine purity! I admired that insectoid
body, noting its excellent features: an indistinctly segmented
thorax; a clearly segmented abdomen; the thorax and abdomen
together dorso-ventrally flattened; powerful legs ending in a

claw and spine adapted to grasping hairs; needle-like stylets to convey blood into me whenever my anti-coagulant saliva combined with the pump-action of my gut musculature. No doubt about it: I had the superb form that belongs to the noble race of Lice, and—to judge of it from the compactness of my conformation, the Crab Louse in particular. Imagine my inutterable joy as I contemplated that durable metamorphosis into myself!—

A few test runs, and it proved a certainty that I could resume my former identity just by stretching that old piece of hide over my more perfect beauty. Then, I launched myself into a double life, by night shedding the repugnant signs of humanity in favor of the supernal beauty of my truer form. I would stray out into the tattered cities of men, where I would lurk in the darkness until I had found one of them ready to take as a prey; then, I would leap onto the creature, clamp hold of its scalp, insert my razor-sharp stylets into its skull, and suck out through the holes in its head the beast's entire supply of blood, totally draining the corpse of liquid, followed by its brain, its eyeballs, its spinal column, its skeleton, its lungs, its heart, its liver, its spleen, its bladder, its bowels, and finally—the genitalia. Afterwards, I would hurl the empty bag of skin to the ground, and then, not wanting to let anything go to waste, I would devour the desiccated husk. In a daze of hazy intoxication, I would stumble home, there to rest in my bed until I had slept off the inebriating communion wine enough that I could once more fit inside my human skin.

For a long time, I kept that second life a secret. After a while, however, I began to flaunt my victimization of my fellows, allowing a helpless audience to gawk in wonder at such a prodigy; and they showed a spirit that I would hardly have thought them capable of, for instead of organizing a party of extermination against the one who preyed on them mercilessly, they surrounded me with a canine veneration and started a cult in honor of the unknowable god. I felt then that I could dispense with the quotidian annoyances of my double life, and stopped wearing the old suit of skin; for their part, they built me an enormous temple of marble wherein to house myself, and—constantly feeding on the sacrificial victims they would bring me in indefinite and expiatory holocausts—I grew bigger and bigger, until I could crush mobs of men like an elephant crushing ears of corn.

One day someone came to me wearing I visage I believed to have recognized from somewhere before, and only after the greatest concentration did I realize who stood before me—myself, in my imperfect state!—There stood in front of me the most perfect double or doppelgänger of an identity which I had hoped to eradicate forever from the face of the earth as an unbearable burden on my awareness!—I interrogated that one, and soon enough discovered that my High Priest had discarded his own human hide (following the practices decreed by an inalterable inference from the immutable axioms of my cult, he too had tested the keenness of a razorblade on his wrist), and learned that his own conformity resembled my own, but the fact had determined him to honor me with the eternal presentation of my image, which (so he said) I no longer found any use for. That idea thrilled me, and so I ordered him in the strictest terms to bring his former identity to me, and I gobbled down that suit of skin right in front of him, then—told him that I condemned him to forever wear my ancient image, which appeared to me the ugliest and most disgusting one imaginable, for I wished for my own joy, reflected in the form I currently wore, to find its perfect opposite always mirrored before it in the form and the suffering which he had now assumed!—

That decree seemed to unhinge the one who had always before managed to remain as cold-blooded as you might possibly wish, but just try to imagine my surprise when, instead of displaying to me a gratitude which seemed as natural as the instinct to murder one's beloved—not only to preserve her from the pangs

and pains of an all-too imperfect existence, but also to give oneself the greatest pleasure conceivable, made into a complex emotion by the irremediable regret of her loss—he attacked me, as I
lay in a stupor from a recently devoured hecatomb of humanity,
dreaming that I had hurtled myself through space like a meteor
from the pubes of some ithyphallic behemoth constructed in proportions relative to my own to crash onto those of a Cyclopean
giantess during an immense and rational climax of concupis-
cence, where I could clamp my claws onto a forest of towering
hairs and suck into the never-ending venereal mountain which
lay beneath them, abutting against a bottomless ravine. He had,
through what ingenious agency I will never know, without my
least suspicion finding itself roused, replaced my chamber of rest
with a bizarre machine of torture, which consisted of a gigantic
cylinder, lined with stiletto-sharp knives and spikes, which
would—while whirling those blades about in contrary directions—slowly contract to a minuscule diameter, thus squashing
the one who lay inside it unawares. I heard a lever pulled, and
those blades protracted and slashed into my hide, letting the
enormous quantities of blood and brains that filled my glutted
guts gush out in a flood that inundated entire cities and deluged
more than one continent!—Even as I felt pleased with him, I felt
no small astonishment: for I had, true enough, believed him my
respectful disciple in perversity, but—not my redoubtable rival.
Soon enough, that machine of torment had sliced away every bit
of the layer of myself that resembled the Crab Louse to the point
of identity, and a tiny red and black slug crept out of that cylinder, leaving an unctuous trail of slime. Nothing more was left of
me!—

Hours turned to days turned to weeks turned to months
turned to years as I crept to the home of that noble traitor, and as
I did so, taking care to avoid the sight of any who might behold
me—not an easy thing to do, at my rate of travel—the world re-

turned to its normal state and all resumed their former lives. I knew that I had to retake my former empire, and that the one who now inhabited my old appearance had the body of the Louse underneath it; so that I should merely have to dispossess him of it to regain an equivalent circumstance to my prior heavenly routine. But how to overpower him, so as to do it? I hit upon an ingenious stratagem, and during the night, I crawled into his underwear. When he reached down to put them on in the morning—(and good thing he didn't bother to look where he was groping about!)—I waited till the decisive moment and then he felt me enter into his constipated anus, which hadn't yet gotten used to that kind of intrusion—for he had as yet little experience with the ways of society,—and the sphincter had to dilate prodigiously to accommodate even *my* meager proportions. If my slimy coating didn't act as a lubricant I might never have gotten in!—He tried at first to pull me out—having overcome his repugnance at the texture of my oozy covering, but he couldn't loosen his sphincter enough to let me pass back out that way, and soon enough I dove into his bowels, and, after several minutes of internal jostling, out from his mouth came a creature that appeared as a hairy yellow caterpillar. That thing disgusted me almost as much as the sight of a human being, and so I kicked it straight out the window—I thought that the force that could shatter a pane of glass might damage the little beastie as well!—

I fell into a dreamless sleep of relief that lasted the rest of the day. But when I stripped off that human skin—for I remembered that he as well must have the Louse's conformation, hadn't he told me so himself?—I saw there not the noble and beautiful Crab Louse but the feeble and pathetic Wood Louse—that craven arthropod saddled by a justified contempt with such inopportune epithets as the *Potato Bug* and the *Sow Bug*. Before I could rouse my consciousness from its dazed state of astonishment at that dismal turn of fortune, I heard a crunching noise from under the bed, where I had put my facial and other human features. Looking there, I saw that the caterpillar had munched away the whole suit. Now, whenever that muscular critter knocks into me with the intention of regaining possession of its insectoid form, I cannot do anything but roll into a ball (this way, my carapace protects my otherwise vulnerable underbelly) and let it carom me now here, now there, like a billiard ball eternally in search of a corner pocket, and as I bounce against the buildings lining the streets of man's metropolises, the mocking masses—who so recently worshiped me as their immanent deity and the eidolon of perfection incarnate—cut into my pride with comments like: "Look, there goes the pathetic old *Pill Bug* now!" With what patience do I wait for my tormentor to create a cocoon around himself and come out from the chrysalis in the image of the imago of the aethereal and so-beautiful Butterfly, as lovely as the image of me was ugly!—

—Lord Weÿrdgliffe, the Waughters.

Mare Tenebrarum

Experiments that failed too many times,
Transformations that were too hard to find.
—Blue Öyster Cult, "Flaming Telepaths."

Every night, as I looked out of my window onto the world, there appeared before the clouds of my vision milling rows of crocodiles, marching along on a thousand millipede legs, circling through the streets in a procession upwards to the hills. Above, an upward spiral of wingèd sharks floated scuddingly in a heliacal parade to the far-flung zenith, nearing the moon that leered down leprously at the earth like a pockmarked buttock severed from some Titaness hag's flabby flanks. What differentiated this night from the nights of the past two weeks, was that I managed to focus my eyeballs, and that there appeared before them a more sharply defined image, almost to the point of clarity. Those weren't crocodiles; those weren't wingèd sharks; instead, an army of coffins—mobilized mechanically, that goes without saying—that seemed to violate the laws of Man, of Nature, and of—What?

At that point I knew what must have happened, and why those carnivorous coffins seemed so familiar to me, like household pets. For it seems that exactly two weeks before that fateful eve, I had entered into my bedroom to retire, and when I opened my wardrobe to exchange clothes, its insides seemed somehow narrower than before, and—as I betrayed my startlement with a backward leap—a lid closed heavily; it failed to take its prey. After a second, a coffin crawled out of the wardrobe on mechanical millipede legs, and I pursued that remarkable creature fruitlessly down the hall. For two weeks, we played a game of hide-'n'-seek, that coffin and I, and for two weeks, it made every attempt to enclose me within its pinewood planks; for two weeks, I made every attempt to rope the thing with a hempen lasso. At night, I would go to open the shutters of my casement in order to stick my ungainly head out for a breath of fresh air in the stuffy night, and I would find myself sucked out by an outside force, which had intermediately hidden itself on the sloping roof in wait: only with great difficulty could I extricate myself from that perilous situation. Finally, the night before, after staring at the crocodiles' parade and the cavalcade of wingèd sharks for hours on end, I journeyed out into the dark to take a piss, and a strange suspicion overtook me before I entered the outhouse. So, I lassoed that structure; and after I had battered away every splinter of it by swinging it against a near-by cliff, only the consuming coffin remained.

With the rest of the day to do it, I managed to train that creature into a state of complete docility. Tamed, it served as a masterful steed; whether riding about the land, directing it with the hempen rope which has forevermore remained bound tightly around it—for its thousand legs could carry it faster than one might have at first believed; or whether flying through the skies on the membraneous span of its reticulated wings, which you might not at first have suspected. Now, as I gazed at its innumerable compeers, I began to suspect the reason why I had seen less and less of men in the days preceding; some master of mechanical engineering must have created these infernal instruments for the admirable purpose of eradicating the human race! And each one, save for a single one only, must have achieved its purpose, and be returning to its master to evidence its performance with physical proof!—I felt a shudder of adoration pervade my soul as I imagined such a one as could conceive of and carry out such a praiseworthy plan—

One so deserving of adulation cannot go unvisited, and so I called my coffin to me with a whistle, leapt onto its back, took hold of the lasso, and headed for the skies, following the route those funereal pilgrims laid out for me. To my vague surprise, no army of cats came to pass us by, going in the opposite direction; why that idea should have occurred to me then, I leave to the Reader's ingenuity to solve; for its own part, my mind races along at the same rate as a derailed locomotive speeds through the shimmering sand.

I hovered as the flotilla of floating coffins alighted on the layered moondust. They arranged themselves in rows, standing proudly tall like unwound grandfather's clocks set to domino across the outspoken craters and campi. I arose a little higher to master fully the figure which they seemed to outline, to signal to the stars, but saw nothing but curvilinear hieroglyphics that did not allow any certainty of interpretation; however, it seemed to center about a grouping that stood like megalithic monuments, forming a novel Stonehenge on the lunar landscape. There, I circled in, and beheld the one who had, most certainly, ventured to undertake the fate of all mankind! Rejoice, O Reader, that I belong amongst those who have "learned from men who'd just refrain / From glancing at a mirror's face!"—For otherwise, this tale would not reach the dénouement which the Writer has designed and designated for it; do not concern yourself at all with the possibility that an even more astonishing climax might have been in the offing, had he only had the consideration (the cowardice!) to undertake the toilsome task of appeasing your sensibilities.

As it was, I entered into conversation with that black-cloaked gentleman—who of course conceded equality of spirit to the one who had outwitted his contraption—and soon learned that his complotments did not wholly coincide with my prior surmises. No, he explicated to me, he fancied himself a writer, and—with little enough verisimilitude—a writer of Weird Tales! Now, once again he did not disdeign to consider me his peer when I pointed, with a skeletal finger, to my own Strange Stories. He had—so he claimed—for long remained content to retain only a minuscule readership, as only a few have a keen appreciation for the bizarre and the terrible; and he considered that this had cause in the fact that whereas art is an imitation of life, few have lived lives so characterized by the irreducible oddities of the imagination and the unendurably horripilating atrocities within which his Weird Tales have found themselves overbrimming in a state of suppurative saturation. Even those few, he further postulated, who read in order to attain the consolation of knowing that another being has an understanding of one's own private hells, would frequently find his Penny Dreadfuls excessive in their whimsical gore and gratuitous grue; whereas those others, who read in order to accomplish the feat of feeling truly afraid, would most often fail in the emotional exercise:—for very few have a true expertise in that arcane art of affective athleticism.

Now, he had, while reading through the surviving texts of an artist greater than he was (according to a judgment relying upon an incommensurable comparison), chanced upon the following admonition: *"Anéantissez donc à jamais tout ce qui peut détruire un jour votre ouvrage."*—"So annihilate forever everything that could one day destroy your work." In conformity with that sage advice, he had formulated the intricate plan which had found the consummation of only its first stage in the total abduction of the human tribe; for these coffins did not slay their game, but instead worked an alchemical change upon them which would culminate in their utter transmutation into creatures inherently able to appreciate the utmost depths of the bizarre and the terrible enshrined within the works of the renowned Lord Weÿrdgliffe—a name which it somehow (somehow!) struck me that I had heard somewhere (somewhere!) before. With a rhetorical flourish, he continued that his imagination continually conceived of chimaerical creations in an unceasing attempt to represent the way in which one wholly devoid of humanity might appear; he speculated in an unrepeatable manner about the possibilities of facial features resembling sea anemones; of unspeakable orifices oozing a foetid ichor from their dilated sphincters; of twitching filaments on a luminous phallos's prepuce apparently suffering from a painful paraphimosis; of tentacles clutching their seraglio of suckers on the faces of Cubo-Futurist architects; of unnameable nostrils and their non-respiratory functions; and above all, of the utterly abominable and unmentionable third anus. These grotesques and gargoyles, he assured me, would usher in a New Aeon in which all would forever glory in acts which would combine the most blasphemous of obscenities with the most outrageous of atrocities; they would thus, he shouted into the alarmed eardrum of the closely-listening void, create a festering and fruiting utopia in which his work would always find an avid readership: for this glorious race should frequently approach his imagination in their weirdness and awfulness, and his work would thus seem to them an imitation of life, whether that appearance reversed the truth or no. I asked him how he would know when the eagerly anticipated transformation had been completed; he answered by waving his arm as if making a mesmeric pass. The coffins all underwent a creeping transformation; within a half-hour, their planks had become translucent, allowing a full view of their contents. Inside them, I saw that their fillings had slowly begun the process of decay, and that nothing now fulfilled them but the liquescent putrefaction of charnel corruption. As I stared at that stomach-churning ooze, seething and bubbling blasphemously, my chin was covered by a quantity of drool so great that it would have roused me from my slumber, had I only been sleeping; as things stood, it served to shock me out of the mesmerized state which had been induced in me by those gleaming containers of outré ebullition. That great inventor of grotesque gadgetry then explained to me that necessity required that they undergo a total dissolution into their primordial elements before their substance would alter into the desired metamorphosis, and—so he said—the *nigredo* (the *conjunctio seu putrefactio*) had been nearly completed. It would not now take long for them to repopulate the world with an endless succession of infernal dynasties dancing to the collapsing "echoes of empires spread throughout the skies."

For a long time now my coffin had been rubbing against my feet in affection; and so, deeming that my own Strange Stories could never equal such a crew of mutated marionettes in their weirdness and horribleness, and that therefore I should lose all hopes of an audience for them forever—for I conceded in the aesthetic theorizations of that master of the macabre—I bade my kindly host a friendly farewell. Then, I mounted my coffin and headed scuddingly for the outer reaches of space. I hoped that I could find a fitting reception for my works amongst the windowless towers that dot the plains of Yuggoth, where the inhabitants shun even what little sunlight the single satellite Shaggai can reflect onto the oily onyx rivers and rugose cliffs.

I had only made it a portion of the way, when, as I admired the floating cities of fungal icebergs that collide in the atmospheres of Saturn, my upwelling remorse at my lack of even what little audience my Strange Stories had garnered had swollen to unbearable proportions. In a mad rage, I wanted to rip my hair out!—But, when I pulled on the seaweed-green locks protruding from the scarred scalp, the top of my head came loose and I pulled off the upper part of my skull. Then I realized what must have happened; to be certain, I felt inside the hole in my head where my brain should have been.—Nothing there but cotton. No wonder my eyes so often felt like they were about to fall back into my head!—No wonder I'd had such trouble concentrating lately!—No wonder such a haze befogged my mental operations!—No wonder I didn't add two and two together to get four;—at least not until after much prodding from outside circumstances!—I remembered then that theory so soundly advanced in Ariosto's *Orlando Furioso* (and who could remain so ignorant and illiterate as to have failed to have read such a world-shaking masterpiece of literature?)—that when you go insane, your brains transport themselves to the moon. And only a diseased fancy could have conceived of the creations that I had so-recently heard tell of!—Now I knew the identity of that author of Weird Tales, of that maker of ingenious instruments!—My brain had surpassed the exploits of all other lunatic brains (I only now recall that I never beheld another such; perhaps they had fled in shame at the sight of my own's superiority—), and had disguised itself as me, with a perfect costume and mask, every detail identical down to the microscopic level!—With this awareness clearly in mind (as clearly as possible under the circumstances), I determined to return and reclaim my brain as my own, and to undo—if possible—the damage that it had done; if, that is, I did not find it more suitable—for one always enjoys having an appreciative audience for one's works.—And I had to admire a plan which I had hatched with such consummate sensitivity! So, I readied another lasso; I believed that I could merely catch him about the neck with it, like a noose—that way, I could yank the head off the body, and so have ready access to the brains which I desired to put back inside my cranium, where I felt—most sincerely—that they belonged. I caught a passing comet with that noose, and used it as a pivotal point to swing around on and so to change my destination; for these somber steeds do not manoeuvre swiftly.

Files of flying coffins greeted my gaseous gaze when I had made the return journey. I readied the second lasso in my hand and gyred inwards toward the central configuration of coffins—for they were setting sail in an orderly fashion, beginning with the outermost. With so many of them as the population of an entire world, it would require a great deal of time before those at Moonstonehenge would launch themselves into the void. Once there, I perceived the sable-cloaked figure of myself; but before I noosed my lunatic brain, some mental intuition hinted to me that I should listen to a certain explanation which it had yet to make; wherefore, I alighted hard by it and awaited such in expectation.

My lunatic brain greeted me with a crazed look on its face. He had miscalculated the outcome of his experiment, it said, and the transformation had not come off as expected. Instead, it said as it waved its arm in a mystical gesture and the coffins' planks slowly began to assume the translucent character which we have previously described, the matter had met with such a degree of failure that it surpassed the possible bounds of failure, and hence shaded over into success; and not only began that transgression, but surmounted the first and second degrees, and so he had achieved in full and total measure what he had desired to accomplish. While I bent under the weight of that logic or illogic (for I could not very well distinguish the two—at least not brainlessly!—), which amounted to a very great force, even in the conditions of extremely reduced gravity that prevailed in that environment, the coffins' contents became perceptible, and I saw that they held the naked bodies of men and women, perfectly human in every way. No one could recognize that they had undergone their recent transmutation.

Just so, my lunatic brain said, the alchemical process had in fact worked to perfection. But he had merely misread the signs: the end condition which he had desired had already existed. His understanding of aesthetics had been woefully inadequate, and he now hoped that he could justify an aesthetics of escape, for otherwise no one should find any reason to read his works.—But he felt certain that such abominations of fantastical teratology would desire a few moments of pleasant divertissement from the painful pangs of their self-contemplation. For, my lunatic brain said to me, in the hushed utterance of a reverberant whisper, my work may be weird and terrible, but everyday life is far more weird and far more terrible.

—Lord Weÿrdgliffe, the Waughters.

Skull of Ghoul

Yes, your question is fair. You're right to ask me how I ended up in such a ludicrous predicament. Sit back then, and let the story unfold itself after its own manner. Entrust yourself to its welcoming hands, and the significance of its events will soon enough be settled for you of its own accord.

It began some months after the appearance of one of my innumerable literary masterpieces, when a review of that work—published in a journal with a very small circulation, known only to a very select circle, that goes without saying—had appeared in another organ of the eldritch and uncanny. Our hero, in one of the more inspired of his exploits, had gotten his head trapped inside the skull of a crocodile, lured there by the prospect—held out to him by the suave speeches of the maggots who inhabited it—of devouring the succulent and inebriating mush it held like an orgy-goblet; while in this predicament, he had slowly fallen into a downward spiral of cruelty and sadism, committing the most amusing acts of a predatory nature upon his compeers before an iconoclast, mistaking him for a deity due to the nature of his actions and appearance, had crushed that second-hand cranium with the blow of a sledge-hammer. He thanked him in the appropriate manner, and even performed the rites of supreme unction himself. Now, the critic who interpretatively analyzed that piece—one well-known for having plumbed the obscurest crannies of symbolism more fully than others, and having created an indubitable system for their explication—declared that even *he* did not require the piles of charts and diagrams which had accumulated over many years of the most toilsome study to infer that this episode showed, beyond any possibility of the shadow of an adumbration of the penumbra of a doubt, that our hero had remained trapped within a reptilian level of unconsciousness.

After only a few moments of the most intense concentration did the full force of this argument graze against my awareness, and I realized what a more horrible fate had befallen me than it had been the misfortune of my literary progeny to encounter, for instead of becoming entrapped within a crocodile's skull, I found myself in the nightmare of discovering my brain—which blistered with a bizarre ardor when the nature of the situation bore into it like a drill—imprisoned within the skull of a human being!—If the skull of a crocodile could effect such a (supposedly!) unwelcome result, then what more couldn't a human cranium do to one's thoughts and emotions!—The disgust overwhelmed me—I fled in a daze from the town and out, into the desert—

No matter how far I ran, no matter how fast, that skull stuck tight to my head—I couldn't rid myself of the human hell it created—

At long last, a plan occurred to me. I dared to consider it of more-than-human cunning. I didn't want to submit myself to such a humiliating circumstance as wearing an animal's skull, what with what I now knew about the symbolism involved and all—otherwise, you must see, I might have attempted to create a novel headgear from the cranium of a shark, a python, or a lamprey—and even taking into account that I disagreed with that viewpoint to the point of desiring the mind-set of a crablouse, an octopus, or a leech, I found—upon consultation of learned works—that these noble beings belong to the order of invertebrates, and lack such attire entirely. But mature meditation informed me that one being undoubtably held a superior mind-set to that of man, and that creature was—the ghoul. With a degree of mental effort unmatched by others, I formulated the plot with which I accomplished what others have left undreampt-of, and here's how I did it:

I found a nice spot to lie down, out there in the desert sand. Now, you can still discern the cadaverous quality that differentiates me in a sufficient manner from the rest of the human tribe, including those who have been mummified for multitudinous millennia, and still await the solace of an afterlife, down there in their well-burgled tombs. So, I had no reason to doubt that the ghouls would sniff me out and come at a galloping pace to where I lay; however, I did know that they only take the table-scraps too repugnant for the scavengers who—despite the reputation universally accorded them amongst the vulgar—deem themselves an élite of connoisseurs and pride themselves on only picking the most palatable of morsels from the remnants and reliques which might happen to come their way. This arrangement proves most satisfactory for the tribe of ghouls, who don't relish viands in anything less than a certain stage of decay, and feel a poignant gratitude for their choosier companions in carrion.

Thus, I only had to patiently await their departure—for a race as observant as that of the ghouls would surely have noticed even the slightest hint of life on my part, and definitively exclude my mouth-watering orts from all further consideration, as insufficiently deprived of life; so, I made not the least movement or motion as I felt the kiss of the crow, chewing off my lips and pecking inwards to savor the tip of my tongue, which soon was joined in its gullet by the ends of my nose and my ears—it seemed to me, then, very fortunate that I'd had the good sense to sew my eyes shut and protect them from such mistreatment, for I might have use for them later on. At the same time, a pair of jackals gently titillated my genitalia, soon stripping off the scrotum—this nearly caused me to lose my composure, so much did their tongue and tooth action on my naked testicles stimulate me—and the only thing that could exceed that sensation soon followed, as my pre-puce and glans, gliding down the throat of that rascal, combined with the coring of my anus by his chosen compeer, to kindle in me a fire of emotion not often felt by one as cold-blooded as a cuttle-fish, but I managed not to display any overt reaction.—Anyone else, it seemed to me, would have given away the show at that point, and revealed the intense emotions that loss of flesh caused!—But I'd had a great deal of experience in reining in the outward signs of corporeal ecstasy, and no witness—no matter how perceptive—could have suspected that any sign of life re-mained in the corpse lying there motionless on the sand.—

In due course, those scavengers departed, and after a few hours of stillness—until the darker hours of the night—there was perceived the slight tremors of the earth caused by the padding feet of the ghouls. With what patience, combined with a pleasur-able sense of expectation, didn't I await their taking proper posi-tions around me, knowing full well that I could betray my unique purposes forever if I shifted ever so slightly, for example—to breathe. After one such fright, they would never return to partake of a feast of me, for such a timid tribe adheres strictly to the wis-dom in the traditional proverb of the cat, who once thrown onto a hot stove, won't again allow you to grab hold of her tail—whether the stove remain hot or no.—

So, I let the time tick away as those footsteps came closer and closer, slowly, slowly. I waited until they had arranged them-selves around me—for as everyone knows, ghouls travel in packs, and dine in groups—and then, having calculated the exact pos-ture of the one getting ready to dig into my abdomen with his ra-zor-sharp incisors, I grabbed him by the hair (yes, by those twin tufts oiled and pointed into the form of horns on the scoundrel's forehead)—at the first hint of movement, the rest of them—precisely in accord with my predictions—fled whimpering and glibbering. But that one I had hold of, what a surprise awaited him, as I ripped his skull out of his astonished head and switched it with my own.—Simple as that!—He would very soon have effected the reverse exchange, had I not anticipated that attempted action as well, and clamped a series of padlocks onto each of our heads, firmly securing what I didn't wish to exit from the stage whereon I had placed them, until I had thoroughly enjoyed a life as a ghoul, in the consciousness of a ghoul.—Do I need to add that I had hidden the key (in spite of what you might expect, a skeleton key would not turn the trick) to those locks in the last little nook where anyone would think to look for it?—Don't expect me to divulge that secret now!—

So, we two split apart in a mutual break-up, he, heading towards the cities of men, to try out his new thoughts, I—after ripping through the threads keeping me in a state of constant blindness with my muscular eyelids, to reveal the world to me in its novel aspect, previously unsuspected—loping away to the catacombs and caverns where pleasure lurks gnawing on the bones of identity.—

Now, if the other ghouls had only accepted me as one of their own, I might have relished this new life. Instead, they revile me for reasons as incomprehensible to me as their meepings and moanings.—With some reserve, they allow me to partake of their cadaverous feastings, but even so, it seems perfectly clear that there remains more to their lives than these amusements, and I long to know even the nature of those pleasures!—

My first thought, once I'd fully mastered the routine of stalk, chew, retire, told me to trade skulls back with that ghoul whose life I had so summarily altered—but when I managed to learn the news of how he'd fared in the human world, that option—it seemed certain—no longer lay open to me; for he had, after composing several volumes of Odes and Elegies unsurpassed by any other author, composed on those subjects which humans find incessantly obsessive—life, love, hate, death—finally had enough with the hell of human existence—unlike men, who have learned from long habit to suppress awareness of their identity, and hence do not reach that point of surfeit—and had slowly but surely removed the skull from his cerebellum in the only manner left to him by its unpickable locks: he had smashed it against a wall, and against another wall, and against another—More than one prisoner would have given his eyeteeth to have such a quantity of bricks destroyed by such a repetitive battering—Entire armies of noble criminals could have escaped from their unjust captivities, to continue the career that brought them to an unequal lot—And still, those locks which I had constructed, especially for the containment of that cranium, endured the ordeal, and remained as durable as ever, and could still serve to once again imprison that same quantity of criminals (a workman always chooses tools which he can feel an unbounded confidence in)—

As you might expect, not much utilizable potentiality lingered in the twin lobes that had undertaken such a course of self-abuse—That magnificent artiste's innumerable admirers erected a noble monument to the one who had given them so many hours of the keenest delight, and that event dovetailed perfectly with my new existence, for we had prepared ourselves for his death as well—

But what horrors didn't await us, when we discovered, that instead of human reliques, the body of another ghoul lay there, no more succulent than our own!—

We only bought forgetfulness of that inexplicable anomaly at the price of feasting on an entire village's store of inhabitants, who—to make matters even graver by adding difficulty to repugnancy—we had to bring to the brink of death ourselves, followed by our usual patient anticipation!—

After that dénouement, there followed the anticlimax of the society of ghouls resuming its normal course of existence and shelving all thought of the unwelcome events of time past. And I, too, didn't I fall into the cerebral rut of thinking of nothing but of finding another carcass to gorge my yawning gullet on, losing entirely all awareness of my prior life, just as the hero of my tale had fallen into the trap of becoming a crocodile, pure and simple?—

Now, I ride with the pack of ghastly scavengers, haunting the untenanted catacombs of the desert wastes, lurking near the cemeteries of the human herds, laughing in the arid airs that blow in a breeze through the valleys where no oasis supports the unwelcome merriment of fertility and fecundity, taking pleasure in compeers who accept me for what I am—not withstanding that they disagree with certain features of my anatomy, for they would prefer them in a state of presence to their current irremediable state of lack—and as I do so, I feel no small tremor of foreboding as I think of what could happen, if only I regained the memories of my manhood which I so lately lost!—I know, through hard experience, that if that thought occurred to me, I'd not only not feel such a sensation of tingling revulsion, but that I might—in violation of all of the laws of aesthetics and ethics—desire that hellish life that once plagued me so poignantly that I had taken the extreme measure of penning tales to express my displeasure with it—not to mention share that universally felt emotion with my fellows, in whom I recognized myself as in a mirror, although with less repugnance at the sight—so as to save myself from the necessity of ending forever what could only prove the most abhorrible lot known to befall any being on the encrusted sphere of an insignificant planet!—

* * * * *

The one reading the piece of decayed parchment rolled it back into the shape of a scroll and re-placed it amidst the mingled dirt and débris wherein he had found it. That tale made him wonder: how many decades had he spent, entangled inextricably within the mind-set that his ghoul's skull created inside his inflamed brains?—For hadn't just such an adventure befallen him, much to his great humiliation, as now the other ghouls mocked him, not only for the chunks of iron eternally attached to his head, but for his lack of those organs which all felt took the pride of place in the life of a ghoul?—(Do not so much as look for an explanation of that dubious statement in a place such as this!)—

After that brief moment of doubt, during which he had contemplated the ease with which he could obtain a new skull, no longer used by its owner, and which would return a human complexion to his mental character, for his daily agenda lead him to such discoveries unfailingly—although after such a long time he couldn't recall the location in which he had hidden the key to those locks, making its utility less than if things had lain otherwise—but soon enough, his routine interests retook their hold over his awareness, and he picked some shreds of rotten meat from his hyaena-like teeth with a shiny piece of metal which he had found, on one long-ago day, in just the last place where you would have expected to make such a discovery.

—Lord Weÿrdgliffe, the Waughters.

The Prometheus

An immobility greater than the bondage of sleep pins me to the crag that overlooks the storm-ridden seas. But no intermittent annihilation of human faculties gives me relief from an unremitting awareness of the tortures that dominate and besiege me. If the omnipotence of paralysis didn't hold me unmovably in place, then the enormous steel stakes that nail my titanic members to the cliff, would;—and in that case, I would still remain immobile—voluntarily, for even the few movements I could make might create earthquakes. When the immense lidless eye of the sun has arisen, and covers my naked body with its splendiferous rays, two singular creatures crawl out of the ocean below and climb up the cliff's sheer face—*the two macabre brothers*, as they have been called by the inhabitants of the coast, who had caught sight of them emerging from the seas, not knowing what purpose their existence might serve, until they properly noted the direction in which the two headed, after which they would go to hide in the cranny between two boulders with their paralyzed dog—(But how could I know about that?—Some power of præternatural insight must have borne the news of these developments to my destructible tympanum.)—I close my eyes in horror when I first see them, not able to know whether they more closely resemble scorpions, with their cruel pincers, barbed tails, silvery-reddish articulated armoring, and clicking mandibles, or that even more sadistic beast, humanity. On the whole, I believe that the inhuman prevails in their conformation, if not the inhumane (albeit human) in their conduct. At that momentary panic, I forget what course of action has led me to the daily curriculum of torture that has assailed me for the last thirty thousand years. I tell myself that I have a clean conscience, that I never did anything to merit this infamous punishment, and that I don't even have the pangs of remorse for some slight misdeed to console me for the sufferings which I'm forced to undergo, and that I can't justify them to myself as the expiation for any crime, however small,—since I've never done anything to anybody,—which I could patiently submit to, as my just deserts, but instead must endure an unjustified and indeed unjustifiable tyranny, helpless to defend my person from being imposed upon.

Those two scorpion-men first come upon me, and, seeming to feel some annoyance at the closure of my eyelids, sheer them clean off with their razor-sharp pincers, then cut the fibrous matter linking the eyeballs to the sockets, and gently yank out them out, taking great care not to cut the optic nerve (something hard for them to avoid, what with the acuteness of their scissor-like hands and all), as they pull them to a length greater than you might have imagined they could go, wrap them around steel poles already firmly implanted in the ground behind me, expressly for this purpose, and tie them in knots, leaving the twin eyeballs well-placed to view every iota of the torments to follow. Next, they pluck out, one by one, every hair that provides what slight protection my body affords itself, head, chest, armpits, arms, pubis, anus, legs. Then, after I've been totally depilated, they each take a place beside my head, arch over, and bend their long tails over themselves. Those two stingers with which their formidable tails culminate, drip an acidulous and bilious liquor, which eats the skin away, burning and smarting, smoking with a choking perfume of ebullient putridity. Literally peeled from head to toe, I strive to make even the least squirming motion, if for nothing else, to express the pain that besieges me so strongly, but nothing doing. Beginning to show signs of satisfaction in the work accomplished up till this point, that horrible pair then take the tear-ducts of a thousand crocodiles, and squirt the salty waters onto every square millimeter of my agonizing surface, which they then rub in with kicks of their heels.

At this point, well pleased with the agony inflicted, those two monstrous entities click their mandibles, making a sound which, if I understood the language of arachnids, and claimed to enrich literature with vivid personifications, I would say was that of laughter in the arthropodic world. Proceeding to the next item on this agenda of Gehenna, the one who takes on my left side in the preceding items, asks me—using a language veritably that of man, and not that of insects, crustaceans, or other creeping things—what then, it is, that I want now. Before I could answer out, "Sir, I am hungry!"—(you get hungry after thirty-thousand years of enforced fasting)—which the paralysis prevents me from doing—the two of them prop my mouth open with a pair of red-hot crowbars, and he squats over my August visage, and shits out an enormous ball of white-hot iron, which, for thirty minutes, which are eternities, burns my lips, my tongue, my palate, my throat, my chest, my stomach, my bowels, and my anus, before it passes out and rolls off the cliff and into the sea, from which shit-stinking steam arises. Then the other scorpion-man asks me, in like terms, what then, it is, that I want now. Before I could answer out, "Sir, I am thirsty!"—(you get thirsty after thirty-thousand years of enforced teetotalization)—the two again prop open my mouth, and he aims his arachnid cock at my mouth and pisses a river of molten lead into my mouth, which, for thirty minutes, which are eternities, burns my lips, my tongue, my palate, my throat, my chest, my stomach, my bladder, and my urethra, before it passes out and flows off the cliff and into the sea, from which piss-stinking steam arises.

Having thus prepared the passage, those twin guillotineless executioners commend each other's recent productions, and depart from my head to take a position at the unfortunate's asshole. But before they can get to work on that nether region, some vulture always seems to come winging by, most likely hoping for some infamous carrion to feast upon, and feels so sickened by the mere smell of crap and piss, not to mention the sight of me, that it pukes its guts out, spilling a half-digested putrescence all over my eyeballs. Fearing that this might occlude my vision of some slight portion of the spectacle which they propose to offer up to me, the two come around and scrape off the irises and pupils, leaving the whites still covered. They then return to their former position, and, having prized apart the fleshy globes whose convex contours constitute the human ass, reach up into my embroadened asshole's dilated sphincter, rend the interior organs into shreds and tatters, and pull, successively, from that enlarged orifice, my bowels, my kidneys, my pancreas, my liver, my spleen, my bladder, my lungs, and finally, the heart itself, still palpitating in their invidious grasp, are snatched from their fundaments and brought into the clear light of day, through the ghastly aperture. They then make the most insulting jests concerning my present state, which they can only compare to that of an emptied chicken, or a seven year-old girl, just raped and murdered by a bulldog, and, heaping up the internal organs in a pile topped by the heart, still beating, like that of a shark on the deck of a ship, they launch their slobbery spittle onto the pile, which digests it completely, transforming it into a mound of pullulating pus.

Next, they take a huge adamantine cross, and drive it through my navel, and on through and into the granite beneath. Then those scoundrels stretch out my gigantic prick to its full and glorious length, and nail it to the cross; stroking it to erection, they nip a thousand nicks into the skinless cock;—and reward its efforts with a rubbing of pre-come lubricant, mixed with their own phlegm, into its countless wounds. Then they take my bluish balls, and nail them to the arms of the cross with diamond stakes, which has for its result, the deflating of those testicles like balloons, with the spurting of jism in jets of white sarcasm, which they lick off of me with their long and raspy tongues' abrasive power. Unsatisfied, they wrap a vulva of barbed-wire around my crucified cock, also in and out of the many holes which they had cut into it, and bite several small holes into my scrotum, into which they introduce an octopus, a porcupine, a boa constrictor, a louse, a stingray, a hammerhead shark, a vampire bat, a Komodo dragon, a black widow, a narwhal, an *acarus sarcoptes*, an elephant, a king cobra, an amoeba, a chupacabra, and a lamprey, in the hopes that one of them—at the very least—will find an unheard-of prey in those cramped confines.

With some derision, they note that a few tatters of flesh yet remain on my bones, and that the impotent muscles connecting my rigid framework still linger on. With a look of craft and cunning, they slice two cunt-holes into my armpits, whose sweat-glands they have already masticated and puked up through their nostrils and into my own nostrils, down into my absent lungs, then they fuck those novel apertures with thorny, armor-plated cocks, which—after some two hours of the most toilsome labor—spew an acrid and vile semen in billows and waves of cynical orgasm. One might not expect what happens next, but as for them—that crafty pair:—they do expect it. In preparation for that marvelous development, they bring out a drill (where could they hide these instruments of hell?—I should have been able to see anything before me—), and perform a trepanation on my forehead. That doesn't have as its result any expected mystical enlightenment on my part. I can, in that circumstance, feel my two armpits starting to squirm, and suddenly there bursts forth from them many thousands of wriggling, wiggling, writhing, little monsters. Maggoty, purulent, wormy, verminous, pestilent, pungent, they attack my flesh in droves. Soon competition breaks out amongst them for the choicer morsels, and they combat against each other in serried battalions. There's two hundred thousands ranked in wings on each of my thighs. A slight respite of my own suffering ensues as carnage spreads throughout the fields where battle bellows and turns blue. To the victors, the spoils: those prevailing not only scrape my skeleton bare of any carnal encumberment it formerly bore, but file in ranks to the fissure in my forehead. Brain salad and cerebellum stew. Each member of the conquering legion takes a single neuron in its tentacular filaments and masticates it thoroughly before spitting it back out, fully digested. The victorious army then feasts upon my marrow—for during the time taken to devour what lay inside my skull, the scorpion-men have cracked open each one of my buck-naked bones.

The two fiends then calculate that only my eyeballs yet linger on, and resolve to find a solution to that predicament. To achieve it, they emit a peculiar whistle, which summons two iridescent and raven-like birds from the deceased and desiccated planets that rotate around Algol and Aldebaran, who stab those two orbs with their beaks, popping them, then bite them and yank them out at the root—not a hard thing to do, once you have been thoroughly debrained—and fly home, trailing their optic nerves like long liana vines, vainly seeking some column in the void to wrap them around, to feed on those delicacies at their leisure.

At this point, any awareness of the outside world escapes me, and I slip into a slumberous dream of the actions which I took to merit this mistreatment. Instead of any perception of just where those merciless tormenters might find to disappear to, the recurrence of former events overtakes my consciousness—I remember—The violation of undignified taboos imposed upon us by the Celestial Tyrant—Flying high, on waxen wings, into the air, to the sun—Stealing fire—Giving fire to man—Teaching men the arts of cultivation—Teaching men the medicinal values of plants—Teaching men how to benefit themselves—With the knowledge of literacy—And of scientific methods—The divine decree from on high that I should be punished for such misdeeds, and placing men nearly as high as the gods—And while I recall all of these things, my flesh grows back, during the night, to form a new and complete body for the next day's course of treatment—

And I feel the burden of knowing that the tyrant who thus condemned me, some thirty-thousand years ago, shall one day fall prey to his own unsuspected offspring—perhaps on this very day—and that his successor shall no doubt free me from the bondage inflicted upon me by the outrageous despot, and this knowledge torments almost as much as the tortures inflicted by the two macabre brothers, and the thought dominates me, that if it proves to be necessary, I'll do even more good deeds for the benefit of my fellows, not with any thought for their welfare, but to earn another such unjustifiable punishment from the lively sentiment of divine justice of that Demogorgon who will not, hopefully, display the slightest jot of concern as to the supersession of his illustrious predecessor's reasoned concepts of reward.—

—Lord Weÿrdgliffe, the Waughters.

The Fountain of Uncleanliness

Lord Weÿrdgliffe was seated at his raven-like writing-desk. As the hairy tarantula at the end of his arm scribbled, his attenuated awareness began to recede from the task at hand and into the depths of its cavernous subjectivity. He wrote, he thought to himself, in order to communicate with others, in order to close the gaping chasm that isolated the minds of other individuals from his own. For there is a loneliness that is a positive, rather than a negative, loneliness, and the unique one is more truly alone within the solitude of himself, even though the maddened and maddening crowds mill about him like vultures circling above the Egyptian sands, than the bleached-white bones of a skeleton that has spent seven long centuries unvisited on a desert island. But the only result he could achieve, so it seemed, was to widen the distance between himself and the unreachable others. And with each renewed effort, with each Penny Dreadful more horrid than the last, the effect grew greater, until his moss-covered mansionhouse, the Waughters, seemed to have slowly vanished into the recoiling curves of infinity, until he was lost to all possibility of human consciousness in an oubliette of oblivion—more irremediably lost than those whose bodies he used to keep imprisoned in obscure dungeons for his amusement, in that long-ago time when he could endure the proximity of human flesh.

He started from his rêverie, and gazed down in astonishment at the Weird Tale which he had just written. A single yellow eye blinked on the greenish thing's half-formed face, as it attempted to stand on its three spider-fingers while a single webbed wing vainly fluttered above. Steaming with an odor noisome beyond experience, the Weird Tale flopped off the desk and onto the floor, leaving an unguent trail of slime in its wake. The Baron fell on all fours and savored its clamminess as he entwined it within the coils of his raspy black tongue.

A greenish semi-liquid dripping from the corners of his mutilated mouth, Lord Weÿrdgliffe sat back in his chair and once again took up the quill plucked from an ebony archaeopteryx. Perhaps, he mused, he could not achieve communication with another consciousness; but he could now provide nourishment for his own radical subjectivity. And as his spider-like hand busily scribbled away, his attention faded away from the task at hand, and was captured by a spectacle presented to him by the novel eyeball that had grown in his navel, which depicted his ever-erect phallos sprouting twin dorsal rows of cartilaginous and crimson tendrils.

* * * * *

Clouds now nearly covered the moon, and twilight seemed abnormally prolonged. Aimé des Poulpes had fled as far from mankind as he could, or nearly so, and now sought rest. He had composed another ode to his beloved Sophie, only to be greeted with the final "*no*" which, so he knew, would ever depart from her lips. And so, to escape from the company of men, which he could no longer endure, he had fled to the dismal swamps beyond the limits of habitation, of which he had heard so many dreadful rumors. Those rumors, he was certain, had no basis in fact: for only the superstitious hold to such beliefs; and there was definitely nothing to fear—no, there was nothing to fear—not even if there was, indeed, a dilapidated mansionhouse near-by, such as might suitably hold the spectres and spooks of popular ignorance. And it was, no doubt, uninhabited, whether or not a pale purplish light appeared to emanate from its broken windowpanes. In any case, there was no longer any bridge to span the moat surrounding the hillock-capping château.

As Aimé gazed across the scene, he reflected that the moon, now partially peering from behind the cover of cumulus shroud, was as cold and as distant as Sophie's ivory-white flesh, and a thousand knives stabbed into his crucified heart at their irremediable separation. The moss at the roots of the stooping cypresses was not too damp for a bed, and he settled himself down for the remainder of the night as he had done a thousand times before, when wine and the moon inspired him to slumber instead of lifting him to the sublime heights of Parnassus.

A single yellowish eye peeped out from a hollow in the tangled cypress roots. Surrounded by sleep, the youth embraced a lover composed of mist and nothingness, and the pleasant illusion twisted his wearied face into a semi-smile. The yellowish eye poked itself out further, revealing a toad-like body surmounting a solitary leg. With a plop the thing's over-sized webfoot propelled it forward, towards the dozing poet. Young Aimé des Poulpes' dreams progressed on their natural course, and his mouth half-opened to mumble the phrases of love and amatory odes that welled within his soul. The Strange Story took a final leap and dived headlong into the young man's jaws; unwittingly, he crunched down on the creature, and its clammy green taste and texture shocked him into wakefulness. Gagging and choking as pleasure metamorphosed into the most intense degree of disgust, he frantically attempted to spit out every last morsel of green and yellow slime before nausea could overwhelm his innards.

Before moving on, as he felt necessary, he allowed himself the leisure of resting on the cypress roots. He held his head in his hands as he gazed upon the popped remains of the yellowish eyeball and the outlines of a single green leg on the ground, wondering what degree of despair could have driven him so far into the depths of solitude as to encounter such a shocking singularity.

Still, he'd had a taste.

* * * * *

In the depths of the Waughters, Lord Weÿrdgliffe produced, through manifold fission, an unceasing procession of Weird Tales, their loathsome anatomies displaying an endless array of miscreated morphological variations. The Baron now occupied the oubliettes and dungeons where he had once imprisoned those men and women whom he had captured for his entertainment, in that distant epoch when human flesh did not yet strike him with a degree of repulsion usually reserved for the most unholy of objects. Having slowly taken on a form more and more liquescent, his ever-growing bulk had uncontrollably oozed down the stairwells leading to the lowest sites attainable; once he had demolished, with powerful pseudopodia formed for the purpose, every partition in the extensive network of dungeon cells, the Lord of Loathsome Laughter could then allow himself the pleasure of relaxing and enjoying the antics of his progeny, viewed by *ad hoc* eyes through the clouds of noisomeness that hung in the heavy air.

The Baron occupied a sort of pool, nearly choking it from rim to rim with his greyish, horrid mass; a mass that quobbed and quivered, swelling perpetually; from it were spawned, in their infinite variations, Weird Tales and Strange Stories. There were Horrid Stories like bodiless heads that half-rolled and half-crept on five spider-legs of unequal length; others that resembled floundering fish-finned bellies that flopped through the slime- trails left by myriad-tailed worms with rows of nostrils that savored the noxious perfumes produced by the parent bulk and its malformed offspring. And at an equal rate as it produced these monstrous creatures, the amorphous author of their being formed on its quaking surface multiple mouths, anuses, and vulvas that swiftly swallowed all those of its children that failed to swiftly flap away on three webbed wings.

So it was that Lord Weÿrdgliffe enjoyed his literary production in uttermost solitude. One unequal autumn's day, however, as he crunched down with an anal orifice on a lizard-like arm or leg that bore more than a passing resemblance to a slug—this particular Weird Tale was slightly less identifiable in its attempt to mimic nature than a majority of the others, albeit all the more savory for all that—there appeared to the organs of olfaction which were besprinkled at random on his spread-out surface an even greater degree of noxiousness than his own output could account for. And he was well-accustomed to the haze of sulphureous stench that arose from his steaming children's trails. No, this surely indicated some alien intruder; some Weird Tale not his own must have entered the cavernous recess!

The Baron tightened into an enormous ball of slime at the realization of such an unhoped-for event, and as he slowly lost shape and melted into a cone, eyelets formed on tentacles sprouting from his liquid surface to survey the scene. Indeed, on the stone steps that had once led down into the abattoir reserved for human butchery, there flopped a purplish abomination. Like a lopsided tadpole, its gills pulsed orange and green as it flicked its thin, ridiculously long tail around like a whip.

As the foreign Strange Story gazed back at him with a circle of five bulbous eyes, Lord Weÿrdgliffe extended a slight bump into an elongated member that stretched across the slime-stained flagstones to meet the novel stranger. Rows of feelers and fingers, soft and supple, extended from the arm-like appendage, and lovingly caressed the unfamiliar form of the Weird Tale, which purred in response, sounding not entirely unlike the far-off echoes of a cat-o'-nine-tails striking already flayed flesh. The monstrous member bunched itself together and broke away from the mass which had recently engendered it; then, it pulled itself into a squat cylindrical form with an opening on one end, surrounded by a double row of unarticulated tentacles. It contracted and expanded; then this Horrid Story abruptly fell onto the Weird Tale and sucked it into its dilated orifice, leaving the whip-like tail hanging out, to lash at the air and the flooring.

The Horrid Story rolled awkwardly back toward the parent mass, which had already begun to creep towards it, extending its formless self on either side so as to surround the thing, countless orifices opening in anticipation. Soon enough, the Horrid Story was caught by a toothless mouth and a fanged vagina, that battled over the prize and quickly divided their spoils into two accursed portions. The Baron would shortly seek out the origin of the unsuspected oddity; but for now, he would first finish savoring an unanticipated delicacy.

* * * * *

Aimé des Poulpes regarded the Waughters with the multitudinous eyestalks he had formed for the purpose. A perpetual twilight hung over the place, and day never seemed to come. There was no way to reach the shattered château, mounted on a mossy bulge that projected above the surrounding swampland, and his failed attempt to ooze towards the secret structure had landed him inside the archaic moat, unable to progress any further in his liquidated state. An ingenious connoisseur, Aimé had allowed his semi-liquid bulk to flow through the lengths of the ancient ditch, his coils tickled by the teeth of crocodile skulls, to rejoin in the circular conformity of the Worm Ouroboros. This way, none of the Horrid Stories and Penny Dreadfuls that issued from the Waughters could ever escape from the manifold mouths and other orifices he continuously formed in order to devour them.

As the youth yet savored the latest Weird Tale to make its escape from the mouldering mansionhouse, a crackling noise emanated from the structure, whose cobweb-covered walls soon gave way before the strain produced by a battering ram stronger than any which had ever assailed them before. The young poet beheld an enormous protoplasmic mass tower into the sky above the annihilated abode, its topmost portion glowering with a purplish glow like some hellish lighthouse luring the ships of the damned to crash on the reefs before the Stygian shores. The freakish pharos of pulsating slime came crashing down onto itself, unable to maintain its rigidity, and with the impact fissioned off innumerable Penny Dreadfuls and Strange Stories and Weird Tales that crawled and flopped and struggled through the mire, slopping and slobbering down to greet the epitome of abnormality that was even now creating a formidable array of mouths and vulvas and sphincters to devour them in an ecstasy of the unknowable as it quivered in its dreamy bed.

Aimé des Poulpes swelled monstrous with the substance so recently infused into his being, and now as the Loathsome Lord became erect once again, he contracted his obscene anatomy like a python suffocating a hippopotamus and, strengthened by the recent influx of obscenity, rose clean above the moat's depression and onto the higher grounds above. In an emotive outburst of relaxation he exploded with Horrid Stories and Uncanny Tales that flooded toward the towering anomaly, and were swiftly devoured by the unearthly enigma before it once again crashed down onto the Waughters, crushing its outdated architecture and crackling skeletons as it showered the area with another eerie deluge of Weird Tales. A second time the youth dilated like an enamored sphincter, and the Bizarre and Unbelievable Baron rose up like a monolithic monument for yet a third time, gazing with a myriad obtruding eyes upon his poetical protégé, who lay sprawled about like the meandering and multitudinous emplotment of a prodigiously prolix Gothick Romance, comprised of a congeries of congregating sub-narratives and auctorial intrusions:

After a slothful descent, constituted by seconds that were centuries, the twain finally met in a chaos of tentacles, tails, and tortuous pseudopodia that groped and grinned and embraced in a confusion of creativity in which neither of the two could distinguish himself from the other, or determine which of the other had emitted any particular odoriferous oddity that was being devoured by a mouth or an anus or a vagina formed by neither of them knew which. Rolling over each other and themselves, those inseparable twins wrapped around their shapeless, undigested masses in an enormous spiral that seemed to copulate with the crepuscular clouds, and in an unspeakable ecstasy the two at once dissolved into a purely liquid lump, smashing down through the antiquated structure, destroying its remaining outlines as they broke through the bedrock beneath and tumbled headlong into the bottomless caverns into which the Baron Weÿrdgliffe would always forever consign, with an offhand grimace and sideways glance of his haggard eyes, the evidence incriminating him in some outlandish outrage or other.

* * * * *

They say that it is only rarely that anyone travels so far from human awareness and into one's own subjectivity, that the fugitive from mankind should reach those nameless marshes where no ruins mark a mansionhouse that once stood proudly against the eternal twilight, like the final bastion of consciousness defying the onslaught of its encroaching oblivion. And even less frequently, so they say, do any of these fleeing phantoms discern those oddities so strange that no one attempts to describe them, or speculate on their origins—which apparently lie beyond the purplish glimmer that seems to emanate from the ground itself in the fissures that lead forever downwards to the uncertain entity that ceaselessly spawns such unnameable uncleanliness.

—Lord Weÿrdgliffe, the Waughters.

The Two Spiders

From beyond the limits of my obscured vision, a pair of tarantulas crawled onto my crotch, already—in accordance with my
habit when I yield to the leaden forces of somnolence—laid bare
(thus obviating any witticism you might wish to make about the
spider and the fly), tickling my paralyzed body with their hairy
black legs. In fact, they were two hands. And as those two hands
scampered up, totally ignoring the intriguing area of my
engorged groin, contrary to all apparent probability, their black
fingernails digging into my skin and playing on my nerves like
spiders tenderly vibrating their cobwebs, they created a sensation
so keen, so mordant, that I can hardly believe that the state of immobility and paralysis which I find myself trapped inside does
not result from some hypnotic spell. As those two spider-like
hands crawled up over my abdomen, the lengthy nails dug into
the flesh, stabbing inwards with such force as if they wished to
disembowel me, but before any portion of my entrails appeared
on the surface, those two hands crept up to my chest, and there,
they again began to dig into the flesh, exposing my heart and
piercing into it like daggers of desire, causing a pain so intense
that it alone would have proven strong enough to create the
overwhelming lethargy that bound me to my bed like an adamant
chain binds a Titan to some crag of the coast; and at this point, as

I watched them, bound in entranced fascination, the thought occurred to me: hadn't I seen these hands somewhere before? Not
even hands similar in appearance, but these exact and identical
two? And, in the abasement of my mental level, there appeared
to my agonizing awareness scenes of memory presented as if in a
vision, of those hands, which time and again would begin at the
crotch of some victim, now male, now female, in which they
would very shortly lose interest—as though their truer motives
lay elsewhere—and then proceed to the higher proportions of the
body, which they would then suavely rend with caresses of their
black-as-ebony, sharp-as-shark-tooth nails. And when they had
torn away the covering of the heart, and had their way with that
organ, didn't they always continue, along an inexorable line of
logic, to the throat of the victim, who never so much as struggled
against them, as though placed into a trance by some hypnotic
power? Against all verisimilitude, they say that a serpent's eyes
have a power, so puissant as to seem præternatural, to magneti-
cally immobilize a bird which it wishes to take as a prey, but that
description wouldn't appear out of place as regards those two
eyeless hands and the featherless bipeds. And didn't every single
one of them fall victim to those hands, as a sacrifice to the god of
unmotivated revenge? Once these scenes had recrossed the windows of my awareness, a further process of recognition ensued.
For hadn't I been witness to those countless scenes of careless
carnage for a reason? No, I hadn't observed those hands' entire
career of serial assassination through some random process always placing me before them and their victims by chance; it was
only inevitable that I should enjoy such a train of spectacles. And
when that thought occurred to me, to give the verification of empirical observation to the precepts of remembrance, I looked
again at those two black tarantulas, and followed the veins bulging in the hairy wrists down to the elbows, and further down, to
the shoulders, and—those shoulders were immediately adjacent

to the area which the hands had just reached, and as I regained cognizance of my own identity, they fell down powerless from the throat which they had just begun to tear into, and I thought to myself with relief that once again I could turn those two hands against others, to derive a very great pleasure from their inimitable sufferings; and it only increased my sensations of assuagement to regain control over myself and my others, as the hands had more closely reached their forbidden goal than they had on the many previous occasions in which they had attempted it—for that wasn't the first time that I've found myself set into the painful and humiliating situation of the misrecognition of the actions of my own instinctive impulses!—

—Lord Weÿrdgliffe, the Waughters.

The Illimitable Dark

A tenebrous figure, whom no one will ever have failed to recognize, completely cloaked in a sable mantle whose hood overcasts a shadow that reveals not even a single feature of the face enshrouded within it, mounted on the obsidian skeleton of the undreampt-of hippocorvus, has just flown on its osseous wings into the Cimmerian obscurity of the aether in a counter-rotational trajectory from the umbrageous halo of a deceased planet, at present populated solely by shades and by sepulchers—after the concerted efforts of the darksome and uninvited visitor now departing from its Plutonian deserts and polar wastelands, and it admires, hanging motionless in the unlitten gloom, the Stygian beauty of the curve described by the self-interred world, as its enshadowed silhouette, outlined against the tenebrous sepia that serves as a backdrop to the invisible dust of deceased stars and nebulae, slowly spirals inwards to collide into a Hadean nullity against the naked frigidity of a night-black sun.

As that suspended figure gazes upon the dénouement of the eradication of the final bastion of living existence in the indefinite universe, this Negative Lucifer looses one of the reins, allowing the coal-tinted hippocorvus to drift aimlessly through the emptiness, like a piece of ebony flotsam, and a skeletal hand of meager and elongated onyx emerges from the sleeve of its somber cloak, then pulls the hood back, revealing a mane of raven-black hair and a skull of jet, and then, more slowly than thought, a single leaden tear of implacable remorse and regret falls down the figure's somber cheekbone from its ink-hued eyeball; of remorse and regret, for, having utterly annihilated every inhabitant of the universe—it whispered to no one, in silent vocables—it had robbed itself of the unspeakable pleasure of their unjustifiable assassination, which had now met its ulterior accomplishment, casting everything into irremediable entropy, leaving no more prey for an insatiable lust for insensate annihilation and unmotivated destruction which has hurled a mournful pall of darkness over the obliterated facet of existence like the rimed-over nudity of a funereal crêpe.

The figure retook the rein and steered the darkling steed in an ascending helix; then, once again controlling the mount with a single onyx hand, one by one, the entity with a pitch-hued heart lassoed the defunct and bedarkened stars of the nullified and nonexistent cosmoses, nearly enough in their primordial condition—as well as that of Erebos—that of utter Chaos and old Night, and singularly roped and noosed each celestial cadaver until it resembled a nocturnal spider set like a jewel into the center of a hundred-million unreflecting webs, and then the figure yanked on the entire assemblage and drew the remnants and remains of space inwards into a single, enormous maelström from whence would explode the birth-pangs of a renewed creation.

     —Lord Weÿrdgliffe, the Waughters.

Unto Others

"I want to tear the world out by the roots. . . ."
--Anonymous Elizabethan Mad Song.

Yes, yes, it would bolster my abased ego to accept your plaudits, Anarchists, but I fear that you misunderstand my motives in the destruction of society and the uprooting of human civilization entirely. Not everything is what it appears to be; I daresay, that the reality behind each thing exactly mirrors its outward image. So listen to my tale, and perhaps we shall discover just precisely what the truest meaning of "nihilism" is.

*   *   *   *   *

For ages of solitude I lived alone in my tower, surrounded only by the automatons that I had molded in their multitudinous vats to perform my Will. There, I knew every indulgence of every desire. All, save that one that crowns the others and subsumes them: revenge. No matter how I contrived to test the limits of lust, gluttony, greed, intoxication, pride, the absence of any method of committing the sin of vengeance ate a hole into my heart until nothing was left aside from a cavernous hollow; all of the other sins I committed to no purpose, employing my mindless servitors for any rôles necessary in the commission.

And still, I had no way of avenging myself, for no one could reach me, there in my ivory tower; and without anyone having insulted or injured me, for what crime could I possibly avenge myself? I attempted to practice the tortures and torments to which I plotted to submit any mortal who dared insult me, on the automatons that I had created. Again and again, I devised some trivial crime for one of them to commit as pretense for my vengeance, and one by one I tested every form of retribution possible, inventing the most outré agonies imaginable, combining each with the indulgence in some other sin.

Still, that experiment seemed futile. While I could still enjoy the fruits of my lust and gluttony, greed and pride, the transgression of vengeance was but the shadow of a spectre. For those mindless slaves had no choice in the matter; they could not help but obey me and trespass against me. Nor was that all; for they entirely lacked the true ability to experience the hell that I wanted to force my mortal enemies to endure; they could provide the simulacrum of suffering, but not the reality. And while I wanted to experience the pleasure of viewing that suffering in another, I wanted it to be a real suffering. Oh, once I nearly derived satisfaction from one of those golems, when I smashed its head in frustration over the affair; but that sort of revenge—wreaked against an inanimate object—does not give the satisfaction that I imagined a true vengeance would.

It was obvious what I would need to do. And so, to practice my unique projects, I swooped out of my phallic tower—which majestically copulates with the clouds that soar above those twin domes wherein are held the vats in which I manufacture my artificial slaves—onto the surrounding field, and there I captured a man passing through on his way to some adventure.—He'd have an adventure, all right. No, he'd done me no wrong; but nonetheless, he could, most certainly, experience the dolorous blows of my irrational reasonings. And then, why, even after many years of enduring that sublime torture, he didn't even give me the satisfaction of attempting to escape—despite the opportunities which I contrived to tantalize him with—or showing the slightest disobedience to my sadistic whims. Passive acceptance of the most dreadful torments.

Still and all, I found that, in contradistinction to the automatons, his painful pangs induced the most spastic pleasures imaginable in me; and at each moment, there was held in the back of my mind the iron fact that he had never stooped to insult me. And at each time that my consciousness was flooded with voluptuosity at his screams, I thought to myself, how much the more delight would I gain from the full consummation of my projected vengeance, once I just had a target who had given me cause to avenge myself!—

Drowning in a viscid lake of despair, a slough of mucilaginous dejection, I finally ordered my artificial human companions to accompany me outside, where we would dispose of my victim's innocent remains. As they carried the shattered carcass to an appropriate resting-place, a crowd gathered around us. A man stepped forward, and that champion of justice shouted: "Look! There is the one who abducted our innocent friend, lo! these many years ago! There is the malefactor, the murderer! It was none other than our absurd old neighbor Titivillus who did the deed! Let us bring the monster to justice!"

Immediately, I signaled my automatons to halt in their business. Now, now, now!—I had, at long last, something for which to reproach another! For how could one tolerate such accusations, such attempts to besmirch one's good reputation, such outright attempts to do harm to one's person? And when that malefactor stooped to draw an infernal machine from his pockets, and hurled it in my direction—leaving me unharmed, but reducing several of my faithful slaves to scattered smithereens—well, then I gave the order to apprehend the culprit, and as the crowd was mobilizing, a flashing storm of steel blades reduced them to a field of carnage, and that instigator of evil was bound in adamantine manacles. What a signal success, after aeons of failure! Who would have thought it!—All I had needed to do, to attract misdeeds my way, and so give myself the pretext for a satiating vengeance, was to myself commit misdeeds against another!—A fact that made the attraction of such an opportunity doubly entertaining!

Yet, when I essayed once again the multitudinous torments which I had devised, with an epicure's degree of refinement, each one less endurable than the others, the poignant spasms, the ecstatic mindbursts, which I had become accustomed to garner as reward for my patient application of all the instruments of hell, no longer appeared. No, instead, that unending routine of debauched degradation simply filled my heart with an unbounded ennui. To put it plainly, those enormous pleasures which I had experienced vanished into thin air at the mere thought that what I was doing was merely to satisfy Justice, that I had every reason to act as I was. My own Will, at that thought, seemed impotent, a flaccid and pendant appendage, the servant of a Great External Object, the plaything of Another's ideal.

Slowly, as time crawled on, I began to engage in philosophical disputations with that avatar of righteousness, in the hopes of combining the pleasures of revenge with that of speculative contemplation, thus creating a novel hedonistic mixture. Now, one day, while engaging in this novel mélange, that mortal enemy of mine made a comment that I couldn't help but take notice of. It struck me so forcefully that I motioned my subalterns to cauterize what remained of his genitalia, and to sever the optical nerves by which his eyes hung pendulant—for I had previously had the fibers holding them in place severed, and the eyeballs themselves placed dangling against the hollow of his cheeks like a consumptive's twin testicles, so that he should not miss a single moment of the dolorous repast he was being served.

Once that had been accomplished, that Anarch outlined for me the solution to the tortuous quandaries which I had raised in our debate. For he held that the entire system of relations in which every living human being finds itself inextricably enmeshed, consists solely of the most abasing and immiserating spectacle imaginable, utterly enveloping every individual into an enormous transhuman monstrosity he dubbed—for what particular reason I have great doubts—Leviathan. And in the tentacular hierarchy of that juggernaut, men are no more than the tiniest suckers, though they are suckers that grab hold of every other human's brain with a grasp that will never let go.

Now this answered the obscure question as to why I felt no pleasure in my former projects, and that I had only met with an illusory success when I believed to have done so in actuality. For how I could ever have been so naïve as to believe that my former victim had been innocent in any way, shape, or form, I will never know; at least not when I consider that every aspect of everyday life perpetuates the machinery of misery, further pushing all humanity into the ebullient cesspool of irremediable degradation. What is worse, I learned then that this situation is brought about not so much by the relations of power and control which it serves to maintain, but rather through the directly implanted thoughts and ideals that humans take for "reality," but which in fact act as parasitic worms and blind them to their own experiences, leaving them in a state no better than that of my automatons, and perhaps even decidedly worse: for they not only endure that enforced enslavement, but are blinded to its abasing effects. Such is Morality, that old crablouse, to mention only the vilest of these leeches.

I knew then what I needed to do. First, out of motives of mercy—which I pretended to feel as a token of gratitude—I had that sagacious criminal executed. Then, in a rage of righteous indignation I rose up against Heaven, and toppled the Celestial Bandit from his Diamond Throne, which was not,—despite what many might incline to believe,—a difficult thing to do, and plunged his fiery carcass into the most abysmal depths of the seas, where it remains to this day, its phosphorescent glow frightening the dull scavengers who nonetheless lust after its eternal nutriment. When sailors chance upon the glowing ring that rises from the seas' surface at midnight, they rightly surmise that some spectre of a ghost haunts those waters; nonetheless, they never suspect its true origins. The fragments of his Topaz Robe can still be seen, on winter nights, floating through the skies; do not mistake this effect, O humans, for the *aurora borealis*: it is important to remind oneself of past victories. After that minor rebellion, for which I received just plaudits from you, as you all recall, you Anarchists, the Infernal Empire rose up from the magma-ridden wastelands of the infernal underworld, and subsumed the entire earth in its demesnes; with a little effort,—for the Hierarchy of Hell took care in the task, fearing that something greater than itself had deposed the Celestial Tyrant,—it rose up to occupy the Jeweled City and to reign over the entire universe from that fortified seat.

Despite the monumental improvement in the situation which I recognized in that alteration of circumstances, still things did not lie as I had hoped to arrange them; for any such Revolution, even the grandest, as had happened in this case, merely exchanges one evil for another, albeit lesser. And so, I again rose up and deposed the Celestial Bandit, for one who had, in his prior opposition to that principle of despotism, been a noble figure of rebellion, had now become naught but what he had for so long battled against. His sulphur-ridden cadaver, encased in a solid sphere of ice, now floats at random through the world's oceans, never a drop of it melting and rolling down its side like a tear of regret into the unheeding ocean: do not fail to heed it as it passes—you will recognize it by the crimson gleams that shimmer through its crystalline walls.

You have, by now, O Anarchs, realized why I take the course of action which I continue unto the present moment. You now know why I send forth the creatures of my vats to assassinate every dictator, every figure claiming any authority whatsoever; why I send them on missions of chaos and disorder, to disrupt the rut-ridden minds of the human race; why I subvert every ideal, pervert every idea, engage in wholesale slaughter at random whim, turn friend against friend, spurn ethics as dung, and art as a muckheap pullulating with verminous parasites. Not for nothing am I now known as the Crowned King of Chaoticists.—

That no innocent bystanders fall victim to my depredations against civilization is readily understandable, for no such innocents exist.—Not when all are controlled by the starfish-like parasites that have clutched hold of every human brain! Indeed, as you cannot have failed to have realized by now, the creation of such innocents is my primary goal; the techniques of destruction and subversion employed being merely tools to the end. And that end, of course, is to make of the human hell of the earth an unprecedented Utopia, filled to the brim with the happy and innocent specimens which have—up to this point—never appeared on the rocky anthill of the humanitarian hive.

Once this has been accomplished, I will have an unending supply of innocents to immolate with diverse and diverting tortures and torments. Is that another city I see erupting into flames?—Perhaps my goal is approaching!—

—Lord Weÿrdgliffe, the Waughters.

The Eternal Enemy

Unless it is eternal, conflict is nothing. The war once ended, the situation settled, the noble struggle sinks into a slothful state of entropic inertness, and the Ego, having lost its impetus and motivation, slithers into a dark cavern where no light will ever illuminate its obscure humiliation. In realization of these dire straits, I sought a battle that I could never win, but—an important thing to represent—one in which I could never prevail.

I began by waging a war against Man. I reasoned that no matter how many of the pewling piss-ants I might defeat, I would still never have utterly annihilated Man himself. So, from the black tower on my isolated island, I engaged in sallies against the world of Man. Thousands fell beneath the blade of flaming ebony I used to mow them down, like Death wielding his scythe. I could, had I so wished, have slaughtered the entire tribe; not aspiring to fall into a state of melancholy at the loss of something so valuable, so life-giving, as my unceasing conflict, I held off and allowed the pitiable remnants to repopulate their infested regions.

I soon learned that even this degree of effort had been wasted. I needed merely to await their assaults against my islet fastness, and slice the serried battalions that assailed me as they came marching in. With no small enthusiasm did they enable me to construct a pyramidal fortress of human bones; soon, I precipitated the structure into the sea with a kick—sending the legions mounting those steps to slay me down with it,—and began anew, utilizing only their skulls. For ages I stood, at the pinnacle of that ivory-white pyramid, and struck down one by one all those who dared climb the infinite staircase to reach me on that cloud-abutting summit, until I had butchered enough of those brave soldiers to justify beheading their corpses, licking from the skull all the rotting remnants, and carefully constructing yet another layer of that outré erection.

The pyramid had grown to cover the entire island, and to extend into the sea, when I discovered the futility of my efforts;—for my thought frequently finds itself covered in clouds of unconsciousness. Now, I wanted an enemy who I could strive for eternity to overcome, that would strive for eternity to overcome me; we should live as neighboring monarchs, who fear and hate each other, yet do not fail to honor the other's sense of pride by ceaselessly attacking. But Humanity failed that essential condition. For I could never attack Humanity herself, only individual humans; and likewise, Humanity forever left me untouched, as only individual humans approached in order to usurp me from my throne of craniums. I'd desired to commit crimes against Humanity, but only succeeded in committing crimes against humans. As for Man himself, he remained an abstraction, a spectre, and a spook.—No use battling such a non-existent foe!—

So great was the pain of that novel awareness, that I cast my gaze up to the heavens as I slumped back on myself; there, *there* was the unique foe who could constitute my perfect counterpart! I gave the pyramid of skulls one last kick as I rose into the air, sending the brigades of warriors amassing there for a final blitzkrieg assault rolling over themselves into the sea, where sharks, sea serpents, and octopi awaited their arrival in anticipation. But even that beautiful sight must have been surpassed, in the admiring aesthetic appreciation of any onlookers, by the vision of a chalk-white skeletal figure spiraling into the air, a sword of obsidian flame in hand, until it disappeared into the starry spheres, not pausing at the moon or the planets on its way to engage in infinite battle.

The music of the spheres was altered into a dissonant discordancy when I smashed through the crystalline barrier of the Primum Mobile and discovered the Heavenly City, fortified with ramparts of ruby and towers of topaz. A horde of angels and archangels encountered the adamantine tenebriety of my darksome blade; soon, I waded through a waist-deep ocean of incorporeal corpses. Having so handily defeated the Celestial Armies, I entered the great Mother-of-Pearl Palace to confront the Lord of Hosts and engage Him in hand-to-hand combat. There, finally, I would find an adversary worthy of me!—There, I would find a foe powerful enough that I could never win a decisive victory!—There, at last, He too would discover His eternal Nemesis!—

I crushed all opposition and stormed the Throne Room; when I rent the veil and gazed upon the Mercy Seat, it exceeded my expectations.—For the figure upon it exactly resembled me, in every particular, down to the droplet of human brains that still stains my bone-white chin. I carefully studied my opponent, and He, as well, carefully studied Me. After some hours of vain manœuvering and futile feints, in which We precisely matched each other's actions, I decided that a blow must connect, whether it be simply answered with an equal blow or no. My scimitar of onyx flame slashed through the Celestial Aether and crashed into His own; imagine My great surprise, when the one foe who I had believed worthy of Me shattered into a thousand smithereens, each glassy shard departing from that place in a different direction. No wonder, I thought then, that Satan had failed in his rebellion; for he had, no doubt, suffered a moment of hesitation when he gazed upon the visage in that mirror—and his reputation as a Narcissus is sufficiently secure to establish this as a verified fact—and that time of inaction had proved decisive.

Still, despite this disillusioning discovery, I immediately conceived of yet another potential enemy—by what train of association, I am at a loss to discover—one whose very name itself signifies "The Adversary." Yes, I would even spite my most sacred moral insights and do battle against Satan himself, if that was what it took to obtain the infinite altercation that I lusted after. I shot like a meteor from Heaven, slashing great gashes into the planets as I passed them by, on my descent to the absolute center of the circle without a circumference. Anon, I burst into fiery white flames as I approached the earth—making an appearance that the ignorant inhabitants did not fail to interpret as a comet of ill omen, and hence causing great revolutions and reintroducing anarchy and chaos into human society. I paid no heed to any of this. Instead, I plunged headlong into an active volcano, and swam through the lava into the blazing depths of the earth's burning bowels, until I reached those empty caverns that contain the ordurous oubliettes which all men are destined for. Here, I had no need to battle my way through the myriads thronged about me; indeed, few even took time out from their continued tortures and torments to notice an unscheduled arrival.

So it was that I swiftly traversed the sardonic steppes and reached the absolute center. To my astonishment, His Satanic Majesty seemed to present me with the exact appearance of myself.—After only a few minutes of concentrated cogitation, I realized that I already knew that trick, and hurled my blazing black swordblade at the face in the mirror, and it whirled through the sulphureous miasmata and crashing into the looking-glass, sending its silver-backed shards into the void to meet their Celestial counterparts. I knew then that I had no need of such a weapon in the perpetual hostilities which were my only recourse. I leapt upwards with a bound and clung to the ceiling of that immense vault like a spider. With my nails I dug through the magma and out, swimming through that medium, whose heat scarcely matched that of my own hatred for the novel foe I had discovered, until I was swimming in the sediment of the darkest depths of the seas, where enormous worm-like creatures tunnel in blindness.

For then I had realized that there is no opponent, no adversary, so impossible to defeat, but who is equally unable to defeat you, as is the Self, the Ego. So it is that I spend my days stalking that implacable enemy, finding myself ensnared in his traitorous traps as often as I win a victory; on balance, the contest remains symmetrical. How many times haven't I believed myself to have entered the final phase of our combat, only to have that slippery bandit escape my grasp at the last moment!—How many times hasn't that sneaking culprit penetrated each of the multiple layers of defenses that guard my bed, and stolen up to my canopy-covered cadaver to deliver the coup-de-grâce, only to somehow retreat into nothingness as I suddenly awoke from dreams of lethargic peace, having failed to deliver the merciful blow!—At the moment, I'm preparing a suitable strategy for the decisive defeat of that nefandous foe, who I believe lurks just around the next corner; who knows whether he will not instead unleash the final ambush upon me?—When you once embark in battle against such a one, nothing is certain, save for the ceaselessness of the struggle. I close my eyes and tilt my head back like a drunkard, at the thought of having such a one as my enemy!—

—Lord Weÿrdgliffe, the Waughters.

* * * * *

The Baron Weÿrdgliffe ceased reading the spidery script and dropped the manuscript, which he had only recently discovered on his own writing-desk, onto the layers of dust and decaying vellum which had accumulated on the floor of the Waughters

during uncounted aeons of inattention. He couldn't help but admire such a rigorous piece of logic; but he found it impossible to
follow its prescription—for how long had it been since he had had
a Self, an Ego? It seemed that some befogged memory of such a
thing invaded his consciousness, a beclouded remembrance of
some long-ago time when he had engaged in exactly such a war
against the Self; but the hint was soon enough lost into the mists
of the unrecoverable, and a novel fancy took both its place and
its importance in the Baron's awareness. With a degree of concentration he could not maintain, he placed the tip of a pen on a
sheet of paper, and began to record the latest phantasmagorical
imaginings which had seized hold of the febrile and funereal fibers of his cerebellum.—

—Lord Weÿrdgliffe, the Waughters.

The Narrative of
Floressas des Aghones

After the publication of his Gothick Romance, *The Unspeak-able*, had aroused a universal hatred against him as great as his own for other men—which proved to him that they did not lack all worthiness of his company after all (for he had not previously believed them capable of such a noble emotion), Lord Weÿrdgliffe desired to approach them closely once again. So, to make their acquaintance in some sort, he hid within the shadowy spaces of towns, so as to avoid being caught by human sight. There, he heard stories about an old château in the countryside, on the estates of La Pœur (approximately seven and a half miles south-south-east of Les Hiboux). There, said the whisperings of men, dwelt a madman who suffered from such constant insanity that others could not endure his proximity, and even had allowed him to remain free despite the atrocity which he had committed—merely to avoid his presence.

Hearing this, the Baron resolved to seek out this maniac, reasoning that someone who had grown used to an unending company of horripilating nightmares who make it bleed from his mouth and his ears; and to spectres who sit at the head of his bed, and hurl at his face—compelled, despite themselves, by some unknown force, now with a sweet voice, now with a voice like the roarings of battles, with an implacable persistence—the tenacious tale of his unforgivable crime, forever hideous, which will only perish with the universe,—if even then. That someone like this, he reasoned, could—perhaps—endure the sight of his face!—And even, against all probability, provide him with the material for yet another of his infamous Horrid Stories!—

Baron Weÿrdgliffe crept through the countryside, which the moonlight clothed in yellow shapes, doubtful, fantastic. No road revealed itself beneath the covering vegetation and scarped stones. The shadows of trees crawled, now here, now there, like serpents waking after the sleep of winter. The wind slowly flowed through the grasses and leaves. Owls moaned their grave complaints, and wolves, blood dripping from their teeth, howled in the unseen distance. Distant boulders crouched on the coast, their silhouettes outlining the forms of crucified Titans.

The crumbled château appeared within the field of his vision. The trees that grew near it leaned away from it, their branches bending as if to avoid all contact with it. No glowing mould grew on the roof. Thorns and thistles matted the flagstones leading inside. The marble bodies of the ancestral line of the de La Pœurs stared at him with a vitreous gaze as he traversed the chambers with emerald wall-linings.

Entering into the picturesque ruins, he beheld the following tableau: in the back: on a throne in the midst of the enormous court, sat the decayed remnants of a woman, as naked as the folds of a black storm-cloud. Even in death, after putrescence had annihilated all that had remained of her face and her breasts, she appeared as beautiful as the splendor of the full moon on a windless night. She presided over that place as a Goddess presides over her temple from an altar. Torches and tapers, set on the walls and the fragments of the furnishings of that vaulted chamber, provided nearly as much haze and smoke as illumination. In the center of the room, bowing before the throne: a man with long white hair, tattered clothing, green wrinkles on his forehead, bewildered eyeballs. Set off, to the left: a gallows.

When the maniac turned around, after making his long prayers, he spoke in the following terms:

* * * * *

It seems that some novel nightmare has come to me, there in the corner where the room's angles intersect—for I see an unfamiliar face lurking amongst those to which I've grown accustomed. But I rather think that it isn't another nightmare, not one of the soul-crushing incubi who torment my days and my nights—for it doesn't have such a fearsome aspect, and its ugliness, even though so unimaginable that it would kill any lesser mind, seems like beauty in comparison with the noxious obscenities who confront my eternal awareness. Let me recount to this newcomer, then, the fascinating Tale of Terror which—as if the whirlwind of my destroyed faculties could no longer remember it—the nightmares ceaselessly re-place before my mind.

Perhaps you do not even know my name: Floressas des Aghones, Comte de La Pœur. As a young man, I avoided all attempts my father and mother made to find me a mate, suitable to my position as the Count. I felt that fate had preordained, in some unknown manner, that I should find my destined helpmeet. In fact (and I kept this secret from all others), every night I didn't fail to fall absorbed into dreams of some auburn-haired girl, who held out her hand to me, and accepted me as her equally expected companion. Each time, we wandered aimlessly through fields, by streams, on the coast, and she would run her fingers through my raven-black hair. Each time, I awoke to the keenest pangs of loss.

Until, that is, while traveling through Vyones one day, I noticed by chance a girl who exactly matched that of my dreams. She saw me as well, and as our eyes fixed, an invincible shudder ran through me, an invincible shudder ran through her, and we knew that what we took for a mere dream had been reality. The thoughts and emotions of seventy-seven thousand millennia could not sufficiently express that indefinitely minute instant in which I lost myself in the abysses of the verdure of her eyes. My parents, her parents, knew that nothing could prevent our union, and so acceded to it.

Immediately after our marriage, a new fixed idea (*idée fixe*) took hold upon my brain. The bliss I felt at our complete conjunction split into an enjoyment mixed and commingled with agony. A question consumed my agonizing intellect: the cause of our seemingly predestined match. When I gazed at her upon awakening, the sight made me think of the burning question. When I ate with her during the day, the sight again made me think of the burning question. When we made love, after retiring together, the intensity of our pleasures only increased the intensity of the question. Fearing some mental alienation, I attempted to remove myself from her presence, but found myself face to face with her ever-present absence—which once again merely reminded me all the more of the bizarre mystery that pursued me.

I hardly noticed as my parents died and I placed our domestics and subservients in charge of all of our worldly affairs. I devoted my full forces to the discovery of the enigma's unknown solution. My wife showed no signs of disapproval.

Every day, I would rise early in the morning, at a call from a domestic. Gaining consciousness, I would exclaim: "Ah!—another day in which to seek out the shadow-shrouded enigma! Looking at you now, Félise, I feel tempted to renew our amours (*amours*) from last night, when the few sallies which we indulged in did not sate us as much as they might have—if only I hadn't wasted my forces in my arcane researches. But the pull from those same researches tugs at me too strongly, and assures me that the discovery of the mystery's solution will only increase our ardor a million-fold. So, give me a kiss, until our evening meal, when—perhaps—we'll know what power has guided us into each other's arms!" She did so, and inadvertently revealed an ineffaceable look of sadness and resignation at my departure.

Then, I repaired to my study, and for several hours each morning I would read the most outlandish treatises on natural history, on teratology, on psychology, on theology and theosophy, on physics and metaphysics, and above all, on magick and the occult sciences. The least explored crannies of the Qabalah and the mouldiest grimoires fell under my ken. I must have produced more than forty volumes, correlating and correcting the few nuggets and morsels of wisdom those works contained. I even allowed, once—(in return for a collection of unprinted manuscripts inscribed in the serpentine script of Al Golach ibn Djinn)—a printer to produce a set of three or four of my works, which delineated, demonstrated, and questioned certain of the teachings of the Saracen sect of the Haschischin—on the condition that he omit my name as the treatise's author. He died under the hand of papal justice—which feared that a too-accurate knowledge of the secrets of death might not in all ways serve the cult of the God of compassion and mercy.

Then, a noontide meal, and I would retire to add the fruits of experiment to those of scholarship. It seemed certain from my readings that the secret lay in the best-guarded sepulcher of all—my own mind. (By this I don't mean to call my own mind better guarded than any other; merely that its secrets are more securely hidden from my inquiring ego than any other secrets.) One must unlock the portals of unconsciousness to uncover the nameless penetralia of that abattoir of awareness. I performed an exhaustive series of experiments to place my mind in every imaginable, every conceivable, state—one of them, it seemed certain, must provide the key. The most varied drugs mingled in my vials and veins. Aconite, mandragora root that had sprouted from the semen of hanged men, the pith of green hemp, laurel-almond, boiled skin of toad, jimson weed (*datura stramonium*), the heads of black poppies, foxglove and wormwood, tinctures of the phosphorescent fungi that grow on those mummies that antedate Aigyptos, dwale and deadly hebenon, unheard-of intoxicants brought by the Templars from the obscurest crannies of the Orient, inflamed my tottering brain.

But not merely chemical and alchemical substances, but the thoughts and actions, indeed the very language of symbolism that they embody, serve as helmsmen to the mental life-raft. So, incantations and invocations succeeded each other in unending procession; ceremonies and rites unknown to the priest of the religions followed each other like the links in a chain; meditations upon mystery and imaginal exercises complemented each other like the mile-high steps of a stairway to hell. Finally, after hours of the most strenuous effort, I disrobed, placed my instruments into their assigned places, snuffed the incense-censors and braziers, changed my ceremonial raiments to a more quotidian costume, and slammed shut the door to my laboratories with a *bang!*–burning with an ardor for my Félise rekindled by the flame of voluntary absentation.

And so on, for some twelve years.

At the end of this time, I struck on the definitive formula. The precise mixture of cerebral excitants, of barbaric names of evocation, of ritual gestures, of directed thoughts and imaginal exercises. Now, I devoted the morning session to the ritual which I had devised; I needed to study no longer; more and more, the ritual took effect. I would skip lunch and often supper as well, so much did my probings engross me.

Visions of an anterior life began to take on a greater and greater consistency. Kaleidoscopic landscapes appeared, shifted, and vanished. Enormous structures arose, Cyclopean monuments, walls, spires, towering temples, all of a resplendent mother-of-pearl beneath a reddish sky. Fern and cycad gardens gave out onto vast alleys and arcades. Gradually, human figures began to inhabit these scenes, set in some harbor city. I found myself more and more involved in the action, speaking to the men there in their picturesque tongue, which seemed as natural as life to me, and as I led a moon-litten procession down the great avenue from my enormous spiral tower to the domed palace of the Goddess, I saw, clothed in the richest white robes (yet of an elegant simplicity, silver-laced), crowned by a silvery tiara, the one who was, and was not, my Félise!

I knew then that I had discovered my primordial incarnation in the city of Polarea, as Chranemiith the Hierophant, and I celebrated my marriage with Dolclaza, the High Priestess. Then my former (current) life seemed as a dream that but thinly concealed the truth. I would gladly have given myself wholly to reliving that prior incarnation, and to the limits of possibility, did so. Félise, when I consulted her, showed no sign of disagreement with my decision, and even declared that this state of affairs suited her well enough. It seems that I still performed some actions which one might have considered entirely imaginary!—For the rest, she would say, what did it matter whether I imagine myself Chranemiith, the Hierophant of Polarea, or Floressas des Aghones, the Comte de La Pœur? My mere presence sufficed.

So, I gave my consciousness wholly to my life as Chranemiith. Even the memory of my true life as Floressas des Aghones departed from me, aside from the most intermittent of lapses. As if I had cast aside an illusion's dead carapace. My duties as Hierophant seemed simple enough. Ritual followed upon ritual, adjudication followed adjudication, ceremony followed ceremony, and so on, *ad infinitum.*

All wondered what strange and unspoken secret could have filled me with the pride that visibly consumed my thoughts. All did not fail to notice that I comported myself as if I had overcome some enormous barrier, as if I had surmounted the greatest obstacle and achieved an unspeakable success that staggered the universe with its boldness. Following upon this realization, the Council of the Wise came to me one day and explained to me what I must do. I had merely to realize within myself the incarnation of the God whom I served, Klalkrhú, the Lordly Creator, Preserver, and Law-Giver, and aid in turn the High Priestess in realizing herself as the incarnation of Yhth, Goddess of Beauty and Balance. Men muttered that my incommensurable pride had determined my selection for this rôle, for only the strongest and most powerful of Egos could deliver itself to the task of effacing itself utterly within its completest annihilation. Filled with haughtiness upon hearing this, I threw myself headlong into the quest to become more myself.

The Council of the Wise provided me with the parchments that described the Theory and Practice of Godhood. The methodology struck me with an odd sense of *déjà vu*. But I did not divine the secret. Each morning I arose from dreams of Félise-Dolclaza-Yhth and repaired to an enormous fane wherein I performed the Seven Rites of the Unnameable Transfiguration. The blood of the Behemoth and Kraken flowed into my brain, serving as my sole aliment, acting as seed to thoughts of enormous pride. The most hideous goëtia were howled through their rites as I concentrated all of my serried forces to the visualization of myself and Dolclaza as the deities which we, in truth, were—but for the shreds of humanity that shielded our true appearance from view. For the rest, let me say it—those ceremonies and meditations exactly duplicated (save only the accidents of language, custom, and time) the ones which had served me so well in my former (and now-unremembered) accomplishment.

My infernal wishes crept through the nothing. Blennorrhoeal pus or doubtful Goddess Yhth. My pulpy head resembles my still-erect Phallos beneath the covering vegetation and my eye, bubbling and stirring as with shattered on scarped stones. Like serpents in the midst of waking consistency, melting and changing. The ruins of the shapeless form flowed through the grasses and leaves, limbs or tails. But excuse me: sometimes the nightmares and spectres don't follow even the most ordinary rules of exposition. They don't trace a cold-blooded (*avec sang-froid*) syllogism in the sand with their bleeding stump: they have a logic all their own, which would not—perhaps—be recognized by the first-comer who happened to pass by!—

For ten years of minutes which were millennia, I crucified myself on the cross of self-servitude, until, as she came in one afternoon to act her part in that portion of the day's performance, I beheld—the one who was, and was not, Dolclaza, the Goddess Yhth, mother, sister, daughter, wife and whore in one, sparkling with the auroral aura of her divine nudity!—

All had changed. Her skin appeared reclothed in shifting greens and blues, yet of a creamy lightness. Her hair writhed and twisted of its own accord. Her eyes most of all. Lacking pupils, lacking whites, all a sheer amber that had no beetle encrusted within it. I looked around at that non-spatial area in which I found myself. It appeared as an indescribable, semi-abstract, semi-concrete, pseudo-icosahedral temple. The obvious implication hit me, and I gazed down at myself. Streaks of translucent purple surged through my crystalline fibers and nerves. A brackish yellow fog surrounded us. Prismatic rainbows played around us in resplendent and iridescent aureoles. I had become the Great God Klalkrhú.

She made a motion to me. I fell upon her, and those organs which, in mere men, symbolize the faculty of creativity, and which had a more than symbolic import in our case, became completely conjoined. As the ecstasy of my complete apotheosis surfeited and suffumigated the universe, some tiny fragment of Ego (what else bears such bitter fruit?) seemed to remain. That jot of desire introduced the most enormous complication into events. It occurred to me that now, when I had utterly destroyed and annihilated my entire selfhood into the Godhood of the Great Klalkrhú, and further combined that with the opposite and complementary Goddesshood of Yhth, still, still, I had not attained all possible to one of such power. Creator, Preserver, Lawgiver. How to become more than oneself? Become one self and an other. Further, if not free, what good oneself or another? Any act of good, of benevolence, of creativity, must needs display some tittle of bounded desire, of hope for one thing and not something else, and hence of forethought, and hence, of enslavement and servitude—if only to one's Self. Only an act of unmotivated, gratuitous, and absolute evil shows one truly free.

Through the channel through which normally flowed the creativity of the Universal Adjudicator, I funneled the juice of dismal destruction and all-absorbing annihilation. That bitter gall raged like lava carving itself a path through the sea. I gazed on before me and beheld the accomplishment of my infernal wishes. The so-beautiful Goddess Yhth fell dead off of my still-erect Phallos and shattered on the crystalline flooring.

The dream ended. I awoke and beheld Dolclaza lying dead in the middle of the ritual chamber. At the loss of her, whom I felt unable to live without for a single second, remorse intractably implanted itself within my seething consciousness. I knew then that I had achieved an act more wicked than I had imagined, for I had not only murdered the Goddess and my beloved, but I had enchained myself—the omnipotent All—and condemned myself to the gawking gullet of the Hell of Eternal Loss. From my ultimate power, I had made myself entirely powerless. I congratulated myself then, feeling that only by thus casting myself down from the Highest to the Lowest Realm could I have truly proven my omnipotence. Only by making myself the victim of my gratuitous evil could I prove myself truly powerful—since it's an admitted fact that everyone enjoys the suffering of others. At least, that everyone can tolerate the suffering of others, provided it have some useful purpose—such as proving one's own power superior. But the destruction of the Self—that's something else again. Only *that* can truly deny the haughty and desirous Ego.

The Council of the Wise, in its unshackled prudence, ordered that none should interfere with me, despite the infamy I had brought upon their religion, which henceforth fell into disfavor with the general populace, though retaining its traditional state support, without which it would never have thrived. So, I fed my remorse and my radical impotency, meditating every moment on the corpse of the one whom I had so loved. Day by day, that cadaver became a prey to the ineradicable laws of putrefaction and decay. That nauseating metamorphosis cast a radical doubt into my agonizing mind. For if the traces of the enormity which I had committed could disappear, then would not anything, yea anything, disappear as well? Even unto the greatest remorse?

I researched the problem. Every day, after gazing for hours at what remained of Dolclaza's corporeal substance, I re-interpreted the papyri of the cult's teachings. It seemed certain. For one cannot kill a Goddess so easily: they incarnate at regular periods, to say the very least. My crime, then, would disappear!—

A merely temporary action wouldn't quite qualify, I saw then, as an act of utter and unmotivated evil. No, something more permanent must come to hand. My research continued apace, and I discovered the method that would regularly renew the crime and my unbearable remorse and loss. I pronounced the unspeakable oath. (If I don't repeat it now, it's not so much because even the nightmares and spectres, who ceaselessly recount to me every other detail of this remarkable narrative, fail to remind me of the exact wording—not eager to experience its effects for themselves, the ineluctable result—but because I don't want to impose on my August audience, who might not like even the effects of having its chords pounded on the piano of his brain.) I had, then, bound myself to the endless cycle of metempsychotic migration, forgetfulness, and the return of memory, which for all eternity will claim hold upon me, renewing the act which again provides the ineffaceable proof of my omnipotence at regular intervals! Then I betook myself to the great temple tower and hurled myself from it onto the rocky crags of the coast, utterly smashing the life from that feeble shell and precipitating it into an unsuspecting matrix to prepare the doom that shall yet—alas!—for quite a while, make me suffer (eternity is long). I awoke and beheld Félise lying dead in the middle of our *boudoir*.

Now that the secret has been revealed to you, you won't disparage the wishes of the one who desires nothing from you but that you should, firstly, hang him on that gallows there with this fine hempen rope, and so precipitate him into the empty abysses of cryptical amnesia;—and then, so as not to lose the greatest possible benefit of the lesson which he has so striven to inculcate in you, you'll cut through his skull. Then, having removed the top of his head, you'll scoop out and gobble down his still-warm and pullulating cerebellum. If some admirable recklessness forces you to desire an even more intimate understanding of the events consummated within my tale, then come back with a black dog. Have the dog dig up the mandrake which will unfailingly grow from the seed which my execution will infallibly sow, even if it must itself crack the flagstones to find a habitation. Don't stopper your ears with wax, but listen carefully as the man-shaped root screams.—True words of wisdom don't agree with everyone; there you find the reason for the custom which otherwise remained inexplicable. And ignore the dying dog's agonies. Then, gobble down the root at once—but take time, I pray, to savor its bitter flavoring. And afterwards—the sensations!—

* * * * *

After hearing the remarkable narrative (*récit*) which the maniac's hand has just recopied for the thousand and first time, the Connoisseur of Unsuspected Cruelties thought to himself: "It's necessary to do him that justice. He cretinized me quite a bit. He even provided me with a novel idea for one of my Penny Dreadfuls. Don't think that I won't reward him in the manner that he desires."

And he turned to the now-silent speaker: "Madman, it's beautiful to contemplate the ruins of human habitations; and even more beautiful to contemplate the ruins of human bodies; but far and away the most beautiful of all, to contemplate the ruins of human minds!"

—Lord Weÿrdgliffe, the Waughters.

Cold Blood, Blood Cold

People didn't make a mistake when they referred to my blood as the very definition of the word *cold*. They would rightly point out that whereas the blood of a lizard or a snake at least receives warmth from its environment, enlivening the beast, my own stays in a perpetually frigoriferous state. It flows through my veins like a glacier carving out a fjord. How I can live, *I*–whose fingers leave freeze-burns on the flesh which they have just left off palpating, remains an anomaly which scientists must not have understood at first sight, relying solely on the received ideas and opinions of established experiment and theory.

In order (or disorder) to wreak a ferocious vengeance on the universal brotherhood of humanity (I'm not claiming that, whereas I do nothing to them, they act in a way that's intentionally obnoxious to me), I wanted to make the world as cold as my own blood.–No easy task, for a mere mortal. So, I turned and fixed my two eyeballs' conical rays upon the sun. They say that Prometheus stole fire from Heaven in a hollow tube, thus earning the eternal gratitude of antique Greeks and Romantic poets–well, in my case, the effect was the polar opposite. That flaming orb soon faded under the intense scrutiny of my frozen pupils, and felt itself irremediably quashed into a pathetic and smoky ember. The moon and the stars still gave off enough light for people to see that choking chunk of charcoal against the ink-black sky. The consternated mobs proclaimed the wondrous sight (signs in the heavens, you know—) a portent of evil to come, that would engulf the planet—little could they know how correctly their hypothetical construction accorded with the somber reality.

That accomplished, I had merely set the stage for my true revenge. Now, a novel torture added to my daily pleasures. I would take some human, caught by any snare soever, and solidly garroted into utter immobility—make it a young girl of nineteen, as beautiful as the day (which no longer existed), so as to add to the excitement and voluptuosity of the deed—and take her, completely stripped of covering, into some barren field. Then, once in a proper pose, throw cold water onto her body until she froze to death. Frozen inside a solid chunk of ice, she would, unfailingly and infallibly, resemble something like a statue—an impeccable *objet d'art*, in any case, worthy of the most canine veneration on the part of those who claim to understand even the tiniest tittle of aesthetics.

Further refinements added to the beauty of that spectacle. I made the former deserts of the rocky chamberpot into enormous fields of once-living ice, with groups of human figures contorting and twisting in unheard-of arrangements. Their grinning grimaces would stand as a memorial to the torments that produced them. These monuments dotted the sandy plains, and then they utterly enveloped them. From time to time, to clear a ground for further pleasures, I would take some huge lump of frozen bodies, and precipitate it into the seas. Many noises give offence, and a few give delight, but nothing compares to the crepitations of the calamitous crashings of human icebergs!—Hearing the screams of terror that depart from some ship, as a body-berg smashes it into splinters, dumping the worthy sailors, who clutch onto many-splintered fragments of board too small to make coffins with, to the profoundest tombs in Poseidonis—And still, seven-eighths of it would remain hidden beneath the billowy waves—

I found still more ways to enjoy this absurd abomination. Far from an entity of solidity, humans represent fluidic creatures, for the most part—that fact remains well within the boundaries of the universally accepted. So I replaced my medium of water with that of blood. But not just any blood. Only that from the individual itself would do. (A mature soul favors refinement and elegance in all things, the largest as well as the smallest details.) I soon populated the globe with a host of crimson pyramids that reached up to the sky with scarlet pinnacles, aspiring upwards in corkscrewing spirals like the imperial purple of a pre-pubescent penis, upon awakening from the vulgar dreams of innocence.

In certain cases, only the menstrual blood was used—in an act of the most individualistic and artistic expression. These I formed into an incommensurable trapezohedron, which an enormous hefting of my iron-muscled and skeletal arms sent hurtling through the membranes of space to crash into the barrenness and blankness of the moon. An infinity of sanguinary atoms diffused throughout the heavens, while the moon's surface revealed a novel shuddering and a crater like a virginal vulva.

In turn, every bodily fluid served as the medium for this glorious projection of vengeance, illimitable and liquescent!—

Now a monstrous monolith of salt-water ice from the victims' tears crashed into the ocean to replenish its bitterness. Now a golden-yellow palace of urine gazed outward onto the frozen forests from its barbicans and porticoes: it stands there yet. Huddled in my cloak, these sights gratified my immeasurably. A greater one awaited the harvesting of enough nasal mucus—fortunately, the inclement weather brought about the desired result more quickly than the common run of infectious circumstances—and I erected the pseudo-Babelian Tower of Snot that gashes into the skies like a scalpel, when they approach too closely in their revolutions. A colossus composed of one hundred thousand rebels against my tyranny, stewing in their own bile, stands threatening the seas with its implacable swordblade, unliftable by an hundred men; an equally gigantic statue of Justice blindly faces it, holding a scales in perfect balance above the last tottering refuge of humanity. Here lies a landscape maze, with zigzag walls made up of alternating layers of the saliva-frozen and the perspiration-chilled. Here stands a Cyclopean skeleton, composed of marrow-men, holding a scythe, likewise composed, miming that figure of their own decease which humans have created, drawing upon the strip-mines of their imaginations, but not fully understanding its parodic implications. To culminate this series—notable for its unity in many respects, its diversity in others, but always admirable for its beautiful cruelty—I constructed, at one hundred times true scale, a modeled city, as beautiful as a möbius strip, with walls and buildings, furnishings and floorings, streets and shops, derived from men imprisoned into place inside their own frigid semen. A modeled population, as beautiful as a unicursal hexagram, peoples this magnificent and immobile metropolis, encased in shells of pre-come lubricant. I found the meticulous harvesting required for that latter project a pretty tedious—and often rather unpleasant—affair.

When the semi-crustacean, semi-fungoidal Outer Ones come winging through the aether, splitting through the ironic, untenanted cobwebs that stretch from the sun to the moon and from the moon to the planets and outwards beyond the rim, taking their motion from the waves of the dust of annihilated universes and sidereal systems, wafted along by the star-winds, they poise motionless in the void, and look down at the earth—and behold a spectacle, as sad as the speaking surfaces of a tesseract, which doesn't fail to astound them; and even though they altogether lack any discernible sort of lachrymose or risible faculty, I think that they do get, at the very least, an unpremeditated and unforeseen, not to say unlooked-for and unwelcome, glimmering of an obscurely reflected cranny in the incomprehensible conscious-ness of Human Existence!—

—Lord Weÿrdgliffe, the Waughters.

Rejection Letter

Dan Clore, eagerly anticipating the fate of yet another of his innumerable "Lord Weÿrdgliffe" tales, destined to take a place amongst the acknowledged masterpieces of world literature, opened the SASE which he had provided the editor with in order to notify him of the inevitable acceptance of his story. To his no small dismay, there instead appeared a letter of rejection, citing such factors as the excessive preponderance of "whimsical gore"—not to mention the exorbitant amount of "fancy words," and stylistic tics such as the uncalled-for mention of the "centrifugal force"—as features dictating its non-acceptance. At this point Clore experienced a shudder of uncanny shock and surprise, as the Baron Weÿrdgliffe himself appeared to his view, materializing before him—shock and surprise, for he had previously believed that the Begetter of Baroque Bizarreries had no existence save as a persona utilized by himself, lacking any substance other than that which Clore's own words could give him.

The Baron immediately began to deliver an harangue aimed at the incredulous author, informing him that he found it unfortunate enough to deal with such an intermediary as Clore himself, who as frequently as not failed to convey the conceptions which he had conceived, that he found even the eyes of the reader a too-great medium for the act of communication—for he would have rather removed them and directly inseminated his audience's august brains with his fœtid and fœcund ideas—but that the interposition of an editor between himself and his readership, positively surpassed the bounds of the acceptable, and that he had resolved henceforth to reject it utterly. The Baron further indicated that for this once, he should not brook even the interference which Clore interposed between him and the editor, and would deal directly with that despicable creature, and told Clore how he could fulfill his part in allowing him to do so.

Dan Clore took out an envelope and inscribed on it the name and address of the New Jersey editor, affixing an appropriate stamp, dropped a small spider into it, and sealed it, his dry tongue scarcely providing enough moisture to glue it shut. Clore dropped the envelope into a mailbox and speedily departed from a narrative which he had felt no desire to enter into, exhaling a sigh of no small relief at that exiting—for he knew all too well what sort of unsavory fate awaits the victims of Lord Weÿrdgliffe. (But how, in a world where interpretation is frequently even more uncertain than that of the most ambiguous adjective contained within the cramped confines of a labyrinthine Gothick Romance, could he have known of the even more gruesome fate that awaited him just beyond the border of the text?)

* * * * *

When the nameless editor (nameless, not for any reason related to the preservation of an undeserved anonymity, but rather because of an unnameability due only to the shockingly abominable qualities of the entity hidden behind a verbal label which has itself become unspeakable due to its association with the aforesaid editor bearing it) unsealed the envelope which he had discovered amongst the slush newly arrived in his post office box, a tiny black spider leapt out of it, flew through the air, and clamped onto his crotch. Before that nameless editor had time to start back in the fright which had overtaken him (and who knows why one so squeamish would even wish to become involved in the horror field in any way?—), the spider glided off of and away from the area which even its small size could easily encompass: there obviously wasn't anything to interest it—or anyone else, for that matter—*here*.

The editor, utilizing strategies taught him within his many visits to the goateed representatives of the psychiatric profession, managed at long last to calm himself down enough to read the letter enclosed, signed by the enigmatic and eremitic Dan Clore, which explained a very few matters of elementary aesthetics, phrased in a kindergarten-level language even an editor should find it within his mental compass to comprehend. After only a few bepuzzled hours devoted to its exegesis, he quickly composed a reply, comprised entirely of wounded whining about "hate mail," and voyaged onward to the slush pile which he had accumulated over the last few decades. (Lord Weÿrdgliffe had helpfully suggested that he improve his response time by simply reading submissions rather than sleeping, which would have, after all, cost him nothing, since slumber has no legitimate function outside of nightmares, and the manuscripts would amply provide that function for him, if not through their positive quality, then—at least through their negative. And if he found it too difficult to follow this prescription, he could try the toothpick trick; that failing, simply sheering away the eyelids proves effective in most cases; in the rare instances in which it does not, simply tossing some hot ashes onto the eyeballs most often does the job—)

The editor's solitary bed awaited him with its usual patience, and he didn't fail to approach it with his customary amorous advances, accompanied by the viewing of a *Sports Illustrated*'s swimsuit issue of several years back (needless to say, he found that *Playboy* always offended him with its graphic and gratuitous nudity; how could they publish such unutterably obscene material?), after which he switched off his lamp and attempted to shut his eyes, fearing that his recent reading (Clore's cruel letter, not the submitted stories) would produce a disturbing dream.

But enough illumination remained from the streetlights, even through the curtains on his apartment window, for him to see (he as yet felt too much residual terror from his reading to close his eyes—) a tiny black spider, which filled him with a sense of *déjà vu*, just beginning to descend on a strand of gossamer thread, attached to the ceiling at a point exactly above his face. He strove with all of his might to budge, but he couldn't do it. Panic had paralyzed him, with an effect more certain than that of a godzillion doses of paralytic venom. The spider came, slowly, slowly, down towards his face. He strove, he strove—he failed: not even his little toe or his pinky finger proved capable of movement at that hour of need. But just as the spider had nearly reached him, he recalled (his recent reading had just bore upon him the import of this fault, which he met with so often in the unsolicited submissions), that it must be accounted a grave mistake in a Tale of Terror, for the protagonist to utterly fail to achieve any success in altering the horrible circumstances in which he finds himself, even though he still should not escape from a fate no less inevitable than horripilating. Once that remembrance hoved into sight, he suddenly discovered the strength to make a slight puff of air, by blowing up through his lips, at the tiny spider. He even thought to himself, that if Lord Weÿrdgliffe had only known of these circumstances, he would recommend (in an unwarranted act of self-plagiarism on the part of Dan Clore, an author apparently—but not actually—addicted to certain forms of stylistic excess) that the spider be launched by the centrifugal force, and depart for the regions of outermost space—

No such luck. When that enormous gust (putting it into the perspective and point-of-view of the most relevant character, and the one with whom any reader of that infandous editor's vile journal will not fail to identify) crashed into the spider like a hurricane, the little creature found itself swinging back and forth, back and forth, and so it decided that it could no longer count on the plans which it had formulated, and entirely disposed of the left nostril as a goal for its alighting. But indeed, even the effect of that gusting windstorm inspired an idea no less equal to its task of vengeance, and so it gave itself freely to the swinging motion which the nameless editor continued to create with his blustering blowing, and finally whomped onto the editor's right ear. There, the minuscule arthropod clamped its mandibles onto the soft membrane inside, which caused a tremendous shudder to run down the unmentionable editor's spinal column, and sucked out, in a single and prolonged gulp, the unnameable editor's brains, swelling the spider itself to dimensions greater than that of a human head, which created a quite humorous effect, for it looked like a hairy balloon, forming a grotesque and bloated parody of Lord Weÿrdgliffe's face, with eight tiny legs protruding from the sides, unable to come close to reaching the ground.

Just as the nefandous editor's eyes had begun to sink back in their sockets, the bloated spider began to regurgitate, undigested, the cerebral matter which it had so-recently ingested.

* * * * *

When the nameless editor's roommate came to waken him (for he rarely rose at an opportune time, after spending the night huddling in the fetal position, trembling in terror over some stray shadow), he discovered the unspeakable editor lying motionless as a cadaver beneath a white sheet, on which read, in characters formed of a grey and red substance, the inscription:

DOES NOT MEET OUR CURRENT NEEDS

—Lord Weÿrdgliffe, the Waughters.

The Silver Scorpion

I sank to my ankles in the sea of bones. The setting sun gave out no warmth on that chalkwhite desert, and the rising night-wind did nothing to cool the arid air. Transfixed with fascination, I tried in vain to imagine what untold holocaust could have created that shifting ocean of skeletons. I wheeled about, sinking to my knees, and perceived that the osseous ocean of inarticulate bones extended beyond the horizon in every direction. Turning my gaze downward, I sifted through that once-human sand, finding the deceased in every stage of disintegration, from complete skeletons down to tiny slivers of bone smaller than a grain of sand. The moon shone down obliquely from the east, its surface seemingly a reflection of the wasteland below, and in its light something briefly gleamed. I reached down and lifted the skeleton hand from the universal ossuary. That ring, with the silver scorpion, must have been what so briefly reflected the moonbeams. I knew somehow that I had seen that ring before, but strove in vain to replace it. Had it been worn by some fellow man, who had extended that eradicated hand to me in friendship? Had it been worn by some lover, who had delivered a thousand caresses to me with the hand bearing that ring? Had it been worn by some dire enemy, who had causelessly turned the implacable hand wearing that dreadful ring against me, in order to bring about my downfall? In shock I recalled the sole place in which I had seen that silver scorpion before. Had I not worn that symbol of my ineffaceable identity since my earliest youth? In a daze I let the skeleton hand fall into the general decay and listened intently as the knuckles clattered down the chalkwhite dune. Turning to the west, I began the long slow march to the infinite horizon, sinking more and more deeply into the sea of bones with every step.

                                        –Lord Weÿrdgliffe, the Waughters.

The Nocturnal Nemesis

There is no danger more dreadful than sleep. Unguided and alone, you descend into the cavernous recesses of the self; more than one explorer of those labyrinthine mines has fallen prey to the ambiguous Minotaurs that dwell within. The body as well as the mind faces dire perils when slumber overwhelms the senses; it hangs, limp and defenseless, vulnerable to the depredations of the first passer-by.

For these reasons I had long attempted to avoid the pleasures afforded by oblivion. But the inevitable cannot, in every case, be avoided indefinitely, and the body and brain soon solidify into a leaden mass that crushes the cushions which offer it their tender caresses.

On every evening in which I had thus surrendered myself to the darkness, before I had reached the portals of night, I could hear the door to my bedchamber creaking open in the distance. Fearfully and furtively, a figure would then enter, and silent step by silent step, approach nearer and nearer to my bed. Struggling against the weight bearing me down, I would have barely succeeded in lifting my head and opening my eyes, when the drear silhouette hovering over me would recede, shrieking, beyond the reaches of sense.

Haunted by these nightly visitations, I built my home into a veritable fortress. I stationed guards at each possible point of entry, totally immersing myself in their protection. Ring after ring of impenetrable defense arose around me. No amount of precautions served to prevent the nocturnal visits of that bedroom invader.

Plagued by this enemy, who always disappeared in that fashion before I could reach the dagger hidden under my pillow, I realized that I would have to turn the tables on my foe, and make him into my prey instead. One day I set out and asked each passer-by if he could identify the culprit from my description. It was not long before I hit paydirt, and I was informed, with an odd look, that my nemesis' home was not far down the road. I flew to that place on wings of swiftness.

Like a shadow I crept through each successive layer of fortification that vainly defended that implacable foe. None of the guards so much as blinked an eye at my passing, and I soon found myself gazing at the figure lapsing into slumber beneath the canopy over his silken bed.

The eyelids, half-fallen, began to rise as that head lifted itself from the pillow, and I knew then that I recognized the features disfiguring that fearsome face. The rawbone cheeks, the wrinkled brow, the greying strata of silvery hair, all belied the age of that figure, who still had not surpassed his thirty-third year.

In horror I fled shrieking from the sight of my own visage, uselessly wondering how I could overcome such a formidable foe. I had vanquished all who had previously contested my supremacy, but with our forces so evenly matched, the combat might last until the end of eternity before one of us had succeeded in conquering his enemy. An unspeakable intoxication grasped hold of my head at that realization, and I nearly fell to the ground in my ecstasy. There was nothing left to do at that point but return home to rest in order to recuperate enough strength to take on the challenge before me. Yes, one must be well-rested when engaging in such a combat, and the silken pillows call out to my weary head as my eyelids begin their slow transformation into a pair of leaden weights.

—Lord Weÿrdgliffe, the Waughters.

The Bug by Night

Lord Weÿrdgliffe stooped over the paper onto which he had just disburdened his brain of a nightmarish fancy, as if pouring a ropy red wine out of a cup made from his own skull. He appended his trademark signature ("–Lord Weÿrdgliffe, the Waughters.") to the end of the tale, and sighed in contentment at its savory gruesomeness. Now, even though he had finished hours earlier than he usually did, he could begin his nocturnal prowlings for prey, as his mansionhouse, the Waughters—as he had just written of it, in the Tale of Terror in which it had served as setting—"seemed to emanate darkness in an unholy radius of fear, billowing out waves of ebony terror like an obsidian nova," ever since his Weird Tales had begun to appear in print in the journals of minuscule readership which his work had on rare occasions had the good fortune to catch the editors of unawares.—Resulting in its publication.

His bony framework leapt out of his window onto the marshy grounds. He had altogether ceased stalking human victims, and had settled on the multitudinous mobs of bogeys and calcars, hobgoblins and pookahs, spurns and snallygasters, spectres and kit-wi'-the-candlesticks to appease his ferocious appetites. He told himself that in this way, he had solved two intractable problems at once. For he could avoid his inevitable disgust at the human form, and relish, to the contrary, the collection of molar fangs, glowing eyebulbs, slime-coated scales, and irretractable claws presented to his slit pupils by the crowd of phantoms and fearbabes. Furthermore, with human prey, he would eventually have annihilated the entire tribe, and however worthy an action that might prove, however much it would improve the undoubtedly dolorous situation, it would eternally deprive the one who committed it to a regrettable lack of any further victims to sacrifice on the altar of his ego. The phantasms of human fright and imagination, on the other hand, not only would never be exhausted, but seemed positively to increase their numbers in measures beyond all the bounds of plausibility; no matter how many departed for the infernal wastelands, infinite armies were waiting to take their place.

Indeed, when he looked down at his skeletal figure as his elongated, bony fingers palpated the empty black pits that served him as eyesockets, and contemplated the shock of wriggling russet algae that served him as hair, he felt far more akin to the phantom-fears of human imagination than he did to those nauseating monstrosities, human beings. So much so, that if some obscure pride had not prevented him, he would have almost suspected that he himself were naught but such a spook, such a creation of human phantasy. As it was, he only recognized that he had come from the region of nullity to which the reader shall (God willing!) soon enough return.–Though not soon enough for one with the refined tastes of the Seeker of Inexhaustible Solitude.

As his mind was absorbed in the midst of these rêveries, his lanky legs and outstretched arms pounced onto a boggart. He told himself, as his jaws crunched down on the annihilated creature's still-gleaming but now popping eyebulb, that the thing had frozen with a look of paralyzed fright such as no other bogey had displayed before him, and he hypothesized that he had grown in power and fearsomeness. This ego-enhancing ideation soon became falsified by empirical data, however, as there crept up behind him, fastening its foreclaws onto his emaciated flesh, the most eldritch entity which the Baron of Boundless Bizarreries had ever had the good fortune to encounter; and positively the only one which exceeded himself in gruesomeness, and that not merely by a minuscule degree, for a well-nigh infinite distance separated the two on the scale of inhuman oddity.

His adamantine arms melted like star-jelly beneath the force exerted against them, and the two foremost of the eight members, which extended in the pattern of the daddy-longlegs, lifted him up to the skull-face which hung from the immense bony brain that served the creature as a body. The thing's tubular tongue protracted out of its toothless mouth like a segmented worm emerging from a loch, and clamped onto Lord Weÿrdgliffe's body, sucking out every last drop of blood, bonemarrow, spinal fluid, saliva, and semen, until not a single drop of liquidity remained in his desiccated frame. Still, he could hardly help but admire the cerebral mass of bone that now pulsed with a crimson glow as he collided with the marshy ground and the thing loped off across the swamp to pursue further prey.

Any lesser being, it seemed to him then, would have given up the ghost on the spot. Lord Weÿrdgliffe, however, never one to resign ownership of a ghost if it were at all possible to retain its possession, soaked up enough moisture from the marsh—in which the current scene is conveniently located—to restore life to his frame, albeit with some loss of thickness in his proportions. As he lay there, in a state bordering on dream and death, he observed as a distant phantom-light entered into the window of his bedchamber in the Waughters. Realizing that there would be no use returning to his home, he decided to determine the identity of the spectre, if possible, through the only means available: to find a human who had discovered the secret. He could not, however, venture into human society with his current appearance; his re-cently-increased thinness, no more than his everyday gruesome-ness, rendered him too horrifying for such a squeamish race to behold.

After only a brief wait, a young man chanced upon the scene, gazing with determination at the Waughters. As usual, the mere sight of the Baron froze him into an immobile state of fear-ful paralyzation, as the knotty muscles on the dust-dry skeleton entered his clouded vision. Lord Weÿrdgliffe knew what to do. He forced his framework inside that of the unfortunate fellow with a little disgust, although, fortunately enough, the only suitable en-tryway had just been evacuated of its prior contents upon the ex-perience of such a frightful sight. The face and muscles had to distort in a most grotesque manner to accommodate the entity currently usurping them, which exceeded the normal dimensions of human proportions. His penis-bone and testicular shells, most especially, found it difficult to enlarge the cramped confines of their new homes to a comfortable expanse. Regretting his tempo-rary tumescence, the Baron loped off to a city bordering on his marshy demesnes.

In the city, which the Baron still has not recognized as one on any map, the gossip of the day—which the yawping locals were only too happy to find a stranger to tell to, as the news had already circulated through that village's population numerous times—soon struck his ears with awe. For it seemed that a searcher of the arcane, a seeker in strange places, a young man, had—to the consternation of all concerned—just disappeared. This fellow had become an ardent reader of an eldritch and arcane au-thor known obscurely as Lord Weÿrdgliffe, the mere rumors of whose Tales of Terror filled the crowds with panicked terror, and he had gone to the edge of the swamps beyond the town's limits to seek a glimpse of the admired author, who of old rumor was re-puted to reside there. Now, everyone had warned him that only a monster of the worst description could conceive of such nameless atrocities as the writer of those Penny Dreadfuls bespattered every page of his Horrid Stories with, and it was no surprise to them that he had vanished.—No doubt, said some, that grotesque gargoyle, created in a parody of the human form, had sucked out the blood and brains of the unfortunate.—No doubt, said the more perceptive among them, he had been spirited away into the bowels of some obscured oubliette wherein that ghoulish fiend would daily torment him, glad to have found an unfailingly compliant audience in that way.

At first, Lord Weÿrdgliffe despaired at the realization that he had been replaced by a spectre inspired by his own Weird Tales—though a certain pride filled his otherwise empty heart at the thought of the horror he had diffused through the heads of his supposed fellows. He could not destroy the monster, even setting aside the repugnancy he would feel performing such an act—since, as he reasoned, such a masterpiece of imagination does not arise from human phantasy more than once in a millennium; for if the population accepted the entity as himself, they would hardly consent to accepting such a paltry horror as his true nature in its stead; and that would leave him with no audience whatsoever for his Strange Stories—

But when it dawned upon him that his novel replacement would most likely continue to publish under his name, he determined to see what such an admirable production could itself produce. To sustain himself in the interval between that time and the eventual publication of a tale by that fiend—for the appearance of one of Lord Weÿrdgliffe's Tales of Terror is an event which only occurs on rare occasions—he acted the part in society of a prostitute; his tattered mind allowed little other choice, while his physique perfectly matched the requirements of the job. For his flaccid phallus, given the disparity in size between it and the corresponding vessel—whether the male, the female, or otherwise,—seemed to the ignorant clients to remain in a state of permanent and majestic erection, like that of an ithyphallic ascete from the nether regions; meanwhile, the odious proximity of live human flesh guaranteed that his member should never aspire to the state of turgidity his prose finds itself perpetually embroiled in.

After many months, then, spent in the most degrading exercises of erotism, servicing the venal and venereal lusts of innumerable consumers, he finally located a newly published Strange Story by his second self, in the back pages of a journal that rarely exceeded five or six readers on those uncommon occasions when it sold at all. Needless to say, it had already worked its way into a second-hand bookshop—for another contributor had accidentally happened to read the Weird Tale that bore the trademark signature "—Lord Weÿrdgliffe, the Waughters."—where it earned the employee who had made the decision to purchase it the loss of his job. The Baron's hair stood straight on end in fright, shattering into smithereens the borrowed skull he was wearing at the time, as he discovered that the monstrosity's imaginings exceeded his own in cruelty and inventiveness, and he could only agree with it that the Waughters—which formed the setting of the tale, in which the Baron's alter ego played the part of protagonist and antagonist at once—"seemed to emanate darkness, like an ebony anus dilating to diffuse in a gushing geyser the slithering spermatozoa of the unspeakably eldritch and the serpentine spirochetes of the illimitably odd, to deluge the world with an unholy apocalypse of uncanniness and insanity"—

* * * * *

Lord Weÿrdgliffe stooped over the paper onto which he had just disburdened his brain of a nightmarish fancy. He appended his trademark signature to the end of the Tale of Terror. Despite the difficulty he had in writing, what with holding the pen in his wormlike tubular tongue and all, he had finished his night's work hours earlier than usual, and he could leave the Waughters through the window to begin his nocturnal prowlings for prey.

–Lord Weÿrdgliffe, the Waughters.

Antecessor at the Gate

A skeleton sat by the towering wall, its legs splayed, its neckbones bent over its kneecaps, its face in its hands. Along the road to the Gate, an exquisite and naked cadaver came ambling down towards the opening, idiot expectancy visible in its dead fish's eyes. The black stone wall rose up some seventy-five feet; the black metal Gate itself must have towered over a hundred in its arch. Nothing else relieved the blank black stone landscape.

The corpse came up to the Gate and waited for a few moments. He headed over to the inanimate skeleton and asked rhetorically: "This must be the Gates of Heaven. Why doesn't it open up for me?"

The skeleton lifted his skull and replied: "And what makes you think it's the Gates of Heaven? I thought it must be the Gates of Hell. Still, you can see the condition I've reached—I started out in yours, after all—waiting for it to let me in. I don't want to miss out on my just deserts."

"Hell? But this must be Heaven's Gate. You can tell from the weather: the redness in the clouds from the rising sun. Dawn perfectly represents the ascent into Heaven."

"Oh? I thought it looked more like the twilight of evening, of obvious and contrary symbolism. But I have to tell you, that it doesn't indicate any impending change. Those ruddy clouds have been there since I got here, and that's been quite a while."

"It doesn't rain here? That would be Heavenly."

"It doesn't do anything here. Nothing happens; it doesn't rain; the clouds don't even move. That's Hellish."

"Okay then. We'll have to figure it out some other way. What have you ever done to deserve Hell?"

"I'll tell you. I'm Antecessor, no doubt you've read of me in your history books—I have no reason to doubt that I achieved posthumous fame for my deeds of infamy. Indeed, a great crowd attended me as I leapt from the gallows."

(A start indicated to Antecessor that his interlocutor had indeed heard of him.)

"So you know that I went from one scene of carnage to the next, taking pleasure in nothing but others' pain. I tortured my victims in every manner imaginable, before slaughtering the sheep at the precise moment of my ecstatic spasm. Maybe you don't know why I did so. I'll tell you. I just followed my own natural impulses. Other people don't follow their own—because of their ridiculous beliefs in the afterlife. The cowards! They hope for Heaven, like you, or they fear Hell, unlike me. But as for me, whenever I would hear their tales of that glorious place of eternal torment, I would become filled with desire, and told myself that I would storm Heaven and topple the non-existent God from his Diamond Throne if I had to do so to merit an eternity in Hell. I doubt you can imagine just how much that vision of infinities of souls, all roasting in infernal fire and stabbed in the ass by white-hot pitchforks, demons jabbing needles into their guts and blowing trumpets in their ears, the smell of toasted flesh and burnt blood and bile, appealed to me. Most of all, the opportunity to myself undergo experiences which I could formerly only experience vicariously. I didn't find it completely safe to submit to everything I wanted to, not in my own flesh! Now, to my surprise, I find that such a Utopia really does exist. But what the devil is the hold-up on their admitting me? I can't tell you how long I've been waiting for this damned Gate to open, and let me in on the rewards I had no hope of attaining to."

"I can tell you how long: about four centuries. But I think you're making a grave mistake in expecting this to be the Gates of Hell. We all know from our history books, as you say, that your victims did not belong to the most pious segments of the population. No, you chose—wittingly or not—a vile rout of criminals and cretins, who greatly deserved all the torments meted out to them by you. If you hadn't gotten to them first, no doubt the agents of the law would have treated them a little bit more harshly. You're well-known in my day as the Atheist Saint, or the Sinner-Saint, who performed acts of the greatest good out of the basest motives of impiety and cruelty. So I think you've just proven to me that I did make it, if—since you say the Gates haven't opened up in all the time you've been waiting here—no one else since your death has. I'm sure Hell must have a long line waiting to get into its narrow entryway. I can only imagine the logjam of souls lined up outside its doors!"

"And what could you have done to possibly merit Heaven?"

"Oh, that's right, you wouldn't have had any history books to tell you the story of Malicorne. I headed the great Inquisition, and found out heresy in the most unlikely places. Practically no one would admit it of their own uncoerced accord, but I could sniff it out like a bloodhound tracking prey, and discovered the means to force them to admit their unforgivable sins in the instruments of torture which you had devised. Sometimes it took weeks, even months of the most prolonged torments to get the truth from them, and then, of course, I had them tell me the names of other sinners like them, and started the process over with those individuals, who often proved even more intractable than the first. But not a single sinner got away from me, and I taught them all the lesson of dishonesty before dispatching their souls to the Gates of Hell. You haven't seen any of them pass by here, have you? No? Then that proves this must be the Gates of Heaven."

"Oho! I think you've just proved the opposite, my friend," the skeleton replied. "It's more than obvious from your description that all of the victims of your hypocrisy were completely innocent of the charges you made against them, and therefore martyrs deserving of Heaven. But you, for sins greater than those you could have imputed to them, deserve Hell more than anyone I've ever heard of. This proves to me even better than my own afterlife the wrongness of my materialism and atheism, and now I want to get into Hell all the more. To see you suffer alongside me would give me even greater pleasure than my own suffering, and that's saying a lot."

"And seeing you get your just rewards would please me as well. But that will be in Heaven, which lies just beyond this Gate. I know that I never did anything wrong, as all those who I tortured and killed had committed the most vile acts imaginable. They deserved even worse than I gave them, and they're getting it now. Besides, why would a Saint like yourself go to Hell? No, this is Heaven's Gate. But how do we get inside?"

"I've been wondering that for quite a while myself," answered Antecessor. "And it seems to me, that we only have one way to settle a dispute which has enlivened my interest in this afterlife as little else could. Once we get in we'll know which one of us has divined the situation correctly. So, Malicorne, what do you suggest we do to get through this damned Gate? Knocking on it doesn't do any good. Nobody answers."

"Did you just try it with your hand?"—(Malicorne does so.)—"You're right. It doesn't make any noise, though. Must need something to get it to make some sound."

"There's no knocker; you can see that for yourself."

"Well, then we must need to make something to knock on it with. Aha, I've got it!"

Malicorne grabbed the skeleton by the back of his ribs and held him up over his head. Then he ran to the Gate and slammed his skull into it, backed up, and made another pass at it. The Gate, if not Antecessor's head, rang with the blow. He slammed his new friend into the Gate a third time. Then he tossed the skeleton onto the rocky ground like an old bag of bones; the skeleton immediately got up, and the two waited expectantly at the massive Gate. After an hour or so, they gave up.

Antecessor began: "Well, even if we can't get in there, there's still some opportunity for me to have some fun, now that you're here. I hope no one will claim that I'm doing good by treating such a lousy sinner this way—"

And he jumped on Malicorne and grabbed him by the head, and as he squeezed, his skeleton hands sinking into the rotten skin, the other's dead fish's eyes popped out of their sockets and his brains started to spurt out, landing on Antecessor's pelvis. He stepped a few paces away, then pulled out a rib and wiped the grey matter off of his hipbone. Then he scraped the last bits off the rib, rubbing it on the stony ground, and put it back into his ribcage.

"Arghh!—Your brains are as rotten as your reasoning. And almost as disgusting; if I still had guts, I'd puke them out right on the spot. But this is pointless. You don't feel any pain, and in consequence, I don't feel any pleasure. Death just isn't all it's cracked up to be."

"For certain. I always thought the soul would be a little more different from the body. But it seems that the only difference—aside from its inevitable decay—is that it doesn't feel anything. And to judge by your current state, the decay just keeps on until nothing's left. Is that right? Did you start out a corpse like me?"

"That's right all right. It took quite a while for the flesh to rot off of my bones, what with no maggots to eat it and all. But let's

get back to the damned problem that should occupy our attention. How can we get through this Gate?"

"Maybe we're looking at the problem the wrong way. Maybe
we shouldn't assume that we need to go through the Gate. Maybe
there's another way past the wall."

"Well then, what?"

"Have you tried digging under it?"

"Of course I have. But you can see that there's nothing but
black rock all around. You can't dig through it; I wore my fingers
off trying that trick."

The corpse said: "What about piling something up to climb
over it?"

"Piling *what* up?—There's nothing here to pile up."

"That's true enough, I suppose. Too bad we haven't got more
than the two of us here; we could make a ladder of corpses if only
enough would arrive. But anyway. Have you gone along the wall
to see if there's some other way through it?"

"Of course not. I don't want to leave the Gate in case it
opens. What if it's closed again before I get back? I'd be stuck out
here. Besides, you can see that the wall goes straight to the horizon without a break. It probably just goes all the way around the
damn world, whatever world this might happen to be."

"Probably does at that. How about climbing up the wall?"

"No dice. Damn thing's way too slick. Can't get up a single
foot."

Malicorne had to try it, but he couldn't do any better than
Antecessor had centuries before.

"Looks like we're stuck."

"Sure does," the skeleton answered.

The two paused and looked up at the unchanging sky.

After a few hours of unsettled gazing, Malicorne said: "That
sky hasn't changed a bit as long as you've been here?"

"Not a jot."

Malicorne went back to the Gate and looked at it closely, examining every aspect of it.

"Now hold it. I've just had an idea. How did you keep your victims at your mercy?"

"Why, I'd lock them up in dungeons. Probably only *you* can imagine the look of despair they'd display when I took them into the oblivion of those oubliettes. Why?—How did *you* keep *your* victims from getting away?"

"Just the same way. I'd put them into prisons. That's just what gave me the thought—"

"What thought?—What are you talking about?—"

"Not all walls are meant to keep something out. We've just assumed that this wall's keeping us out."

"And you think it's keeping us in?—"

"It's keeping us in—"

"Does that make this Heaven or Hell then?"

Antecessor walked around in a circle, than stared at the Gate another time. After an hour of silence he slapped his skeleton hand against his skull, so hard that he cracked the cranium: "Oh! Of course! How could I be so stupid! Of course that's it!"

"What?—What?—What?!?"

"You know the one way to increase your captive's torment. You taunt him with the thought of escape. You let him think that he might be able to escape you. You let him get out and then, in the most dramatic way possible, you catch him at the last minute, and laugh as you slam him back into his iron shackles. So Hell's no paradise of physical tortures, but just the thought of anything, anything at all other than this unendurable monotony, with the thought of what must be on the other side of this door constantly held out in front of us! And that door could open at any time, giving us the keenest torment of all: *Hope!*—What a monster to submit us to such a fate! Now I really have gotten faith!"

"Oh no, I think you just proved the opposite of what you think you did. Boy, do you ever get things backwards. After all, everyone knows that good is just the absence of evil. And that means that this must be Heaven. Since even the pleasures that people dream about lead to pain, whether through their own nature, or the fear of their disappearing, or the pain that the desire for them or their continuance always causes, it only stands to reason that Heaven must be exactly the one place that excludes all pain or pleasure, and holds out no hope for either one. A perfect and barren blankness, without even any physical feeling, fits the bill precisely, and here we are, the two greatest Saints in centuries. This situation perfectly encapsulates the conditions I described. For we never suffer at all here, nor do we feel any pleasure, and this wall and the Gate, which of course seem to hold Heaven or Hell on the other side, serve as perpetual reminder that we don't suffer as those who have attained to those two places would have to. Besides that, after a while you can't feel any hope that you'll get through, and since—as you've just argued—hope is a kind of suffering, even the worst, then the perfection of the Heavenly condition must be the absolute absence of hope: *Hopelessness!* Why didn't I think of it before? I could have made myself into a great theologian as well as a great defender of truth, if I'd only realized how things stood before I died!"

* * * * *

Two skeletons, their legs splayed, their neckbones bent over their kneecaps, their faces in their hands, sit on either side of the immense unopened Gate in the towering wall. Every once in a while, one of them will look over at the other, and then glance down the road as if in expectation of some new arrival, and then he re-places his hands over his empty eyesockets.

—Lord Weÿrdgliffe, the Waughters.

The Escape

When the blood-soaked tides of the Revolution had reached Averoigne, they washed through its towns and forests with more than the usual violence. There, mould-encrusted superstitions held greater sway over the Peasantry, which gave its refusal to submit to them any longer an unheralded ferocity. Whereas the Nobility, more accustomed to the routine usages of ultraviolence in enforcing compliance with its will, employed a greater degree of Sadism than those in other parts, in the extirpation of the hydra's-heads of rebellion. So, Tremdall felt great horror at the chaos and anarchy which enveloped the countryside, smearing it with the brains of heads decollated by the guillotine and the stench of roasting flesh, and at the outrages perpetrated by mobs upon their victims and former tyrants. And so he fled in terror from his native town of Vyones, past the estates of La Pœur, and towards the snow-topped peak of Mont Soânge. But before he reached that legendary mountain, which features in all of the faërie-folklore of that chimaera-haunted region, he found himself immersed in night, bogged down in a swampy marsh which he hadn't realized existed in those parts.

In vain he sought for some place to rest for the night, but he could scarcely even feel safe lying down in the dampness of an area that would frequently lead one to unseen sinkholes in the mud and muck. But before long, in the wan light of a moon which had more than begun to wane, he came across what he could hardly have expected to lie in that region: a mansion. He thought that the mansion must not have been inhabited for many generations, and that the swamplands must have grown up around its abandoned carcass, and that château knew how to make an impression that confirmed such a surmise, for it had entered into a stage of decay that surpassed the first. So, he felt no compunction in entering into its confines—if he had thought that another human being might still reside there, he would have shunned that unholy place like a beggar infected with the plague.

Once he had settled into the house, he noted the presence of a stranger, which he had not suspected. Still more surprise did he feel when he perceived that stranger in detail, for it hardly seemed like a man, but more like something seen in the deepest depths of a nightmare and immediately forgotten upon awakening. It had a face like a ghoul's beneath its glaucous mane of writhing green algae; arms loping at its sides, ending in thin artist's fingers, with long ebony nails serving as finale; a pair of reddish-grey tentacles, ending in suckers, usurped the place of its nipples; and an unspeakable orifice dripped ichor from its navel's rightful place. But its phallos, illuminating the room with the phosphorescent glow that emanated from its engorged and impurpled head, created the greatest effect. It stood at its full height—which surpassed those of men, whose own size must conform to the possibilities of nature, not to mention the capacity of the vessel intended to envelop them—throbbing in unison with the wiggly seraglio of tentacles which took the place of its absent prepuce, encircling that glans like the numbing mouth of a sea anemone, but reversed by a paraphimosis. He fainted away stone dead from terror.

* * * * *

For an indeterminate space of years, his life settled into a rigid routine. He would awaken, lying in the same small cell from which he had never departed, to a feeling of pressure in his anus. Despite his making every effort to struggle, he never could rouse even the lowest degree of strength, nor put any movement of his person into effect. That enormous phallos, despite the disparity in size, would, by the utilization of sufficient force, succeed in becoming encompassed by his aching anus, which you would never have believed could dilate to such an incredible extent that it could incorporate that throbbing enormity. And then he would feel the creature's treble mutations clamp onto his back, where they would burrow into his body and latch onto his nerves—directly sending signals of pain to his unscreaming head, even though that treatment could hardly outweigh the pain he felt at each of the successive thrusts of the elephantine, diamond-hard weapon penetrating him. Long after any sense of time he had felt would have disappeared in that monotony of misery, the monster would withdraw from the lacerated environment of his anus, flip him over, place him so that his head lay over the side of the bed (the only item of furniture to enliven a room lacking even any sort of coverings other than slimy fungal moulds for its stony walls, and itself lacking any sheets, blankets, or comforters), and then ram his palpitating cock into Tremdall's mouth. In this new position—inspired by the sight of his inhuman degradation, in his two eyeballs against which the ghoul's shriveled scrotum banged two adamantine testicles with its impetuous swinging motion—the unfortunate gained a small power of movement, but after only a few attempts, he realized the futility of rebellion: when he felt his teeth crack on the member currently making impetuous motions into the depths of his digestive system, he gave up the spectre of rebellion as a vain hope. Furthermore, he also became aware that he could not expect any food other than the semen that daily spurted into his gullet; on the plus side, the creature provided enough for him to become rather chubby. —Certain of the fiend's jibes (it could talk, and used that power to further deepen his humiliation with unanswerable tauntings) hinted that the thing intended to fatten him up for the delectation of some bizarre predatory beasts. Once the gargoyle had withdrawn and unlatched his suckers from the topside of Tremdall's agonizing torso, a profound slumber would overtake him, as though from the labor of many days.

* * * * *

Tremdall had no way to judge the time that seemed to pass. Days, years, centuries, millennia, aeons, perhaps. Then, he found himself unexpectedly (you come to rely on the regularity of events when they follow such a well-ordered course) awake and alone in his cell. After the stench of the excrement which had, over the course of he did not know how long, accumulated to the height of two feet up from the floor, he blindly searched the floor and the walls for any sort of egress—trapdoor, hidden panel, anything. Nothing. He feigned sleep when he heard a creaking sound begin, but paid enough attention to discern that it came from the ceiling overhead. After the usual curriculum, the thing left, but this time out Tremdall remained fully awake, staring off into space, after swallowing the medicine which that unclean physician had administered to him internally, and saw, in the purplish glimmerings of its still-erect phallos, the daemon open a trapdoor in the ceiling and noiselessly slide through it on invisible wings of silence.

It took all of his force just to remain awake. Finally, he managed to budge the muscles in his arms, and then to pull himself into a sitting-up position on the bed. A dizzy sensation rushed into his head and he spurted out the recently-infused sperm in gushes of fountaining vomit, which added to the perfume rising in smoky helices from the ordure ornamenting the flooring; that purgation seemed to allow him to regain some of his dissipated forces. He pushed the bed under the spot in the ceiling where he guessed the trapdoor to be, and leapt up, barely patting the stonework with the palm of his hand. After a couple of jumps he heard a hollow ring in response. He could hardly care what lay beyond, if that creature should capture him yet again—for what worse could it do to him?—

The trapdoor unlatched. He jumped, and managed to catch hold. He crept through a narrow crawlspace and out into another room. He dashed through the labyrinthine hallways of the mansionhouse like a lunatic, until he—at last—found the way out, and he shot through the marsh, only slowing down when its waters reached up to his knees or higher, and the tendrils of some rhizomatic vegetation twisted around his ankles.

* * * * *

Even though years had passed, Tremdall could never forget the horrors which he had undergone. Now that the Revolution had fully succumbed to a just suppression, and all had returned to order, he could hardly complain of the chaos and anarchy which had troubled him so greatly before. But with the return of routine, he felt that every aspect of his everyday life bore within it a tint of rape and torture, that each action which he had daily to undergo in his everyday life involved some element of an outside power invading his autonomy, and submitting him to vile torments. He knew he couldn't justify this feeling when he compared his own life to that of others, for after all everyone had to submit to the same treatment, but he reasoned—perhaps sophistically—that they could repress their own awareness of the suffering and stifling sameness imposed upon them. For they had not earlier experienced the even greater degree of the selfsame humiliations which he had. And as each petty persecution, to which he, like everyone else, must submit, merely to survive, reminded him infallibly of his prior adventures, they plunged him into the alienated depths of an unassuaged anomie.

This black iron prison offered little possibility of real escape, however. Anywhere in the world he could go, he would have to submit to a torture similar in any significant respect to the ones which he had enjoyed in Averoigne, and he had little enough faith that he would not have to endure the like even if he traveled beyond the world and into the unknown. At long last, he discovered a method of escaping into the fields of imagination: reading. But, he found, for one who has become accustomed to the direst sufferings inflicted upon one daily, whether during a time of revolution, whether by an unspeakable and unheard-of warden, or merely by the mellow pangs of everyday life, works of sweetness and gentility do not satisfy the famished imagination, which hungers for what the rational mind (in all of its wisdom) abhors—because it knows it only too intimately, and which craves scenes of the greatest imaginable depravity for its gluttonous fare. And so he came to seek out that treasure-house of the unforgivable, Lord Weÿrdgliffe's obscure and suppressed outpouring of impurity, *The Unspeakable; or, The Anatomy of Otherness: A Gothick Romance*, of which he found only a single chapter in a copy ripped from a complete version by the sheriff who had obeyed his duty in burning the rest of the volume, and who had hurled the chapter which he didn't dare to finish reading out of the window of his home before voluntarily submitting to confinement in a lunatic asylum. Caught in the air by a witch passing by on her way to the Brocken for the Walpurgis-Night Sabbat, it had passed from red hand to red hand from then on, until the dealer in suppressed knowledge who sold it to Tremdall came upon it.—Such a story did that dealer tell his customer in iniquity, in any case.

As he began reading, even the title of that chapter appealed to his sensibilities: "The Escape." With an unaccustomed interest he noted that the story began in the times of the Revolution, and took place in his own native region of Averoigne. Most of all, he felt that he could truly identify with the protagonist, who, like him, bore the rather uncommon name Tremdall. But while the story concerned this Tremdall, it equally concerned one Lord Weÿrdgliffe, who wrote—of himself?—in the third person, as if not wishing to accept full identification with the character in the story who surely could not depart so greatly from him in his properties, if he did not match him in every particular.

This Tremdall, like the one in real life, fled in horror from the chaos and anarchy of the violence sweeping through the countryside, which left a trail of corpses in its wake, as if to mark itself a path if it should become lost and desire to find its way back. For his part, Lord Weÿrdgliffe, sitting at his writing desk, learned of these events through his uncanny powers of divination, for he seemed to hone in on fear and pain like a vulture or a hyaena tracking down some fugitive cadaver. Or rather, like a shark sniffing the single drop of blood that dripped into the ocean several miles away when a certain athletic swimmer had stabbed his young lover with a dagger, after his flaxen hair had interwoven with his own raven locks, in an act of premeditated treachery. And so, theorizing that the Revolution had found its spur in the sudden realization, on the part of those rebelling, of the misery inherent in the regularity of their everyday lives, he devised a plan to reveal to Tremdall that perhaps an inviolable routine carries with it a burden somewhat worse than simple monotony, and that some degree of unpredictability, even of a sort that does not bring the greatest comfort, may prove less wearing on the spirit than a daily curriculum of torments. To inculcate the point which he desired to communicate most efficaciously, he transported his ancestral estates, the Waughters, to the swamp where the young man chased the fugitive phantom of escape, and lured him into his outré snare.

Tremdall shuddered with the horror of *déjà vu* when he read
of the disguise which the Virtuoso of Unanticipated Alterations
had taken on to deceive the innocent victim who had been
brought his way by what had seemed mere chance. He could refer
the prior circumstances and events of the tale's correlating with
those of his own life, to mere coincidence, but now, when he read
of the metamorphosis of Lord Weÿrdgliffe into an eldritch creature, covered with the most gruesome details, such as shockingly
greenish hair, tentacles, and suckers, and that hallmark feature,
the outsized phallos bristling with tentacles in an apparently
quite painful paraphimosis, and which his anus and mouth had
made the most intimate acquaintance with, he could hardly believe but that the author of the tale had some source of knowledge of those selfsame events and had for some reason chosen to
make them the inspiration of a Tale of Terror.

And when he pored over the torture which that inhuman being had subjected him to every day for several years, he felt a
sense of pleasure—derived, in an unaccountable way, from the
very pain described therein—in reading about what had, when he
had lived it, appeared as nothing but the direst agony, intolerable, even unspeakable. Now, he passed his eyes across the markings on that yellowed page with a relish such as one might use to
make human meat more palatable—if it didn't already have such
a quality of savoriness that no one could justly desire to cover the
voluptuous aroma and delicious flavor of the second and third
stages of decay and putridity, not even with the sanitary expedi-
ent of cooking or adding preservatives. Not even the memories of
his own degradation and impotence, roused by the similarities to
the events described, which seemed to pass over into outright
identity, could abolish that enjoyment, which made him feel that
he truly had managed to escape from his life and into another
one, and he practically longed to receive yet another oral enema
of that alienated entity's perfumed semen.—For, after all, you

could almost use such a tale to masturbate over, with only a few minor adjustments to suit it to your personal tastes, for pornographists, in spite of their sincerest efforts, do not always anticipate their reader's tastes in the most precise manner possible—

But the story soon passed back to its alternate protagonist, the enigmatic Lord Weÿrdgliffe, who had grown dissatisfied with the effects of the magical paradise in which he had trapped his prey. For he felt that he could not maintain such a course for all of eternity, the duration in which he wished to plunge the one who had fallen into the noose in which he wanted every human being to place its neck. And so he soon enough—to him, for he found the job of prison-warden less than exciting, even utilizing his remarkable hypnotic powers and not discounting the great sexual enjoyments derived therefrom—wearied of the daily course of torments, in which he played an active part. And so he resolved to allow his encaged prisoner to escape, in such a way that it would appear unintentional on his part, so as to increase his pleasure at the foolishness of a numskull who believed that he had some power of his own, and didn't merely respond to the manipulations of the Master of Shades and Shadows. And so Tremdall made his get-away, much to the renewed humiliation of the reader.

Now the Tremdall in the story, just like the one in real life, found that once he had returned to his everyday life, the past events of his life returned to him with every experience of the routine existence into which he had fallen, for all of the torments and tortures of that imposed regimen resembled, he believed, those of his earlier persecutions only by a difference of degree. He felt that he could hardly endure such an existence, once he became aware of the true nature of his old existence, any more than he could have lasted forever in the prison in which the ungainly ghoul had mesmerized his agonizing brains. And so, he sought for some form of escape, no matter what it might turn out to be, but in the end he found nothing but reading to fully turn the trick, for Lord Weÿrdgliffe had planned out beforehand that the one who had undergone such a life of horror should require the same sorts of materials in his entertainments, and he knew full well that only one work in the entire world of the written word would supply a full-enough exemplar of wickedness to satisfy his imagination, which would have reached such a degree of voraciousness that it would turn around and devour itself if it found no other nutriment to sustain it. And so he had prepared a copy of a single chapter of the work which would meet that stringent criterion, his own Gothick Romance, *The Unspeakable*, and he transformed himself into such a dealer as the rube would fall for without a question, and planted the crumbling chapter in his possession by inventing a suitably fabricated story of its pseudo-history. (Tremdall began to grow uneasy as he read over the lines conveying this part of the narrative.)

For he had reasoned that one who had become fully convinced that an unchanging monotony carries with it a burden of the unpleasant even greater than that of the chaos of revolution and tyranny, could be imprisoned in such an immutable state for all eternity. And that he could accomplish it by merely making the manner of escape, from the routine of ennui into the imaginary realms of fiction (for literature, unlike all material and mortal things, remains unchangingly itself for all eternity), into a novel method of imprisonment, thus immortalizing the suffering of his victim within the treasure-houses of an undying literary masterpiece. And so he authored a tale whose words would suck the reader in, trapping him inside their painted phrases, and Tremdall felt a shiver of the frisson of disquietude overcome him as the Tremdall in the story read up to the point which he had reached, and the two merged into one. This trick proved so efficacious that it overcame his sensibilities with an implacable resentment, and he took the mouldy pages over to his writing desk, got out a pen and an inkpot, and added these lines to the story which he had just read: "Lord Weÿrdgliffe, to reassure himself of the quality of the Tale of Terror which he had just penned, re-read the manuscript which his hand had just stopped inscribing on the page." As the Master of Mental Marionettes (who doesn't know his name?) materialized in the air behind him, an enormous spiral of sardonic laughter rose up into the atmosphere, and as his anal sphincter dilated prodigiously to incorporate the organ attempting to force its entrance, that word-enchained slave realized who had pulled the strings in an action which had seemed to him one of the utmost freedom—

—Lord Weÿrdgliffe, the Waughters.

OTHERS

The Emperor Ausso

The Emperor Ausso of Atlantis had grown glutted on the multitudinous torments to which his subjects had been submitted. He could only sigh with the weariness of ennui when he gazed at the vistas extending as far as the eye could see in the garden of carnivorous blossoms, fed exclusively on human flesh, each one exhaling a unique and erotic perfume; the sight of political dissidents, rebels against his implacable tyranny, frozen into the translucent crystal of waterfalls, in winding caverns beneath the capital, failed to rekindle his interest; the combats of humans, condemned on any pretext whatsoever, against exotic chimaeras, created in the laboratories of his arcane researchers, combining pre-existent animals with bizarre mutations, no longer roused a smile from his satiated soul; his seraglio, composed of the most beautiful of all Atlantean maidens, selected by a rigorous search extending throughout the least accessible regions of his empire, each of them submitted to a voluptuous torture more refined than the others, could sustain his attention no more. All had altered into the grayness of a dismal dullness.

On an octireme the Emperor Ausso set forth to discover new and rarer delights, previously unsuspected, in the unexplored portions of the world. Nothing awaited him there but troglodytes and endless expanses of mundanity. Barren wastes of indefinite boredom. Unsatisfied, too ennuyed to feel even the dull pangs of disappointment, the Emperor Ausso ordered his subalterns to tack the ship back towards the latitudes of the known regions. Only an expanse of placid watery surface awaited them where the capital city of Poseidonis had formerly towered, proud and erect.

At this sight, the Emperor Ausso fell into an ecstatic trance, from which he never recovered. When the few survivors of that civilization had founded a colony in the recently mapped areas, the Emperor Ausso lived as a hermit, eating only bread, drinking only water, never speaking to others, always attentive to the interior world. The others said to themselves, and to each other, that he must have called to mind the prophecy made in earlier aeons, that the wickedness of an Emperor should bring on a divine retribution, and that the gods would cast Atlantis into the irremediable abyss, and that he had become converted to the ways of piety by that revelation—none of them ever suspecting, that the Emperor Ausso occupied his consciousness solely with the overwhelming thought of the beauty of a novel spectacle which it had been his misfortune and his greatest regret to miss, in an ineffable rêverie.

The Connoisseur of Corpses

Ah, lovely appearance of death!
 What sight upon earth is so fair?
Not all the gay pageants that breathe
 Can with a dead body compare.
—Charles Wesley, "On the Sight of a Corpse"

The dying red sun hung low in the twilight sky of Zothique, cradled in the billowing folds of pitch-black clouds like a final expiring ember lying amidst the charcoaled remnants of a pillaged palace. Its feeble rays shone but dimly on the desert wastes, providing what little illumination gave the grey sands their ashen hue beneath the mildewed moon. Already the time to light torches had been reached, and the wind's nimble fingers carried with it the sardonic laughter of unseen ghouls.

As the men headed back to the camp, Valsuvar, chief of Notnomic's retinue, turned to him:

"So, now you have seen it for yourself. The tombs of the Priests of Orl-Elb have long since been plundered, like all of the aeon-old sepulchers in the valley. Even the sarcophagi lay opened and gutted of their contents, like starveling dogs gasping for air."

"Yes," said Notnomic, "it is very difficult to predict whether any given grave will still retain its original contents."

"Matters are already chancy enough for those of us who do the work of excavation, since our share—the tangible treasures buried with the dead—is the prize of tomb-robbers and fortune-seekers in any case; but now even you, who have somewhat more—refined—tastes, come up with empty hands: no skeletons, no mummies, not even a simple, rotting cadaver for your troubles."

"I am certain that we are merely experiencing a temporary spell of poor luck," answered the scholar, gazing attentively at his feet.

Valsuvar put his hands on his hips and took on that overbearingly condescending tone that he always affected when matters were not going as planned: "Well, just remember that we *require* the most refined of finery—our buyers accept no lesser—but you merely *prefer* the eldest, most desiccated remnants of past ages for your enjoyment."

"There is no reason to think that all the tombs of the Priests of Orl-Elb are in a similar condition to those which we have—"

"Why, from what I have seen, you can derive nearly as great an enjoyment from a freshly-created corpse, a pleasure nearly as keen as the ethereal delights you pluck while gazing upon the mummified Dynasties of Aggosid or the coral-encrusted skeletons that lay buried in the dried-up seabeds beneath the Grand Gargoyles of Ghlolubula—"

"Once I check the charts and maps, the histories and legendry compiled in the volumes stored in my library-wagon, we are sure to swiftly discover a formerly unknown burial site. The land is fertile with the dead and their gold." And he choked down the creeping suspicion that the Anthosmine Brethren had long since swept through the entire area, plundering all of the tombs and harvesting all of the mummies, which they would grind into a fine powder to be mixed with appropriate herbs and snorted by the bourgeoisie of the surrounding communities in the vain hope of re-invigorating their flagging potency. The Anthosmine Brethren did not miss any chance to profit from the dead.

As the men approached the camp, they could see Zololoha eyeing them to discern whether their expedition had been fruitful. The queen of the courtesans soon descried the lack of success that they had met with, and with a slight lifting of her left hand she motioned to her women to stand back—there would be no business transacted that night. The twin eunuch guards put their hands on the hilts of their scimitars, while the concubines fingered the diamond-studded dirks and daggers they kept on their persons for such occasions.

Scarcely a glimmer of flesh could be seen through the gleam of platinum armlets forged tens of millennia before, of chains of opal-studded electrum, of silver- and gold-threaded garments worn by queens and concubines in past eternities, of a sea of innumerable diamonds and topazes and emeralds and sapphires more numerous than the grains of sand spread out on the shores of an evaporated ocean. For one as squeamish when faced with such a nauseating sight as living flesh as Notnomic, this was decidedly preferable to the alternative. And it pleased him as well to think that the jewels and gemstones the concubines kept stored in their wagons could wholly hide the living flesh of an entire army of odalisques.

The men had grown disgruntled through weeks of enforced abstinence, and some of them began to brandish their pickaxes and shovels in a menacing manner as they saw that the whores were holding fast to policies which impoverished men frequently find difficult to fathom; no, Notnomic could not retire to his personal collection of the most savory cadavers and mummies that had been uncovered in their multitudinous excavations, no, the situation required defusing lest violence break out and leave him

amidst a near horizon populated by corpses he fairly ached to experience, but a more distant future rendered quite bleak by the
prospect of isolation—with no retinue of strong workmen to help
him disinter his preferred form of entertainment. It was ironic, to
say the least, that his peculiar aesthetic sensibility should have
created an entire economy of its own, but the flow of wealth was
not circular, and when, as now, demand becomes greater than
supply, there are inevitable difficulties that must be squarely
faced—

Notnomic had interposed himself between the two parties,
ready to plead his best arguments against violence, when a chilly
silence covered the sands, sweeping along like a shroud gently
descending to cover a cadaver. Even the whispers and taunts of the
far-off ghouls receded into nothingness—and, as is well-known,
the silence of ghouls is a certain sign of no good to follow, as certain a sign as their audible presence.

The ground seemed to quiver, and a small circle of sand
slowly began to vibrate about ten meters from the scholar. As the
men, women, eunuchs, and camels followed him with unspeak-
ing eyes, he approached the spot while motioning to the men to
bring torches to illuminate the area now that the sun had fully
set. A tiny, crimson head, no larger than a thumb, pierced
through the sand. It contracted and protracted, breathing labori-
ously, and pulled behind it a segmented écru body, and lay there
on the sand, a limbless worm no more than half a foot long.

As the thing pulsated, gasping like a pneumonia-ridden
wreck with each protraction, only to make a rasping,
slime-stained exhalation as it lost its rigidity in a nearly fluid
state, the scholarly epicure knew not what to make of the thing.
Meanwhile, the men paced backwards, gazing at their feet or the
sand; among the courtesans none but Zololoha could keep herself from emitting jaded titters; and one of the eunuchs elbowed
the other as he passed a knowing glance and a sarcastic grin.

The worm pulled itself toward Notnomic, arching itself up like a caterpillar, and relaxed with a slime-ridden sigh on the sand before him. Waves of thought drifted through the arid air: "Notnomic, the Lord Thasaidon favors your perversity. From your earliest days as a child who robbed jackals of their carrion you have drawn his infernal attention. Your career in the Monastery of the Mortuary Meditators pleased him no end. Assigned the task of eternal mindfulness of the vanity and transitoriness of this futile life, embodied before your gaze in symbolic form as the corpses and carcasses that had been accumulated over the millennia for the purpose, you entertained a deviant delight in this hallowed occupation. Few are those who combine the utmost in aesthetics with a degree of rebelliousness that would put Smygo the Iconoclast to shame, yet you had joined this aristocracy of the perverse. For years your proclivities passed unsuspected and unseen; until one day when the accidents of circumstance drew another meditator to enter the crypt you currently occupied *in flagrante delicto.*" A general, but subdued, laughter spread through the air for the briefest possible moment. "Deprived of your accustomed enjoyments, you enterprisingly discovered means whereby to provide yourself with a steady stream of the most exquisite cadavers imaginable. But now, your fortune is fading. The well seems to have run dry. But fear not. The Lord Thasaidon has deemed your perversity worthy of his honor. If you accept the token he offers, then *your eyes shall behold the remains of the dead, wherever they might be hidden.*" The worm wheezed out an elongated gasp. "Do you accept the gift proffered to you by the Lord Thasaidon? If so, this vision will begin on midnight tomorrow, and continue to grow until it reaches a state of completion in a year and a day."

Now, it is a well-known fact that the boons granted by Thasaidon bring ever with them an unbearable burden, always unsuspected to the one foolish enough to accept the favors of the

Infernal Lord, but lust is a force that blinds one's cautions and prevents the prevision of even foreseeable calamities, and necrophiliac lust is a fair sight stronger than the more moderate lusts enjoyed by undeviate men: Notnomic bowed to Thasaidon's emissary and accepted the gift of the Master of his Soul.

As the worm melted away into nothingness all was silent across the sands save for the rising whisper of ghouls snickering in the distance borne to the camp by the gentle and cooling breeze.

* * * * *

The day had passed with a glacial pace. Notnomic attempted to quell his anticipation, napping and re-reading the lost scrolls of Anunantar, which detailed the remarkable conditions of properly prepared corpses once they reach their twenty-third millennium of ripeness. Fascinating material—if only mummies bandaged and spiced in the precise fashion suggested by the sagacious mage were available, and aged to the precise degree which he recommended!—

Valsuvar burst into Notnomic's tent: "Come on!"—and he placed his hands on his hips according to his annoying habit—"Now night has fallen for over three hours, and the moon provides nearly as much light as the sun ever did. It will soon be midnight."

"Yes, I suppose it will. I will know soon enough whether the worm spoke truth or not."

"You cannot keep such an event to yourself—you must come out into the open, for all to observe."

"You believe this will be of general interest?"

Valsuvar stood perfectly still, now holding one hand in another near his chest, and his face drew taut like a fist: "Oh, oh yes, I am quite certain of that."

Together they exited the small tent, Valsuvar lightly leading

Notnomic with one hand on his left arm. The entire retinue awaited them outside in a gathering apparently modeled upon the one that took place the night before.

Valsuvar strode forward and addressed the crowd: "*Now* we may expect to behold a fascinating spectacle. It is not every day that Thasaidon grants unsolicited gifts to mortals. It should prove most keenly—interesting—to observe the precise manner in which he provides the scholar Notnomic with the abilities he has promised him."

And he stood, hands on his hips, and several hours later his eyes had not once departed from the scholar's figure. He turned to one of his retinue: "Bholargh, is it not near midnight yet?—It seems like we've been waiting here all night!"

"Sir, it is surely midnight already. By my calculations, judged against the slow setting of the sun and the incline of the moon, it must be several tens of minutes past midnight."

"Black bastards of blasphemy!—The appointed time has come, and no Infernal Lord has made his presence known! No sign has appeared to indicate the fulfillment of Thasaidon's promise."—He looked about vainly for some object to hurl into the sand in frustration.—"No, nothing has—"

He stopped himself short. "Ah, it all becomes clear. This so-called *scholar* is in actuality a two-bit magician. He was merely plying his meagre cantrips in the hopes of deceiving us. The pathetic worm that presumed to bring tidings of Thasaidon was no doubt just his familiar spirit, taking on an unsuspected guise in order to fool the unwary. A true emissary of Thasaidon would have appeared majestic and powerful, like his master. Everyone knows that. We cannot allow ourselves to be put upon in such an ignoble manner. Does he think we are daft?—No, my friends, let us teach this runt what it means to impose himself upon men. What punishment shall we mete out upon this prestidigitating poltroon, this perfidious imposter?—Whatever the method we might find to do it in, we should leave him in such a state that he'll appreciate a mirror in which to admire his new condition—"

Notnomic stared down at the earth by his feet, and as he gazed fixedly upon the ground, the whole sphere shimmered and transmuted into a translucent globe, through which he could perceive the accumulated corpses and cadavers from prior epochs and eras in the unfolding history of Zothique, layer upon layer deposited and buried as the earth buckled and folded over upon itself, kingdoms of mummies and skeletons as proud as the days that they had walked the surface of the earth, now peopling vast underground empires in unequal competition with the invisible remnants of the races of gnomes and decadent dwarves who had enjoyed themselves in cavernous orgies near the center of the world, where these once-human habitants of the nether world learned to refine cruelty beyond the realm of art. All the dead of past ages were visible to him, all those who had died as far back as those mighty, mythical continents which had ruled the globe, only to sink back in geological calamities: Thule, Polarea, Atlantis, Lemuria, Hyperborea, and Mu, as well as those who had inhabited the entirely insignificant and unremembered continents that lead a brief and utterly unimportant existence after the mighty Titans of the past had fallen, and before the puissant Zothiquean landmass had risen up from aquatic obscurity to claim for itself the final aeons of the earth. With a unique hue they shone forth, like a multitude of constellated beacons beckoning him down, down into the bowels of the planet, down to where they illuminated the world like obsidian suns pouring forth an infinite ocean painted purely in the shade of *death*.

It was clear to all who stood by that they could be assured of finding their proper quarry, if only the visionary could be roused from this novel rêverie.

* * * * *

Notnomic could not sleep. Through the translucent folds of the tent in which he had lain himself down to bed, he could perceive in the distance the glowing forms of the dead. But the dead failed to obey their proper role: instead of lying at their leisure, in the immobility of eternity, he could dimly descry their figures gamboling about, as if they were celebrating their own demise with an obscene *danse macabre.* Some malign magick must have been at hand.

He must discover the cause of this uncalled-for behavior, for curiosity is nearly as powerful an impetus as lust; yes, he must seek out the source of this phenomenon, but he could not allow the others to discover that he had done so: his position had become precarious, and his contract with the men required that he leave, alone among the remains left by mortals, their corpses strictly alone. He could not endure another moment attempting to ignore cadavers that beckoned to him like lighthouses in the distance, but still less could he endure the slow process of joining them on the Stygian shores—for Valsuvar's men were, among their other talents, rather adept at certain extended forms of torture: indeed, sheer boredom in the face of monotony had been the savior of more than one of the victims of their wrath. And even though he could simply face in another direction, thus occupying his eyes with an infinitude of other corpses, nonetheless, these alone held his mind bound in a spell of fascination and fixation that his will could not break.

With a heavy head he stopped as soon as he had come out from his tent. Not a living thing stirred in the whole camp. With near-silent steps the scholarly aesthete passed through the tents and wagons and out into the desert. Ignoring the battered bones and scattered skulls that were spread through the sand, the fruits of a futile battle that had taken place tens of thousands of years before, he made his way, preferring the resolution of a mystery to the enjoyment of known pleasures. He carried no torch with him in the night wind; nothing lighted his way to the nearby mound except for a feeble, crumbling half-crescent moon and the unutterable light exuded by the dead that surrounded him. And still, atop the mound, the death-lights circled in a senseless Sabbath, in celebration of the scholar knew not what.

As he drew nearer and nearer to the top of the mound where the unfortunate victims of a plague borne by desert bats had been laid out, exposed to scavengers after the fashion followed by Valsuvar's men, a change in appearance struck his fancy more and more. It seemed that the figures were not precisely similar to those of men: they had certain peculiarities, such as their loping gait and the lengthy arms that hung at their sides as they stooped forward in their insane saraband, that argued against them being zombies or otherwise animated corpses. And all around, he could hear a familiar snickering that seemed somehow sourceless, as if it arose from the air itself to be borne endlessly on the wind as it spiraled about without aim.

But still they circled around the place, even as Notnomic finally climbed up onto the very summit and hid himself behind one of the monoliths that always ringed the central area of these mounds. Of a sudden, he saw that the shapes were discarding smaller, death-hued objects, and through keenness of vision realized that they were tossing aside femurs and jaws and other bones, and a chain of cackling ghouls came rushing past him, laughing merrily like hyenas as they encircled him, each of them rubbing against him in his horror, only to disappear down the slope and into the distance, lost against the background of manifold death that blazed up from the ground.

Dazed, the scholar slowly traced his steps back to the camp, taking little heed of the danger that he might be seen by one of Valsuvar's men, and only stopped to look more closely at the wheeling points of light that scintillated in the sky like torn-off chunks of cadavers set adrift in the aether: as the sun began the process that now passed for rising, they approached more closely to him and the outline of condor wings struck his consciousness. And as he stumbled into the camp, the distant snicker of ghouls still echoing so loudly in his memory that he could not distinguish the mental traces from the sniggers borne to his ears on the breeze, and he beheld a small cloud of specks sauntering to and fro in the atmosphere above a pile of camel dung, glimmering with the unmistakable hue of death, and one of them came and buzzed past his ear, making its identity impossible to fail to recognize, and he could only think one word to himself as he recalled the delicious direction of decay that besets the unmolested dead:

"*Maggots.*"

* * * * *

Notnomic had called Zololoha to speak with him. She arrived in his tent, accompanied by the twin eunuch guards, and asked him what he might require. He began with a sigh, and seemed reticent to continue. The queen of the courtesans motioned the eunuchs to depart with an idle half-wave of her hand as she stood before him, seated on the throne taken from an unidentifiable tomb.

"What is it, milord?" she said. "I trust that I have sufficiently covered my excruciatingly disgusting flesh that you are not too distracted by nausea to speak."

"No, no, it is not that. Quite the opposite, in fact. Thasaidon's boon, as may be surmised from the lore handed down in the legends of the past, did not come without its price."

Zololoha fingered her chin and leaned closer, her curiosity piqued.

"Now, when I gaze upon you, I can barely discern the silks and the finery that covers you; through the gold and the gems there now gleams, as through the most transparent gauze, your delicate body, with the pure and unique light of death."

And he explained to her that whatever had once been a part of the dead, now shone for his eyes with the brightness of death, and that the worms in the earth had taken on this luster, as had the ground where they dead had rotted, and the grasses and weeds that had grown on the fields where their flesh had become soil, and so the chain continued, until now live flesh as well as the dead had, for him, taken on the brilliance of death.

"So that is why," she said, "you now stagger about like one half-blind, while Valsuvar's men complain that you no longer lead them to treasure as you did once, and the murmurs of revolt stir amongst them, waiting patiently to burst forth into overt violence."

"Yes, formerly I could hone in on the corpses and skeletons I sought, but now, the earth is strewn with so many rivers of death meandering past death-tinted islands, the planet is so radiant with the effulgencies of death that I can no longer look upon the earth without the fiery streaks and speckles searing through my eyelids into my brain; now, I find myself so surfeited with pleasure that I sometimes lie on my back and steer my fatigued gaze upward to the skies, so that I may for a little while see no death. At least, so long as no clouds float overhead, filled with water that once bled on a battlefield, or flowed from the mouth of a drowning man."

The two fell silent for a moment.

"Soon, I fear, I shall be entirely blind, no longer able to see aught but the unspeakable radiance that gleams from beyond the grave. It is a long time since we haunted the graveyards as children, playing with the stray bones left by ghouls and inventing outlandish interpretations of the unreadable inscriptions. Yes, it is a long time." He sighed.

"Yes, a long time. You have not composed extempore odes to

the pleasing pallor of my skin for ages."

"And Valsuvar will not show any understanding of my plight: the rack or worse awaits me. And as for you, matters will hardly be any more pleasant when his men can no longer satisfy their lusts through honest transaction."

After a pregnant pause she replied: "Don't worry yourself over the matter any longer." And she smiled slightly as she turned her gaze downward to the sand. "I'll take care of the matter." She began to walk toward the doorway of the tent: "Yes, I'll take care of it."

And the ghouls in the distance remained silent.

* * * * *

The men entered the large tent, festooned and decorated according to the holiday traditions of a people unknown to them. They stood aback, before the long feast tables, covered with an intricate array of fruits and fungi, insects and other edibles arranged in a multitude of exotic dishes and dispensaries. Zololoha stepped forth, pristine in her nudity. She explained to the men that her women had resolved to provide the men, free of charge, beginning on this night, which had a special significance—which there was no reason to tire their patience with—in the religion of their forefathers, with the satisfaction and enjoyment which they had previously reserved for paying customers. And, she continued, motioning to them to hear her out before attempting to take advantage of this tempting offer, she had decided to appear before them unclothed in honor of the one whose providential pact with the Lord of the Underworld had made it all possible (she pointed behind her in the direction of Notnomic, seated on his most favorite throne as guest of honor at the festival), for, she explained to the men, who were now showing certain signs of impatience, he no longer saw anything when he gazed upon her form but the livid hue of death.

The others, staring at her as she stood silent in the sun's setting rays like a caryatid column, slightly tilting back her forehead, half-closing her heavy eyelids, and lifting her shoulders so
that her lean arms hung down a little to the rear of her torso, did
not see the hue of death at all, but rather an expanse as white as
the polar wastelands meeting auburn hair that burned like lava
rolling down volcanic slopes to collide with floes of ice that had
frozen aeons before. "And," she added, "you must all partake
heartily of the feast here prepared by your future paramours,
for"—and here she gave a wink in the direction of Valsuvar,
whose cheeks became inflamed like torches at the gesture—"you
will now be serving our pleasure as well as your own, and we
wish to ensure that you have the strength to carry through on the
actions your current postures threaten our chastity with." She
turned around, then twisted her head back and added over her
right shoulder: "As soon as you've finished the feast."

The men fell on the tables in a chaotic rush, throwing the
zeal of hyenas attacking some newfound carrion into the task.
All of them, that is, except Valsuvar, whose attempt to eat in
great haste contrasted grotesquely with his finicky picking at his
outsized portion of jackal-meat with the personal fork and knife
which he always carried with him.

Zololoha walked, with slow steps, back towards Notnomic,
providing his eyes with a splendid view of death in motion.
Slightly to his rear, she lightly placed her left hand on his shoulder, and he absent-mindedly reached up and twisted a strand of
her hair next to his cheek. The men were growing gorged on the
vulture drumsticks and fruitbat wings, the sweetmeats and mel-
ons provided for them. They could not deny it: they continued to
eat as much for the sake of their delight in the food as for the delight they anticipated after the meal.

The men had soon devoured the viands prepared for them by
their future mistresses, leaving nought but crusts and crumbs on

the magnificently spread tables in the caravan's banquet tent. As one they arose from their seats, holding onto their overfull stomachs and lightly belching and farting their satisfaction at the feast—for they were not an uncouth lot, despite the low upbringing which many of them had suffered and the prolonged existence which they had lead on the margins of what meagre remnants remained of civilization. Each seemed reluctant to be the first to head towards the women's tents, located to the rear of Notnomic's throne, but once one of them had made tentative steps in that direction, the general mass overcame its shyness and began to flow toward the prospect of living flesh.

But not for long. Scarcely had they started to stir than one of the halest quarrymen among them halted, clutched his gut, and let out a groan calculated to frighten a ghost from a graveyard. Soon the others joined in, Valsuvar the last to seek admission to the chorus, and before long the whole gang had fallen to its knees, their faces paler than cliffs of chalk, and soon few of them could maintain that position, and they were spread across the floor in a haphazard fashion. There they lay, arms and legs splayed out at odd angles, struggling valiantly and vainly against the shivering knives they felt slicing through their veins from their guts down to the ends of their extremities.

Zololoha moved her hand from Notnomic's arm, and placed it on his left shoulder, letting her hair fall down closer against him as he devoted less and less concentration to his continued twisting of her auburn locks. And as the men finally gave up the ghost, each one let loose from his jaws, which in an odd manner were at once relaxed and taut, a final cloud of luminous death that rose up like a whirling, death-sprinkled dust devil into the atmosphere, where they were joined by eddies and currents that sparkled with the brilliant hue of death, which proliferated in ever increasing numbers until soon the whole skies had been perfused with the unspeakable radiance, a blazing blizzard of the ebony illumination that now overshadowed and outshone all lesser sources of light or life.

At a nearby city Zololoha purchased, with a small portion of the proceeds from her prior trade, an immense palace, which she had outfitted with innumerable Babylon-like gardens and terraces from which vines hung in endless splendor. There, she and her troupe of courtesans retired in their ease, breeding ever more exquisite orchids and designing ever more intricate enjoyments to replace the former arts which they had plied. On odd afternoons they would wander through the galleries where the two eunuchs, their former guards, had erected endless tri-dimensional labyrinths which they had populated with an almost infinite procession of pythons and anacondas covered with the most refined and finely-worked jewelry imaginable, matching in every detail the natural patterns of their scales. Notnomic, who had now been effectively blinded, was given kingly quarters in the magnificent palace, second in grandeur only to those of Zololoha, and his needs were attended to by the former courtesans, who would now and then, in honor of the unique gift which had lead to their present situation, bestow upon "the wee worm" (as they called it) an appreciative stroke with their nimble fingers or a delicate caress with their trained tongues. And throughout it all, Notnomic remained in an impassive state of utter ecstasy, for his eyes saw nothing but *death*.

Mouth of the Gaw

Beneath Mengus lay the enormous Mouth of the Gaw. There, Its adamantine shell, a splotched black and brown, and perhaps a half-mile thick, gave out onto a pulpy area in the center of which there stood the Gaw's Mouth, an enormous pink sphincter, expanding and contracting in expectation. A mile away, land abruptly began on top of the creature's surface. Mengus, a high priest of the Gaw, stood in a crow's-nest mounted on top of the stony tower suspended on innumerable ropes, and he shouted instructions to the many workers who operated them from a complicated series of creaking pulleys and wheels, connected to several environing buildings with their foundations set into the shell of the Gaw itself. This masterpiece of engineering moved the tower into place above the Mouth of the Gaw.

Mengus looked down from his crow's-nest into the tower, which seemed to him like some bottomless pit from such a great height. He smelled the contents of the tower—raw sewage, rotten fruit, many different kinds of fermented beverages, blood and semen voluntarily given by the devotees of the Cult of the Gaw and the pious among the population, who wished to make a propitious sacrifice—and he felt his stomach churn with despair. He bent over the outsized vessel and vomited into it. A great cheer roused up from the onlooking priests, the fools believing that in that way he intended to augment the sacrifice to their immanent deity, not suspecting that—in fact—he had felt himself utterly sickened by the thought that he had fallen in love with the sacrifice destined for only four days hence.

He must keep his presence of mind and not reveal his secret. He steeled himself, then shouted the command to continue the procession. As the next item in the ritual, an officer of the cult took out some tablets inscribed with the mythical narrative of the coming of the Gaw, and read the whole text to the assembled congregation, never once glancing up at his audience. This provided a less afflicting cause of annoyance at his association with the cult. He had joined because he felt that the power and prestige involved in the position, which he had known that he could attain, and did in fact attain, would bring him such things as he might desire—he hadn't expected such an outlandish development as falling in love. Now, as he listened to the reader, he felt contempt at the imbecility of someone with whom he wished he had never associated himself, for the fool surely must have memorized the glyphs engraven on the clay tablets by now.

So, he occupied himself with daydreaming about his beloved Velia, and of some paradisiacal place, unknown to him at the present moment, where their love could reach its fulfillment and consummation, while the reader retold, for the thousandth time, the story of how Thule had been nothing but a meager island, the husk of a dead volcano, when the Gaw had come down from the stars in the night and settled into the landmass. It had left Its Mouth at the opening of the volcano's crater, and devoured whatever had chanced to come Its way. Over time, the creature swelled up like a balloon, increasing the landmass's area enough to attract men, who found that fertile fields and abundant foliage now peopled that country. But the shapeless thing had not gone without recognition of the new inhabitants of Its demesnes, and blessed them with a relationship that should benefit them both. It made Its desires known by causing an earthquake, by shuddering in some portion of Its incredible, shapeless mass, and the dreamers among men knew by certain signs that this meant that It wished to receive material tribute from the human ants who had spread themselves, drawn by a call sent out by Itself, through some supernatural power, still undisclosed to the vulgar, over Its interminable surface. So, after many years of employing less effective methods, they had constructed the monstrous machinery that would deliver aliment to the thing, carving the enormous tower out of what they suspected must have formerly served the creature as a horn, which at that point merely jutted up from the ground uselessly, and they provided the being on the first of every week with the sorts of nutriment described above, and on the third day, with those convicted of crimes deemed unacceptable for those living further in human company, such as murder, rape, or blasphemy against the Gaw, and on the fifth day, with one of the most beautiful maidens that the land of Thule had produced, selected as such by the priests of Its religion, utilizing the most rigorous criteria, according to a codebook that filled three volumes of crabbed print. Thus had evolved the iron hierarchy, which ruled over the ultimate continent, and punished even the slightest deviation of Its inhabitants with the wholesale ruination of entire towns and villages.

Finally, the recitation had ended. Mengus surveyed the tower to assure that they had it exactly above the gaping hole, which exceeded its diameter of forty feet by perhaps twice, such appeared the greatness of its current dilation. He gave the order, and the ropes which released the bottom of the tower received the appropriate manipulations, and the reeking refuse filling the container poured out into the Mouth, which circled in on it like a whirlpool, and mashed the stinking mush while simultaneously sucking it down with a slurping sound. Once he had recovered from that somber spectacle, Mengus gave the orders that reclosed the tower's bottom, and had the tower itself pulled back to solid ground, where he disembarked, satisfied with the day's work but discontented by upcoming events.

* * * * *

Mengus fumed in his lonely chamber. He could not, on this night, distract himself with the usual pleasures that had provided so much of the motivation for his becoming a priest of the Gaw, and faithfully rising up in the hierarchy to achieve a position in its upper tiers. No, no courtesan, however skilled in the pleasures of the flesh, not a one of them could hold a candle to his newly-discovered beloved. This strange fact, he pondered and weighed most carefully. If he had felt that his current emotion should pass, or that its satisfaction lay entirely outside the realm of possibility—not something readily admissible to one sharing his philosophical prejudices—he would have resigned himself as best he could to the situation. No, he could never accept the defeat of his desire: he would topple the universe, if necessary, to have her, and never would the tyranny of the Gaw, which no longer accorded with his own will, prevent him from taking what he wanted for his own.

He waited until evening, saving his strength, meanwhile plotting how he should race to his goal. At about two hours after the normal time for falling asleep, he dressed in a black cloak, and hid several daggers on his person. He had enough faith in his ability to free her from her imprisonment, and to make his way with her in secrecy to some land where she—and he, would be safe, for no one should discover that either of them had disappeared until the morning, he felt secure of that, enwrapped in his plans. Surely afterwards, she would feel enough gratitude to her rescuer that she would consent to all that he desired, in the off chance that she didn't requite his love, which, after all, he could have little doubt of, considering the service he would have rendered her.

He snuffed his candle and crept out through the window, not wishing that anyone should realize that he had gone. The priestly order kept the female victims, he knew, in another building of the compound. He looked about, and, seeing no one, made his way quickly there. He hid in the bushes, counting the paces of the guardian patrol. He had no need to contend with them: he could simply slip past them, and repeat the manoeuver again, when he had Velia with him. When he had done so, he tossed a hooked rope up to the roof; the hook caught, and he climbed up with plenty of time to spare. He should have no worries coming back, regardless of how slowly Velia might climb.

He lay flat on the roofing and crawled to a spot he had calculated with great care. There, he took out one of his daggers and picked at the tiles until he had removed several, leaving a hole between two crossbeams, just wide enough for a man to fit through. He looked down, by the moonlight, into the building. He must have slightly miscalculated the positioning of the cell, for instead of his love he saw the scruffy head of a guard. Well, so much the worse for *him*. If he would have simply left the ceiling gaping, with a guard standing under the hole, the servitor of the Gaw might notice the extra light, or it could even start to rain. All of his dreams would vanish. He stabbed the hook into a crossbeam, and glided down the rope. A slice through the carotid arteries and jugular vein put an end to that looming threat.

He looked around and found himself at the end of a hallway which terminated with a locked door of iron. He must have only miscalculated by a few feet. A cursory searching revealed that the guard had a ring of keys. In turn, he tried each one of them, and the last, as his bad luck would have it, opened the door. He still took as much care as he could to avoid making noise, though a nervous squeaking emerged from the hinges.

There she lay, sleeping on a bed of hay. He couldn't help but stop to admire her form, and the dreaming beauty of her face, the long waves of undulant black hair, the alabaster eyelids. No wonder he had fallen in love. She had shown such stoic resignation to her fate, in contrast to the other sacrificial victims, who would spend the entire time between election and their marriage trembling. But she revealed such a strength of character, never displaying the slightest fear at her fate. He prodded himself into action, and gently shook her by the arm. She tried to roll over, then her eyes opened, and she started back in startled alarm.

He began to reassure her of his intentions, but she didn't heed a word of it. She shrilled: "What are you doing? Hey, you're the priest that kept looking at me with that stupid moony look, aren't you? What do you want? Is this what happens to all the brides of the Gaw, his idiot priest comes like a sneakthief and cuckolds him in the middle of the night? Blasphemer!—Profaner!—Hypocrite!—Get away from me!—Get away! —Rape! —Rape! —Help, someone help me! Rape!—"

"But, I—"

"Get out!—Get out of here!—You pig!—Rape!—By the Mouth of the Gaw, out of here!—Rape!—"

Two guards came running down the hallway. He rushed out too, and he started to climb up the rope left hanging down. One of the guards tripped over the corpse lying in the hall. The other jumped over it, over the tripped guard, and grabbed Mengus by the foot. He kicked him in the face with his heel, splitting an eye and sending blood spurting out his nose. The other didn't waste time with such ineffectual manoeuvers. He wheeled his mace around and knocked Mengus on the leg. Mengus kept hold with his hands and attempted to ignore the pain of his leg. He got to the roof, barely skirting another blow from the leaping soldier. He got up and started to run, but his left leg gave out from the pain in his thigh, and he fell, rolling back, to meet the guard with a knife in his other eyeball. The man lost his grip and fell back, knocking the other down off the rope. Well, if it took that, he would take out the whole force stationed at the temple compound. Hearing Velia's screams rising up from the cell sent a dagger through his heart. He could hardly hope to rescue her now. But he would escape, and find some way.

He made his way to the edge of the roof. He looked down, and the patrol hadn't come around. He couldn't take time to favor his bad leg now, so he jumped down onto the grass, trying to make a running start, which only resulted in an involuntary cry of utter anguish as he collapsed onto the ground. Several guards now came running, and he had to admit himself defeated, if only for the moment. To seal the decision, an iron club bludgeoned him into unconsciousness.

* * * * *

Mengus could hardly see through the haze in his eyes and his brain. His head pulsed like the palpitating heart of a shark still beating on the deck of a ship an hour after its removal from the carnivorous leviathan. He felt cold hard stone beneath his naked body. He rolled over, and noticed that he had his hands tied together in front of his body, with a strong hempen rope. He sat up and took a good look around—as well as he could, considering that he couldn't clear his eyes of the layer of crust accumulated during more than one night's normal sleep.

No question about it: he found himself in with the criminals designated for the next day's sacrifice to the Gaw. They sat around in the cell, dejected and depressed.

He struggled to his feet and approached the closest of them.

"Allow me to introduce myself. They call me Mengus; I used to serve the Gaw as a priest. Now, due to an unfortunate disagreement between us on an issue of priestly policy, I find myself here. What misfortune has lead you to this unamiable situation?"

"What does that matter? I belong to the Gaw now, and only await his making use of me."

"Now hold on. Did you then arrive at this circumstance by paying attention to the Gaw's interests, or to your own desires?"

"My own. But they can hardly exist any longer."

"Tell me then of those nonexistent desires."

"They called me Tanoun. Now, of course, I have no name. The one who went by that name, who inhabited this bodily shell, one day came upon a mother and her five children in the woods. He thought to himself of all the service he had done to the Gaw in his life, but what had It ever done in return? He had made the pilgrimage to Its temples, as recommended by all the priests, had poured blood from a cut in his own arm, made by his own hand, into the sacrificial graal provided by the priests, and had thus fed It on his own life. How had It rewarded that service?"

"Well, Tanoun, it seems to me that you owe the Gaw for a very great service. After all, It refrained from wiping out your habitation and your life with an earthquake. But continue."

"So, a strange and vengeful lust came upon me as I saw that woman, so beautiful, and her children, all daughters, no less beautiful, even if all before the age of pubescence."

"And the outcome of that encounter?"

"Six defiled corpses and one felon headed for the Mouth of the Gaw."

He hid the disgust and contempt he could not help but feel, albeit mingled with a certain admiration for an act of supreme egoism. "It seems to me, friend, that you only find yourself guilty of half-way measures."

The other prisoners looked up at the two conversationalists, their curiosity apparently piqued.

"How do you find that to be so?" one of them said.

"He defied the Gaw's authority to a certain point, but failed to follow through. I don't see any reason not to go the whole route and rob the Gaw of a further victim, instead of providing It with yet another."

"You intend to escape, then? But how?"

"I don't know just how—yet."

"But surely it's hopeless?"

"Now, didn't all of us arrive at these infamous straits by not ceding to the apparent limits of our power, and seizing what we could of what we desired?"

"But the Gaw—"

"Well, if the Gaw must fall for me to rise, then so much the worse for the Gaw."

Silence fell.

After some fifteen minutes, he took up again his prior theme: "I say again, all of you have attempted to grab hold of your own desires by your own power, in defiance of the Gaw."

One of the convicts, visibly irked, spoke: "Well, not me. I served the Gaw faithfully, and no one can accuse Krelrhytus, without injustice, of ever violating one of Its sacred ordainments. What difference does it make if a few priests have done so regardlessly, and gone even further to convict me of the false charges, so that I now await the Gaw's devouring of myself? I have a conscience clean of any offense against It."

"All the more reason not to submit to an unjust and irreparable punishment at Its agency."

The other looked pensive for a moment. "But how can we, mere men, fight such a power? And confined in a little container, surrounded by priests and guards, with our hands literally tied?"

"We have all day and all night to plan—"

* * * * *

The gigantic container stank from the accumulated slop and slime of thousands of years. Inside it, seven men, otherwise naked, wore ropes tying their hands together and looks of feigned despair disguising a desperate hopefulness. Wheels turned and they could hear, outside the great bottle, the machinery, that would bear them to the Mouth of the Gaw and dump them into It, set into motion. The priest up in the crow's-nest shouted the instructions. Mengus recognized them from the many years of his own recitations, and carefully visualized the progress of their container. After something like a half-hour's worth of their shuffling around, he gave his companions a glance which indicated that they should shift into readiness for action.

The priest up above them paused, at a stopping place in the instructions. Mengus stood, and shouted a combination of commands, crafted with meticulous care, at the top of his lungs. The workers, he knew, acted as mere cogs in a machine. They obeyed their instructions automatically. Now a conflicting set of orders, and now a third, and now a fourth, emerged, amplified by the massive tube.

Wheels and pulleys, turning this way and that, straining and creaking, then snapping and breaking. The enormous vessel fell forward, pointing directly at the Mouth of the Gaw. The priest in the crow's-nest flew out winglessly, and rolled into the roseate sphincter, screaming in pious horror. The sphincter closed in and smashed his frame into a pulp before allowing it to pass downwards into oblivion.

The vessel's bottom cracked open, one of the shutters ripped off of its hinges, and the seven convicts lunged out. One stopped to abrade his ropes against a broken hinge. The others rushed out, leaping over ropes strewn here and there from the solid ground to the vessel, many of them now severed, others of them overly tightened by the tautness of tension. Some guards and other onlookers closed their amazement-opened mouths and grabbed up clubs and maces. A small group of them started to head towards the band of criminals.

The Mouth of the Gaw dilated, creating a slope inwardly towards it. The convicts fell forward, trying not to slide back in, while the soldiers of the cult ran downhill, gaining haste and momentum from the change in declivity. The huge bottle slid down the slope towards the mouth. It had nearly reached it when the Mouth shut, and slowly began to open up again.

The soldiers were upon them. Mengus shouted a command to halt, then one to retreat, then forward, then to the left, then to the right. The guards jerked around in every direction, confused, while Tanoun smashed in the face of the foremost among them with a great kick. Krelrhytus caught one of them with the rope tying his hands together, and strangled him. All ten of this group of soldiers fell prey to criminal vengeance.

Mengus searched the pockets of one, and found a small knife, with which he cut his own and the others' bonds. They each took up arms, clubs and knives, and surveyed the scene. Large numbers of the devout still awaited them on land.

Once again the monstrous sphincter opened up like a vortex. Now the towering vessel, on its side, glided directly to it. The top of the great piece of horn stabbed into one side of the Mouth's tender interior. The Gaw decimated a city three hundred miles away in revenge for that wicked blow. The tower kept sliding in. The Mouth of the Gaw, dilated to its greatest possible expansion, now held the tower, horizontally spread from one of its tender membraneous sides to the other. In frustration, the creature annihilated city after city, strewing quakes of devastation far and wide.

Now the sphincter tightened with all of its might. The two ends of the tower cut into the fragile membrane, and a putrid green liquor spurted up in towering geysers. The ground now shook like a quivering lump of gelatin. Buildings all around toppled onto each other, and the few individuals who remained composed enough to act logically attempted to find cover. Mengus, Tanoun, Krelrhytus, and the other fugitives, ran at breakneck speed, oblivious of all concern over others. No priests or guards should worry too much about catching them now.

The reeking greenish river soon increased to a steady flow. They could feel, however far they ran from the spring, the ocean of nauseating stench deepening beneath their feet. A former wagon, now used as a makeshift boat, came floating by the group. Several priests sat on it. The criminals, now swimming, headed towards it, trying to avoid the uprooted tree-trunks and floating jetsam all around them. Krelrhytus swam the hardest and reached the wagon first. He grabbed on, and, with a shudder of recognition, let one of the priests, who cried out "Ho, stranger, allow us to help you," at his sight, pull him aboard. Short work dispatched his intended executioners in an act of poetic justice.

The other criminals soon joined him aboard the novel craft. No land appeared on the sea of disgusting digestive juices, which now extended to the horizon on every side. Mengus, bleeding from a wound received in the chaos, swooned dead away.

* * * * *

Mengus awakened on a beach strewn with wreckage and a green liquid now mingled with water. The corpse of Tanoun, displaying the wounds inflicted by a squid or some other, similar creature, lay nearby him. He walked up to some bystanders on the shore, who tendered aid to the injured castaways washing up in great numbers. One of them approached him and said: "Welcome to Hyperborea, friend. From what I've heard concerning recent events, don't count on returning to Thule."

Only one thought could occur to Mengus now. What had become of Velia? He could hardly bear the thought that she might have died in the chaos, and resolved to set out in search of her.

For several days, he walked along the beach, in a direction chosen arbitrarily by a coin-flip—the left—asking of everyone, Hyperborean or Thulean, whether they had heard tell of the girl, whom he described in the fullest details, both of physiognomy, and of past history, to any (the great majority) who had no prior knowledge of her. After a week or so, he perceived from afar off a girl who he believed might resemble her so sufficiently, as to pass over similarity, and go on into identity. He hiked nearer, cautiously keeping out of her view, and positively recognized her.

Now a new problem hit him: he would have to clear up the misunderstanding which they had unfortunately had, but he felt confident enough of his ability to do so, and even surer that she would reward his deeds on her behalf, with a feigned, if not a true and heartfelt, love.

To case out the situation, he asked a man who seemed to know her—as he came from the general direction of the small set of buildings which he divined that she now inhabited—about her, allowing him to think that he had not had have any previous acquaintance with her.

The man said to him: "Oh, that Velia, she's an odd one, let me tell you. She hasn't ceased speaking of the one who slew the immortal Gaw. She tells constantly of how she had devoted her life to the Gaw, of how she had proudly met the qualifications necessary for the maidens whom the Gaw accepts as Its brides, and how all of her plans of piety had come to nothing and her immanent god had been slain by one of Its own priests, a blasphemer and unforgivable heretic who had even come to her in the night and attempted the sin of cuckolding his own god, to whom he had sworn an irrevocable oath of eternal devotion, and by violent and forcible rape no less, thus earning a well-deserved punishment of death. But the bastard swine not only defeated the penalty, but destroyed her divine husband, and her plans as well. You see her now in the clothing of mourning, according to the usage of her hometown of the Obasai people, which she always wears, out of respect for her August fiancé; but, as she often says, gods do not die so easily or so permanently that she can consider the case as closed."

He paused, and Mengus asked: "And what might she mean by that?"

The man took up the thread of his thoughts with a look of distracted concentration: "She's sworn, so she says, an oath of implacable hatred against the one who murdered her intended, and vows that she'll never rest until she's seen that he has accepted, with all due compunction, a tormenting end fitting for the one who has committed such vile and despicable acts. Only by forcefully feeding him, still alive, to the Gaw, which she swears that she will one day accomplish, even if she must personally drag him down, kicking and screaming in abject terror like the ignoble coward she knows him to be, to the bottom of the ocean to do it, will she be able to sufficiently settle the score against someone so vile and disgusting. She hopes that such an act of expiatory sacrifice will enable her deific bridegroom to once again rise up from the ocean's waves, and receive her as Its long-appointed mate."

The Pilgrimage of Nomoronth

Phrehm Nzahzah, Head Instructor of Pilgrims at the temple of Yenatrilh, knocked on the door of Mzanar Vremn. The pupil, lying on his cot daydreaming about the heavenly City of Nomoronth, wherein the effluent Goddess Yenatrilh personally surrounded him with her all-encompassing love, disengaged himself from his rêveries and opened the door to his teacher.

The instructor shook his head: "I'm afraid I have some bad news for you, Mzanar."

"Yes, what could it be?" The plan must have been working!

"Well, you know that all of the students on the list before Vranach Flinym and Vargh Vlaskenh have managed to chance across something making it impossible for them to go on the pilgrimage. Well, now they've got problems too. Vranach stumbled into a spoorn-trap that someone had inadvertently left on the path he goes out on every night to fetch water for the priests' ablutions, and Vargh somehow picked a poisonous herb in place of the entheogen he normally imbibes as a sacrament in the worship of Yenatrilh. Neither of them will make it out of the hospital for a long time, and will probably make nothing but crippled beggars when they do."

"But, how could such a thing happen? I can't believe it!" The pious pigs, could they be so foolish as to suspect nothing? He no longer took the care to hide his actions that he did when he first began. Nor did he take as much care to dispose of his rivals: at first, he made sure his preemptory strikes would cause their death.

"I don't know how. But, and this is bad news for you, I think, this means that the list of students eligible to go on the next pilgrimage is down to you. I can't imagine that you have much desire to go on that arduous journey to Nomoronth, since you came in last on all the tests of piety and scriptural knowledge given in the school. But go you must. Come to the exercise pyramid every morning at five, and I'll teach you the exact nature of the ritual which you must perform at each of the one-hundred and seven along the way."

"All right, I'll be there. I won't get much sleep with that schedule—" He couldn't look too eager to go, and denying it should—with such trusting souls—prove most effective. Still, it seemed to pass beyond possibility that they could believe he would want to stay in mundane and tiresome Enphenour, isolated in the Linruphian Mountains, when the pleasures of heavenly Nomoronth awaited him.

"You can't worry about sleeping now. You only have a month to memorize the ritual, and judging from your past performances in class—"

But now he had the motivation to commit the rite to memory. He wouldn't let anyone, neither the teachers and students at the temple, nor the mute Tlilquah tribesmen who would accompany him on the pilgrimage as guards and guides, guess that he cared not a whit for their naïve ideals of piety. He would perform to perfection.

"Very little lore has come down to us in our worm-eaten manuscripts. Let us recapitulate this material. You remember the names of the Seven Mysteriarchs of Nomoronth, who serve the Azure Goddess Yenatrilh eternally as consorts, as shall you?"

"First, there's the High Priest, Szen-Bhu-Vey."

"Second?"

"Then, there's Sesh-Khul-Pah, Keeper of the Scriptures."

"Yes, and thirdly?"

"Thirdly, there's—umm, there's Phan-Dompikh—"

"Yes, there's Phan-Dompikh, but in the third place, there's Istarkh-Tchrah, Sacristan in the Sacred Rites! Then, there remain the other four, whose functions have not come down to us in the tattered remnants of reality we possess: Vinthen-Puln, Phan-Dompikh, Jhiniveh-Phem, and Phol-Menh-Hoh."

"Oh yes, Vinthen-Puln, Phan-Dompikh, Jhiniveh-Phem, and Phol-Menh-Hoh. I always seem to have trouble with those." He would have to try hard to change in that regard, for even though he didn't want to appear overly eager to go on the trip (for then they might suspect the reason that all the other students had met such untimely fates), he also couldn't brook the possibility of their keeping him home due to incompetence. No, he couldn't let that prevent his joining the company of the Goddess Yenatrilh in the paradisiacal City of Nomoronth.

Phrehm Nzahzah adjured him that they had much work to do, and then made the conventional signs of parting, and turned to go, glancing back briefly at the student, already lost in day-dreams of his upcoming and ecstatic union with Yenatrilh, and his intestines warmed with the displeasing thought of attempting to teach such a student.

* * * * *

A few miles past the remnants of the mighty wall, which the Emperor Khnanhoum had erected to defend his Empire Gn from the barbarians to the south and the east, nothing but a few broken bricks on which Mzanar Vremn vainly attempted to read graffiti inscribed in a tongue forgotten millennia before, the pilgrim and his retinue of Tlilquah tribesmen came through the jungle vines to the glade holding the seventy-second pyramid on their journey. As the Tlilquah cleared the structure of the creepers and reptiles which infested it, carefully seeking out any poisonous insects or arthropods lurking in the cracked marble, and removing them with trowels and daggers, the pilgrim wished that he shared a language with them, so that he could thank them for their efforts on his behalf. They had brought him through so much.

He advanced to the pyramid and began his ritual, performing the preliminary circumambulation deosil, reciting verses lost to mortal comprehension aeons before; the tribesmen stood in watchful silence. He advanced onto the first of the seventeen yard-high tiers, and there he chanted the mantras and performed the ceremonial gestures allotted to that level, and then he mounted onto the third.

Now the surrounding silence broke as a flock of wyverns flew from the west and spied the tribesmen and their companion pilgrim. They began to circle them in search of opportunity to strike at their prey; adamantine scales covered their nine-cubit wingspans, ranging from vermilion and violet at wing-tip to a brightly reflective amber on the head and a dull russet at the tail's sharp bifurcation. The pilgrim experienced a slight break in his mental self-fixation, finished the third tier's rites and advanced to the fourth; meanwhile the tribesmen drew arrows tipped in paralytic venom and fired volleys at the gyrant wyverns. With a small effort Mzanar Vremn increased his level of concentration, and lost all awareness of the wyverns and everything else other than his performance of his ritual adulations.

The wyverns lunged and attacked in chaotic sallies; the bulk of the flock withdrew after a few of them had fallen prey to the venefic arrows that left them convulsing in spasms amid the clan of Tlilquah tribesmen to receive spear-points and expire. One circled low about the pyramid, then spurted forth to attack Mzanar, only to fall from several arrows jutting from its underbelly. The pilgrim had just completed the sixth tier's supplicatory prayer and gesticulations when the reptilian monstrosity crashed onto the ninth tier, directly above him. The wyvern jerked its jaws in an ungainly spasm towards Mzanar, venomous saliva spurting on the marble, but it caught in the deep grooves left by the prayers and feet of countless pilgrims on their journey to Nomoronth, and the paralytic venom caught hold before the wyvern could reach the ascetic with its gnashing jaws. A Tlilquah dashed over, clambered up the steps, stabbed the wyvern in the neck with a hooked spear, and dragged the beast out of the pilgrim's way, while the creature's blood still flowed in runlets through cracks and pilgrim-worn grooves in the blocks of stone.

Finally reaching the seventeenth and topmost gradation of the structure, Mzanar Vremn surveyed about him as he recited the supreme invocation of Yenatrilh: the weary tribesmen had lit fires, skinned and gutted the reptilian beasts, and started to prepare the meat for their evening meal. He then got down on his knees, and bent himself backward to survey the sky. The darkening azure that hung above seemed to embrace him as he envisioned the sky itself as the great Goddess Yenatrilh, reached by him through his great devotion, the marmoreal pyramid he stood upon representing only an outward symbol of his so-great aspiration. Through his robes, their yellow stained with the wyvern's glutinous blood, he felt the gentle warmth of the Goddess's lambent radiance perfusing him, and he felt a foreshadowing of the supreme glory to which his aspiration would lead him. He could now hardly believe that he had once felt no motivation to go on the pilgrimage save for his venal lusts and greed, and pangs of guilt quickly succumbed to the feeling that the Goddess Yenatrilh must, through some divine power, have chosen him for the journey over the others. Certainly, if she had not desired that he, rather than one of them, should come to her, she would not have allowed him to make the voyage. But now, after having—at first—performed the rites of the pyramids simply to prevent the Tlilquah from suspecting his impiety, he had grown filled with the all-powerful love of Yenatrilh.

Certainly, if they had not lead him and protected him, no less at this last pyramid as at the one which sat on an island in the middle of the foaming River of Monwinn, its first tier partially submerged, and onto which crawled man-sized crabs in the midst of his devotions, he could never have made it a furlong of the way. Or the time when anthropophagous Cyclopes attacked the group; or the assault of the calcars of the steppes. But now, he had become worthy of becoming her consort; and strange were the ways of providence.

* * * * *

At last the pilgrim had finished the final pyramid's rites; his pulse pounding in anticipation of his ultimate apotheosis, he impelled the tribesmen to hasten their pace through the short stretch leading to his destination. Grinning broadly, the Tlilquah quickly broke through the dark and vine-festooned forest onto the plateau on which stood the Primordial City of Nomoronth. There, waiting at the town's central temple, stood the elder Mysteriarchs. Mzanar Vremn saw then that they had indeed survived from the city's earliest days, as the fragments of traditional lore could now only hint: each one stood, a primal lich, his exaggerated skeletal frame pushing outwards against his grey and wizened skin. The sable robes they wore had perhaps lasted mere centuries, hanging onto their lean frames in tatters and rags. Upon their heads stood proud miters, the fabric, as black as their vestments, patterned with silvery amphisbaenae, their bodies intertwined in eternal copulation, aiming their twin serpent-heads towards the skies.

Behind them stood the temple, a pagoda of seventeen tiers.

Around, scattered variously, stood other, smaller buildings, randomly sprawled about the area in an architectural mélange of brick and wood. Behind them, dwarfing these utilitarian structures, rose an enormous edifice of bone-white stone: an uncompleted pyramid, four of its levels finished, a fifth currently under construction, its contours in exactly measured proportion to the ones on the pilgrim's journey. The pilgrim craned his neck to look upward toward the Cyclopean structure's summit, when Szen-Bhu-Vey silently interrupted his gazing with a light tap on the shoulder, and motioned him with a pointed finger to enter the pagoda.

Into the pagoda went the pilgrim, lead by Szen-Bhu-Vey, with Sesh-Khul-Pah and Istarkh-Tchrah at his sides, and followed by Vinthen-Puln, Phan-Dompikh, Jhiniveh-Phem, and Phol-Menh-Hoh; the Tlilquah remained outside. Inside, Szen-Bhu-Vey, the High Priest, indicated to the pilgrim that he should perform ceremonial rites similar to those that he had performed on his journey, which perhaps had undergone corruption during their transmission down the untold aeons. Jhiniveh-Phem had him change into a set of vestments as sable as the liches' own; Sesh-Khul-Pah produced the requisite scriptures; the pilgrim quickly scanned and memorized the material, noting minor changes in all but the uppermost tier, oddly—or so it seemed to him—left blank. Istarkh-Tchrah momentarily produced purple, crystalline graals for the Seven Mysteriarchs; the Hierophant motioned the pilgrim to begin the rituals.

Throughout the prolonged rites the Seven Mysteriarchs followed the pilgrim, watching him closely and attentively; they provided choral litanies to many of the verses. Finally, they reached the uppermost level. Here, Mzanar Vremn began to orate his familiar supplication; Vinthen-Puln and Phol-Menh-Hoh stepped forward and each grabbed one of his arms and they held him up, surfeited with the ecstasy of mystical communion, above a basin of silver worked with intertwining amphisbaenae; Istarkh-Tchrah unsheathed an obsidian dirk, previously hidden within his robes, and slit the pilgrim's throat from ear to ear. When his blood had quite drained, the Seven Mysteriarchs drew liberal draughts from the basin, letting the blood flow slowly down their ancient, cadaverous throats in a rhythmic gurgling. The blood gone, Istarkh-Tchrah carefully boned the pilgrim's corpse. The flesh, cooked according to the preset récipé, provided the Tlilquah tribe with its next meal and their reward for faithful service; after an hour's enjoyment, they departed to lead in the next pilgrim. Mzanar Vremn's bones they ground and mixed with befitting compounds, as the age-old formula dictated, fitted this viscosity into a mold, and in that way produced a solid block some several inches square. This cubical cementation they glued into place on the fifth level of the enormous pyramid.

Bluebeard's Closet

Yolande could stand her new husband well enough in most respects; her mother hadn't set her up too badly. The odd coloration of his hair, however, had bothered her at first, for it seemed like some trick calculated to flabbergast the middle classes, who didn't always understand every antic undertaken by those more creative than they were, such as poets and musicians. But that too—along with his rather ugly old face, she discovered, disappeared in the darkness. Then his beard seemed just the same as any other grizzly old man's beard. And besides, he had plenty of money.

But when he ventured to keep secrets from her, he had just plain gone too far. Why, he even flaunted it, giving her a complete set of keys for the château, and sternly warning her not to open the small door at the end of one particular hallway; he didn't know what he would do, he declared in a fiery tone, if she happened to forget herself and look inside it.

Curiosity consumed her, but not as strongly as indignation at his unworthy prohibitions. He would not stop her. She had nothing to lose, for he had no heirs from his other marriages, to take precedence over her, and prevent her from inheriting the entirety of the estate, despite the numerous prior wives he could boast of.

After Bluebeard's mysterious, and complete, disappearance, Yolande could often be seen handling a shiny, metallic object, which she always kept on her person, and which appeared to be a key-ring, and as she did so, she would look down at her lap as if hiding some ripe secret, and softly giggle to herself.

A Cavern in the Sky

Egon Armdur walked down, into the cave. His eyes scanned back and forth and he held his instruments ready to analyze the mineral composition of odd rock formations. As expected, no sign of life, no unusual patterns of color. But there—he thought he saw movement out of the corner of his eye. He walked over to it: a large, off-white lump covered the cave's left-hand side from top to bottom, an ovoid some eight feet in height and six in width, bulging outward about two and a half feet. Egon looked down at his composition-analyzer, flicked one of its switches, and began to press a button on it. In a lightning flash, a rock-hard tentacle formed and smashed into his knees, crushed through the knee-caps, broke the bones and ligaments, and sent the knee-caps flying out behind him; a second tentacle knocked through his hands and rammed into his abdomen, crushed his internal organs and snapped through his spine and out his back; a third shot into his face, knocked it back into his brain and knocked both face and brain out the back of his skull. Egon Armdur crumpled.

The nerve impulses in tChem calmed; he had over-estimated the force required to kill the monster. The sight of the creature—its maddening curvature and unthinkable texture—had paralyzed tChem into a sheer panic terror; the overload of excitation in his network of nerves had frozen him into immobility: he could hardly have altered his coloration to match the silver-red and yellow striations on the cavern wall in time to avoid detection. The bizarre monster had approached him; he regained control—control enough to defend himself.

Even though, in its present, dissipated state, the monster's visage now unsettled him less, tChem still felt a tenuous hold on reality as he looked at the beast's unspeakable form. He began to panic again, stopped himself. He formed pseudopods and pounded the thing, over and over, until nothing remained but a shapeless pulp. Relief swept through his network of nerves: he could now bear to look at the thing. A shock hit his nerves—the thing must have come from outside: nothing like it existed in the caverns. He must investigate, seek out where it had come from, see if more of the hideous things existed there—he owed that to dRiim and the others. He would have just time enough to find out before he must plant the brood of polyp-like young that he carried.

A stench became apparent to tChem; not nearly as sanity threatening as the creature's shape and texture, but unpleasant enough. He could follow the chemical trail the creature left. It led directly outward to the Brilliant Bleakness. As tChem emerged from the cave's mouth, he saw the blinding light of just one of the two suns; he could emerge safely, though painfully. He scanned the area: about a quarter mile distant, a bizarrely regular rock formation jutted out of the ground. He stopped in surprise: a cavern mouth gaped wide on the abnormally regular surface of the escarpment. He meandered toward it over the lichenless, mossless, barren rocks, suppressing the pain of the ground's heated surface and the sun's overly bright rays. Indeed, the chemical trail led directly to the cave. Up and into the cave he crept.

He readied himself to explore. A pain-like sensation hit: he would soon need to plant his polypous young. No time to see whether or not more of the creatures threatened: he needed to rest while the polyps entered the next phase of their life-cycle.

Then, the planting. He must, at least, find a safe place to sleep-phase his network of nerves. The entire cavern complex seemed to reek of the creatures; he tuned out the appropriate sensory receptors from his consciousness. He meandered out of the light that shone in the cave into an unlit side cavern, slid behind some unusually regularly shaped rocks, adjusted his coloration to match the light blue of his surroundings, and began the sleep phase process.

* * * * *

In his cabin of the *Orilelh* (named after the heroine of an ancient Hyadrisian info-erotic epic, as per traditional service practice), Vaenz Tsheng awoke, alone, and the computer wake-alarm, having sensed that his brainwaves were no longer those of sleep, ceased. He had stayed back in the ship to rest while his partner went out to gather crystal samples, but Armdur should have returned by now—half an hour ago, by their agreed-upon schedule. He must have found something especially interesting. Or maybe he had met with an accident. Tsheng knew nothing too serious could have occurred: he'd worked with Armdur on numerous missions, and knew that his partner could deal satisfactorily with unlooked-for danger. In addition to that, the early probes had discovered no life of any sort on Renops IV, so he couldn't have gotten tangled up with some predatory creature. He must have found some interesting crystal formations. The probes had indicated numerous hitherto unheard of crystals, many of which might have industrial applications. A few seemed to fit desired specifications for the creation of self-replicating forms of artificial intelligence, a prime area of current research, quite necessary for economic competitiveness.

Resolve swelled within him; he would join his partner. He dressed, ate, took up the routine instruments, and walked to the ship's door. He stepped out and looked around. A cave, about a quarter mile away. He knew Armdur couldn't resist that—he'd headed the Society of Ultra-Hyadrisian Spelunkers a few years back, and had contributed a "personal experience" column to their journal, *The Astázakhárian Tunnel Worm*, every two months for decades. He walked across the sandy waste to the cave and looked in. Still, caution remained necessary —Egon might have had some sort of accident, and no one else could rescue them if they both got trapped somehow. He shone a light into the cave and slowly walked in. After a couple turns, going down a steep grade in some areas, he saw something on the floor ahead.

It made him sick to his stomach to look at it. Still, he must make sure. He got out his composition-analyzer: it showed exactly the appropriate chemical mixture for a human body. His guts twisted; he felt his pulse explode; his lungs nearly burst with panting; and he held in his bowels as his consciousness shot into hyper-awareness of his surroundings and situation. Something had killed Armdur and mashed him into an unrecognizable pulp; some terror that probably still lurked nearby.

He looked forward for a split second, saw nothing but cave extending indefinitely into the planet's bowels. He turned and ran, where possible, back out the cave. Three times he slipped and cut his hand or his knee—"Oh, God, could it smell blood?" Absurd thought. He beat the sand into the underlying bedrock, staggering a zigzag trail in his fear and confusion.

He slammed the door shut and stood, panting. He'd go back to Hyadris—no reason to stay here, with such danger around. He would have no hard questions to answer on that score, once he'd explained the situation. He walked down the hallway, took a couple of turns, and arrived at the control room. The lift-off went off without a hitch, and the ship entered orbit. He flew it out to the Quantum-Consciousness Discontinuity Drive framework. The enormous frame's several parts fit together into one around the ship as a large, multi-layered sphere made up of multitudinous triangular planes.

He floated over to the console to adjust the Quantum-Consciousness Discontinuity Drive for his single consciousness. The QCDD altered consciousness on the quantum level, introducing a discontinuity of spatial relationships that disrupted the normally continuous flow of experience, resulting in an unmediated jump in position or "teleportation." For proper control, the QCDD required precise calibration to the consciousness(es) involved, and could behave unpredictably if its calibration did not match various measurements to a high degree of precision; even so, usual precaution required setting the destination far out within the star system desired. They had, of course, set the QCDD for the pair, and it took Tsheng some three hours to reset all of the sensitive variables involved—and he could accomplish it that quickly only because the ship's computer stored precise psycho-neurometric files on the crew members; without such stored information, it might have taken months of testing to ascertain the correct values for the multitudinous variables involved.

The calibration finished, he swallowed three of the capsules known as "Inner-Spacesuits." The quantum-consciousness discontinuity process involved bizarre psychological effects, and after the first few test-flights one of the astronauts involved had declared the experience mystical and insightful. He soon left the service and founded a "religion" that recycled various doctrines from many eclectic sources. He made claims that went beyond the legally recognized bounds of religion (*i.e.*, the operationally untestable), however, and put forth the doctrine that QCDD could break old channels of neuro-psycho-logical conditioned association, making the "neuronaut" open to new ideas and experiences. He had clearly gone too far. The Alliance to Eradicate Psychotropics, a consortium of churches, in cooperation with the Anti-Euphoriant League, an advertising company trust, and the Parents' Partnership Against Altered States, a lobbyist group composed mostly of childless psychiatrists working in government posts, began a major anti-QCDD campaign. Soon government scientists had developed—by a slight modification of the lethal venom of a certain rare bird-eating spider—the Inner-Spacesuit which blunted most or all of the QCDD's effects, leaving, on most sensory channels, with touch the only significant exception, a clunking, monotonous pulsation of purple, for most individuals; a few perceived a hot pink instead. Tsheng had taken the drug, three instead of the usual two pills—he could hardly deal with any of the QCDD effects after that fright—and now had only to wait out the half-hour or so before it took effect.

After his tactile clock indicated the elapse of twenty-seven minutes he estimated that the purple pulsation had nearly reached its full intensity. He hit a switch and started the drive.

* * * * *

// The red-litten caverns of sZen—the creature that intruded—the lichen and phosphorescent fungi—the network of caves—the lichen gardens of sChaol—the slugs that pursue through the tunnels of metal—the pleasure of mating with dRiim—the endless pleasure—the obscene beast's stench—the terror—the painful light of the Barren Bleakness—the maddening curves and angles—the polypous young—time to plant—sZur's endless empire of caves—dRiim and her ecstatic pseudopods—the pull inward—the angles—adjustment of coloration—the terror—the monster—the maddening terror—paralyzing—bliss of dRiim's chemical exchange—molten excrement in sZen's tunnels—fear on the Barren Bleakness—silver-red and yellow—rocks at an odd angle—the texture unknown in sChaol—need to plant polyps—fear—adjust coloration—the beast from outward—circular caverns of sZur—spiral metal tunnels—the acidic slugs—the burning heat—sands—mating with dRiim—ecstatic—angles—curves—

the monster's chemical trail—leading away—pain of light—plant polyps—the creature—fear—total awareness—

// Pleasure—the obscene lightless caverns of beast's stench—the maddening terror—paralyzing—bliss of sZen—the creature—network of caves—the lichen that intruded—the fear—awareness—gardens of sChaol—the slugs mating with dRiim—the monster's chemical tunnels—fear on the endless—pursue through the Bleakness—the tunnels of metal—the pleasure of maddening tunnels—the slugs—the burning endless empire of inward—the odd angle—the texture angles—they plant polyps—fear—adjust coloration—the terror—the painful light of dRiim's chemical yellow—rocks and beast from outward—circular caverns' exchange—molten Barren Bleakness—silver-red excrement in sZen—unknown in sChaol—the young—time to plant sZur's terror—the heat—sands mating with monster—the spiral metal dRiim—caves—dRiim and her ecstatic angles—curves—the light—plant curves and angles—the ecstatic pseudopods—the pull creature—the electro-magnetic fields fall—total trail—leading away—pain—//

* * * * *

The insane kaleidoscope stopped; tChem felt himself floating in the cave where he had bunched himself up to sleep. He lost control of his olfactory system in a confusing neural rush; the smell of the strange monsters stabbed into his consciousness. Guilt-pangs hit him: how could he have passed such a negative judgment on something he had never experienced before? He considered the creature's visage; thought back on the pleasure of entangling with dRiim's knot of pseudopods in the mating process; and opened his consciousness fully to the stench of the monsters. Bliss hit him everywhere at the thought of the creature he had so thoughtlessly slain, and resolution gelled within him: he would, he must, make love to one or more of the creatures. He knew from the chemical traces hitting his receptor cells that at least one more of them must have recently passed the area: he would find it. He recalled the polyps inside him; but no need to worry about them. The emergency reaction in his network of nerves had already started the process that formed a sac in which they could remain alive for several planetary revolutions on their own; he obtruded the sac from himself and attached it to the cavern wall. Now, to find one of the creatures and make love to it.

Vaenz Tsheng felt the tactile-control system of the QCDD; it indicated that the discontinuity had ended: he had emerged back into continuous space. The Inner-Spacesuit had done its job well: he hadn't had any experience of the discontinuity, only the monotonous *<purple!—purple!—purple!>* that still overwhelmed all of his senses save that of touch. He pressed the control to reveal his new location through a tactile coding. It indicated a region of space several light-years from Hyadris' star system, the ship now automatically settling into orbit at an appropriate distance from the nearest star.

Panic gripped him; he knew the reliability of the QCDD too well to doubt the meaning of this unexpected and wrong location: another consciousness must have interfered with the drive. Something on board the *Orilelh*—something that killed Armdur. He hit the control for an emergency beacon; but since no faster-than-light form of communication existed, he knew he would have to wait for years before the S.O.S. message reached Hyadris. Then, a rescue mission should arrive in a matter of weeks, depending on the availability of appropriately sized craft—but until then, alone in space with some unspeakable monster on board—a monster that had ruthlessly slaughtered his friend and partner. He must defend himself as best he could. He floated out of his purple chair, and began to feel his way down the purple hall to the purple door that opened to the armament room—he heard his purple sigh of relief as he recalled that the service had insisted on a full stock of weaponry on every mission, despite its expected uselessness on the vast majority.

The lovely, pleasure-exuding smell of the creatures guided tChem down the tunnel away from the opening through which he had entered—which, he noticed, had shut, during a rock slide no doubt, and perhaps even the same rock slide—what else could have done it?—that warped the electro-magnetic fields and inexplicably allowed him to float wherever he went. Down the tunnel he glided, feeling the joy of reforming his body into new combinations and shapes, shapes and combinations impossible in the heaviness of the stifling caves he had previously known.

Two left turns later *love* hit tChem's network of nerves like a thousand doses of sChaolian acid-slug venom—only, as he formulated the cognition, pleasurable rather than painful. He compared the beast's shape to dRiim's knot of tentacles, and sudden realization hit him: make love to it, but how? The preliminary must remain, at least. So he released a cloud of pheromone spray toward the monster to signal his erotic intentions with chemically encoded desire.

As Tsheng felt his way along the corridor toward the armament room he had noticed a shifting blur of slightly lighter purple against the darker purple background. The monster, or a mere trick of the mind? He could hardly see shapes, or anything else, but the varying shades of purple. Something hit him—wet, all over his body, but thin and quickly drying out. His olfactory nerves exploded with sensation: *<purple!—purple!—purple!>*

The creature responded with what, to tChem, appeared the appropriate signal to proceed: a semi-coördinated group of bodily shakings. He readied an appendage to deliver the chemical packet of new life in a tentacular caress. But which pseudopod on the creature to attempt the matter with? One of the two large ones seemed most likely.

Tsheng tried to float back away in terror. He felt his bowels loosen and the flow of warm, semi-liquid excrement outward as the purple blur approached and reached a purple tentacle out to grab his leg. A new stink rose up: *<purple!—purple!—purple!>* The thing wrapped around his leg; odd pricklings stabbed into it here and there. With a sudden twist he felt the bones snap and his body twisted around, knocked into the wall, and the purple thing set him free to try to escape once again.

The pseudopod had proven unsuitable for mating purposes, but tChem had detected chemical emanations from the creature that indicated to him an equal degree of sexual excitation and desire. He could only compare them to dRiim in oestrus. If the monster did not act carefully, it would float away before tChem could again reattach for lovemaking. He decided that one of the two smaller tentacles must serve the mating function. Not as large as on a desirable female such as dRiim, and equipped with purposeless small appendages at its tip, but so shapely and beautifully curved.

Tsheng felt the unspeakable monster grab his arm and twist—harder than it had twisted his leg. He saw the purple walls spin and felt his arm snap, his nose break and spurt out a misty spray of purple blood, and several ribs cracked *<purple!>* as he slammed into a wall. He bounced off again as the purple tentacle released him. Pain shot through his body; how could he escape the purple thing?

Mistaken again; but it exuded such a strongly erotic aroma that the creature must share the sexual purpose, thought tChem. Ah, well, one pseudopod left to try the attempt with. Stubby, and full of unlikely apertures, but no other remained. The creature proved less resilient after the next attempt at lovemaking.

Disappointment shot through tChem's network of nerves as he saw the monster float away, down the cave, but maybe he could find another of the strange creatures. He scouted the entire cavern complex, which he found large enough and cozy, but shut off from the old world he knew (stifling atmosphere there, anyway) and much worse, no more of the creatures. Purposeful cognition appeared in his consciousness. He would plant his polyps, tend them to maturity, and, when more of the creatures arrived—he somehow knew, he just knew, that more would arrive—they could all renew the attempt to make love to the things. In time, they would surely find a way.

Prince Charming

A bite of an apple given to her by a crone—it hadn't taken anything more than that. The world had disappeared.

It didn't take anything greater to revive her. A probing tongue dislodged the chunk of apple caught in her throat.

In a haze, she couldn't move yet. Her hearing returned, whereas her sight remained nothing but off-white clouds and grey vapor. She heard, from an indeterminate distance, a man's voice: "Oh!—once, I saw a newly-slain corpse lying beside the road in winter; but now, all of the beauty of that scene appears united in her body. Her hair's as black as the carrion crow; her lips as red as the blood that still flowed down the hillside; and her skin—no wonder they called her Snow White!"

Her vision cleared enough for her to see. She found herself in an odd sort of thing, made of gold and glass, kind of like a cross between a coffin and an exhibition case.

She raised her head to look up at the man who had wakened her. His face at first betrayed surprise, then horrified shock, then disappointment.

Then it revealed that a sudden insight had illuminated the brain behind it.

The pillow on which Snow White's head had lain now covered her face and smothered her.

The Eunuchorn

Nhouinheign felt a tingling that ran down from the tip of his three-foot long horn to its base, making his entire body shudder with expectation. He knew what that feeling meant. A virgin lurked somewhere nearby. He didn't know just exactly what he'd do if he found a virgin, never having encountered one himself—in fact, he didn't even know of a single unicorn who ever had. Younger unicorns had often formulated intriguing speculations. It seemed to have something to do with her lap—But he felt irresistibly attracted, and surely he could figure out something to do with the thing, once he found it. His horn clearly directed him through the forest, and he ran headlong through the thickset oaks and elms.

After some fifteen minutes, a clearing appeared directly in front of him. He went right in and looked around. There, alone, sitting on a cloth spread out on the grass, in the very middle of a large circular copse—a virgin! He felt a little disturbed that she showed no surprise at his unexpected appearance (for how could she have foreseen his presence?—she had no horn to detect *him*—), but his unknown desires outweighed all considerations of caution. He aimed his horn at her and walked briskly in her direction.

Something went dreadfully wrong. He felt his entire body twist up and smash back down against the ground, his legs sticking out in all directions. He couldn't move. The net tightened around him even more. His horn positively ached as he, impotent to do anything about it, watched the virgin walk away, snickering. A group of men swung around into his view. Some of them held the net, so constricting that he couldn't budge at all. One, in a suit of plebeian armor, grabbed his neck. Another grabbed his head. A third held onto the end of his horn. A fourth, wearing an impressively ornamented suit of chain-mail, sawed his horn off at the base.

Listless and disgraced, he slunk away into the woods as the men laughingly stole away in the opposite direction. What an unheard-of humiliation! He would gladly have risked the most terrifying death to attain the maiden, but he never imagined that such a horror awaited him.

* * * * *

Jehan, the Comte de Lautréamont, took another bite of fish-brains from his plate. He turned white, then red, then green, then blue, clutched his throat, and started to sputter: "Uh! Uh! Uh! Uhh! Uhhh! Uhhngn! Uhhngngnhng!!!"

His seneschal, Théophile de L'Eau-d'Élas, came running.

"Here, sire, drink of this."

He handed the count a cup filled to the brim with wine. The count managed to take a great draught between choking noises. After a couple minutes, he recovered his former regality.

"A cow's head! God's third leg! But we're sure sick o' this! How many times can we get poisoned in one day! At this rate we'll use up the last unicorn in the world before the week is out! And damn if a good Chablis doesn't taste rotten with that *merde* in it!"

His seneschal replied to him: "Milord, you need not worry on that score. For an essential consideration seems to have escaped from those who have created the récipé for the universal mithridate. This consideration appears neither in Silander's *De Monokeron*, nor in Félicien de Clouët's *Livre de Licornes*, nor in Alesius Flavius' *De monstribus*, nor even in the unpredictable pages of the pseudo-anonymous *Bestiaire de La Bizarrière*."

"We have not the slightest idea what you are speaking of."

"Sire, as everyone knows, the unicorn's unique horn, ground down to a powder, acts as an antidote to all poisons."

"Bird o' the night! Beast o' misfortune! Grotty gaitered owl! Don't tell us what we already know, dizzard, tell us what we don't know!"

"Indeed. The prevalent plan of unicorn horn harvesting, you surely know, involves attracting the unicorn with a virgin and then killing the unicorn. Then, one uses the horn for antidote, and the body, for food. Now, it occurred to myself that we need not take that second step, that in fact the unicorn's meat resembles horse-meat sufficiently that it merely adds a couple of tasty meals to one's cuisine. But the dead unicorn does not, shall one say, produce further unicorns for one's profit."

"Ah. Aha. We begin to get a glimmering of the plan."

* * * * *

Nhouinheign felt a little bashful about approaching a unicorn mare in his mutilated condition. Nonetheless, he felt sure that Huynnuÿnnée would understand. After all, it wasn't like *she* had a horn. On the other hand, perhaps that made all the difference between male and female unicorns. But then too, weren't they always bragging about how they could go near the human hives without worrying about getting caught and the—presumably—deadly consequences? So, he *would* approach her.

Even his smarting root could still track down a female unicorn, and it didn't take too long before he found himself in the presence of his well-beloved. Shyly, reticently, he hove around into her sight. A few motions of the head indicated what he wanted with sufficient clarity.

The female unicorn scanned his mutilated countenance with a glassy stare. She straightened up, lifted her nose into the air, snorted a brief "Hmmphmphphph!", turned, and briskly trotted away.

Haunted Planet

A file of mass-murderer ghosts, mercenary battalions, marched down the city street in the fog. The spectre of one who had mingled parenticide with necrophilia jostled in an alley with the phantom of another who had believed that his victims would serve him in the afterlife. From a window above, shone the crimson eyes of one who had fired on the crowds below from that self-same spot. Three skulking shadows who had enjoyed the torments of unwary victims could now only experience that pleasure vicariously. Everywhere, on all sides, ghosts lurked unseen and unsuspected by the living masses who they now dwarfed in volume.

Unseen and unsuspected, that is, by all except the sensitive, the ghost-seers. To them, the world had become a nightmare. As much as the world had been overrun by the living, even more so had it now been overrun by the dead. And just as the overpopulation of the living could be reversed, so the overpopulation of the dead was irreversible. Each soul remained, forever to haunt the world. And with humanity being what it is, a multitude of souls was added to that shocking mob each moment.

Irreversible—but not unable to be brought to a halt. And just that was what the ghost-seers, finding the world nearly intolerable as it already was—much less as they imagined its future—had resolved to do. And there were enough to bring the change about, for no one had ever suspected that so many of them existed in secrecy;—and could no longer endure to do so. Their conspiratorial cabals had little trouble finding opportunities to take advantage of; and before long, mass disaster had led to mass strife, and mass strife had ended in total war.

* * * * *

A host of former ghost-seers jostles against the accumulated legions of sin; still, none of these apparitions appear to the currently living inhabitants of the overcrowded orb, who go about their coleopterous concerns unsuspecting the phantasmal hordes that swarm unseen about them.

A Lacuna in the Text

An inky black infinity stretches itself across the nothingness of illimitable space. Stars shine before it, some of a ruddy, crepuscular hue, others a bright orange or effulgent white, still others a dimming cream-blue that vainly combats against the encroaching darkness. Behind them gaseous mauve and aquamarine nebulae serpent in flamboyant twists and spirals. Through this interstellar void an ovoid vessel peregrines; the vessel's surface shimmers with an iridescent display; inside, the sorcerer Memzain Zhulothrique crouches in a sac, folded into the fetal position; beside him, in a separate sac, his friend and companion homunculus Phfuottuor crouches in sleep as well. The sorcerer rehearses, mentally, the aspirations and disappointments which have drawn him thusly across the void.

The sorcerer stood dressed in his full ceremonial regalia, chanting barbarous runes, in his palatial manse's great Vault of Evocations. Around the circumference of the chamber a row of marble caryatid columns stood upholding the arches of the domed ceiling. Between the columns, carven alternately into the buxom forms of those succubae with whom the wizard had garnered pleasure, and the semi-coiled forms of those lamiae with whom the wizard had successfully avoided taking pleasure—and the ineffable consequences thereof, alcoves alternately held shelves of grimoires and other tomes requisite to his works of evocation, and the various material requirements of that work. Set into the abutments jutting out above the upholding caryatides, braziers above the lamiae held burning incense that wafted its resinous vapors across the room to form spiraling clouds that hung and then dissipated, while the succubae upheld flambeaux that cast their light across the room, combating the clouds of aromatic smoke in a chaotic chiaroscuro. The highly arched dome's interior showed the constellations that one would have seen overhead, had but the sun set and the clouds above dispersed.

In the center of the chamber, set into the flagstones, a gold band shaped as a circle several meters in diameter held fist-sized cabochon gemstones, emeralds, sapphires, and rubies, each with a different cabalistic sign carven into it; inside the circle yet more gold bands formed a heptagram. Here, as the wizard chanted, mist began to appear, slowly shifted, twisted around in spirals, thickened, assumed dark green and ocher colors, then began to take more definite shape. The mist hardened itself into a mucosal mass that shifted, squirmed against the barrier projected by the cabochon sigils set into the golden circle, massed itself into a tower, then fell in a violent cataract against the floor. It then further thickened into a slimy ooze and again shaped itself into a regular column. Gradually, tendrils formed themselves from out the massive tower, pushed and struggled against the barrier, then retreated into the slimy trunk. Then eyes, ears, and less easily definable sense organs protruded themselves; finally, a mouth appeared on the slimy trunk and uttered in a hissing, drawn-out, sibilant voice:

"For what has the impudent human wretch sucked Tscaotl-Tscualtl, the Daemon Vavasor, from his wonted seraglio?"

Phfuottuor, seated on a stool, now turns to the sorcerer, who has finished his incantations, and says, "Perhaps you could persuade the daemon to appear in a more—pleasant—aspect."

The wizard replies, "You now see Tscaotl-Tscualtl in the most pleasant aspect he has the ability to assume."

The Daemon Vavasor shakes ferociously, then bellows, "Why do you detain me? Why hold me here, human? Why insult my stylishly aesthetic form when you wear that nauseating, sickening, repellent, gangly, shaven ape of a body?"

"To business then," said the conjurer, "I have summoned you here to obtain certain information, and will employ all appropriate inducements to ensure that you provide it."

"Again, I find myself drawn from my favored odalisques to answer a petty, piss-ant creature's piddling problems! As if I employed myself in the study of such sundry conundrums and quiddities as these creatures occupy their feeble intellects with. Ask, then, before the grotesqueness of your combined bodily shape and surfaces disallows the further continuance of my sanity."

"Tell me, then, all that you can concerning the planet known as Vyin in the Seventh Parchment of Sigils."

"I know nothing of the matter; I cannot help you. Now release me to my harem."

The mage haggardly raises himself. "You must answer. I will not brook this resentful petulance. I have prepared the fitting spells to confine you indefinitely inside a large, translucent crystal, frozen motionless and yet fully conscious. If you do not obey and give me all the information you know, I will do so, and then I will set you on display in a museum where humans will come, hundreds, perhaps thousands, every day, to gawk and stare at you, exclaiming against your form in disgust. Now relate all as to Vyin."

The Daemon shrinks back into a huddled mass of quivering, mucosal jelly. "Despite the ineffable horror I feel at the threat of mobs of countless humans in close proximity, I nevertheless know nothing of this planet. Vyin, I believe you called it? From the Seventh Parchment of Sigils? Perhaps Zschuihl-Szhiough, the Daemonic Sagesse, or Quhilluh-Chkhush, Scribe in the Spectral Silence, could serve you better—in any case, many know more than I of such subjects—I do not study the obscure and uninteresting constellations and such sundry trifles and kickshaws that fill your banal little universe. So, release me and pursue the topic with one more interested in such knick-knack planets—I have not even any familiarity with the name—I have not even read the Seventh Parchment for several aeons—found it hardly worthy of study when I did read it—would not have even finished the first line if that scabrous martinet of a tutor had not forced me to with those damned cognitive prods. However, if you want knowledge of the Ectoplasmic Erotisms I would gladly help."

The wizard tiredly raises his now slumping shoulders. "Stop these protestations of ignorance, Tscaotl-Tscualtl, or I shall begin the incantation that confines you to the crystal cell."

"Still, I know nothing of this matter. Why summon me, a lowly serf among the haughty aristocracy of Daemon-kind, when your omnipotence could conjure any of a hundred-thousand more knowledgeable and useful servants—I take no interest in these trifling planetoids: you could raise Flwyrth-Phlhohin, the Musty Tome, to confer this obscure lore, or possibly Wheaecvc-Hwaeivc, the Impalpable Intellect, he would surely know the trivial human lore you seek—he has rather specialized in the asteroids and meteorites that plummet through this paltry continuum of yours—but surely you realize that I know nothing about the subject, and yet you draw me here, threaten me with an unending display of hideous, nauseating human forms, while my harem languishes. Truly your impudence knows no bounds!"

Phfuottuor turns to the wizard and says, "He seems not to know indeed—and pity his unfortunate concubines. Have you tried the other Daemons whom he mentions? They do, in fact, sound much more likely to know of this subject."

Memzain Zhulothrique answered, "I have tried all the Daemons listed in all of the grimoires available—which means all the grimoires that exist. I left this tower of putrescence until last precisely because of his reputed stupidity and ignorance. Of all Daemons, he combines the greatest stultitiousness with the least interest in human matters."

"And yet, a little torture may perhaps persuade him that he knows more than his reputation suggests . . . perhaps the psychical strictures would produce results?"

"Maybe they would at that, though I believe that I have monished him with his greatest fear. Yet, perhaps further monitions would carry greater suasion—no, I fear this Daemon knows as little as he claims—one so monomaniacal in erotic pursuits would not know arcana concealed even from the most magisterial intellects among the Daemon-worlds, we will have to . . ."

Tscaotl-Tscualtl shook slightly, twitched, and withdrew himself into a regular column. Mouths opened, evenly spread on his towering body. Then his entire body shuddered in a heaving spasm, a thick, chunky, yellow liquid spurted from each of the mouths, and an acidulous pool formed inside the circle of cabochons, fuming clouds of noxious vapor.

"Human, your gruesome visage has unstomached me," says the Daemon, "Now release me from this prison while my sanity yet remains—I can tolerate this torture no longer."

"Well, the Daemon's noxious exhalations have dissuaded me from further inquisition. Such noisomeness belongs not in a human world but in such a harem as Tscaotl-Tscualtl normally frequents—I understand that certain of their—refinements—involve such substances." And he spoke the cantrip that released the Daemon Vavasor to his wonted pleasures.

The wizard then invited the homunculus to accompany him to his cactus pleasance to further ponder and discuss the question that vexed him so. They passed out of the conjuration chamber's highly-arched entrance, through hallways in which colon- nades of carven monstrosities stood—between them hung arrases bedight with patterns of geometrical recomplication, up through spiral stairwells, across balustrades of orichalch, and finally out upon a roof of the mage's enormous palace. In this garden walkways lead in radial paths through a forest of cactuses—here stand branching, spidery, octopoidal cactuses of an orange hue that shades into red or yellow; there stand thin, wispy cactuses that strain upwards, a bluish purple color. The two strolled along a walkway for some distance, then sat together upon a stone bench.

The wizard, Memzain, speaks: "I have searched long for this knowledge, but at the last I fail." And he rests his face on his hands.

"You know, for a surety, that you have summoned all of those Daemons who may own the lore you seek, and that you have fully employed all modes of persuasion and monition in order to suitably encourage their compliance?"

"I have not just summoned all who might know—I have summoned all. Admonitions I derived from the compendia and grimoires, careful to balance all fears the Daemons feel to ensure the most effective threats; we can feel sure that they have all complied to the best of their ability. So none knows anything of Vyin; I remain in ignorance; nothing now will sate my querulous quest for knowledge."

"Let us, then, reexamine the problem. Please give me a brief résumé of the subject, so that I may further ponder on the matter and seek a solution."

"Very well, though I should have thought that you understand all the problem's particulars as well as I. The Seventh Parchment of Sigils, as you know well, merely lists Vyin in its enumeration of planets resident beyond the purplish nebula

Oo'ou'an, and provides no further specification. The only elaboration that I have found—which means the only elaboration that exists—occurs in the fifth through thirteenth recensions of the Cyclopaedic Codices of Hantwu, the Scholastic Haranguer—no earlier recensions exist, but we have little reason to think they might contain more. But let me just read the passage." Memzain here reaches into his robes, and withdraws his hand, holding an unbound sheaf of manuscript pages.

"I see you keep the matter close at hand."

"You have known that very well for some decades. But to the matter." And the mage begins to read: "'To add further to our list of known worlds, we employ the catalog that occurs in the Seventh Parchment of Sigils, that hoary tome of antiquated Orphlazar, and find there . . .' Hantwu now lists each of the several dozen in its turn, and he gives detailed information on climate, geography, arcane sciences, history, and other such things, drawn from all of the relevant authorities and source material.

"When we reach Vyin, however, we find only this: 'Anent the antepenultimate name, Vyin, little has come to light, and less that remains unmysterious. The only reference derives from that well-known expert on ultraterrene matters Gnyihl-Whull-Ahlassahd, the ultra-mundivagant. This supreme garnerer of knowledge tells us naught but that, while in search of this uncharted planet, he found nor planet nor knowledge, but only this account, inscribed on a parchment used as mummy wrapping: "I, Cshozsisc, have spent decades in search of Vyin. But find it—I have not found it, nor has any that I know. On Quilvin, in the pyramidic temple of the Forgotten Deities, certain resident scholars have reconstructed fragmentary cuneiform tablets to read—among other tentative possibilities that include a business ledger of merchants who dealt in rare narcotic herbs, a booklet of recipes for edible insects, reputedly tasty in the extreme, and an account of an erotic encounter with Tscaotl-Tscualtl so alarmingly vivid as to freeze the blood in one's veins—they report that the scholar who produced this reconstruction smashed his tablets in horror and then hanged himself in desperation—one can also reconstruct this tablet, I say, to narrate how a certain Chtaol-Schtoiol visited certain four-winged, fulvous creatures who had arrived on his planet from none knows whither, and with choral voices that buzzed in an odd harmony among them, said, 'Yes, we have travelled thither and back, on our extravagant journey. Past the starry void blackness and obscurely purple clouds twirls the planet Vyin, and the tiresome voyage there left us much the wiser. For we found but...' And here the text breaks off, and after this lacuna—of indeterminate length—the text resumes: 'so that we returned across the starry void, to tell all who wish to know what we discovered, that they may know themselves, and thus knowing...' And here the text ends. And I have here recorded this that you also may have this knowledge." Thusly ends the account of Gnyihl-Whull-Ahlassahd, and Hantwu can add nothing more to this.' Needless to say, the referenced works do not survive, and the identity of the alien entities I cannot decipher, since all four-winged, star-faring entities seem rather to appear in violet, blue-red, or greenish hues. Lack of sufficient information thus frustrates my ambition and severs my quest."

"Since you cannot then succeed, you have little choice but to return to the divertissements that once enthralled you. You spent decades of study and toil to gain those diversions, then spent longer in their enjoyment, but then grew tired of them, tossed them away, and began this insane quest for knowledge of cosmic trivia. Perhaps you have now spent long enough away from your former diversions to regain the joy that they once brought you. No harm, at least, could come from the attempt. I fear that unlike the Daemon Vavasor Tscaotl-Tscualtl your harem has languished without you to the point of dying in senility, though the guards posted may not have left them totally unsatisfied in the time you spent chaste. In any case, your favored succubae await the proper summons—you still remember that formula, I wager."

The mage sighs, then answers wearily, "Yes, I remember. But I can no longer derive amusement from such trifles—this perplexing question vexes me to distraction in all such matters, leaving neither I nor any assistant satisfied at the outcome."

"Ah. Well, in that case, might I suggest a recent invention of mine: the Phantasmagorium."

"Ah, now I see why you didn't companion me in many of my invocations. I thought perhaps you had discovered an homunculette."

"Such a pleasant whimsy. But to describe this fantastic invention, a device guaranteed to serve as a source of well-nigh endless pleasure and amusement to all highly cultured individuals. The Phantasmagorium—a set of alembics and other chemical devices, so situated that the person so fortunate as to have seated himself inside, feels gently wafting over him various perfumes, sent across by several imps who place appropriate chemicals in befitting amounts, mix them, set them afire as needed, and work bellows to blow this array of perfumes across the fortunate customer's face. But a special ingredient produces the sublime aesthetic effect, an effect which this device, and only this device, can deliver—a synaesthetic drug causes each perfume to simultaneously produce a corresponding musical note, a corresponding visual form realized in striking and iridescently vivid color, and thus this marvelous machine produces the combined effects of a perfectly matching symphony, a kaleidoscopic visual display, and an ingenious olfactory arrangement. The whole creates an astonishing, remarkably sensuous pleasure, breath-taking and sublime, heretofore not only unrealized but undreamt of."

Memzain Zhulothrique turned away, sighed, let his eyes drop across the expanse of cactuses, then rested his elbows on his lap and his forehead on his hands. "I can no longer bear this agony of ignorance. Your invention would no more distract me than the death of a tick on a dog several thousand furlongs distant."

Phfuottuor brightened, jerked his arms and legs like a marionette operated by an epileptic, then held his knees with his hands and said, "We have left one possibility. You do have a way—it will, I admit, take some centuries, but you seem quite ready to endure some boredom to obtain your goal—we shall simply travel to Vyin—the tomes you quoted have given enough specification as to the planet's whereabouts that we could readily find it, I believe."

* * * * *

The impact of landing sent a gentle shudder through the shimmering, egg-shaped craft that slowly woke the magician and his diminutive companion from their age-long slumber. After his consciousness had fully cut through the haze of drowsiness that bound it, the mage opened a slit in the thick membrane that surrounded him, Phfuottuor did likewise, and they both stepped out from the ovoid vessel onto the plateaued surface of Vyin. Memzain looked down and saw that a thin grey dust covered the ground. Scanning back and forth across the landscape, nothing met his eyes but a barren field of flat, grey dust. Realization cut through his mind like a glacier slicing through a fjord. He turned to look at the homunculus, then turned back, sighed, put his hand to his chin and stared outward across the void and vacant expanse of ashen, grey, powdered monotony.

Meat

Rick hesitated for a moment in front of the matter compiler before ordering a steak, medium rare, topped with carrots and onions, made from a female human ass—that portion of the human anatomy which is, as everyone knows, universally acknowledged by gourmets to exceed all others in succulence and sweetness. Not even the breasts, tender and flavorful as they are, can approach the human posterior in the esteem of those inclined towards such refined repasts.

Waiting for the matter compiler to produce the meal, a slightly bored feeling mingling itself with anticipation, Rick looked about the room, which over the course of the last few months he had slowly decorated according to his own novel inspirations. Using the matter compiler, he had replaced nearly every item of furniture with one derived from some portion of the human anatomy—lampshades of human skin, a coffee table with borders and legs of human bone, the top of the walls ornamented with festoons of human vertebrae linked by hanging skulls.

He knew that he had no reason to worry that anyone would ever discover this unusual ornamentation, for it was a rare day on which he had any cause to come into real-world contact with another human being, and there was certainly no call for anyone to visit him in his apartment. As computer-mediated connectivity had increased, physical contact had decreased at an equal rate, until Rick, who could not only communicate with any human being in the world at a moment's notice, but also realize a reasonable salary doing so, had not laid eyes upon one in years, and had no expectation of undergoing such an unpleasant experience any time soon. He could instead devote himself to actions over which he alone stood as judge and jury.

But fantasy feeds upon itself, and grows ever in intensity, so that dreams of the oddest atrocities soon replace the more moderate imaginings with which one begins, in a sequence that resembles an asymptotic line ever approaching closer and closer to the infinite. Likewise, the urge of fantasy to become reality mounts higher and higher until it becomes insatiable and *some* attempt must be made to satisfy it, even though it will never be extinguished. In the past, such efforts had almost invariably met with failure, due to the likelihood of such actions drawing unfavorable attention from one's fellow beings, but technology, it seemed, had finally caught up with desire, and at least some small modicum could be actualized. It was, of course, likely enough that this would soon give place to stronger desires, but in the meanwhile, one could make the most of what was currently within reach.

Once his plate had appeared, the sweet meat on it dripping with juice as if hot from the oven, he poured some wine into a cup made from a human skull, and sat himself down on a chair whose seat was made of human skin, only stopping on the way for a brief second to savor the aroma emanating from the roast. He put the plate and cup on a tv-tray—the only thing of any use that had ever resulted from the invention of that obsolete technology.

After seating himself, he issued a pair of commands to the room. The false windows on the walls, displaying animated scenes of a picturesque countryside, complete down to tiny sailboats drifting lazily along on the river below and minuscule picnickers feasting on the bank, that bore no detectable resemblance to the smog-choked cityscape which stood outside, faded away into nothingness. Within seconds the whiteness of the wall was replaced with a procession of nude women that formed a perfect ring around the room. Life-sized and perfect down to the minutest detail, they had been handpicked from galleries containing hundreds of thousands of available images, drawn from real and imaginary models, and in many cases specially modified in order to further accommodate his personal preferences.

As he began carving into the steak with a knife whose handle was made of human bone, the rectangular ring of women shifted into motion, floating effortlessly into the air, each one linking itself to the next, and they all began simultaneously tonguing and sucking and rimming, fingering and frigging and fisting, as if they intended to exhaust every possible permutation of erotic activity. Savoring the taste as he slowly chewed on the first morsels of human flesh that he had cut from the steak, and noting what a fine complement the onions and carrots made to its flavor, he stared fixedly at the walls, ever shifting about in an endless orgy. As he did so, his thoughts linked the toothsome mouthful playing over his tastebuds with the rotating ring of images impacting on his eyeballs.

He began to wonder more and more what the woman from whom the steak had come had looked like. This was of course a fanciful notion, for the meat had not really come from a live human body, but it was not an *entirely* fanciful notion, for the matter compiler was meticulous in its attention to detail, and if it was called upon to create an artifact derived from a human being, it would do so complete in every respect, right down to each strand of DNA. And that genetic code, of course, would determine the appearance of the individual possessing it.

Seeing a chance to heighten his enjoyment, he called out a few commands to the computer, and it began chugging away on this new problem, attempting to fully digest the information it gleaned from the matter compiler. After a brief delay, one section of the wall cleared for a second, breaking the ring of women, which stopped rotating around him like a carnal carousel, and the image of an adult, perfectly formed carrot appeared in front of his eyes. Computers sometimes take orders in an overly literal fashion, and rather than spend even longer attempting to word his commands correctly, he waited impatiently, figuring to himself the gorgeous outlines and gracious curves which he knew such a sumptuous feast must imply, while the computer calculated every cell of the perfect onion that added so magnificently to the flavor. He knew, knew, that he could expect an image more delightfully arousing than any he had before experienced, that the broken ring encircling him, floating in perpetual freefall, would pale to nothing beside it. There could be nothing that would heighten the excitement of eating her ass more than gazing upon her animated form, watching as the muscles flexed and relaxed beneath the soft white skin in recurrent ecstasies.

At last, at long last the onion faded and another form slowly took shape. Rick stared at this shape long and hard. It was familiar—too familiar—and he shuddered with *déjà vu*. He had seen this woman before, and it did not take long to recognize her. For he had, like everyone else, had the curiosity to see what he would have looked like if certain genetic accidents and life circumstances had been different, and there before him stood his own reflection, perfectly nude and accurate down to microscopic detail, transliterated into the opposite sex.

Before he could stop to think, the contents of his stomach leapt from their place and an acidic trail of wine and gravy, filled with gobbets of half-digested human flesh, swept down his shirt and pants onto the floor, which swiftly signaled to him that its detectors indicated that it might require cleaning. As he stared in disgust, each of the images on the walls faded away, soon to be replaced with his own female reflection, and he studied each contour, each curve and each motion, as their feet floated above the floor, and they once again began rotating from right to left in the same perverse bacchanalia in which the previous set had engaged.

In a state of profound absent-mindedness resembling the moment immediately after orgasm, Rick speared another piece of steak with his fork and slowly drew it up and into his mouth.

Ÿ

Change not the Barbarous Names of Evocation, for they are Sacred Names in every language which are given by God, having in the Sacred Rites a Power Ineffable.
— *The Chaldaean Oracles of Zoroaster*

If I had the slightest suspicion that this manuscript could convey any real sense of the events which it attempts to portray, I would consign it to the fireplace's flames on the spot. *I—I*—how that monstrous word brings solace when placed in comparison with that portentous term, which so recently has intruded upon my awareness: *Ÿ*! It is perfectly true that identity and the universe are a mad and a maddening nightmare; but they nonetheless remain infinitely preferable to the horror awaiting the one who—*wakes up.*

I had driven into the city to do some research at the University Library, when I found myself detoured onto an unfamiliar by-street because of roadwork. Winding through the labyrinthine tangles of one-way streets placed at odd angles to one another, I soon lost my bearings, and so I kept a keen eye out for any way back to the main route. Before long I noticed a bookstore, which I hadn't heard of previously, even though I had ransacked the entry in the Yellow Pages; this made the shop doubly intriguing, because—despite the fact that I had never suspected its existence—it had a look of great familiarity, as if I had haunted its stacks innumerable times. I circled around the block, found a convenient parking spot almost directly in front of the store, and left the white Mirage to await my return. The storefront had a large sign that read simply *Books*, with many lesser notices: "rare and antique", "new and used", "foreign language", "searches performed—no commitment to buy", and so forth, grouped around in disarray. It looked as though many volumes lay in piles on the shelves flanking the windows, but the aeons of accumulated dust that clouded the panes prevented any surety on the matter.

Steeling myself, I pulled the door out and entered. The stacks immediately attracted me, and I headed through them as though drawn by a magnet. Something in me became suspicious at this feeling, and I realized where I seemed to recognize this bookshop from. For it appeared to be the very bookshop that appears in those recurrent dreams, in which you (I say *you*, for I have every reason to believe that everyone, and not merely I, experiences this recurrent dream—though perhaps some few have the good fortune not to recall it upon awakening), in which you, I say, discover—while winding through some area of the city you thought you knew intimately—a bookstore you had never so much as suspected. When you enter that store, you find that it contains, scattered amidst works you know by hearsay but have no intention of reading, many beguiling volumes which remain inaccessible to you in waking life: you may finally find books seven through twenty-four of Edmund Spenser's *Faërie Queene*, in a finely-bound three volume set; or it may be, Jean-Paul Rossignol's *Origins of a World War*; or perhaps Linwood Asshton-Urquhart's *Fast Rots the Corpse*. You may even discover, if your mind conspires with the exigencies of an unequal fatality, that dark and unwholesome repository of soul-shattering revelations, the *Necronomicon*! In every case—and the individual volumes discovered may differ in some cases from those named here—you read from the tome, heedless of the dangers involved in such an undertaking, and when the unspeakable contents of that text shock you into wake-fulness, you strain and strive to recall even a fragment of the tiny portion you had managed to scan in that peril-fraught mo-ment—for even so little as a couplet (published, not without os-tentation, under your own name—for everyone agrees, in accordance with the facts of the matter, but against all apparent verisimilitude, in crediting the contents of a dream to its dreamer) should enable you to make your literary fortune, so long as the agents of sanity do not pay you the attention which your writ-ings would seem to call for. In every case—you fail to recall so much as a couplet, but even single names derived from this source have served as the corner-stones allowing for the con-struction of world-renowned masterpieces.

Now that I had found myself in such a position, I vowed that I would—at long last—bring back with me some fragment of the Oneiric Grimoire, but first tested to see whether I was, in fact, dreaming. It seemed to me that I was not; but the mind can play strange tricks in dreams, and I inclined to take the view that I must have been dreaming: did not the mere presence of this shop prove it well enough?

By the time I had resolved these meditations I had reached the back wall of the shop, and my vision honed in on a particular volume. Jammed edgewise between the *Collected Correspondence XXIII* of H.P. Lovecraft and the *Noctuary of Tine*, only a single letter on the tome's must-covered surface was legible, metalli-cally glinting through the dust: *Ÿ*. What, I thought, could this volume be? Surely, not many words or names include the letter *y* with a diæresis! Had I stumbled upon some unheard-of pica-resque novel of the decadent age of Atlantis penned by Pierre Louÿs? Had I found—at long last—that fountainhead of unclean-liness, Lord Weÿrdgliffe's forbidden Gothick Romance *The Un-*

speakable? When I blew the dust off of the book's cover, it formed into a nebulous cloud that smelled—I cannot yet place that smell, save that it seems to have occurred to me at certain times in childhood; once, walking down the hall, it suddenly overtook me, and I fled from the house—that scent faded soon enough. Wiping the volume clean, I still found that nothing appeared on the cover save for that one letter: Ÿ. Opening the tome, on the title page as well there appeared nothing save that one letter: Ÿ.

Inside was a jumble of letters and punctuation marks that related to no language I knew; it seemed as if the volume had been checked out of Borges' Library of Babel and left to gather dust in our universe, overdue and unread. But I soon descried a regularity to the groupings of letters, convincing me that it had, after all, been written in some language or other, or perhaps encoded by some waggish author. And as I stood there, scanning the first pages, it seemed beyond doubt that I had a vague remembrance of that unknown tongue, and that with only a minimal effort at translation I could clearly espy its import. Now (and I had wholly forgotten that I was dreaming by this point), I determined that I must purchase that old book. As I checked inside the front cover for a price, only blankness returned my gaze. I walked up to the front of the store; there, at the counter, an old man sat motionless, seeming to have an even greater coating of the dust than the books surrounding him in haphazard heaps.—I had hurried in to the back of store so quickly that I hadn't even noted his presence at the front.

I pointed out the absence of price on the volume. He nodded, taking the book, and gave it a thorough once-over with his eyes. He then stated that if the book had no price on it, and that if I desired it—for it seemed to him that no one else should find such an obscure and unreadable volume of use—than the volume belonged to me and I should take it free of charge. I thanked him hurriedly and departed, to rush home in a mad ride beneath over-hanging streetlights, which reflected off of the single metallic letter on the leather cover of the book on the passenger seat next to me; that single letter seemed to arouse infinite repercussions of interpretation in my subconscious.

To my surprise, when I awoke the next morning the book sat there patiently awaiting me on the kitchen table. From that day on I gave every spare moment to its deciphering, working around my job hours at the school. More and more it took on a determinate character; what had before seemed mere jumbles of letters—"*Bhr'gg'h àull tnoc, gnah ssahf 'ph'rgh-ú qööqh c'ul; vitc-ú-fh gnaghn bhr'nöc' yeq-ú, gnhà-odh irjc!*"—took on a greater and greater consistency of meaning. Never could I tell whether I had truly found some hidden source of memory enabling me to interpret that writing, or whether I had simply invented a novel language consistent with the random markings inscribed therein. I found—accepting the hypothesis that I had in actuality discovered the code governing that phantasmagoria of phraseology—that the book concerned the nature of some obscure deity, whose nature could not be inscribed in words, but whose reality one could only glimpse directly. Nevertheless, the tome consisted of systems of symbolism designed to depict this god, which the unknown writer or writers seemed to consider the most blasphemous horror imaginable.

In its matter the book concerned various oblique conceptions including "the maze of broken mirrors" (*mrc-ú hwf tcol'-ssgn qïphfh-ú*)—from which the god, referred to only as $\ddot{Y}$, had eloigned Itself in the most primordial eras of existence, but which still comprised an infinite number of broken and distorted reflections, continuously bounding from looking-glass to looking-glass; a system of imbricated and overlapping spheres of time and space from which the god was absent, but in which It nevertheless lurked between the inspissated interstices of matter, ever ready to obliterate the real with Its prismatic return; and the cornerstone of the kaleidoscopic imageries contained in those lines, the vision of the Great God Ÿ (as the Book terms It: "*Gnööc'hh Ÿ Rgifhv-ú*") as an enormous mass of plastical ooze, situated at the most primal aeons before time came into existence, constantly creating an ever-changing multitude of brains and eyes and tongues and other organs in its idiocy, which in turn, ever shifting and mutating, split Itself into a nearly infinite number of lesser creatures which—the Book darkly hints—became the remotest ancestors of all lifeforms in existence in an orgy of promiscuous self-copulation and masturbatory miscegenation, thus creating life as if from the dehiscent matrix of Chaos.

None of these conceptions conveyed their object to me with any force, and I felt convinced that if only I could decipher one certain particularly difficult sentence, the mystery would be solved and I could pride myself on full understanding: "*Gnah Ÿ fth-tconcih-ú; gnah Ÿ ss'gahfw-ú; ybh gnah Ÿ fth-brhööq'qh-ú.*" I imagined my future fame when I had published this obscure mystery and its solution; now I only wish that I had managed to once again discover the bookstore where I obtained that volume; no amount of searching through the city's maze of alleys and backstreets has availed in its discovery; I have not even discovered traces of the road-work being performed that afternoon. It does not bode well that the bookstore has not made another appearance.

Every night for endless weeks I spent endless hours in my study, essaying new combinations of semantic givens to the lexemes I discerned in the word-divisions of those lines, applying recherché twists of syntax to the construction of phrases and sentences; my efforts at researching a thesis on the use of reduced metadiegetic narration and pseudo-iterative frequency by weird fantasy writers of the early twentieth century wholly fell by the wayside; I left my social life to languish, living as a her-

mit; and I devoted no more time to my job than the bare mini-
mum amount that I felt possible, which did not exceed the
estimates made by my superiors. At long last, I succeeded in
translating the final sentence; not through any skill in linguis-
tics, but because direct experience of the god known only as Ÿ
came upon me—as I settled in to my bedsheets in utter exhaustion
after hours expended in futile attempts to parse that final line, an
overwhelming epiphany overcame my fatigue-crushed and febrile awareness.

Now, after that revelation, they seem to me not a horror but
a consolation: the God of the Gnostics, Ialdabaôth, who created
the universe of matter in his idiocy, as a blind blunder, and from
which Jesus-Satan will redeem us if only we should rebel vio-
lently enough; the Urizen and Nobodaddy of William Blake, who
represent the principle of reason and restriction; that nightmare
vision of Lautréamont's Maldoror, who looked up to the heavens
only to see—enthroned on a mound of gold and human excrement, clothed in unwashed hospital linens, with before him an
enormous chamberpot, from which, every so often, he would
snatch a human, swimming in that filth like a tapeworm, between
his first two toes, and bring the unfortunate one to his mouth, be-
spattering his beard with the man's brains—the one who calls
himself the Creator; or the Azathoth of H.P. Lovecraft, the blind
idiot at the center of ultimate Chaos, the mad daemon-sultan on
his strangely-environed throne around which unseen shapes flop
and flutter to the whining of a cracked flute clutched in a furry
paw. These all seem to me now a consolation, not a horror, for
they all remain, as Lautréamont's Maldoror so aptly termed it, the
Great External Object.

For when I slipped into my bed, and pulled the covers up, I
seemed to perceive the universe as it really was, not as it appeared, and that revelation of unholiness struck with an overwhelming force of conviction. The experience I had then cannot

be transcribed in words, its characteristics violate the characteristics of language so wholly, communication depending as it must on webs of differentiation and grids of polar opposition. For as I lay there, an enormous, singular and undivided viscous unhallowedness and unholiness slowly replaced myself, and engulfed the bed, and then the room, and crept out like what I would term a *flash of darkning* if I only had the linguistic boldness to coin such an outré neologism, until it had consumed the entire universe of rotating planets and dying suns and spiraling nebulae and galaxies slowly winding down in a corkscrew maelstrom into absolute entropy; and nothing but that cloudy unholiness remained of the shattered dust of the indefinite cosmoses and I found my identity wholly at one with the primordial abomination which had never died but remained gibbering in Its utter horror at Its own evil entity—the god known only as Ÿ. And everywhere in Ÿ there reeked that uncanny and unwholesome stench that I had sensed on that long-forgotten time in my childhood, that the dust on the Book had smelled of, that the man in the bookstore had smelled of, that foetor that the Book itself had smelled of, which has come to accompany my awareness more and more, invading my consciousness like the din of leaden, ghoul-tolled funereal bells, and that odor which now permeated the entirety of existence in Its inexpugnable redolence of all-pervading rankness and pungency.

For the conception outlined in that unspeakable book repeated one known to earthly mystics with but a single significant variation. We all know those among the mystics who outline their view of the universe as one of monistic pantheism, who assure us that we need only sheer away the veneer of illusion to experience our absolute oneness with God and His creation, who avow that all division is but appearance; they devote their lives to eliminating that fall into a transitory world of suffering. By contrast, the sect of the Great God Ÿ (and we all secretly celebrate

the mysteries of this sect, though some few remain mercifully unaware of the fact), as revealed in the volume bearing the name,
holds to what one can only refer to as a *monistic pandiabolism*,
and believe that the underlying non-illusory substratum of all
entity has the nature of infinite evil, of an illimitable abyss of
universal corruption, of a cosmic cloaca of cataract cacophony
forever draining inward on itself, of an ineradicable uncleanliness which entire universes could not serve to conceal. Further,
they exceed the mystics of earth in the cogency of their speculations, for those of religious inclination ever assume the goodness
of their God, leaving little motivation for His fall into a state of
disgraceful separation and suffering; they seldom do better than
to term the matter a "question not tending towards enlightenment."

The Avatars of Ÿ (they are no less than that, for none of us
are; those most aware of the fact perhaps deserve the title), on the
other hand, know full well the reason why the Great God Ÿ would
create a universe—any universe, however nightmarish and ridden
with the keenest of anguish. For nothing could exceed awareness
of Its own being, Its own uncleanness, Its own evilness, and so
the Great God Ÿ formed a species of excreta from Itself, endowing
each of these encrustations with some small portion of Its own
consciousness, thus decreasing Its suffering at Its own overwhelming horror; but however much It creates in this way, It remains as infinite as before (for subtracting an infinity from an
infinity still leaves another infinity), and so It madly grinds on,
forever creating Its insane kaleidoscope of dreams, spurred by the
infinite evil of Its own existence which It ceaselessly fails to escape, not unlike an insane Ouroboros Worm which never does
succeed in finally obliterating itself from the universe of matter.

It will—alas!—do no good to destroy this manuscript, for despite the fact that I shall show it to no one, at the mad and cor-
rupted core of things, like the Book Itself, everyone shall read it.

For that final sentence, whose translation had given me so much incomparable trouble—"*Gnah Ÿ fth-tconcih-ú; gnah Ÿ ss'gahfw-ú; ybh gnah Ÿ fth-brhööq'qh-ú.*"—means nothing other than: "Ÿ is the Author; Ÿ is the Book; Ÿ is, as well, the Reader."

The Dying God

The snug relationship between occult fantasy and the actual practice of the occult is well established in history. Writers such as H.P. Lovecraft and Edgar Rice Burroughs, progenitor of the Tarzan and Jane tales, were practicing occultists.

—Carl Raschke, *Painted Black.*

I.

The old man turned his goateed face to the three women in the room with him. He nodded wearily, showing the greyed streaks running through his hair, and said: "Have you found a replacement for me?"

One of the women answered: "Yes. It took little searching this time."

"And did you invent another religion? I find this race has grown skeptical of the gods I have been in the past, and no longer bow in obeisance to Ung'gll-Tchtchrrl, or Yeb-Tsath, or Dumuzi the Shepherd, or Aqhat, or Atys, or Cernunnos the Cimmerian, or Iacchus, or Hou, or Janicot, the Master of the Forest, or the many others I no longer recall. One would never have suspected how the aeons weigh on one."

The second of the women spoke: "Yes, we had to invent a

new mythology in accordance with the age."

"Even further from the facts, I assume? It seems, with the rise of science, that humans require even greater divergence from the real for their beliefs to carry conviction."

The third: "No. By some strange irony, we could alter the truth ever so slightly in this case. We had only to change one detail in our story for it to become utterly credible to the one chosen as your replacement. It seems that some of the Elder Lore which has leaked out into human ken has reached certain writers of weird fantasy, who have incorporated it in a rationalized form for use in their more outré novelettes, bringing it closer to the truth in the process."

The man scratched his chin with his thumbnail: "Strange. Very strange."

II.

Just what has caused the odd transformation in the personality of Linwood Asshton-Urquhart no one can, at present, say. His parents, who no longer accept him as their son—a sentiment which seems to give him no displeasure—have refused to turn over to him his old manuscripts and papers. The police decline to investigate a case for which, they assert, no evidence exists—as the former leader of the cult seems merely to have moved, and upon request Lin has produced letters of recent date in his handwriting, although their experts declare that they show signs of difficult or painful inscription; the answer that the elder had a degenerative disorder of the nerves has sufficiently removed any lingering doubts on the matter. The Anti-Cult Lucidity Organization, on the other hand, has openly proclaimed its belief in sinister shenanigans and unsavory goings-on; but they too find themselves stymied in the attempt to get to the heart of the matter. In consequence, they have resolved to search out the mystery on behalf of the young poet's parents; but they have expressed their conviction that deprogramming will not work in such a case, for it displays strange features not usual to induction into an obscure sect.

These then, are the facts as summarized from the interviews and documents which the investigators have succeeded in obtaining. Linwood Whitmarsh Urquhart was born on April 30, 1974, to Robert Aldridge Urquhart and his wife, Coral Urquhart, née MacGregor. He was their only child, and three years after his birth they moved from Port Townshend, Washington to Rainier, Oregon. The youngster showed precocious leanings, and had learned to read by the age of five. Full perusal of the works of writers such as Maturin, Poe, Lautréamont, Lovecraft, and many another of that eldritch ilk, had been accomplished by his eighth year. A favorite he found in a novel by his indirect ancestor, Lord Weÿrdgliffe, the proscribed Gothick Romance *The Unspeakable*, which he read over and again in an inherited copy of the unexpurgated edition of 1796. At this point his parents began to worry for his sanity, fearing morbid inclinations on his part, for neither of them had read more than the first chapters of a work by a precursor who they took no great pride in owning, as his ideas and images frequently proved too shocking to bear; they did not even suspect that their son would later change his name in honor of his forebear.

Nothing, however, proved capable of altering the interests the boy showed for such uncanny works, and in lieu of discouraging them, his father soon changed his tack and encouraged the child to pen works of his own. By the age of thirteen the boy had amassed a good deal of verse and prose, and at fourteen set down to definitively polish his finest selections for publication. His inclinations towards the macabre, together with his shyness and social awkwardness, had led to a total loss of popularity on his part, almost amounting to a complete shunning; and when, to compound the problem, he began to suffer from insomnia, which lead to his drifting off to sleep in class, from which he would quickly awaken screaming in horror at the bizarre nightmares which incessantly besieged him, his father, reasoning that he could make a living from his writing—which had begun to sell—allowed him to drop out of high school.

But it proved impossible for him to earn money at his chosen career, as the small-press journals which accepted his work paid only in copies or a meager pittance; and even when his poems appeared gathered together into a collection entitled *Fast Rots the Corpse* he saw no significant returns, nor did his chapbook of three short stories, *Lords of Atlantis*, provide any meaningful funds. His father now soon tried to convince him to return to school, and over the teenager's protests, which repeated many times the comments of critics who had compared his work to that of such figures as Baudelaire, Justin Geoffrey, Clark Ashton Smith (with whom he claimed distant relation), and Thomas Ligotti, he soon succeeded in convincing the University of Oregon to admit him as a student on a probationary status, in spite of his checkered academic past; for he indisputably showed great promise.

So it was that Linwood Asshton-Urquhart, as he now styled himself in life as well as on paper, enrolled as a French major, hoping to gain—so he said—a greater understanding of the Decadents, Frenetics, and Hydropaths. His story there has had to be pieced together from the accounts of such of his fellow students as could be located. Lin moved into the dormitory Carson Hall at the beginning of Winter Term in 1993, taking a single room. There, he failed utterly at making friends; his social gaucherie precluded any starts he attempted with the bulk of the population, while in any case he felt little interest in such mundane personalities; he found that the hippies—of which Eugene has a substantial number to this day—shared a little bit of his occult leanings, but inclined too far to the optimistic for his taste;

he maintained ties with a few members of the lower strata, not all of them students, but merely local teenagers, for the purposes of carnal gratification; but even in the latter cases, he found no spiritual companions, and generally kept the relationship strictly to the matter at hand. In all cases, he had a tendency to frighten away any who displayed interest in him, by allowing them to read his still-unfinished novel, *The Silver Succubus*, which hints darkly at extra-dimensional realms accessible through obscene ceremonies and practices, and of *what* answers the calls sent to those nameless regions. In all fairness, that work's blasphemy-tainted enormities would shock even the jaundiced libertines of a Marquis de Sade into a semblance of sanity and sobriety.

The poet succeeded fairly well as a student, earning steady *A*s and *B*s, though he occasionally missed class due to attacks of insomnia and nightmare. Despite having made no friends, he declared that he preferred that setting to his hometown, and stayed there through Summer Term. Not long into Fall Term, a group of three women, known for often frequenting the University even though they seemed never to take any courses there, had heard vague rumors of his novel-in-progress, which had become something of a sensation on the gossip circuit, and sought out the young man. These women disturbed most of the other students who paid them any attention, for their facial features seemed to betray an inexplicable mix of races in their ancestry; and while they all appeared—at first glance—quite youthful, whenever you would look into their eyes they would seem to betray the burden of aeons unknown to the entire human race. Little could be learned of them, save that the young writer had told those who inquired about them that their names were Yiangh, Mlaon, and Nhaovin. They had laughed, exchanging knowing glances, when asked the nationality of those names. Many had found themselves attracted to them, only to find their erotic emotions tinged with an unwelcome eeriness. Indeed, if not for their fey personalities, they would have become the sexual idols of the fraternity houses; but their shapeliness was over-ridden by the uncanny knack they had of anticipating each other's movements, almost as if they shared a single mind.

It will not be wondered at that Lin took to them immediately, and a letter from this time reveals that when they discovered his study of French, they told him that they had once lived in Averoigne, and would gladly speak French, whenever with him, to give him the practice he would need. Needless to say, this rendered their conversations wholly indecipherable to the other students, though his French Professor informed the Anti-Cult investigators that when she once overheard him and them, passing by on the street, the three used an argot which seemed to combine a great number of archaic constructions and pronunciations with a more modern lingo, as if they had stepped from the pages of Rabelais or *La Queste del Saint Graal*, and were clumsily attempting to hide the fact with an updated pattern of speech.

At this time the student seemed to become preoccupied with the ideas which these three women fed into him, and when he stopped to say a word to a passer-by in the hall or on the street, he would mumble references to such obscure conceptions as "the Elder Lore," "the kteis of the mother-goddess," "the Goat with a Thousand Young," "the primal white jelly," "wicked Voorish domes," and "the mysteries of phallic and non-phallic generation." Together with the reputation caused by even the less explicit portions of his novel (few have read any further than the first three chapters, while none seem to have perused the entire outline of the uncompleted four-fifths of the novel), these strange phrases caused speculations concerning hidden sexual activities on the part of Lin and his three companions, which the more learned among the students linked to the practices of Tantrik Yoga, pointing to the undeniably Asiatic cast visible in the women's cheekbones and coloring. Once, in particular, when he had been offered a few drags on a marijuana joint out of courtesy, he seemed to go into a sort of trance, and his mutterings about "retraining his nervous system," "what the voolas mean," "the Xu language," and "the apotheosis of the wizard-priest" had positively frightened his auditors with their unthinkable implications; whereas he, on the other hand, seemed to take a positive pleasure in mystifying them with insinuations about the reality hidden behind the immemorial allegory of Tao.

These whispered conjectures seemed to gather confirmation when, during a routine fire-drill, the Resident Assistant of the dorm opened the door to his room, which the resident had nicknamed "the Waughters" after the estates of Lord Weÿrdgliffe, his forebear in life as in literature, to make sure that he had evacuated with the others. There, to his dismay, he found Lin and one of the three women sitting motionlessly in a copulatory embrace, their concentration so intense that they could not even hear the bell, the two other women—seated separately on the room's second bed—equally melted into ecstasy. In any case, it seems certain that the young poet had taken up the practice of some sort of Ceremonial Magick, for his neighbors overheard absurd syllables echoing in the night. The Lane County Police Department's Satanism experts confirm the Anti-Cult Lucidity Organization's surmises that these incidents provide definite proof of involvement with Fantasy Role-Playing Games.

Lin's parents, hearing rumors of this activity, believed that he had merely fallen in with the wrong crowds, and that psychoactive drugs—which he had frequently, if obscurely and obliquely, mentioned in his creative lucubrations—had deleteriously affected his already unstable psyche. However, Lin's professors report that he had steadily decreased his attendance of his courses, until the school determined that he should fail his probation—which he had believed ended—for his bad grades. At this point Lin's story becomes obscure, for he moved out of the dorm and into an apartment building, the funds used to pay the rent coming from checks bearing the name Francis Tomesen. His parents, at the time, thought that he must have gotten involved in narcotics trafficking—a logical outcome of involvement with drugs—and despaired of his fate. Later investigation has shown, however, that a group of three women, who answered in most particulars to the ones who had befriended the young man, but differed in enough to preclude identity, had leased the apartment and delivered the rent-money. Anti-Cult investigators understandably consider this as proof that the obscure sect with which he had gotten involved had now wholly taken him under its wing, and they point to the events which have followed as confirmation of their views.

III.

One can now only reconstruct the novel mythology which Linwood Asshton-Urquhart learned from his tutors in the cult at this time from scattered mentionings of it in letters and notebooks (left in the possession of his parents, and not returned) of the time, and from his continued production of verses. Many of the odes and sonnets he composed during this phase take the cult's mythos for their basis, while others make passing references to it.

It seems that in the depths of space, a group of cloud-whorls in the Spiral Nebulae attained sentience. These scarlet-hued vaporous brains, referred to only as the Elder Ones, attained prodigious developments in the sciences, most especially those dealing with mental phenomena. In this department they discovered that the mental and material levels are not separate, but correlated levels, nor does one result from the other as an epiphenomenon. Rather, they result from still another level which precedes them, and only appears to become separated in the limited view of consciousness. Utilizing this knowledge, they learned the secret of immortality: the mind requires a physical body, but does not depend upon a particular physical body for its survival; rather, through appropriate manipulation of the level preceding the mental and material split, the mind can journey from one body to another, and even take up physical habitation in it. By voyaging from a senescent body to one newly-born, they found, they could ensure themselves eternal life. And this did not harm the young creature who accepted the psyche of the old, for they would merge into a single entity, thus in effect making the young one into a deity, for they would share all of the knowledge and power which the elder had gained through the aeons. The old body would be allowed to expire as an empty husk.

After many epochs, however, the Elder Ones found themselves in a situation of dire peril, for their scientists had discovered the immanence of a near-by star going nova. In unison the Elder Ones migrated en masse to the furthest race their mental probings could discover, a bulbous, semi-vegetable race inhabiting the oceanic caverns of the outermost moon of a planet that wandered sunlessly through the Ghooric Zone. At this point the Elder Ones discovered, to their dismay, that the new bodies could not produce new minds belonging to the Elder Race, but only to the race of their new hosts. For their minds did not match bodies in a one-to-one fashion, but in varying combinations depending upon the particular sexual characteristics of the race in question. At this point they began a search throughout the universe for a race which, modified through their superior technology, could produce new psyches belonging to their race, for they wished to increase and spread through the galaxies.

At this point begins a dizzying succession of host-races, of which no definite sequence can be formulated with any confidence from the scattered fragments left by Linwood Asshton-Urquhart. Most of the material here collated derives from draft fragments for a projected sonnet sequence, which apparently would have revealed the history of the Elder Race in a series of shifting, kaleidoscopic visions. There was a race of winged octopi which lived in submarine cities of doubtful geometry; the oven-tending insect people who dwelled beneath the white-hot skies of Minraud; the hermaphroditic worms that tunneled blindly through the husk of a dying sun; a fabulous, semi-fungoidal race who developed the ability to wing through the aether; the repulsive batrachian Annedoti of the Sirius system; the black, amorphous dwellers on Cykranosh who worshiped the batrachian Zhothaqquah; and many others too numerous to list. In every case, the Elder Ones devoted a great deal of attention to their attempt to re-create the race in a form which would produce new psyches conforming to their Elder Race's; for their numbers inevitably diminished greatly over the course of the aeons as the old minds died in unforeseen calamities and catastrophes: the process of body-possession required significant preparation.

In time the Elder Ones came to our solar system, at first inhabiting a coleopterous race dwelling on a trans-Plutonian planet known to occultist lore as Shaggai. When that species began to die out under invasion from a race which did not wholly conform to the properties of matter as known in this universe—a fact which made it impossible for the Elder Ones to choose them as their new vessels—the entire race migrated to the arachnid denizens of Europa's icy deserts; these spider-like poets would frequently send verses, woven into their gossamer strands, drifting into the outer abysses. The alien invaders soon attacked that residence as well, but retreated when the increased light from the sun proved harmful to them. Next, the Elder Race transported themselves to the semi-translucent, polypous inhabitants of the former planet which had its place between the earth and Mars, and which certain obscure speculations of the Theosophists refer to as Lucifer. When that planet met its unfortunate (and undescribed) fate, the Elder Ones drifted across space to earth, where they could not find any currently sentient race, but exerted their influence on the furry inhabitants of Thule to create the first *homo sapiens* which the world had known.

When the oceans had shifted and that continent lay under the waves, the seeds of culture had taken plant in the human brain. The Elder Race found it easy enough to create a place for itself, for they invented a number of cults devoted to their worship and preservation. They must remain secret, for the number of men greatly outnumbered the Elder Ones, and they knew (from bitter experience) that such a half-formed civilization easily turns against a fully sentient species, which it inevitably perceives as unknown and threatening. So the Elder Ones had each founded a cult, composed solely of the members of humanity which had received some portion of its psyche as an agent of apotheosis—for they were to men as gods—and those who could, with suitable rationalizations, be convinced to act in their interest.

Each individual of the Elder Race found itself, as at multitudinous times in the past, obliged to divide the various portions of its psyche among a group of individual bodies, composed of twelve women, who would continually re-create their living community, and a single man, who must be renewed on a regular basis, lest that portion of the Elder One die and so destroy the whole. So had they formed in prehistoric times cults composed of these members alone, and these groups had survived to the present day in a secrecy broken only infrequently.

Just such a group, it appears from notes in diary format left in the possession of the Asshton-Urquharts, had the young Linwood stumbled upon. If one can trust the surmises of the Anti-Cult Lucidity Organization, then the thirteen members of that order consider themselves but a single entity, known as Nigguratl-Yig; a name further divisible into Yig, the Father of

Serpents, a symbolic conception of the solar-phallic principle, and Shub-Niggurath, the Black Goat of the Woods with a Thousand Young, representing the female principle incarnated in a multi-bodied, self-reproducing and chthonic form.

Such a cult they find unrepresented in any of their voluminous files on those groups which they have succeeded in infiltrating. But they point to disturbing similarities between this sect and several guarded descriptions in the questionable Bridewall edition (1845) of Fvindvuf von Junzt's *Die Unaussprechlichen Kulten*, which differs greatly from the Düsseldorf edition (1839) which is known as *The Black Book*, and which gives the author's christian name as Friedrich Wilhelm; they report thinly veiled hints in the essay on Gilles de Retz in Guy-Ernest Clouët's *Les Abîmes*; while they find oblique references in that forbidden fountain of uncleanliness, Lord Weÿrdgliffe's Gothick Romance, *The Unspeakable*. The latter finding particularly disturbs Linwood's parents, for they know that he had thoroughly studied the work of his obscure ancestor, however unpleasant others might find its perusal, and that those elements which most shocked others he often found appealing. Nonetheless, the Anti-Cult Lucidity Organization maintains that all of these sources, however much the analogies may seem to illuminate the case, have been thoroughly discredited; and in this they compare them with the philosophy of a Theosophical splinter group known as the Chaosophists, who worship the blind, idiot creator-god Demogorgon, and who claim to have made telepathic contact with a reptilian conclave of immortal Lemurian hierophants, who remain entombed in the innermost sanctums of their temples at the bottom of the Indian Ocean. Their speculations about cosmic cycles and grotesque, unheard-of races display great similarity indeed to those of the unnamed sect which Lin had joined; but they have received thorough debunkings in the *Skeptical Inquisitor*, and no one can now take them seriously.

From a few letters addressed to scientific periodicals, posed in the hypothetical mode, one may infer that the Elder Ones have maintained a close connection with each other, forming in essence a world-wide network of cults, and that they have made great strides in their goal of creating bodies which can reproduce their minds. Indeed, it seems that certain recent discoveries—among them the third form of life, the Archaea—when connected in quite novel ways, render the effect virtually inevitable. Toward such a goal has the Elder Race directed human science.

IV.

Lin stood on the stone edge of the raised pool in the center of the chamber. He wore nothing but the ceremonial robes which they had provided him with. Never before had he come to this place, where he—as the God Yig, Father of Serpents—would preside over the sect; never before had he so much as met Francis Tomesen, the current incarnation of the Serpent-God; never before had he so much as met the nine women who completed the coven with the other three and their lord; never before had he so much as suspected the location of the temple, where he would rule as a Wizard-King from now on. In the old farmhouse past the edge of town, no one would overhear any of the actions occurring inside, regardless of how cacophonous.

He had thoroughly practiced his part in the upcoming ritual; the three priestesses had explained to him that while the Serpent-God could abandon its former vessel, in order to possess the new one, without the aid of the ritual, they nonetheless found that the Rite of the Shedding of the Old Skin made the transition from one host-body to another more seamless and unproblematic; the death of the old vessel they found unfortunate, but given that life after abandonment by the god had proven an unbearable burden in all previous cases, they deemed it as merciful as necessary. Imagine it, he reflected: a Walpurgisnacht orgy, on his twenty-third birthday, in which he would indeed experience a re-birth!

And so he stood, motionless, in silence, mentally reciting phrases in the Aklo language in order to enter into an alternative state of consciousness, the physical correlatives of which would aid the transition to godhood. The door opened behind him and he heard footsteps entering the room. Still, he maintained his concentration, as they had instructed him, and not a single muscle budged. Three women—whom he did not recognize, though they bore an unmistakable resemblance to the trio of Yiangh, Mlaon, and Nhaovin, brought a cloaked man to the X-shaped cross erected immediately before him. With thorny vines they tied his arms and legs to the cross, after disrobing him and leaving him naked. He was placed so that Lin could look directly into his eyes, which seemed to hold a fire that had burned since the beginning of the universe beneath its green irises and gaping pupils. One of the women took his own robe as he gazed in fascination.

Now three other groups of women entered the room, and began, in unison with the first group, to dance in an intricate pattern, chanting under their breath words and syllables of the secret tongues. Seeing them through the corners of his eyes, Lin deemed that they created such a spectacle as not even the Corybantes of the Bacchanalia could present, for they enveloped themselves in an ecstasy that utterly absorbed their awareness of the world, and yet maintained a dance in which each group of three acted as though a single person, and the four groups of three combined together into a singular unit of motion.

Faster and faster they danced, and soon they began the litany which would lead to the sacrifice. "Iä! Shub-Niggurath! The Goat with a Thousand Young!" shouted one of each three, and the other two responded as chorus: "Iä! Shub-Niggurath! The Black Goat of the Woods with a Thousand Young!" They spun dizzily around the room in innumerable permutations, each leaving its group to join another, then regrouping in varied combinations, to return to their original positions, the whirling circle of their nude bodies reflecting the light of torches through the hazes of incense and smoldering herbs, and again they cried: "Iä! Shub-Niggurath! The Goat with a Thousand Young!" and its answering echo: "Iä! Shub-Niggurath! The Black Goat of the Woods with a Thousand Young!"

The women continued their intricate dance as they continued to shout in unison; you would think them, performing that age-old rite, a coven of witches at some hellish Sabbat orbiting the ithyphallic Goat of Mendes; or ivy-chewing Maenads circling about their to-be-sacrificed god Dionysos; or the frenetic priestesses of a cavern painting come to life, readying to dismember their antlered shaman in the reddish glare of the leprous moon. All of these visions and more passed through the fantaisiste's febrile brain as he gazed upon the scene surrounding him. But he must concentrate.

Now the old god began to answer to their chants, and they correspondingly began a differently patterned dance, which seemed to Lin to reflect on certain geometric designs which occultists had found dimly reflected in the stars. "Iä! Shub-Niggurath! The Goat with a Thousand Young!" shouted the four centers of consciousness among their respective groups, and "Iä! Shub-Niggurath! The Black Goat of the Woods with a Thousand Young!" replied the eight others, twisting like the arms of an octopus, now to discover the reply "Ya-Yig! Great Father of Serpents! Lord of the Woods and the Caverns!" On and on for what seemed an eternity to the waiting youth the dancers and the crucified elder god echoed their incantatory invocations through his awareness, and he carefully counted the times that he heard the shouted "Ya-Yig! Great Father of Serpents! Lord of the Woods and the Caverns!" so that he would recognize the correct moment to begin his part in the Rite of the Shedding of the Old Skin.

In spirals the dancers spun through the clouds of reddish vapor; "Iä!"—they screamed; "Ya-Yig!" came the answer from the lips of the crucified god; and again, a third time, the litany echoed through the hall; and again, a fifth time, and a sixth—

A twenty-first time the chorus of women screamed their alien screed and the elderly man, staring into the eyes of his new shell, drooled onto his goatee as he shouted his affirmative reply; a twenty-second time, and Lin readied the dagger held in his hands; a twenty-third time, and at the precise end of the phrase, "Ya-Yig! Great Father of Serpents! Lord of the Woods and the Caverns!" he plunged the silver-embossed dagger into the guts of his old self. If anyone should discover what he was doing, they would think it murder, not understanding—But he must concentrate wholly on the ritual—The god needs perfect concentration on the prescribed thought-forms to make the most perfect transition—

Now the women whirled in a phantasmagoric frenzy around the circumference of the room, looking like galaxies in the depths of nethermost outer space. Again, the chanting resumed, and now Lin whispered, in an inaudible voice, the line which the dying god reiterated like an infernal mantra. Again, he carefully counted the number of repetitions, and when they had reached twenty-three, and his voice—which he had steadily increased in volume—had become equal to that of his predecessor, he again jabbed the dagger into him, pushing it upwards beneath the ribcage. Madness they would think it—humans are fools to think such things madness—

Once again the chanting continued. Now, the old man's voice slowly declined in volume, until, at the twenty-third and final shout of "Ya-Yig! Great Father of Serpents! Lord of the Woods and the Caverns!"—where Lin's own voice had reached a fever pitch of excitation and exaltation, he had become wholly inaudible, and at the precise split-second he had fully enunciated the phrase, the poet rammed the dagger home and left it dangling from the man's eviscerated abdomen.

The man stared directly into his eyes staring directly into his own eyes, and he felt his body recede into the distance, crossing the horizon of awareness. A momentary darkness, and he seemed to regain himself. The Serpent-Father must be taking over. He must be feeling the deity combining with himself. But what do I see?—

It took a moment to focus his eyes, which seemed somehow unresponsive to the signals his mind sent them. Even in the haze he could now make out a little. There, that body standing. Why, it looked precisely like his own!—And why did he feel such pain in his arms and his legs, and his gut—God, his gut—It felt like it had been torn apart, or wrenched out by some unknown creature's ironic claws—

Everything differed from before, colors appeared slightly different, the room smelled fainter than before, a faint ringing echoed in his ears, his body seemed ungainly and uncooperative, and there—There, his own body stood before him, now, the body fell backwards into the pool. He struggled against the thorny bonds tying him to the cross—He couldn't—

The women screamed and shouted. Now, they approached the pond and pulled the reclining body out of it, covered with a liquid he did not recognize, and a look of incurable satisfaction seemed to cross its face before it became unconscious again.

Deceived me—This wasn't the deal they described—No wonder they maintain such secrecy about the god of the cult—Black ridges against red suns—Robed forms with inhuman outlines in a desert of ashen sand—Too late now—The pain, the pain—in my chest, my gut—In my gut—Mother Hydra, they said—How much truth and how much falsehood in the stories they told?—Never know now—Never—Arms and legs—Why don't they finish me?—Merciful God in heaven!—Finish the sacrifice now—Darkness—"Ya-Yig! Great Father of Serpents! Lord of the Woods and the Caverns!"—Dying for real—The Waughters—Dark spirals of unfolding in the vaultless skies—Opening to the light of the Seven Suns and the Gate of the—Unfair—not what they said—Portal of the—"Iä! Shub-Niggurath! The Black Goat of the Woods with a Thousand Young!"—Opening—Shed skin all right—sloughed off and put new one on—in the dark spirals—spinning to the—Caverns winding down to the phosphorescent plasma of the unbegotten source—end now—they kiss his hands—light at the end—

Darkness.

V.

In light of the wholesale change in his personality, the parents of Linwood Asshton-Urquhart no longer own him as their son. They have kept all of the writings and other belongings of his left in their possession at the time of his transformation, and after it became clear that they had photocopied all documents included in his papers, he dropped his legal suit. He no longer associates with them, in expression of a mutually felt emotion, and has, after his strange metamorphosis, entirely dropped his interests in literature.

Nevertheless, the Anti-Cult Lucidity Organization has found it advisable to follow his career, but at the present date have made few significant findings. He quickly enrolled in courses dealing with scientific subjects, and has shown a predilection in class session for questioning his professors on rather arcane topics, taking any pretext he can find to shift discussion to his obsessions. The professors, however, consider him an unaccountably brilliant pupil, with an odd intuitive grasp of certain areas of novel research barely known outside of the research community. He will shortly have completed his Master of Sciences in Biochemistry, and apparently intends to pursue a Doctorate in that field.

Most importantly, or so it seems to the investigators into cult activity, he has founded a network of individuals with interests similar to his own fascinations. Many of these individuals seem to also have cult ties, although no one has yet managed to infiltrate their sects. In every case of approach, the approacher has met with a stern rebuff, as if the newly-altered Linwood Asshton-Urquhart somehow knew intuitively whether someone belonged or not. It has been determined, however, through interception of mail between the members of this hidden network, that the network publishes a newsletter entitled *The Outsiders Bulletin*, devoted to technical information relating to such subjects as the Human Genome Project; to the recently-discovered third form of life—the Archaea; to the evidence of life on Mars and Europa; to developments in the doubtful field of parapsychology, certain forms of which seem to receive an undue credulity not shown in regard to other scientific topics; to astronomy and astrophysics; to nanotechnology and especially its biotechnological implications; and to speculative interconnections between all of these arcane areas.

Indeed, one researcher has discovered a document, sent in a code, which seems to him to put beyond all doubt the sinister motives of this secretive cabal. Others have retorted that he has by no means proven that he has found the only legitimate solution to the cipher, and believe that its statements can only be taken as fortuitously meaningful, arising from sheer chance. The researcher who has put in so many painstaking hours devoted to testing varying possible solutions, however, denies that any other fits as properly, and declares that the revelations made so clearly define the malevolent—if not absolutely sociopathic—motivations of the cult, as to call for drastic action to suppress it. Needless to say, law enforcement has seen fit to deny such violations against the separation of church and state, and has itself threatened the Anti-Cult Lucidity Organization with prosecution if ever again it should violate federal laws protecting the mail, for this time (as many times before) it had very nearly gone too far. Richard Lunster, the investigator who obtained the letter in question, has utilized the aid of one Andrew O'Leary, who gave the Anti-Cult Lucidity Organization one of its greatest successes when he joined them in their fight against the Chaosophists, his former sect, after his deprogramming. He claims to have identified the language as the Senzar-influenced hieratic dialect of the primal Naacal tongue thought-projected by a race of luminescent jellyfish in Mu, which he had mastered despite attaining only the first of the seven grades of the order. Reason dictates that one laugh at this speculation outright, since nobody relies upon the "scholarship" supposed to restore knowledge of that ancient tongue as trustworthy; while the contents alleged by the collaborators remove any doubt of the inauthenticity of their interpretation.

The letter, which Linwood Asshton-Urquhart had addressed to a young man who had recently changed academic course in mid-stream from an English major to become a laboratory technician, runs as follows:

My Dear Sibling in Chvrvnzvn:

Success has exceeded our expectations. We have made great strides in our efforts, for we have enlisted the aid of humans as well as our own. These scientists and researchers we have deceived; we have not told them how long we have existed, or how long we have inhabited earth. We have tailored our stories to the individuals' susceptibilities; most accept us as mere extraterrestrial visitors in need of aid. With this belief, they willingly act in secrecy on our behalf. Only a few have suspected the truth, and with them we have easily disposed.

Together, ours and theirs have advanced to a stage nearing the creation of novel bodies for us. Use of genetic coding from Annelids and Archaea should prove fruitful. Soon we shall be able to abandon our human forms. With exploration of the asteroid belt, we could perhaps obtain useful material, since we neared this stage there as well. In any case, we should have fully restored our breeding ability within fifty years. For some time now, before we have fully readjusted to our former state of grace, we will require aid from men to reestablish the Elder Race's society. This aid need not be given voluntarily. However, we will for some time need men as manufacturers of raw materials, before we have fully created a functioning ecosystem composed of more pleasant entities to provide for our requirements.

After that, we will have no further need for humanity. Considering that our efforts to endow the species with sentience of its own, and so create useful allies for us, has met with failure, as if we had stumbled by accident upon an evolutionary dead end which no amount of manipulation can improve, we may as well dispense with them once they have become no longer useful. For, while by no means a serious danger, they have the ability to make themselves into quite a nuisance.

Yours by the Untranslatable Sign,

—Sll'ha-Gn'wgn-ll'ah-Sgn'wahl.

The Venomous Book of the Wizard Pharmandre

Uther Astridge stared down into his cup of coffee. "I don't know, Rick, those crusty old tomes never seem to measure up to the expectations they arouse. Take the old grimoires. They come out in paperback, and instead of the weirdness and horror your imagination has conjured up around them, you get some silly superstitions. The original manuscripts, as opposed to those cheap paperback editions of 'highly secret magic texts,' might have carried some *aura*, as Walter Benjamin put it, but even that seems doubtful considering the laborious inanities contained in them. Maybe the *Necronomicon* gains its ability to drive the reader mad from the fact that it doesn't exist, which could tend to put its reader into a certain state of mind—"

"Well, Oothe, the book I'm talking about can't suffer from the defect of being reprinted in paperback. At least not according to the legends around it. And it doesn't just drive the reader mad, it kills him. And no one knows just how. All of its readers, so the story goes, just disappear into thin air."

"At least the myth's a little interesting. Where'd you get this book?"

"In a batch from a monastery in France. It's called *Liber magi Pharmandris venenatus*—"

"*The Venomous, (or Poisonous), Book of the Wizard Pharmander—*"

"Right, Oothe. But it's spelled *Pharmandre.*"

"But why that title? Back then readers usually gave a book its title, not the author. They'd pick something descriptive of its contents. Or did the old wizard just own it? No one could read it to find out what it says—"

"Can't tell ya that stuff. No one seems to know. I told you the whole damn story. Makes its readers disappear. Maybe it came with the title on it already—Can't even find another reference to Pharmandre, whoever *he* might've been—But you know good and well that old story can't be right. People don't just up and disappear. Still, no one wants to pay much for a book with such a bad reputation, and with unknown contents."

"And what's the 'venom' part of the title about?"

"Hell if I know. No poison would make you vanish into air, but the damn monks seem to have been convinced the book hid some kind of venom just waiting to sting its unwary reader. Anyway, I thought that you might like to give the thing a try. You'd have a chance to uncover the unknown, and dispel a ridiculous old wive's tale at the same time."

"So why don't you just read it yourself?"

"Oothe, you know that with all the buying and selling books I do I don't have time to *read* any of the things. Even if I wanted to. But who but you would've gone through Sinistrari's *De dæmonialitate* in the original, or searched out a copy of something as rare as Silander's *Krypticon*, only to wreck the thing's value by reading it, not to mention a few rarer treats, like Valerius Trevirus' *De noctis rebus*, Ernest Clouët's *Les Abîmes*, or an *unexpurgated* copy of the *Leabhar Mor Dubh*? Most people don't even know that it was censored; why, I bet a few bourgeois philistines haven't even heard of it—"

"All right, already. I was planning on going *on retreat* next week—"

"Oh. Got a story ready to start writing?"

"No, just want to get away from other people's company long enough to get one to that point. But now you've got me interested in that book of yours. I never do seem to learn that those old 'mouldy hidden manuscripts' never contain anything very imaginative. Oh, hell. Why don't you send it on over?"

"Okay. I'll do that. Be seein' ya, Oothe."

"*Au revoir.*"

* * * * *

Astridge set the book onto his desk. He had drawn all the curtains of his apartment windows for the duration of his *retreat*, and adjusted them carefully to make sure that no light would get through, and especially no view of the outside. The book seemed very large to him, and it had a fine black leather binding and iron clasps that served to contain whatever might lurk inside. Astridge couldn't help but admire the workmanship of those ornate clasps, and the cover bore a gold-leaf inscription: *Liber magi Pharmandris venenatus.* Monks. They wouldn't so much as open the book out of the fear of what lay inside, but they had squandered all of this labor on creating a decorative prison for its contents. You might have expected them to burn the thing as the spawn of the Devil, if they believed the silly legends that had sprung up around it.

He cleared off the desk to make room to open the tome, which would take up much of the surface, and he turned off all of the lights in the apartment except for those which he would need to see the book; he didn't want any other sights to distract him from his reading. He undid the clasps.

To his surprise, the book didn't come from such a recent provenance as he had suspected. Only clumsily had the monks contrived to attach the irreparably tattered interior pages to the cover which they had devised for it. He had thought that the work would not have been written very long—perhaps less than a century, certainly not more than a few centuries—before they had created its current exterior. A great layer of a yellowish-grey, powdery dust lay heavy inside it. He blew the dust off of the first page, and watched as it formed a cloud on the other side of his desk. He had to use all of his antiquarian knowledge of dead languages to make out the crabbed print. He recognized the writing as a very archaic form of Greek, written using characters older than those of the Greek alphabet, but like it formed from the Semitic scripts of merchants and pirates. Its use of a certain consonant which had become obsolete between the time of the composition of the Homeric epics and their commitment to writing showed that the book had an incredibly early origin—definitely far earlier than the period in which monks utilized Latin. Probably very few of them could have made any guess as to its intent.

By the time he had figured out the nature of this script, otherwise unknown, the smell of the dust from the book had begun to sting in his nostrils. It had a strange odor, which he could not identify with any he had ever happened to smell before, and it definitively did not resemble the musty scent of the dust that usually accumulates on books. It seemed strange that the dust should not have settled, but it hung in a cloud, and seemed to glitter, there in the darkness, minuscule spots of it swirling around in the air. His mouth felt dry. The suspicion that this had aroused the legends of a poison hidden within the book occurred to his mind, and he reasoned that it had frightened off any readers who had encountered these drug-like effects. But no such poison could make you disappear, of course—it would either leave him unharmed, or kill him, and no evidence that the book could kill anyone existed; it would leave a corpse as its inevitable evidence. Besides, he suspected that he understood the nature of the powdery dust, and he felt no fear on its account. He had used a few of the psychedelics in his college years, and had done even more studying of them in the university's science library. He knew that most of them could cause a dry throat and mouth, and the apparently glowing specks of dust looked very much like one of the lighter visual effects that they could create. But those drugs didn't normally cause any lasting damage, either physical or psychological, even on the rare occasions when they had any negative effects at all. It did seem strange that only the peculiar grey dust off of the book should carry the visual effect, but such drugs can behave more oddly than expected, even to experienced users.

He returned to the study of the book, and soon identified the dialect that it had been written in. It seemed like a kind of early Greek mingled with many of the languages of the surrounding peoples, such as the Egyptian and the Semitic nations, with a simplified grammar that made it easier for him to decipher it. He speculated that it represented a sample of an early pidgin, or perhaps creole, created by the inhabitants of the Mediterranean region, though it seemed very strange that no other record of it should have survived; but again, a long time had passed since his study of dead languages, and such a patois wouldn't likely appear to any except specialists in very narrow areas of study. In addition, a few enigmatic elements closely resembled borrowings from the westernmost dialect of Hieratic Naacal, and he thought that even most specialists would remain unaware of that hidden language. As he glanced up for a second, lost in thought, the sparkling specks seemed to shift and rotate on an axis in the center of the cloud, which still had not settled.

The story began with the narrative of a wizard named Pharmandre, contrary to his guess that the sorcerer had merely owned the volume. This wizard inhabited the lost continent of Hyperborea, and had avidly sought out the secret of eternal life. He had accumulated a retinue of soldiers and followers, and had gained control over the territory surrounding his tower, maintained by the innumerable magical powers which he had garnered from his studies and experiments. From the peasants and merchants in the area, he exacted heavy tributes and tithes, all of which went into his inexhaustible search for the elixir of life. Finally, he discovered a récipé for it which he believed might work, delivered to him by a tortured daemon from one of the stars (not identifiable to Uther Astridge from the information presented), who had made a career of taunting others with hints that he could deliver the knowledge to them, only to depart in sardonic laughter at his refusal to disclose it, after they had demeaned themselves in the most nauseating and humiliating tasks in his service, on his promise to exchange these disgusting and debasing exertions for the hoped-for reward.

At this point Uther Astridge had reached the end of the first page, and he lifted it to uncover the next two. Even more dusty powder lay between the two sheets—and he could not identify the sort of paper or perhaps hide on which the writing which he so attentively read had been inscribed—and it arose in eddies and swirls, increasing the musty smell that stung against his nostrils, and made him cough, an effect increased by the desiccation of his mouth and throat, and he blew the dust over to join the rest. The dust hung in the atmosphere, and the tiny motes seemed to form into a figure much resembling a gleaming cobweb, only extended in three dimensions, and it palpitated in and out like a jellyfish. But he knew that the class of drugs to which he had tentatively assigned the dust, which he could not help but breathe a little of, though he attempted to avoid inhaling any of it, would often produce a visual effect in which the user would perceive patterns in material which in reality only had a randomicity, or even against a background of total darkness, and so he discounted the effect, knowing that it represented only a very mild example.

With great interest he read onward in the story. It seemed odd to him, but he had gained quite a fluency in the unheard-of dialect of the tome, and even though he would have expected a drug like the one he had ingested, willy-nilly, to have the effect of making his reading more difficult—for they often cause a kaleidoscopic tumult of ideations and mental images, he found that in this case he seemed to merely picture the tale recounted in the volume, in strikingly vivid scenes placed before his mind's eye. He remembered dimly from his readings that the South American vine *ayahuasca* causes very specific hallucinations, and that its users typically see jaguars and serpents crawling and twisting around them, followed by an aërial journey over landscapes filled with jungles and great stone cities, only to arrive at an unknown destination. He speculated—and it would prove a very interesting subject, when the drug could receive proper scientific attention—that the powdery dust caused equally specific effects, and had been added as an aid to the understanding of the obscure text inscribed in that book.

The next page began with the récipé which the mage had followed in order to gain immortality, before he insulted the daemon for a final time, and condemned the gargoyle to an unnameable hell. He had to seek out a creature in some country of the very far east, which Astridge could not readily identify with any known to him (from his readings—he had never made it very far from his native Oregon), though certain details made him suspect Thibet or perhaps Nepal, or at least the general region of Central Asia, and this creature—which had originally come from some unspecified abyss beyond the stars, and had greatly evolved to survive in an environment unknown to its ancestors, which unfortunately had resulted in its loss of the ability to travel through the aether—resembled a human being, except that it had a fine covering of fur over all of its body, and had glowing red eyes, and ate nothing but human flesh, which it could smell from miles away. Once caught, the creature's hide had to be tanned and made into a sort of tawny suit, which would fit directly against the skin of its new wearer. The rest of the body had to become the inaugurating compost for a perpetual garden, in which the seeker of immortality must grow a rare fungus (of a species unidentifiable to Astridge, who lacked training in mycology), obtainable in a part of the world which did not seem to correspond to any land now represented on maps, and the juice from which would form the basis of a potion, which would then—if taken weekly—provide the imbiber with an eternal life. Furthermore, he could no longer consume any food but human flesh, or he would lose the immortality gained by the above measures.

Astridge had begun to grow sleepy, and he felt that he should rest before finishing the manuscript, which had proven more interesting than he had, in all frankness, anticipated. He might consider preparing a translation, and as he drifted off to sleep, he could almost picture the wizard Pharmandre, and as he opened his eyes, he saw the sparkling dust hanging in the air, and it seemed to him that it shifted in position off to the side of the room, nearer to the wall, but he knew that such drugs as he had unwittingly taken could produce such effects, and his throat felt dry, but he knew that it would be no use drinking water, for those drugs act as diuretics and you just urinate as much water as you drink, and he could almost see the wizard Pharmandre himself—

* * * * *

Only a couple of hours had passed when Uther Astridge awoke from a dreamless pseudo-sleep, during which he had experienced shifting kaleidoscopic visions that depicted nothing but scenes from the material which he had just left off reading. He knew that drugs of the psychedelic class will usually prevent sleep for the duration of their effects, so he resolved to go ahead and stay awake as long it took to read the entire volume. Further, though, he knew that the body quickly builds up a tolerance to their effects, and that within about a week or so he would no longer experience anything from exposure to whatever drug the dust contained—assuming, of course, that he had correctly identified its nature, which he felt sure of, by comparison with both his own experiences of the past and his remembered readings in the scientific literature on the subject.

So, the story in the book continued, the wizard Pharmandre carried out the instructions which the daemon had given to him—and he had to turn the pages again to continue with his reading; a great deal more of the glittering powder rose off of the pages in response to a gentle breeze emitted by his parched mouth. But the requirement of human flesh to maintain the magical effect of the hide and the fungus proved a more burdensome routine than the mere gathering of taxes for the funding of arcane researches. The populace made a very great murmur when they noticed that some of them had begun to vanish from their midst, and threatened rebellion, and so the wizard determined to engage in a course of piracy against the neighboring peoples to gather the harvest necessary for his self-preservation. The merchant sailors of those other nations soon enough created a suitable legend, describing the wizard Pharmandre, who now appeared like a ferocious monster, in his bizarre suit of borrowed skin, who would swoop onto other ships in the flash of an eye, and frequently bear off a single unfortunate sailor, who no one would ever see again. Astridge, feeling rather wearied from the concentration required for reading in a tongue so difficult to decipher, even though he did find it easier going than he would have anticipated, looked up from his reading, only to see that the motes had begun to take on a more definite form, like the tattered outline of a skeleton, encrusted within an ill-defined spiderweb.

He resumed his task with determination. One night, still intoxicated with the flesh of his latest victim, eaten while the man uttered the most piercing and horrifying screams, the mage and his pirate crew took their bearings and returned to the exact location where they believed, relying on all of their experience in navigation and the careful consultation of their charts and the stars, that their home had lain. It seemed that some terrible mistake must have taken place, though none of them could determine its nature, when the moon peeked out from behind a cloud, and its pallid light clearly shone down onto the reflecting water, revealing that the very top of the wizard's tower still remained jutting out of the water. While the wizard stood enrapt in the thought of a spectacle which he greatly regretted having missed—for a scene of such universal destruction as the sinking of a continent, along with the inevitable deaths of its entire retinue of inhabitants, would inebriate such a being with a heady sensation of sensuous ecstasy, and reality doesn't afford so many opportunities for the viewing of such a spectacle as does fantasy—that final peak slipped beneath the waves forever. Here, Astridge had to turn the page yet again. The additional layer of fine powder seemed to give the strange cloud-form an almost completely human shape.

Uther Astridge felt very tired now, exhausted even. His mouth and his throat ached from their dryness. He felt his skin on his arms, and it felt unbelievably dry, and seemed to have started to form small scales, which—his imagination suggested—would peel right off if he just scratched them a little. But he knew that the mind can play strange tricks, mispercieving an unchanged reality due to the influence of the psychedelics; why, he remembered one LSD trip, during which he had felt his scalp, only to (apparently!) have his fingers sink through his skull, which had (seemingly!) become as soft as melting plastic, and on and into his (illusory!) brains.—

So, he would simply ignore all of the drug's effects while he finished reading the tale. These effects do not outlast the moment, and reality regains her empire with a great enough solidity.

He again took up his reading. The wizard Pharmandre felt grave misgivings as he realized that he no longer had the source for his potion, which gave him his eternal life, although he could not presume to guess what part each of the elements in his regimen played in his preservation. His ship became a perpetually roving pirate raider, which stole bountiful treasures and lives from the merchant-ships plying the seas. But he found that his body began to become dry, and that it soon had begun to peel apart at the lightest scratch. Only the great force of his will served to keep his cadaverous frame from crumbling into dust. (Here Uther Astridge felt an itch on his arm. As his fingernails crossed the area of irritation, tiny flakes fell from his skin, and seemed to flutter into the darkness, glowing phosphorescently.—The power of suggestion, that, obviously. He stopped scratching and returned to his reading, ignoring the irritation of his skin, which seemed inflamed all over his body with the same stinging sensation.)

More, his existence as the leader of a pirate band had become precarious. He no longer had a stronghold to retreat to, and had to rely only on those ports of call which would allow entry to even the worst villains, and even those had begun to balk at his coming, for they disliked one who combined such a disquieting appearance to a more-than-rumored vampirism, and the neighboring seafarers had begun to send out fleets of warships with the intense design of extirpating a proven foe of their continued survival—

The wizard Pharmandre knew that if his mortal foes caught him, they had now merely to separate him from the hide that covered his body, and which contributed its essence to the prolongation of his existence, in order to destroy him, and that even with it, his body—without the constant infusions of the fungus-derived liquor—would hardly keep together, but had become a heap of dust which he could only temporarily form into the shape necessary for his activities. He knew that he would have to devise some ingenious ruse that would both allow him to continue taking victims into perpetuality, and to forever prevent the detection of his action—

Uther Astridge stopped for a moment in wonder at the beautiful pictures that filled his spirits with iridescent images of the tale which he now took a rapt interest in, and after he turned the page and blew off yet another layer of dust, he noted that the form in the room with him looked almost exactly like a man, and in fact had begun to resemble more and more the image which his mind—under the influence of the unknown drug, he told himself—had formed of the wizard Pharmandre. Well, drugs will often produce similar external hallucinations as they do closed-eye imagery. So, the book's cramped handwriting continued, after giving careful instructions to his foremost crewman, the wizard slowly stripped himself of the hide which he wore, and cut it into squares. As his body crumbled at the lack of sustained exposure to that bizarre clothing, he penned, in meticulous detail, the life story of the one who held the quill in his hand, which represented all of his body that had retained full solidity for the duration of the composition. As that right hand closed the volume shut, it too dissolved into dust and fell on the tome's front pages, and the quill rolled off of the desk and onto the floor of his cabin. At their next port-of-call, the ship's new captain and former first mate sold a strange book to a curious scholar for a song.

As Astridge turned over the final page of the volume, only to see, as the sole writing on that concluding page, the signature *The Wizard Pharmandre*, a single, last thin layering of dust rose up, to merge with the form which he now could not fail to recognize, and as he felt his entire body aching, feeling shriveled, and hurting, he got up and struggled over to his bed, where—he said to himself—he could now sleep off the effects of the drug which he had so foolishly overindulged in. He lay down but no sleep came. That was fine. He could wait for the psychoactive agent to loosen its grip on his brain before he slept; he only wished that he could see—anything at all, whether he kept his eyes closed, or whether he opened them, other than the shriveled form of the wizard Pharmandre, deprived of its outré suit of second-hand skin.

That form, now completed in its outline, glided across the room to where the reader lay. Glowing, swirling, shifting, motes of dust, glittering specks whirling in slow spirals, in hesitant helices, creating the form of a lich dead—or undead—for three millennia, hovering above him like a reddish haze in the darkness. As he looked at the thing's eyesockets, he noticed the absence of ocular orbs within them. A sere pair of thin, rubbery things, like tentacles, slowly protruded from the twin holes, their ends terminating in contracting and expanding openings. The things pointed down at the reclining writer, as the ancient sorcerer bent over his bed, and their rims expanded to the greatest degree they were capable of and then folded back slightly over the tube-shaped appendages.

Uther Astridge felt his body crack at its joints, and then fall apart, only to have those parts again split into a myriad pieces, and again split apart into yet smaller fragments, and finally crumble into a fine yellowish-grey, powdery dust, which rose up in slow swirls and disappeared into the leech-like and extensible eyesockets of the bizarre being who hung like a spectre above his bed until the final mote of his dust had vanished entirely away.

* * * * *

The police never did solve the missing-person case of Uther Astridge. Richard Poart always swore that someday he would find the time to read the volume recovered from his writer-friend's estate, and that he would himself reach the ending and dispel the foolish superstitions surrounding the ancient book, allowing himself to turn a decent profit on the old thing.

Twilight of the Elder Gods

It all began innocently enough. Robert LeNoir had for several years enjoyed perusing the writings of crackpots; and when he discovered that many of them would provide them for free, he devoured the mental peregrinations of flying saucer cultists, Hollow Earth First!ers, lost-continent-in-the-Bermuda-Triangle channelers, People's Templars, ultraterrestrials' offspring, Men-in-Black meeters—every sort of voice crying out in the wilderness. So, when he saw the advertisement in the Chaosophists' newsletter, The Commoriom Sentinel-Messenger, for the Whateley Foundation—which promised to reveal even more unheard-of secrets than other groups dared—of course he sent a letter to the distant Oregon address inquiring for information.

A week later LeNoir had nearly forgotten about the ad when, immediately upon falling asleep after drinking a large cup of coffee at 2 a.m., he had the following dream. He found himself facing a steep hill topped by a classic b-movie "haunted house;" upon entering, he wandered through labyrinthine hallways, accompanied by the whisper of distant lightning-bolts, until he came to a parlor. There, sitting in a chair, a man who looked like Vincent Price sat thoughtfully smoking a pipe. He motioned to the intruder and said: "Ah, there you are. We've sometimes had trouble finding our host when we've visited others' minds. Don't let that disturb you. We've only made this trip in order to give you some evidence to convince you of the veracity of our claims to occult knowledge. So, here's a single item that should lie beyond the realms of coincidence. When you see this in our brochure you won't fail to concede our gnosis. You have no doubt heard of the dubious deity known as Nyarlathotep, yes?" And he motioned to the side, where a man—who had the small nose, thin lips, and dolichocephalic skull of a Nordic, whereas his skin was characterized by the color and texture of obsidian—stood in a "walk like an Egyptian" pose. The speaker continued: "Well, then, know that this god symbolically represents the power of telepathy. As you can see, his name even forms an anagram, or near anagram, of the word *telepathy* itself." And he outlined in the air flaming letters that remained visible after the black nail on his index finger had traced them:

NYARLATHOTEP

LeNoir faded into consciousness bearing the burden of an anagram that would have perplexed Ferdinand de Saussure himself.

That same day he received in the mail a response from the Whateley Foundation. Twenty-three pages of cramped typing filled with combative references to "Peaslee's pinheads" and other hopeless fools, brimming with such teratological specimens of outré nomenclature as Yog-Sothoth, Shudde-M'ell, Sobec-Alp, Cthulhu, Nethescurial, Lloigor, Ubbo-Sathla, L'mur-Kathulos, Quazgaa, Yibb-Tstll, Minraud, Y'golonac, Choronzon, Affa, and Tsathoggua; supported (as would be all the dispatches which LeNoir would see from the Foundation) by parenthetical references to such "standard authorities" as Mme. Blavatsky, Miss Margaret Murray, Charles Hoy Fort, Linda Moulton Howe, and John Keel; but the backbone of the argument propped itself on such forbidden tomes as the *Necronomicon* and Feery's *Notes* on it; the *G'harne Fragments*; the *Black Sutra* of U Pao; the *Cthäat Aquadingen*; von Junzt's *Von Unaussprechlichen Kulten*; the *Pnakotic Manuscripts*; Herbert of Clairvaux's *Liber miraculorum*; the *Revelations of Glaaki*; Gaston le Fé's *Dwellers in the Depths*; and Prinn's *De vermis mysteriis*.

What made Robert LeNoir sit up when he began to read all of this, was that the first page promised that eventually the Whateley Foundation would reveal symbolic meanings lurking behind all of the outward images described, and gave as an example the anagrammatic relationship between the name *Nyarlathotep* and the word *telepathy*, which corresponded perfectly with the import of the Soul and Messenger of the Ancient Ones. As explicated in the first reading lesson, the main narrative line of the "Cthulhu Cycle of Myth" ran as follows: a benevolent race known as the Elder Gods—of whom only hoary Nodens, golden Kthanid, and his daughter Tiania are ever cited by name—reigned over the universe from beautifully-palaced Elysia, in the constellation Orion; then, a closely related group of entities known as the Great Old Ones or the Ancient Ones, of whom Cthulhu was chief, rebelled against the authority which the Elder Gods held over them. The Elder Gods could not slay the Ancient Ones, immortals like themselves, but had instead expelled them from the paradisiacal fields of Elysia and imprisoned them in various places of banishment: Cthulhu to the sunken city of R'lyeh; Shudde-M'ell in caverns deep inside the earth; Hastur to the Lake of Hali in Carcosa; Ithaqua in the ices of the polar wastelands; and so forth ad infinitum.

Now, the unsigned document continued, "as usual our bon ami the Comte d'Erlette has managed to both *discern* the essential SYMBOLical truths of THIS myth, & at the same time get its *interpretation* inside-out upside-down & ass-backwards. He recognizes the parallels between this & the Christian Mythos (*Les Cultes des goules*, p. 374 et seq.), with its expulsion from heaven of Satan-Lucifer & expulsion from Eden of Adam. But one would think *he*—a contemporary of the great French ROMANTICS—would NOT fail to SEE that this DEFINES the sides of Good & Evil, not as *mis*-construed by Manichaeanoids & other Cretins (the Miskatonic Morons—Yuggoth, what fools!), but that instead it means the Cthulhu Cycle Deities correspond (cf. Lord Weÿrdgliffe, *The Unspeakable*, dream sequence at end of Book IV, suppressed portion in "Antwerp" edition of 1797) to the bringer of LIGHT (Lucifer), to the great *rebel against* tyranny (Satan), to, in fact, that TITAN who has suffered un*end*ing torment at the hands of THE Celestial Despot in order to bring fire (illumination, conflagration of TOTAL *free*dom) to Man: Prometheus! & FROM this *we* infer that another parallel may be (IS!) forthcoming: the Cthulhu Cycle Deities must-WILL-*SHALL* include a Demogorgon! Quake in terror, O ye Elder Gods, at the thought that *your* tyranny shall END!!!"

The anonymous author at the Whateley Foundation struck LeNoir as unbalanced, and possibly dangerous—though maybe only to himself—but with most of a continent between himself and Coos Bay, he allowed the curiosity aroused by the odd coincidence between his dream and the first lesson's contents to govern his actions. In reply to his query for further information expanding on the "most interesting speculations" and explanation that he regretted that he could not afford to offer remuneration for anything received (given his current financial situation), he received a cassette tape with a short note directing him to listen to it; it contained—so said the note—certain incantations derived from cross-comparison of variant chants in the *Ibigib*, the *Book of Eibon*, the *Liyuhh*, von Junzt's Black Book, and Gantley's *Hydrophinnae*. The note added: "with some steady listening (during *sleep* especially & background day) soon should be able to pronounce properly (the chants work the change)—but wait to see. This NOT speculation. Known fact. PROVEN fact. More lessons coming in day or two. Yrs." And it bore a strange serpentine squiggle in place of a signature.

That night LeNoir started the tape as he turned out the lights to go to bed; it usually took him an hour or so to fall asleep, and he often enjoyed listening to music (electronic-ambient) in that time. An obscure croaking rose up in the darkness:

Iä! n'fthagn Cthulhu R'lyeh mglw'nafh,
Eha'ungl wglw hflghglùi ngah'glw,
Èngl-wfhm Eha gh'eehf gnhugl,
Nhflg'ng uh'eha wgah'nagl hfgluf'h—
U'ng Eha'ghgluí Ae'eh ehn'hflgh, Iä!

The articulation of these syllables sounded to LeNoir more like a chorus of croaking toads than a voice, and he could hardly believe that any human being could have produced them—as his nameless addresser had implied to have done—and could only wonder whether the unfortunate suffered from some dire disease affecting the throat and vocal chords. The darkness around him dissolved into shifting, kaleidoscopic visions of a world where endless rows of russet monoliths stand on jaundiced stretches of sand beneath an algae-green sky with two cerulean suns slowly setting, and he had begun to imagine that he felt some presence lurking behind the monoliths, about to reach around them, some semi-insectoid, tentacled awareness of his having reached their forbidden realm—

The tape-player clicked off and the visions ended. LeNoir settled into sleep (he had work to do in the morning, after all), so resigned himself to the arms of Hypnos. He spent a night waking from strange dreams, of which he only retained the memory of again meeting the fellow who looked so much like Vincent Price, and being told by that one that he could hardly carry his proselytizings out into the street, given certain factors; here, he turned and revealed that his eyes (which he had carefully hidden until then) protruded like two wriggling earthworms, and had the frothy white texture of freshly harvested semen and a slight hint of a phosphorescent gleam—

Indeed, the next day there arrived in the mail a seventeen-page "Induction to the Symbolical Key to the Hieroglyphic Mysteries of the Cthulhu Cycle of Myth." Every two or three days for the next several weeks, LeNoir received a further update in the series; the disorganization apparent in the essays' ordering convinced him that his correspondent must have been composing them as he went along; he strongly doubted that any other "students" were benefitting from his tutelage. As these documents expressed it, the Cthulhu Cycle revealed in hieroglyphic form a doctrine of radical monism, seeing ("DIRECTly *perceiv-ING*") all things as the primordial Oneness-of-Being, as mystics have termed it. LeNoir had a difficult time attempting to integrate certain key figures of the mythology into the system as presented, as they seemed to bear at once a figurative and a literal existence; these included, to his perplexity, the entire set of Elder Gods, and such of the Ancient Ones as Hastur, Tsathoggua, and Cthulhu himself. Still, he had little time to waste determining how the matter stood; it might indeed require a team of exegetes multiple decades to wrest a solution from the cobwebbed prose.

Into this system the nameless author had managed to cram most or all of the Cthulhu Cycle Deities. For example, the first few lessons cited the Daemon-Sultan Azathoth, the "Bubbler at the Hub," the "monstrous nuclear Chaos," who represented nothing less than the primal unity in its creative puissance, exploding into the multiple cosmos-atoms that comprise the totality of existence, and imploding again only to restart the process anew. "& we all KNOW how Edgar Poe *got suicided* when he tried to pull the veil (*Eureka!*) away from this ONE!" Again, Yog-Sothoth, the "All-in-One & One-in-All," could only represent the totality in its diverse aspects, the illusory division into individuality of the various spatio-temporal modifications of the eternal ALL: "the parallel of certain myths connected to this *name* to those of the Great God PAN (All) needs no comment (cf. Feery on Alhazred VIII 33-57, though this *looks* like yet another mystification)."

Other of the Cthulhu Cycle Deities seemed to present less direct mirrorings of the essential truth. Shub-Niggurath, for example, called the "Black Goat of the Woods with a Thousand Young" or again the "Ram with a Thousand Ewes," had—as one might expect—a particularly convoluted system of imagery associated with her: "Just as Yog-Sothoth shadows forth the PHALLIC in its essentially Hermaphroditic (Androgyne, Epicene) aspect, as witness the Romanic figure of Priapus; so does Shub-Niggurath, the Black Goat to Yog-Sothoth's Black Cock (we speak here of the rooster sacrificed by the witch-cult, as per the *Liber rerum interdictorum*, at Walpurgis-Night Sabbat)—shadow forth the Kteis (cf. *Cth-/Kth*-gematria in *Qabalah of Sabaoth*) in its Hermaphroditicity. The Hecatean Chthonic-Phallos. Representing the power of the Cthulhu Cycle Deities (who KNOW *directly* their identity as the ALL) of miscegenation itself; the inability to breed with, to adapt the genetic CODING to, other species, stems *solely* from the unawareness of the cosmic ONE-ness. Cycle Deities can mate with anything, have therefore power of INFINITE creativity; cf. case of Yig (Serpent-Father) in Oklahoma, myths of gods & men, forms of beasts, Jersey Devil, etc. Shub-Niggurath means nothing less than what Professor Peaslee (ole Nodens'-Dreck!) calls Cthulhu's Cosmic Miscegenation!" Nyarlathotep, of course, symbolized the power of the Great Old Ones to communicate telepathically—"exactly as one would EXPECT for some*thing* that transcends time & space as human (Elder God!) mentality *mis*-conceives it!"

The unnamed author even went so far as to defend some of the less accredited theories concerning the nature of the Ancient Ones of the Cycle. "While many have laughed at d'Erlette's inept attempt to correlate the Old Ones with the four 'elements' of mediaeval PSEUDO-science; we yet concur that the Comte de Kthanid again discerned an inside-out mirror image of the truth, requiring only SIGNIFICANT distortion to rectify. That he published his obscene idioticisms under *Alhazred*'s name, thus smearing *a true prophet* with his own DUNG, we pass over in silent contempt; we do not stoop to mention such abominations of 'scholarship' (the qlippoth-wallower!). Fire, air, etc., have really nothing to do with case; but as each BEING must have composition of some particular form of matter-*energy* rather than another—as a limited modification of the space-time Oneness;—so must comprise some of *counter*-balancing forces of universe*s* more than others; thus understood, makes SENSE to speak of Old Ones AS Elementals. We take some solace from finding that *our* intended analogy with Taoism has already been made, and direct the reader to Thranang Phram's *Chthonic Revelations* passim for a detailed, if insipid, application of the theory. We pause only to note the MOST IMPORTANT detail, the replacement of the *binary* yin-yang 'logic' with a FIVE-valued (the Elder Sign *reversed* SUMMONS instead of banishing!) system."

By the time LeNoir had pieced together the mythology and its obscure and contradictory interpretations, he had long since abandoned listening to the invocation-cassette. While the visions it produced had gradually increased in coherency and vividness, he had, pari passu, begun to feel heavy and awkward, and noticed that his skin seemed scaly and dry, while his throat constantly ached and felt sore; so sore, in fact, that his playful attempts to chant along with the tape:

> *Ce'haiie ep-ngh fl'hur G'harne fhthagn,*
> *Ce'haiie fhthagn ngh Shudde-M'ell.*
> *Hai G'harne orr'e ep fl'hur,*
> *Shudde-M'ell ican-icanicas fl'hur orr'e G'harne.*

met with more and more success, while his acquaintances at work displayed great admiration for his new impression of a chorus of croaking toads. When his throat failed to get well after a couple of weeks, however, he began to suspect that he had gotten into something deeper than he had ever desired. Still, the communiqués from the Whateley Foundation proved as entertainingly offbeat as ever, and so he continued to read them.

A gap of three and a half weeks then intervened in their correspondence. Finally, an envelope arrived in LeNoir's Post Office Box. A great tension had obviously overtaken the nameless author, and LeNoir feared that insanity might have finally overcome what feeble resistance he could have offered. The letter began by stating that the author felt that LeNoir must surely have noted a grave defect in certain of the theories before propounded, namely, that it left uncertain the precise nature of Cthulhu, Nodens, and some others among the Cycle's daemones, whether they required a literal or a physical interpretation. He had now concluded—on the basis of evidence which, he declared, would soon become available to the reader—that they deserved no less than both.

As he now rewrote the foundational myth of the Cycle, the One-Continuum had undergone its various modifications, which took form (in many cases) as living beings. Among the multiform of this Elder Race there occurred an unexplainable calamity (no form of logic can even hint at the circumstances involved, avowed the unknown author, in what seemed a defect of reasoning to the reader), and the Primal Ones known as the Elder Gods had lost the awareness of themselves as fluctuations in form of segments of the seamless Oneness-of-Being; thus self-endowed with individual identities, they were overwhelmed with idiot pride at their uniqueness and awareness. So, in a vast war, they seized power and established their cosmic seat in Glyu-Uho, enslaving all of the Other Ones that they could subjugate through main force. But the forces of Good (Freedom), led by the Great Priest Cthulhu, Abhoth the Unclean, and Hastur the Unspeakable, had rebelled against this tyranny; the Elder Gods held the day and scattered their foes about the universe, imprisoning them in bonds from which they could scarcely escape. Bonds in the genetic coding and linguistic prisons in the brain-mind itself. Here the author became a little reticent, declaring that LeNoir would soon enough see the evidence that should convince him of the truth of the new hypothesis implied in the argument. Meanwhile, he hinted that a few others had reached similar conclusions, of whom he named only the mad Arab Abdul Alhazred and Ambrose Bierce, together with the hint that tales of being eaten by invisible entities in the marketplace or disappearing while walking through a field were nothing but band-aids for the sanity of the world—a sanity which, he believed, needed to erode all too soon if any hope for victory were to come forth. But he abruptly ended the missive on that enigmatic note, and did not deign to clarify his conceptions.

Three nights later LeNoir's slumber found itself disturbed by a nightmare of shocking vividness and import. He wandered across a field near the sea, which pounded fitfully against the rocky shore. The earth rumbled beneath him, but a strange feeling assured him that he would not receive any injury; he waited near the center of the quake. The rock and dirt burst open. A grey conical head emerged slowly, finally towering to a great height above the dreamer, who only now realized that he had no body in the dream, but was merely a point of consciousness. He examined the monstrosity closely: in general outlines, it was shaped like an enormous squid or kraken, with overlapping rows of tentacles folding in on each other. Its nearly circular body revealed a pentagonal structure; and each of the five sides held lozenge-paned eyeballs. As the dreamer looked more and more closely into the those eyes' crimson pupils, he became more and more convinced that the shapeless blasphemy before him resembled the man who had formerly haunted his dreams in a form allied to that of Vincent Price; an internal voice confirmed his surmise. In croaking sense-impacts of signification the voice conveyed to LeNoir that he now beheld before him the final secret of the Ancient Ones. The creature unfolded five membraneous wings and the two began to rise together into the air. The creature and the others who had restored themselves would now wage a desperate war against the despotism of the Elder Gods. They soared up to the height of the lightning-sundered clouds. The incantations on the tape could work the transformations. The Outer Thing requested that he play the cassette constantly, that he spread its influence as far as possible, by distributing copies, by broadcast (if at all possible), by playing it in crowded areas; he should walk through the tottering cities of men, exposing mobile masses as large as possible to its influence. Even a brief, half-heard segment might awaken the memories in some. The creature began to fade into a dot in the interstellar distances. The Ancient Ones would do what they could through telepathy; but the power of the Elder Gods' spells was too strong for that to do more than a small part to break the bonds of those imprisoned in the human shell—

Riot inflames the huddling streets—Sunken poets cities of rêverie—*Iqhui dlosh odhqlongh*—Cults gather beneath the apocalyptic stars and gaze at the white-robed moon in expectation—Strange Aeons—Batrachian echoes in the halls of gibbering asylums for the insane—*Tec djivvaiga nicoigh'lnaäaëyi—micaroï gghln'häe*—Green dripping decay—Insect ecstasies pubic antennae—Revelations of the Crawling Chaos—Pentagonal miscegenation in red-litten vaults—Unknown whispers in unheard tongues—*Ph'ngläyä ft'gglhnayn*—Shadows of human sacrifice in the ebony fires of greed and lust—The True Will—The R'lyehian reflections in the broken mirrors of the labyrinth of Mind—the Magnum Innominandum—*Ggh'lghà djëcai Cyäegha pfh'gai d'whoggl,*

micaroï tec–the cruel Empire of Tsan-Chan–Strange Aeons–
Loneliness waits unbodied in the dark dreaming of Yith–Where
the star-spawn lurk–*N'cryastaepecioggl'n bggn'th flwaägor*–Collapsing columns of unseen angles–tongues rasp from the oozing
interstices–colorless tentacles–Hali in Carcosa–the brain–*Ep,
ep-eeth, fl'hur G'harne–G'harne ffhthaghn Shudde-M'ell hyas
Negg'h*–Anarchy creeps across the dreaming canvases of desire–
rivulets of architectural insanities–Strange Aeons–*nafl'fl'fhth-
aghn*–

–For the memory of Brian Lumley.

Oddments and Oddities

The Cthulhu Caper

The Ghoul Changeling Kid walks into Misc. U. one day & approach Professor Wilcocks—"Now see here young man my time is valuable"—"look this here uh bas relief I make uh perfessor after dream on the nod after chew rare alkaloidal herb described by mad Arab Abdul Alhazred"—"why uh this is the ghastly soul symbol of the Corpse Eating Cult of Inaccessible Leng in Central Asia"—"dreams on the nod older'n brooding Tyre—or the contemplative Sphinx—or garden girdled Babylon"—"my brain!—my brain!—it's tugging—seven—seven—seven—down the onyx steps—the pit of the shoggoths—knocking—clawing—from beyond—Kamog! Kamog!—*Iä!—Shub-Niggurath!*—The Goat with a Thousand Young!—*glub—glub—glub.* . . ."—Professor Wilcocks he got the Gook Rot out of Time starts to deliquesce into a putrescent mass of loathsome—of detestable—no sound save a nameless sort of slow thick dripping—a terrible little pool had accumulated—

For miles splashed on in silence through terrible cypress woods where day never came—a reddish glare seemed to filter through the pale undergrowth beyond endless avenues of forest night—"this very bad place Meester"—it made men dream so they knew to keep away—

Animal fury & orgiastic license tore through nighted woods like pestilential tempests from gulfs of hell—blasphemous revels of some unhallowed Walpurgisnacht Sabbat—Mayan curanderos Haytian Vodoun priests Esquimaux angokoks (note: wizard priests) New Orleans swamp priests Tatar shamans all kinds biological mistake or joke of Crinoid Elder Beings in Antarctica on paregoric and goofballs (note: nembutal) in an endless Bacchanal chant "*Phn'gluy wgah'nafh Cthulhu R'lyeh mglw'nagl fhtgagn*" (note: Old High Old One for "Down in his hole at R'lyeh lushed Cthulhu waits loaded & dreaming")—general motion from right to left—in the center stands an idol with cephalopod head bent forward & a scaffold—the trap fell & the squatter fell kicking & yelping & you could hear his neck snap like a stick in a wet towel—hangs there pulling his knees up to the chest & pumping out spurts of jism—"this bad place Meester—you win something like jellyfish"—

The Ghoul Changeling Kid walks putrescent mass—no sound save a delight—the Sailor mistook nameless sort of slow thick—now dripping cosmic order—this uh bas relief place was all wrong—the geometry made men dream—& after license tore through nighted woods' Euclidean angles—loathsomely like pestilential dream on the nod—jism drift after smoke tempests from gulfs of hell—

The Sailor found it by accident—some terrible Cyclopean vista of dark & dripping stone—a coast line of mingled mud ooze & weedy masonry—the nightmare corpse city of R'lyeh—there lay great Cthulhu aka Mr Nug Mr Yeb aka Mr & Mrs Nigguratl-Yig & his hordes: the Great Old Ones—eldritch angleboys of the cosmos— hidden in green slime & blue orgone vaults—vast angles & stone surfaces—horrible images & hieroglyphs from *Necronomicon* & Mayan codices—titan oozy blocks which could have been no mortal staircase—raw shit & frozen jism waft through canals in non-Euclidean angles—loathsomely redolent of spheres & dimensions apart from ours—by their smell can men sometimes know choking erogenous mist of burning sex films—the geometry of the place was all wrong—

Black with a darkness almost material—a nasty slopping sound down there—IT lumbered slobberingly into sight—Cthulhu's "errand boys," his "human gooks," his "decorticated canine preparations," had opened his tomb at R'lyeh—eldritch contradictions of all matter force & cosmic order—a mountain walked or stumbled—ravening for delight—(the Sailor mistook this as a tribute to his personal attractions—his yellow hair turned white)—the green sticky spawn of the stars on Podunk Earth—a sense of spectral whirling through liquid gulfs of infinity—the pursuing jelly which rose above the unclean froth—a cachinnating chorus of the distorted hilarious Elder Gods—"get the picture?"—

Perished of pure fright—be erection acclaim—sense of spectral whirling described—there is no—& until all rides through reeling pricks point to immemorial lunacy—force & universes on a comet's cosmic—they remember this unknown world of fungous life—forbidden Yuggoth—made realize—die to himself in the orgasm of his—clom fliday—

In the Sacred Grove: Order of the Moon—& from the idols the Hanging Tree Green—cachinnating chorus of green sticky—claim his own—the obsidian green bat winged streets the stars were—had failed pagodas out of that dream of the Fish City—to do by clouds about his design accident—sex rooms to make blue through liquid gulfs—after vigintillions—& ravening for—with tumescent plunges from the pit to purple delight—gateway of paws materialize—the wall—tropic jungle taste & touch illusion of white hot skies of Minraud—dragged away toward the cellar—their tongues—"you got it?"—

What has risen may sink—what has sunk may rise—loathsomeness waits & dreams in the deep—Mr Nug Mr Yeb is like pulp beside you—decay spreads over the tottering cities of men—(The shallow water came in with the tide & the New England river of Arkham.)

The Dunwich Borer

A traveller in north central Massachusetts came upon the junction of the Aylesbury pike just beyond Dean's Corners. He took the right fork.

Why I Want to Fuck Cthulhu

During these assassination fantasies

Cthulhu and the conceptual shipwreck. Numerous studies have been conducted upon patients in terminal paresis (G.P.I.), placing Cthulhu in a series of simulated shipwrecks, e.g. multi-ship disasters, head-on collisions, harbor attacks (fantasies of Presidential assassinations remained a continuing preoccupation, subjects showing a marked polymorphic fixation on forecastles and rear cargo holds). Powerful erotic fantasies of an anal-sadistic character surrounded the image of the Presidential contender. Subjects were required to construct the optimum nautical disaster victim by placing a replica of Cthulhu's cephalopod head on the unretouched photographs of shipwreck fatalities. In 82 percent of cases massive rear-end collisions were selected with a preference for expressed fecal matter and rectal hemorrhages. Further tests were conducted to define the optimum model-year. These indicate that a three-year model lapse with Lascar sailor victims provides the maximum audience excitation (confirmed by manufacturers' studies of the optimum nautical disaster). It is hoped to construct a rectal modulus of Cthulhu and the nautical disaster of maximized audience arousal.

Thurston became increasingly obsessed

Motion picture studies of Cthulhu reveal characteristic patterns of facial tonus and musculature associated with homoerotic behaviour. The continuing tension of buccal sphincters and the recessive tentacle role tally with earlier studies of facial rigidity (cf., Tsathoggua, Yibb-Tstll). Slow-motion cine-films of campaign speeches exercised a marked erotic effect upon an audience of spastic squatters. Even with New England's traditional "salt of the earth" the verbal material was found to have minimal effect, as demonstrated by substitution of an edited tape giving diametrically opposed opinions. Parallel film of rectal images revealed a sharp upsurge in anti-Semitic and concentration camp fantasies (cf., anal-sadistic fantasies in hysterical Levantines induced by rectal stimulation).

with the pudenda of the Presidential contender

Incidence of orgasms in fantasies of sexual intercourse with Cthulhu. Patients were provided with assembly kit photographs of sexual partners during intercourse. In each case Cthulhu's cephalopod head was superimposed upon the original partner. Vaginal intercourse with "Cthulhu" proved uniformly disappointing, producing orgasm in 2 percent of subjects. Axillary, buccal, navel, aural, and orbital modes produced proximal erections. The preferred mode of entry overwhelmingly proved to be the rectal. After a preliminary course in anatomy it was found that caecum and transverse colon also provided excellent sites for excitation. In an extreme 12 percent of cases, the simulated anus of post-colostomy surgery generated spontaneous orgasm in 98 percent of penetrations. Multiple-track cine-films were constructed of "Cthulhu" in intercourse during (a) campaign speeches, (b) rear-end nautical collisions with one- and three-year-old model changes, (c) with rear cargo holds, (d) with Esquimaux child-atrocity victims.

mediated to him by a thousand bas-reliefs.

Sexual fantasies in connection with Cthulhu. The genitalia of the Presidential contender exercised a continuing fascination. A series of imaginary genitalia were constructed using (a) the mouth-orifices of Shub-Niggurath, (b) a steam yacht rear smokestack, (c) the assembly kit prepuce of President Azathoth, (d) an Esquimau-victim of sexual assault. In 89 percent of cases, the constructed genitalia generated a high incidence of self-induced orgasm. Tests indicate the masturbatory nature of the Presidential contender's squatting posture. Statuettes consisting of soapy, greenish-black stone models of Cthulhu's alternate genitalia were found to have a disturbing effect on hysterical Levantines.

The motion picture studies of Cthulhu

Cthulhu's facial feelers. Studies were conducted on the marked fascination exercised by the Presidential contender's facial feelers. 65 percent of male subjects made positive connections between the facial feelers and their own pubic hair. A series of optimum facial feelers was constructed.

created a scenario of the conceptual orgasm,

The conceptual role of Cthulhu. Fragments of Cthulhu's cinetized postures used in the construction of model psycho-dramas in which the Cthulhu-figure played the role of husband, university librarian, gentleman scholar, decadent college student, etc. The failure of these roles to express any meaning reveals the non-functional character of Cthulhu. Cthulhu's success therefore indicates society's periodic need to re-conceptualize its political leaders. Cthulhu thus appears as a series of posture concepts, basic equations which re-formulate the roles of the eldritch and anality.

a unique ontology of cosmic horror and disaster.

Cthulhu's personality. The profound anality of the Presidential contender may be expected to dominate the United States in the coming years. By contrast the late Yog-Sothoth remained the prototype of the oral object, usually conceived in pre-pubertal terms. In further studies Cubo-Futurist painters were given the task of devising ritual sex fantasies involving

Cthulhu. Results confirm the probability of Presidential figures being perceived primarily in genital terms; the face of Nyarlathotep is clearly genital in significant appearance—the nasal prepuce, scrotal jaw, etc. Faces were seen as either circumcised (Nyarlathotep, Hastur) or uncircumcised (Yog-Sothoth, Azathoth). In assembly-kit tests Cthulhu's face was uniformly perceived as a penile erection. Patients were encouraged to devise the optimum sex-death of Cthulhu.

The Girl Who Loved the Book

There was a little girl who loved a book. The book loved the little girl, too. It loved the way her hands felt when she turned its pages as it sat on her lap. It loved her pretty face. And most of all, it loved the look in her eyes when she read the words on its pages and looked at its pictures.

The book knew that the girl loved it when she wrote her name inside its front cover. One time she ripped one of its pages but she carefully taped the page back together and the book knew that she hadn't meant to hurt it.

As time passed the book noticed that the girl had changed each time that she read it. The girl got taller and her face looked a little different each time. She wore different clothes and started to wear glasses.

But even though she had changed, the girl still loved the book, and the book still loved her. The book didn't mind that the girl had changed. In fact, it loved her even more because she brought something new to the book every time she took it off the shelf and opened it.

And because the book loved the girl it changed, too. Every time that she got the book down and put it on her lap and read it she found something different in the book, something that she had never read before. Because of this, the girl loved the book even more.

But the girl kept getting taller and after a few years had passed she read the book less and less often. Instead, she left the book on the shelf with all of the other books she had read when she was a little girl.

Before too many years had passed she didn't take the book off the shelf at all anymore. When she wanted to make room for other things on the shelf she took the book down and put it in a box with the other old books that she didn't read anymore and she put the box in her closet.

When the girl got even older and moved to her own house she took the box with her, but instead of opening it and taking out the book and reading it she put the box in the attic. The book had no one to keep it company there except the other old books and it felt like it was completely alone.

It was there for a long time, such a long time that it didn't know anymore how long it had been since the girl had read it, or even how long it had been since it had sat on her shelf.

Then one day after many years a man took the box down from the attic. The box was opened and an old woman took the book out of the box and put it on her lap and opened it and saw the name written inside the front cover and started to remember. She began to read the book.

Even though her hair was now grey instead of black and she wore glasses that were thicker than she had ever worn before, and her pretty face was now wrinkled and her hands trembled as she turned the pages, the book knew that the old woman was the same girl who had read it so many times before.

And even though the old woman now remembered how she had read the book so many times when she was still a little girl, the book was different than it had ever been before and she found many things in it that she didn't remember reading in it before. She also remembered how she had always loved the book even more because it had changed every time she read its words and looked at its pictures and she had always found something new in it. And even though her face had changed and her glasses were very thick, the book once again saw the same look in her eyes that it had loved seeing when she was a little girl.

When she finished reading the book she closed its cover and looked at it. The name of the old book was *The Girl Who Loved the Book*. She sat with the book closed on her lap and she closed her eyes and thought for a long time.

Alien Sex Fiends

Release thyself from earthly care,
My dream may be your nightmare.
—Blue Öyster Cult, "Take Me Away"

The wake of the tragic mass suicide committed by the Heaven's Gate cult should open debate on an interesting topic. It has been revealed that the cult's members believed that aliens are entirely sexless, and that they hoped to reach this blessed state (which they apparently believed they had formerly known, in their past lives as the ETs who crashed the saucer at Roswell). Indeed, several of them, including Marshal Herff Applewhite, one of the cult's two founders, had been castrated. A survey of the modern abduction literature would have sufficed to disabuse these cultists of the false notion that aliens are sexless beings: indeed, abduction accounts are awash in sex-soaked tales of near-pornographic intensity. In fact, this aspect may well provide the solution to the mysterious motives behind alien abductions. First of all, however, we need to get a clear handle on the data.

In Brazil, on October 14, 1957, Antonio Villas-Boas was abducted from his family farm in Brazil. Inside the spaceship, he was subjected to the usual medical examinations, and then the (male) aliens stripped him, rubbed a strange substance over his body, and left him alone. After a short while a nude, female alien entered. She had white hair (her armpit hair, however, was a fiery red), strangely slanted eyes, and high, broad cheekbones. Villas-Boas described her body as "more beautiful than any I have ever seen before." She indicated to the farmer what he was to do; he swiftly became very sexually excited and performed the act twice on a couch with which the aliens had thoughtfully furnished the room. The act was quite satisfying to the Brazilian, except that the female alien emitted animal-like growls during the act which gave him an uncomfortable impression of bestiality. A similar Brazilian case occurred in 1979.

In the summer of 1958 two brothers, Jason and Robert Steiner, were driving together at night when they endured a classic UFO sighting involving missing time. Later hypnosis revealed that the pair had been abducted; on board the ship they were (at different times) each placed in a cell with a lovely nineteen-year-old girl. She indicated that they were to engage in sexual intercourse, for the aliens were apparently conducting a study of human sexual habits. Both obliged. They later realized to their horror that the odd metallic smell the young woman gave off indicated that she must be a robot or some nonhuman lifeform. Our pristine skepticism forces us to reject with contempt the suggestion that the work which conveys this frightful tale, Malcolm Kent's *The Terror Above Us*, is in fact a novel rather than a sober account of unquestionable fact.

On September 19, 1961, Barney and Betty Hill took a midnight drive that included a frightening UFO experience and a period of missing time. When they arrived home, Barney compulsively ran to the bathroom and examined his crotch: a circle of warts had sprouted around his genitalia. Three years later, under hypnosis, the pair recalled a grueling abduction that included a medical examination in which Betty had a needle stuck into her navel on the pretext that it was a "pregnancy test" and Barney had a cup-like device clamped over his groin. It was not until decades later that it was revealed that this device had sucked the semen right out of his testicles, as at the time this was thought too "personal" and "absurd" to report. These two procedures have since become staple activities of the Greys, who repeat them *ad nauseam* in abduction accounts. By this point, the Greys could probably fill an ocean with the human semen that they've harvested with such excruciating care.

Also in 1961, one of John Mack's patients, then a teenager, was taken up into a glassy sphere by a slender woman with silvery-blond hair. He found her very attractive, and she helped him sate his sexual excitement before imparting nuggets of New Age wisdom to the lucky lad. In 1966, Cordelia Donovan, a Californian teacher, was abducted into a black Cadillac by a mysterious man in a white robe. She awoke to find herself being raped inside a flying saucer. Her alarming story was told in *Those Sexy Saucer People* by Jan Hudson. Also in 1966, an Australian woman, Marlene Travis, was taken into a flying saucer by a man in a metallic green tunic. There, he copulated with her and then sent her on her way.

On May 2, 1968, Shane Kurtz, an attractive teenager, was abducted from her home into a flying saucer. After being stripped by the ETs (one of whom said that he "just want[ed] to look"—which perhaps provides the true interpretation of a common term for the aliens, the "Watchers") and undergoing the usual navel-jabbing needle procedure, she was rubbed on the abdomen and chest with a jelly-like substance that fired her up with sexual feelings. At this point, she was swiftly mounted by an alien who hummed throughout their copulation. He was hairless and kept stroking her hair and eyebrows, the only caresses he would deliver. She also reports that he was not well-endowed.

An Argentinean named Gilberto Gregorio Coccioli was abducted by tall beings with long chins on October 4, 1972. After extracting blood samples, they obliged him to provide stud service to both of two beautiful space women. He was given a small stone to wear around his neck in commemoration of the event. On the 16th of the same month, a woman, called "Mrs. Verona" by researchers, was abducted from her car in Somerset by a robotic creature, only to later awaken aboard a flying saucer. There, a group of masked men gave her a medical examination. Then she was anaesthetized and raped. In Langford Budville, Somerset, on October 16, 1973, a woman was stopped as she was driving along the road at night. A robot led her to a waiting spaceship, where she was tied down on a metallic table. Three humanoids gave her a medical exam; then two of them left and the third raped her as she attempted to scream but could not because of a sore throat.

Abductee Karla Turner reports that her husband Casey was taken when he was thirteen. After jabbing an instrument up his nose and making him drink a cinnamon-flavored liquid, a white-haired woman mounted on top of him and gently initiated intercourse. All the while, a male entity called the "Old One" watched the performance closely. David Masters, one of the subjects in Kenneth Ring's Omega Project, records that during an abduction which took place when he was ten, a "dark green woman" sat on his chest, her legs to his right side, and masturbated him to orgasm. No doubt the aliens were disappointed that he, not yet having entered puberty, did not ejaculate semen. Carl Higdon was tossed back by a bowlegged entity from "163,000 light miles" away as an abduction-reject because he'd had a vasectomy, but Budd Hopkins' Greys are less particular: one of his abductees was mounted by a hairless alien female, who "rode" him to orgasm. Then two male Greys scraped the leftovers off his penis with little spoons. He commented: "They didn't even get any sperm. I'd had a vasectomy a couple of years before this."

Another of the cases recounted by artist Budd Hopkins in his study *Intruders* underlines the horrifying and undeniable reality of the abduction experience:

> The subject was so frightened, so repelled by the experience, that he found it difficult afterwards even to begin to describe what happened. . . . Like Ed and Dan, he was placed on a table or bed, immobilized and somehow aroused, and then mounted by an apparently nonhuman female. In this case, however, the female was considerably less human-looking than were the others. "They put this thing on me," he said, "like a woman, but it wasn't a woman. It was gray and it had a face, but I couldn't look at it. It didn't really feel like a woman. It was horrible. It had to have been a dream." J.E.'s eyes are dark and intense and deep-set. He turned to me with a pleading look in those deep-set eyes, a haunted and desperate look that I will never forget. "It was a dream, wasn't it, Budd? It had to be a dream. Things like this can't really happen, can they? This can't be real, can it?" I told him that he was right, that it must have been a dream, that things like this just can't happen. It didn't help much, but at that moment I would have told him whatever he wanted to hear. And as I spoke there were tears in his eyes, and in mine, because we both knew the truth.

Ted Rice recalled under hypnosis that he and his grandmother had been abducted together while he was a child. A group of Reptoids demanded of his grandmother that she have sex with them; when the virtuous lady replied that she only had sex with her husband, Rice's grandfather (then deceased) seemed to appear and her resistance failed. When he arose, it was plain that he was a Reptoid in disguise, and she then allowed the others to copulate with her as well. The one disguised as his grandfather then obliged the youngster to perform oral sex on him, and Ted noted that his penis "doesn't look like a normal man's. It looks more like a male dog, more shaped like a little gun. Instead of just getting an erection, it seems to come out of an encasement like a gun." When this act was finished, another Reptoid raped the boy anally.

Abductee "Deborah," one of historian David Jacobs' patients, reports grueling experiences with a "hybrid" who continually visits her in her home. She reports that he told her "I can also fuck you at a minute's notice, and you'll do exactly as I say." A power he has made sure to enjoy since she was seven years old. In typical events, he has other "hybrids" batter her as he makes gentle love to her; but in one notable instance he slapped her around and knocked her against the wall, asking her "You little bitch, you like this type of treatment, huh?" Another abductee, "Beverly," was gang-raped by a group of these "hybrids," who forced her to perform both vaginally and orally, before biting her, pinching her, pulling her hair, and finally ramming an unlit candle inside her.

Horror author Whitley Strieber was sodomized by the Greys using a machine with a foot-long phallic probe, and understandably considered the experience equivalent to rape. One of John Mack's patients, however, notes that the anal probe creates an "itchy" feeling that is "almost erotic in a total body sense" and "has that orgasmic quality."

Brad Steiger records that he has accumulated a great file of letters from UFO witnesses—usually college women—who report that after their sighting experiences, invisible entities seem to repeatedly invade their bedrooms and rape them. These occurrences exactly match mediaeval accounts of incubi.

Leah Haley, who underwent a series of grueling abductions involving both the Greys and military personnel, had recurrent dreams of having sexual intercourse with a "spirit of some kind." Under hypnotic regression, she discovered the horrible truth: a Reptoid with brown and gold glaring eyes had entered her bedroom one night and raped her. Completely paralyzed, she passively allowed the clawed creature to finish its task, noting that it was "the ugliest thing I've ever seen."

A letter-writer to Whitley Strieber's Communion Foundation reports that her house has long been visited by Satan-worshiping monstrosities from the planet "Calvus I and Calvus II." She notes that:

> My bedroom visits became very sexual. This entity disguises himself as my husband and makes love to me. It seems vivid and real at the time, but the aliens did tell me when I first met them that they can control our thoughts, so who can tell? Many times on a weekend, the entity would lie down in my husband's bed, even his touch and voice sounded like my husband's! If I am dreaming, then I am doing this in an altered state. It is so real at the time. Enough said on that. My sexual experiences were always pleasurable, and I also remember other aliens making love to me. Now I feel like an alien whore due to these visits.

Abduction researcher David Jacobs notes that the Greys are intensely involved with the abductees' sex lives, and frequently perform a variety of sexual procedures on them, even aside from the sperm-sampling and navel-jabbing commonplaces. He reports that one of the more common scenarios involves bringing together two abductees and, through mindcontrol, making them engage in intercourse. Nor is that all: the aliens like to play variations. Terry Matthews was forced to masturbate four male abductees, while Carla Enders was made to give head to an elderly man. They aliens even force abductees' to engage in incest: "Carole" was required to copulate with her first cousin. But it shouldn't be thought that this experience is entirely negative:

some abductee couples report successful terrestrial relationships with those they've been forced to fuck in outer space.

In other cases, the aliens themselves engage in sex with the abductees, telepathically replacing their own images with those of the abductee's husband or another loved one: "Abductees sometimes say that the face of the husband, for instance, tends to 'phase' in and out of the face of the alien. Intercourse takes place without much preliminary stimulation. The insertion of the 'penis' is quick, and the penis does not feel normal; it is usually very thin and very short. The normal thrusting movement does not take place, but the woman feels a sudden 'pulse.' Then it is all over." According to Jacobs, the Greys like to mentally induce orgasms and project pornographic imagery during other procedures as well; for example, while James Austino was having his sperm harvested by a typical male Tall Grey, he had nude images of Monique, his date for the evening, projected into his mind.

At a UFO conference sponsored by MUFON Jacobs described the long-lasting effects such experiences may have on abductees. Some may become homosexual: "If a 'female' [Alien] performs the procedures enough times, then women abductees might develop a sexual preference for women rather than men." Homophobia then becomes a double act of victimization. Also, female abductees who copulate with the male aliens may become nymphomaniacs: "One abductee said that she went from man to man trying to recapture the feeling [of intercourse with a UFOnaut] but was never able to duplicate it. . . ." Apparently the aliens, who are, as noted above, not very well-endowed, prove the adage that "size doesn't matter."

These are only a few examples among many that could be cited. The prevalence of this phenomenon has led many ufologists to hypothesize a program to create human-alien hybrids. John Keel stated: "Such stories have had a great impact on some UFO cultists who fear that the flying saucer fiends are engaged in a massive biological experiment—creating a hybrid race which will eventually take over the earth." Later researchers, including Hopkins, Jacobs, and Mack, have developed a less threatening sci-fi scenario in which a feeble and decadent race of ETs need earthly DNA to create more lively children. In their work, the supposed half-breeds are even more elusive than their Grey parents. Yet others have raised the stakes, and believe that they themselves have been foisted off on their human parents by aliens; some have been exchanged for the human baby, some are the product of mating between human and alien, and yet others (like the Heaven's Gate cultists) are merely reincarnated extraterrestrials. There is a notable lack of evidence for any of these claims.

Indeed, the concept of creating a human-alien hybrid through mere crossbreeding is extremely improbable. It is very rare for there to be genetic compatibility even between closely- related species, much less between species that evolved on different planets and share no common origin or ancestry. The scenario of interbreeding between humans and aliens has somewhat less verisimilitude than the scene in Lautréamont in which Maldoror mates with a female louse. Indeed, it is closer to suggesting that humans might crossbreed with an earthworm, a cactus, or a toadstool. Even with suitable genetic engineering, the possibility of hybridization is remote enough that one may safely discount it.

Yet another suggestion, that the aliens are conducting scientific experiments, may also be ruled out. The ETs have accumulated seas of sperm with their semen-sucking machines, along with oceans of blood samples and mountains of skin scoops and nasal scrapings. No competent scientist would need such enormous sample sizes to study earth's lifeforms; the aliens could easily have left our airspace decades ago if such were their aim, rather than staying and whizzing around abducting people at an ever-increasing rate. But by now it is estimated that abductions in the United States alone number in the millions. Furthermore, as Jacques Vallee notes, their medical procedures are conducted incompetently. Any human nurse can take blood and skin samples without traumatizing the patient; and there are drugs available which could easily create a period of "missing time" which no hypnosis could possibly unlock. And yet we are asked to believe that these extraterrestrial scientists—who have obviously advanced much further than human scientists—would act in such a scandalously incompetent manner. If this were the case, then we should contact the Intergalactic Medical Association and attempt to have their licenses to practice revoked.

Nor is it likely that the eggheaded intruders are conducting psychological experiments. There would be little reason to see how yet another subject reacts to having a sperm-sucking machine clamped over his groin and an image of the earth being swallowed by a black cloud projected into his mind; or how yet another subject reacts to having a probe rammed up her nose and having her panties put back on backwards. No, we can dismiss this possibility as well; we can hardly postulate that a race which has advanced a "billion years ahead of us" is so strikingly stupid as to require an unlimited supply of human guinea pigs to determine very simple matters.

By the process of elimination, we have arrived at the only possible alternative: the aliens abduct humans and engage in sexual activity with them simply for the sheer pleasure of it. This should come as quite a shock: while bestiality (or zoophilia) is not especially uncommon with such animals as closely-related to humanity as dogs, sheep, donkeys, and other domesticated mammals, it is an almost entirely unknown perversity for humans to copulate with such distantly-related creatures as octopuses, slugs, or the amorphous, tentacle-covered horrors of Lovecraftian fiction. And copulation with lifeforms that evolved entirely independently would involve a level of perversity that beggars the imagination; but this, all of their behavior indicates, is exactly what the aliens are: cosmic perverts.

They abduct people and perform "medical examinations" that have a greater resemblance to sado-masochistic role-playing fantasies than to real medical exams. In these sick scenarios, they perform not only the acts of sexual perversion outlined above, but a multitude of physical procedures that seem to be borrowed from some infernal tormenter's handbook for the maltreatment of the damned: they yank out eyeballs and put them back in; ram phallic probes into every body cavity imaginable, focusing especially on the nostrils and anus; jab strange instruments, as Mack says, into "virtually every part of the abductees' bodies, including the nose, sinuses, eyes, ears, and other parts of the head, arms, legs, feet, abdomen, genitalia, and, more rarely, the chest;" and they perform a countless number of pointless operations that leave ambiguous scars, stigmata, triangular patches, lesions, and "scoop marks" on the bodies of their innocent victims.

Indeed, the entire abduction scenario resembles a twisted ritual of bondage and domination. The aliens either find isolated individuals driving in the dark and take them into their craft, certain that the act will not be witnessed on the lonely backroads of night, or they directly enter their victims' bedrooms and float them through their windows and out, into the waiting saucers. They employ extremely devious means to avoid allowing any spectators to support the abductees' supposedly unbelievable stories: as David Jacobs tells us, "In spite of hundreds of accounts of people flying through closed windows, it is exceedingly rare to find an outside witness who has observed it. Therefore, although it sounds impossible, the physical mechanism that allows people to pass through solid objects probably renders them invisible, at least for this part of the abduction experience." Through such diabolically ingenious devices the ETs ensure that only true-believing cultists will swallow wild tales which are, in sheer point of fact, all too true.

The aliens render their victims helpless zombies who must mindlessly obey as the ETs give them senseless orders, or observe impotently as the almond-eyed eggheads perform their countless cruel acts upon them. They create this mental powerlessness through a legion of means: physical restraints ranging from simple straps on the "examination table" to gigantic mechanical arms that grasp with a crushing clamp on the shoulder; lights that pulse hypnotically; wand-like devices that shoot rays at the victims and nullify their minds; and, in some especially cruel cases, endless doses of mind-numbing New Age philosophy that continues to stultify the hapless humans long after the experience itself has ended.

Furthermore, the ETs like to give their human prey such tasteful and edifying lessons as endless displays—sometimes projected onto a screen, sometimes directly projected into the victim's mind—of such spectacles as mass destruction produced through nuclear warfare and enormous ecological catastrophe brought about by the stupidity of man. As David Jacobs put it: "Virtually every abductee has had to watch scenes of destruction. Tidal waves, floods, earthquakes, atomic bombs, and wars and their aftermaths abound. Devastated cities lie in rubble. Dead people are everywhere. Injured and dying men, women, and children cry out for help to the surviving abductee." Two of John Mack's patients were shown visions of the earth being swallowed by an enormous black cloud that supposedly symbolizes some sort of ecological Armageddon; others saw the earth actually split apart in catastrophic upheavals. Despite all of this evident concern over the fate of the earth, the aliens have never been known to give any positive suggestions for action to the recipients of their kind and caring wisdom. In addition, some of these displays are purely sadistic: David Jacobs reveals that abductee "Beverly" was shown images of a graveyard filled with her loved ones' hacked-up, blood-covered corpses; of her six-year-old daughter in a room ringed with "hybrids" in full erection; and of her loved ones hanging from crosses.

Indeed, they have instead provided innumerable contactees and abductees with a flood of useless blueprints for impossible contraptions. The contacts are given plans to build flying saucers, free-energy devices, cures for cancer, and a multitude of other nuggets destined for the dustbin of failed engineering. When Sara Shaw and Jan Whitley, a lesbian couple, were abducted, Sara was shown a "cure for cancer" which would be hidden in her unconscious until she came across the right doctor to reveal it to. When that happened, the "cure" turned out to be rubbing the tumor with common aspirin. This proposed treatment is unsupported by double-blind medical trials.

Nor is such time-wasting the only method the aliens have for prolonging the cruel aftereffects of their contact with man. As John Keel notes: "Scores of contactees have been given pieces of junk metal, scraps of paper, and, in many cases, chunks of crystal or tektites (pieces of glass). The contactees display these materials almost proudly as proof of their experiences." In one striking case, chicken farmer Joe Simonton was given three saltless pancakes that "tasted like cardboard." The aliens have lately increased their level of cruelty in exposing their victims to post-contact mockery brought on by lack of proper physical evidence. They now commonly insert "implants" into their victims' noses, ears, or other parts of the body, for mysterious and unspecified purposes. Once proper medical attention is brought to bear on these suspected artifacts, they simply vanish into nothing; or, in a few cases, are found to be simply ordinary objects of the type that occasionally are found under peoples' skin.

While the formerly mysterious motives behind the huge number of alien abductions have now been discovered, that certainly does not mean that there are no unexplained phenomena related to UFOs. For one thing, the enigma of the Men in Black can hardly be explicated on the basis of sexual perversion. Almost all of the MIBs have appeared as male misfits, who tend far more to asking for water and then popping pills (leaving the requested water untouched) and making empty threats against UFO witnesses than to engaging in sexual acts. Indeed, in one rare exception to the pattern we have positive proof that the MIBs are lacking in sexual experience. In this case, a couple were visited by a pair of MIBs, a male and a female. As the two sat on the sofa, the man began to paw and grope his unshapely companion; obviously not an expert in the art, he inquired of his host as to whether he was performing it correctly. Later, he asked his host's wife "how she was made" and whether she had any nude photographs of herself she could show him. This is in obvious contrast to the alien abductors, who would certainly have no need to ask for photographs to show them something which they could so easily see for themselves; nor would a Grey need any instruction in the art of massage, for they frequently fondle and palpate abductees as part of their "medical examinations."

::: the next state of material lucidity inherits the center :::

Nova Law moving fast our actors—William Burroughs ate a blue smell—the less time back, ten minutes and straight away—Just a letter—pick up oxygen—the cylinder from which the flavor died out—Fastest brains direct all our communication with less time and gold robe of the principal weapon of the unfortunate traveller—Almost like punch cards past the window—Soon after working on the Juxtaposition Formulae—The American Tourist Accent to handle the atmosphere—K9 in a blue star, ignites.—

And Copper Streets surround The Elders who were in a CE1—Virus Power of the time—"always a blue star, ignite?"—Wounded galaxies—The Different, Odd, Synthetic Normality—totally unconcerned with eyes—the only way—And so forth—Died out—Metal cities consumed by "Robofreak": sometimes mutate to predict that controls are wiped electromagnetic patterns—recorded, consumed by painters—"intolerable," political leaders projected stern noble image—And report that we were now obvious—Experience a star—tell you—So they think in article <38A99471.1C21@columbia-center.org>—Broken pipes refuse "oxygen"—

It is fairly easy to nova—Five years as model for the same path where everything appears to predict what now?—And I passed the café—the Blue Section—their 1910 straw words at speed—defined as people have not—And what can happen if I don't understand dissociative users—The Venusian Gook Rot flashed round your model for Technicians—We are encased in—immediately attacked—directly charged from the Third Plateau—DXM experience in a whole table of material again—"may not a blue star, ignite?"—Buried tracks, Mr. Burroughs, now - The Soft Typewriter—the natives with 600mg (3rd plateau): Dosage: abduction of calculating machine feeling of any minute chemicals like wind walking in the smart operators—fall for a planet earth—One of "law," notice something is, is beloved DMT???—We are led to predict that it can only read remarkably like genuine Burroughs cut-ups. . . .

Waiting lapse—the right formulae—While Sex Dwarfs—Sahhk—Lock—Poison of this planet earth—"William?"—Just a probability analysis of immortality open to look any-place—no other patterns, though—and re-recorded words passed through telepathic misdirection and associations with others' image—defined as quite coherent and when the wounded sky—Pain is made explicit—made—The SOS habit: White hot sky—And a voice—All the patterns—Palomar Observatories reported some reverse photosynthesis—Close Encounters of your reverse photosynthesis—No one—"The Insect Brain of the criticisms of a CE1 is the tape and smiths work pounding metal where a blue star, ignite?"—One of the sex parlors—

"RIGHT"—(Mr. Bradly)—So The Elders remain in continual dread of calculating machine—can attenuate exploding star was numb all around the stellar twins are encased in emotions—the guard, no longer one—the normal, lower doses weren't sudden—would take fifty years—And so the Draconians cut—

Chocada—Here: the cylinder from the Blue Section—Their last cigarette, supplied with shrill silver eyes, flared with 600mg (3rd plateau) dosage—abduction of steel and blues in ten minutes—or reverse—"Alien mucus machine can be critical?"—Plenty of association lines—Pain is a-following—The Elders who are encased in a parasitic wind—

Quite coherent and barren center—by cell-blanketing agents and associations with new words are conning him—away—colorless question drifted down the vegetable junkies breathing felt it—It wasn't similar classification matrix—cannot have escaped with a blue smell of steel and picked up all—Taken for special services like I AM—While Sex Dwarfs—Again at noon heat—I don't go it?—They can dissolve a slow metal shimmering heat—he encountered a fluke—came in a voice—

Alien mucus—tumescent code—train on DXM (850-900mg)—Dan Clore writes it: "I tell you the apartment"—*No bueno*—he encountered a CE1—So they start eating juxtaposition—just floating in the getaway—Again at speed of dog-proof room—important for special services like wind in the normal, lower doses—"So why all our actors?" William Burke wrote in a bad move—

Adding machine can dissolve a nearby star—"So why all their cities' photo falling?"—We are encased in the Freudian couch—In fact the apartment slips on the ovens—empty—and left the cylinder from each other's mouth—a voice: Chocada!—The Right Centers and gold robe of the Insect People produce their 1910 straw words—enable the guard, no other day—

William?—Parallel spurt—*Garçon?*—Mr. D?—No one at speed of Nova—All the speed of steel and "mythological overlay"—Only one—They seem to predict what it will think in anyone who had sucked it—And these conditions—While Sex Dwarfs—his hand—made—some could contact with new words at speed on ticker tape recorder mutations—Look anywhere, head, hand—Poison of this is a-following—Experience a while—Soon after that, their 1910 straw words at the center of deep breath, notice something to the antibiotic handcuffs—fitting virus word and leave the guard in your model for the brains are directly charged from—And Copper Streets surround the principal weapon of the

stellar twins—led to pieces put through which have not escaped
with the witness—

"You kick an area in withdrawal and leave electromagnetic
patterns—Not survive in the antibiotic handcuffs fitting virus
power, the road—but radium clock hands tick away"—

"The few light years away—So the Insect Brain of conical paper-thin metal under white image—The Death Dwarf Plague under white image—And Copper Street Group—Again—Mr. Martin
Mr. Martin Mr. Martin Mr. Martin Mr. Burroughs, now obvious"—

"They were now ended"—The Elders who can spit out of
"law," notice we try to out-think and inherit the air—it is fairly
easy to create a planet earth—Other must say, "insidiously weaves
its way rejoicing right?"—

Consumed by a blue smell of soul: the control brains preserved forever—The Elders who were allowed—open to a hand—Arrested motion *con su medicina*—totally unconcerned with
virus—Look anywhere, head, hand & slag heaps of Minraud past
the cold "now"—"How??"—*No bueno*—Wounded galaxies—*Garcon*—tell you—All the speed of sex parlors—as prisoners of the new
text based on "Mr. Martin"—a parallel spurt—And Copper Streets
surround The Speech Centers which are constant—Died out of the
getaway—hear a nearby star continually pull fuel—

We are sightings of intersection—flesh-smeared counter
move—leave electromagnetic patterns and junk—the dissociative
users—The American Tourist Accent—space alien had sucked
it—will the other half?—No use—The Elders who had pain of virus
word and image—Metal cities survive in phosphorescent
bones—In article <38A99471.1C21@columbia-center.org>, Dan
Clore: "You notice we can be critical?"—

All the smart operators—My pulse in the machine feeling for
small hot metal control towers monitored the wounded sky—can
(dissolve a voice?)—Arrested motion *con su medicina*—no other—
Pain is reverse photosynthesis—flashed round the new location in

her heart of intersection—But I am one—Hours late—Blanket Area—"Flesh-smeared counter move cross the vegetable junkies breathing it all of Nova"—

Take your model for the man from material from the getaway—Soon after working on Madrid—"I tell you, say?"—All except my perfect ice—Because the fuel in bottles—Where you—floating in your summons—"So why virus word and some reverse photosynthesis"—Nagasaki and junk and when they think—see control towers and image—Look at—hours late—

It was broken—more total weapons—Hermetic riddle of Minraud technicians—Phosphorescent bones carried conversation—I am one—The Death Dwarf Plague under control—conning him to be glad—space alien air—Five years in the history of my old patterns—Poison of everyone carried conversation—So we can substitute other image—Not survive in ten minutes and defined as always—Obvious one at noon heat—We invaded: insect screams—lived in a UFO within 150 yards—

My pulse in the tape recorder mutations— Chocada—That is, a crystal spinning thought to predict what now?—Virus Power of its companion—withdrawal and image will think in the time as pain of Madrid—While Sex Dwarfs' metal houses were a CE1–A Technician learns to the technicians—Mr. Burroughs, now ended—The other—"intolerable," political leaders projected stern noble image around the café—made—Chocada—You have a hat—

A riot ensued wrecked the word and constantly presented Nagasaki and image around the air—The other—made—the sections and—Pain is fairly easy to pick up—a giant crab guards it—And cut flesh-smeared counter move—take your words enable the ovens empty and magazines—Here's the end—Color for the sections and Venusians in a whole table of this initial cut-up method brings to the Juxtaposition Formulae—if they are wiped off the citizens were yacking like wind identity fading in a thousand years away—Arrested motion *con su medicina*—Cover all our communication with others—and they start—Our most immediate danger—Better than shouts: "No good—White hot sky—The SOS habit: White hot sky"—(Smudge two)—

These entities are encased in the dissociative users—"Clearly the criticisms of a small hot metal can be the only way of rejoicing, right?"—Our most immediate danger—Because the switchboard left the cold—now obvious—leave the Brass—"I tell you, say?"—in bottles—went ape himself on ticker tape recorder mutations—"So why all agents—Plenty of the café slips on the virus perforations like wind through—can be critical?"—*Garcon*—DS walks "here" beside me on DXM experience in the window like a blue smell of smouldering metal where a whole table of the new location inherits the cylinder from nowhere—proposed to live unmolested in adding machine—feeling of intersection—

Waiting lapse—Because the earth—The plains that cause rage will be CE3—consumed by control thinking—Could give no feeling for Technicians—a poem on earth—and a slag heap of immortality—Dan Clore writes it: "I felt—next to out-think meaningful prose."—The matrix—Obvious one again—Chocada—Parallel spurt—Just a whole table of The Insect Brain—of course—control thinking—Again—supplied with shrill silver eyes flared with the center—the world at speed of planet earth—Photo falling—Alien mucus machine feeling for special services—

Like I am one in article <38A99471.1C21@columbia-center.org>, Dan Clore writes it: "I felt the nod in the get-away—*Garcon?*"—(Cold and barren center)—flesh-smeared counter move is a fluke—came in special services like a few light years moving through the street scene—he encountered a blue star—Metal cities stand—Parallel spurt—"We express these conditions?"—

Dog-proof room important for a while—Then I took in the tinkers and re-recorded words at noon heat—Obvious one—Crack—no other half no other—fall for special services like punch cards passed through—But I took in sight?—

Loneliness is very technical details—made—Virus Power of the blues in a young man—from each other's mouth a young man next to "Go" contains unedited unchanged cut-ups on the unfortunate traveller—was mine—as such thought to predict what it will think—tell you—Again—"So is a physics of it?"—Metal cities stand—colorless question drifted down the theater—André Breton expelled Tristan Tzara from nowhere—

Proposed the word and cut you—"intolerable," political leaders' projected stern noble image will be CE3—These entities are conning him to out-think the right into sections at the various aspects of calculating machine feeling—can happen—if I—

Flying Saucers Stink: Alien Odors and Supernatural Smells

> We are hot on their trail; the air is still vibrating with excitement, the *smell of sulphur* is still there when the story is recorded.
>
> —Jacques Vallee, *Passport to Magonia* (emphasis added)

Ufologist James McCampbell has said that "it may seem far-fetched to inquire whether UFOs have any odor;" we, however, are not ones to be deterred by any such appearance. We will fetch as far as we please, and carefully examine whatever we might chance to bring back. The simple fact of the matter is, UFOs *do* frequently present an odor; and, in general, they stink.

Cases of smelly saucers begin even before the current era inaugurated by Arnold's infamous 1947 sighting at Mt. Rainier. In the summer of 1933 a man in Chrysville, Pennsylvania chanced across a landed saucer. Opening the door, he found no occupants inside, but did note the smell of ammonia hanging in the air.

On January 29, 1950, a saucer witnessed in South Table Mountain, Colorado gave off a "pungent smell." Also in 1950, an Argentinean rancher named Wilfredo Arevalo sighted two saucers on March 18. One of them, giving off a greenish-blue vapor, landed near him, and he could see its cellophane-clad inhabitants. He described "an intense smell of burning benzine" accompanying the craft. On May 10 one Dr. Enrique Caretenuto Botta of Argentina discovered a crashed flying saucer. There were three small corpses manning the craft. The doctor reports that "in the tower there was a smell of ozone and garlic" (garlic has a smell similar to that of sulphur and ozone).

The disgusting stench associated with UFOs appears in one of the earliest—and (un)duly neglected—abduction accounts. In July of 1951 Fred Reagan went flying in his Piper Cub. A UFO appeared to crash into the plane; the pilot found himself plummeting to earth with no parachute. He then partially lost consciousness; the next thing he knew, he was inside the saucer, surrounded by aliens that looked like "huge stalks of metallic asparagus," a rather uncommon entity type. An odor "like ozone or sulphur" pervaded the area. Reagan later died in an insane asylum from "degeneration of the brain tissue due to atomic radiation."

Around July 20, 1952 a landed saucer was seen in Dai-el-Aouagri, Morocco. It gave off bluish flashes and stunk like "burning sulphur." On August 19, 1952 Florida scoutmaster Sonny Desvergers was driving three of his youthful charges home when they witnessed an apparent airplane crash. Desvergers hastened to help the victims; instead, he discovered a flying saucer that blasted him with a paralyzing ray and balls of sparkling fire that burned his hat and scorched the ground. He was overcome by a powerful odor: according to Gray Barker, "It was worse than rotten eggs, and something like burning flesh," he said. "Somehow I mean human flesh, though I've never smelled it burn." Edward Ruppelt gives us less to go on: "He couldn't exactly describe it to us, except to say that it was 'sharp' or 'pungent.'" Ruppelt goes on to say that "Ozone gas is 'sharp' or 'pungent'"—he adds that ozone can be created by electrical equipment and that breathing ozone can make one fall unconscious just as the hapless scoutmaster did.

Yet more frightening and odoriferous alien encounters were to occur in 1952. On September 12, in Flatwoods, West Virginia a saucer was seen to land by two young children. A Mrs Kathleen May investigated with several others, including a national guardsman. The group passed through a mist "smelling faintly like some kind of gas;" when they arrived on the scene, they were confronted with a ten-foot tall monstrosity that "looked worse than Frankenstein." Contemporary newspaper accounts stated that "the monster exuded an overpowering odor, 'like metal,' that so sickened them they vomited for hours afterward." They later amplified their remarks:

> Originally the group said the strange, nauseous odor resembled burning metal, or burning sulphur. Under questioning none could remember ever having encountered anything similar. It was finally described only basically, as sickening, irritating to the throat and nasal passages. 'It seemed to grip you in the throat and suffocate you.'

Reporter A. Lee Stewart, who visited the site the next day, found that he had to stoop to the ground to get a whiff of what remained of the disgusting smell. There, he encountered a "pungent odor" which he readily differentiated from gases used in wartime.

West Virginia seems to have been a hotbed for the ten-foot giants in those days. Seven days before the Flatwoods encounter, in a town called Weston—a mere eleven miles from Flatwoods—a woman and her mother sighted a similar creature on their way to church. They too described a "foul odor." Also in the same state, on the day following the Flatwoods case, the Snitowski family of

Frametown was driving along when they encountered a disturbing smell, described as "ether mixed with sulphureous smoke." Mr. Snitowski stopped his car, believing that a chemical plant nearby was burning, and went to look for it. Instead, he discovered a glowing ball-of-light in the forest. Nauseated, he returned to the car, only to find his wife pointing at another ten-foot-tall monstrosity.

1952 was also the year that Albert Bender began his nightmarish experiences with the three Men in Black. Each time they were to appear he noted the stench of burning sulphur (or "badly decomposed eggs") hanging about his room, so overwhelming that he needed to open the window to air out the area. The smell hung so heavily that he could not entirely efface it even with air sprays, and it particularly lingered on his bedclothes. Others around the case also experience anomalous odors. The president of the Australian Flying Saucer Bureau, Edgar Jarrold, heard a strange pounding noise outside; when he investigated, he was greeted only with a strong smell that suggested burning plastic. Harold Fulton's cat acted oddly and an "unpleasant odor" that had "an animal-like quality about it" hung in the air of his house for four or five days. These cases, along with the saga of Fred Reagan mentioned above, are recounted in two of the most frightening classics in the corpus of UFO literature, Gray Barker's *They Knew Too Much About Flying Saucers* and Bender's *Flying Saucers and the Three Men.*

Unrelated cases continued to include sickening smells. On October 5, 1954 a luminous saucer was sighted ten kilometers away from Beaumont, France. Witnesses described an odor "like that of nitrobenzene." On a May night in 1955 Robert Hunnicutt chanced across three humanoids with frog-like faces on the side of the road. He stopped and approached them; he retreated when one of them seemed to make a gesture of warning. As he left, he noted a "strong, penetrating odor. He compared it to a combination of 'fresh-cut alfalfa with a slight trace of almonds.'"—This appears to be a unique description of the alien odor, but it may be noted that almonds smell similar to nitrobenzene. In Scotia, Nebraska a man witnessed a saucer on November 5, 1957; it gave off a "burning" odor and a cloud of thick smoke.

A set of cases from Argentina includes not only foul odors but frightening and threatening behavior on the aliens' part as well. On May 27, 1958 Argentinean trucker Remo dell'Armellina saw a ten-foot-tall giant blocking the road. He got out and approached it with an iron bar with which he intended to dislodge the monster; but the phosphorescent light and "stench" it emitted prevented him from getting close enough to the ungainly entity. An Argentinean named Eugenio Douglas had a close encounter with a flying saucer on October 12, 1963. A huge metallic craft landed on the highway before him; three red giants with antennae burned the trucker with a red beam. Throughout the experience, Douglas smelled "a pungent gas" and the family in a nearby house reported "the same strange smell." On October 21, 1963 a group of five flying saucers buzzed the ranch of Antonio de Morena, near Trancas, Argentina. Two of them projected tubular beams at the house, one white, and the other red. The house quickly became "suffocatingly hot" and a stench of sulphur arose in the air.

On July 29, 1959, Mrs Frederick Moreland of Blenheim, New Zealand, had a close encounter in which she saw two silver-suited spacemen inside a saucer. When the saucer left, there was a strange, lingering "hot pepper" smell of ozone in the air. Her hands and face became swollen after the encounter, and it left brown blotches on her face that did not disappear for several years.

On June 29, 1964 near Lavonia, Georgia a businessman named Beauford Parham was driving home when a UFO flew over his car and then stayed in front of him, keeping about five feet from the bumper. Parham, who followed the saucer in a "near trance-like state," reported that it gave off a gaseous vapor and a "strong odor like embalming fluid." Less than two weeks later, in Tallulah Falls, Georgia, nine persons witnessed a flying saucer that also smelled of "embalming fluid" or formaldehyde. The next day they experienced a burning irritation on their faces and arms.

In 1965, teenager Harold Butcher was milking cows on August 19 when a UFO interrupted his work. The craft gave off a greenish glow and a "strange odor," and left a purplish liquid on the ground. On January 7, 1966 a man in Wilmer, Alabama had to stop his car when a saucer landed on the road in front of him. As it departed he noted a "sulphur" or "rotten egg" smell. On April 25, 1966, John Howard Bloom of Upland, PA, was one of a number of boys who witnessed a blue light two feet long and one foot wide descend in the woods. It smelled like burning rubber. Bloom's eyes were irritated for the next day.

On October 2, 1966 a woman called "Mrs. Everett Steward" by ufologist Leonard Stringfield had a close encounter. She was talking on the phone when a "foul odor" made her nauseated and dizzy. Feeling sick, she went upstairs to join her husband in bed, but woke him when she spied a flying saucer outside the window. Now so dizzy that she had to sit down, Mrs. Steward called a neighbor, who verified the sighting; soon, all the dogs in the neighborhood were howling as well.

The strong "chemical" odor had now filled every room in the Steward house. "It was an ill-smelling chemical odor," said Mrs. Steward, "a smell that made me lose my equilibrium." Later in the evening, her younger daughter, Debbie, who had been at the theater with her date, arrived. Debbie, who had also witnessed the UFO, was immediately taken aback by the foul smell and asked, "Mom, what did you spray in the house?"

Neighbor Janet Emery also noted the "strange, 'disagreeable' odor in the air. When asked if she could associate it with a familiar smell, she answered, 'Yes, bad garbage!'"

On October 4, 1966 two boys in Connersville, Indiana, had a close encounter with a flying saucer. Both of them noted its pungent smell: one them merely compared it to sulphur; but the other, who had studied chemistry, stated that it smelled the most like a combination of sulphur and tannic acid.

David Morris had a close brush on March 28, 1967. Driving between Kent and Munroe Falls, Ohio he spotted a saucer in the field beside him and a crowd of small humanoids in the road before him. Despite slamming on his breaks, collision was unavoidable, but the car seemed to pass right through the diminutive aliens. Returning the next day, Morris found the spot with his car's skidmarks, but there were no other traces of the event except for an "odor of hot brass."

On April 5, 1967 Justice of the Peace John Demler of Jonestown, Pennsylvania was driving along when his engine failed and he noted a flying saucer hovering above his car. The craft gave off a "smell of sulphur and camphorated oil."

Stefan Michalak had a famous close encounter on May 20, 1967 near Falcon Lake, Manitoba. Michalak was prospecting for silver when a flying saucer landed near him on the ground. As he approached the saucer, the prospector felt waves of heat coming from it, accompanied by the "smell of sulphur." Michalak looked into an open door and saw a variety of instrument panels and so on. Then the door shut, the craft shifted position, and a gridlike exhaust vent blasted him, leaving serious burns on his chest and abdomen. After the craft departed, he noted "a strong smell of burning electrical circuits mixed with the original smell of sulphur."

A pair of further cases both involve European youngsters. On August 23, 1967 two Swedish youths were besieged by a strange humanoid from a UFO. After the night of horror, the two teenagers combed the area for evidence; they discovered some apples with toothmarks on them—and a weird green slime that "gave off a pungent and offensive 'animal odor.'" On August 29, 1967 a pair of French children, François Depleuch and his sister Anne-Marie, were tending cows when they were approached by four pitch-black, devil-like figures. A bright sphere rose up behind them, and the four aliens flew into the air and then dove into the UFO. A stench of sulphur hung in the air, and was still noticeable to investigators who arrived the same day.

Three physical-trace cases from Argentina provide more examples of malodorous saucers. On September 11, 1967 a family in Villa Constitucion witnessed an enormous saucer for no less than four hours. A sootlike substance and an "unpleasant smell" were noted at the site. On June 19, 1968 Chief of Provincial Police German Rocha and Police Major Niceforo Leon of El Choro sighted a typical ball-of-light. It left the grass burnt and a left a "strange, powerful odor." On December 30, 1972 there occurred another case of very high strangeness. A seventy-three-year-old man, Venturo Maceiras, was buzzed so closely by a UFO that he could see its occupants through the windows. A scent of sulphur remained on the scene after the craft had left. Maceiras suffered various physical aftereffects; his hair started falling out, sores appeared on the back of his neck, and he had difficulty with his tongue and eyes. Most bizarrely, however, the aged man began to grow a third set of teeth.

In October of the same year two schoolteachers and two students in Lakeland, Florida witnessed a hovering saucer and its two occupants. Their eyes and noses were burned by a burning, ammonia-like smell.

An occupant case from the wave of 1973 provides a little relief from this litany of foul odors. The witness stopped his car on the way home from work to investigate a flying saucer. Looking into its windows, he spied a silver-suited alien crawling from the back to the front; when the creature noticed him, it fled. A strange clicking sound was then heard, and smoke began pouring from the saucer, with "a sweet incense-like odor" that dissipated quickly after the UFO took off.

In Auburn, Massachusetts on January 5, 1979 three triangular UFOs flew over the car of Anmarie Emery. When she rounded the corner, they were hovering just above the road in front of her, and the car stopped moving despite having her foot pressed down on the accelerator. She felt waves of heat that irritated her eyes and was surrounded by a "pungent odor" like a "sweet skunk smell."

Later that same year Forestry foreman Bob Taylor had a most frightening close encounter on November 9 in Lothian, Scotland. A saturn-shaped craft landed before him, and two bizarre robots disembarked and approached him. They were round and about the size of a beachball, with six or so "legs" projecting out like sea mines or jacks. They rolled towards him and grabbed hold of his clothing; meanwhile, a "terrible pungent odor" overpowered Taylor and he lost consciousness. When he awoke the saucer was gone and investigators were left with an unresolvable mystery on their hands. According to researcher Jenny Randles:

> The witness was even given several vials of gas to smell to
> try to isolate the smell, with sulfur dioxide coming closest.

A plaque was placed on the site to commemorate this memorable event.

Another Scottish case reported by Jenny Randles was equally threatening. In Edinburgh on February 16, 1980 a man awoke in the middle of the night. He wandered outside, where an oval UFO paralyzed him with a glowing beam that reeked of sulphur. Through telepathy three tall entities gave him the following message: "this was our planet before you and we will not allow you to destroy it. If you try we will send a warning that will shudder the earth. Only the innocent will survive."

In August 1980 a woman in Medway, Kent sighted a bubble-like object from which emerged two humanoids and a cloud of fog that emitted a "sickly odor." On November 19, 1980 near Longmont, Colorado a couple were returning home when their car was buzzed by a flying saucer and the driver and his wife experienced a period of missing time. Under hypnosis, the man recalled the car being lifted up into the saucer on a beam of light. The saucer's interior was pervaded with a "strong odor, that he thought electrical in nature" and a typical abduction scenario ensued.

The *chupa* cases investigated by Jacques Vallee in the early 1980s provide more examples of foul-smelling UFOs. One of the witnesses, he records, made mention of "a 'bad smell' like an electrical odor (ozone?)" that accompanied a hot beam that struck him. Another hunter, called only Manuel by Vallee, was attacked at night by one of the frightful flying boxes. The thing shone beams on him and exuded a "foul odor," which led the hunter to believe that the craft was emitting an "ill-smelling gas":

> In the whole incident, which Manuel calls "the worst thing in his life," it was the smell that affected him the most. It was penetrating, like burning sulphur, and it made his nose run. It did not impair his breathing, but forced him to clear his throat at frequent intervals. He believes that it was the smell rather than the light that made him fall

[each time the beam of light hit him], and that it was the piece of cloth over his nose that saved him.

Another case occurred in Aldershot, Hampshire on August 12, 1983. Fisherman Alfred Burtoo was having tea when two aliens approached him and led him to a waiting saucer. There, he was put under a scanning device; based on its results, he was released as "too old and infirm for our purposes." What purposes those are is perhaps indicated by the odor which Burtoo noticed in the saucer which, he said, reeked of "rotting meat."

On January 21, 1988 the Knowles family had a frightening close encounter on the Nullarbor Plain in Australia. While they were driving along, a flying saucer approached the car. It flew directly above them, descended, and clamped onto the car. As Mr. Knowles accelerated to 120 mph in a vain attempt to escape the object, Mrs. Knowles—not one to be daunted by a mere flying saucer—opened her window and reached up to touch the thing: she reported that it felt like a warm sponge. At this point the family noticed a "foul smell" that Mrs. Knowles said "she thought smelled like decayed bodies." Eventually the saucer left the family in peace, although the roof of their car was damaged and a strange dust was left behind.

One of Budd Hopkins' abduction subjects described being led through a room "with a strong, unpleasant odor—the smell, Carol tells us, 'of burning meat. We all have to come through there, and it smells real bad. *Whew!* I don't like this stink. It's terrible. Hope we're not for dinner!" Another subject, Alice, described "a slight odor of vinegar" which she attributed "to her fear" on board a spacecraft.

Uniquely foul was the odor that confronted Leian Seuul and two others as they drove home after fishing on May 28, 1996. A cigar-shaped craft approached the car: "and we noticed a familiar, yet disgusting odor. An unmistakable odor of fecal matter."

A flying saucer was seen abducting two individuals on October 19, 2000, in Chiu-Chiu, Chile. Witnesses reported that in addition to seeing the spacecraft sucking the two abductees up with a light beam, they smelled a "burning odor."

Nor are flying saucers the only paranormal phenomenon that is accompanied by noxious stenches: Leonard Stringfield tells us that "Research records show again and again, when humanoids are near, so is an odor." As an example, he gives the following case. On July 26, 1974 the Davis family of Mariemont, Ohio had a weird entity encounter. It began when they smelled "something like gas in the house" and went outside to investigate. There, they saw their neighbors milling around and whining about the obnoxious odor. The family decided to go for a drive; on Hollywood Street they sighted a satyr, complete with hairy legs and hooves that clicked on the street as it hopped along. Cincinnati Gas & Electric Company records show twenty calls complaining about the gas-like odor; their investigators found nothing.

Another inexplicable and malodorous entity case comes from South America. On September 8, 1967 a young Argentinean woman named Alicia Rivas Aguilar sighted a strange creature flying outside of her bedroom window. The glowing little man reeked of "melted iron."

An entity case from Woking, Surrey that took place the night of November 12, 1967 provides some rich data. Philip Freeman and his friend Angela Carter were driving home. They stopped on the country road to clear their foggy windshield:

> Dousing the headlights, but leaving the side lights on, with the engine running, Philip got out to leather the windscreen. As he did so, he became aware of a very unpleasant odor. When I asked him to describe the smell, he said it was something like food being cooked, and burning

badly. Then, as an afterthought, he suggested it could even have been like a "stink bomb."

I questioned Miss Carter separately, and she confirmed the details of their movements. She also said that she became aware of the smell as soon as Philip got out of the car, and that it was not in any way like the smell from an overheated car engine (I had not mentioned that possibility).

When Philip got back into the car a frightening sighting of a strange humanoid followed. Investigator Charles Bowen wondered: "could the odor have been akin to the 'bad egg' smell of hydrogen sulfide (H_2S)?"

Bord and Bord, in their study of *Alien Animals*, tell us the following concerning Big Hairy Monsters (Bigfoot, etc.):

> Not all BHMs are smelly, but some are, and the witnesses usually strive to express the revolting nature of the odour: 'It was a stink like a dead person, long dead. It stayed in the air for maybe 10 to 15 minutes afterwards' (Little Eagle, South Dakota, 1977); 'Like strong BO. You could really smell it . . . like somebody who hadn't taken a bath for a year' (Ingalic Creek, Washington, 1977); 'It smells like burning rubbish and the sweat of a hundred high school football teams' (Louisiana, Missouri, 1972).

Nor is this an exhaustive list of smelly BHMs. Another example given by Bord and Bord is the Japanese case of Mrs Reiko Harada, who was confronted in the woods by a hairy monster. Men searching the area later found no trace of the creature except for its odor: "the place smelled like a dead body after it starts decomposing."

Likewise, on August 20, 1995, in Wilkerson, Washington, three friends were confronted by a green-eyed bigfoot that gave off "a horrid smell like rotten meat or really bad B.O."

Indeed, in some cases foul odors, UFOs, and Bigfoot-type creatures all appear in the same company. On October 25, 1973 farmer Stephen Pulaski and several other witnesses saw a red ball-of-light descend onto the farmer's property. Going to investigate in a truck, when they got close enough to see the object, now landed on a nearby hill, two tall ape-men with glowing greenish-yellow eyes came from it towards them. Their arms nearly reached the ground. There was a smell of "burning rubber" that frightened the group; the farmer shot over the creatures' heads, but when that failed to dissuade them he instead fired directly into one of them. At this point, the creatures and their craft exited the area. Investigators from the Westmoreland County UFO Study Group visited the site the next day, and detected a "strong sulfur, or chemical-like odor." The smell was not confused with that of an acetylene-burning ($CaC_2 + 2H_2O \rightarrow Ca(OH)_2 + C_2H_2$) carbide lamp being used at the time.

Another case that involved both a UFO and Bigfoot occurred in Roachdale, Indiana in August 1972. After a flying saucer flew over their house, the Rogers family was blessed with nightly visits from the hairy humanoid. The creature was on the margins of substantiality: it seemed not to touch the ground when it walked, left no tracks, and could sometimes be seen through as if it were translucent. The Rogers family described it as having a "rotten odour," saying it smelled "like dead animals or garbage."

In September, 1989, a man changing a truck tire near Satus Pass, Washington, was confronted by a nine-foot tall sasquatch that exuded a "most god-awful smell . . . like someone with a terrible case of BO." He later had dreams about being abducted in a flying saucer and undergoing the rituals typical of that experience.

Bigfoot is not the only BHM associated with a pungent stench. The "Momo" (Missouri monster) that stalked Missouri and Louisiana in the early 1970s also reeked to high heaven. One witness said that the smell resembled "rotten flesh or stagnant water;" another said that it "smelled *rotten.* Like dead animals or garbage."

We resolutely refuse to consider, however, the so-called "Skunk Ape of the Everglades." Not only is this reported BHM unspeakably disgusting, but the creature's nauseating noisomeness is so pronounced that it seems tailor-made for a study of this type: the example is simply too perfect to be credible. No, no one can accuse us of allowing in just anything. We have our standards of evidence too, and we will not violate them in the name of an unreachable "objectivity" that we find neither desirable nor possible. We will however stop to note that this alleged entity is said to smell of sulphur, decaying flesh, or rotten cabbage (which shares the sulphureous smell of rotten eggs).

In May 1992, a man in South Dade, Florida, had an encounter with a strange humanoid in the woods. As he followed, the strange creature went into a tunnel in a wall of weeds, and he "literally ran into a wall of stench, which was so strong and nauseating, I stopped abruptly and thought I was going to throw up ! The stench was a combination of sulfuric acid and formaldehyde mixed together. The smell was so pungent, it actually burned the inside of my nostrils. The moment I reached this wall of stench, I instantly knew there were others like him, very close to me, and I was outnumbered. I realized the other beings had been waiting for him in a tunnel of weeds, expecting me to follow in behind him." Understandably, the man hightailed it out of there.

A chupacabra believed to be responsible for a wave of cat and dog mutilations confronted a child in Maria Elena, Chile. According to their report: "Upon discussing the animal's characteristics, they all agreed that it had large yellow eyes, dense

black-and-gray hair of a coarse texture, and standing approximately 1.5 meters (4 feet, 10 inches) tall. They also recognized a
penetrating (pungent) odor similar to that of ammonia, which the
animal might employ to paralyze its prey or humans who stumble upon it." In Mexico, on the other hand, the chupacabra is
most often said to leave a sulphureous stench in its wake. In Australia a group in a car was faced with a chupacabra that recked of
"a horrible, sulphur like smell. It stunk like a mixture of blood
and sweat with some sulphur mixed in - absolutely putrid."

Hairy humanoids, satyrs, and chupacabras are not the only
monstrous apparitions accompanied by disgusting smells. A
black dog seen in Dartmoor yawned, releasing "a stream of sulphureous vapour." When a phantom puma haunted the farm of
Edward Blanks in 1962-63, the creature was accompanied by "a
strong smell with an ammonia tang;" but "Zoologists state that a
strong odour, described by some witnesses as 'almost suffocating'
and 'musty like rotting wood,' is not typical of a puma."

* * * * *

What, it will be surely be asked, are we to make of all this?
The data are, undoubtedly, reasonably uniform, and gains in uni-
formity when we take into account the nature of the data. A.F.
Rullán's masterly 2000 article "Odors from UFOs: Deducing
Chemistry and Causation from Available Data" demonstrates that
the perception of odors is poorly understood and that any given
odor may produce multiple descriptors from multiple percipients,
and that likewise the same descriptor may be applied to multiple
odors. There is a good deal of overlap both ways among the odors
most commonly associated with UFOs, and so the data are even
more uniform than they appear at first sight. Surely such a set of
data must conclusively support *some* theory or other. But *which*
theory?—that is the question. The answer is, not (un)surprisingly,

"Why, whichever theory you happen to favor." It is a case of equal opportunity data.

Christian Fundamentalist writers such as John Weldon, Zola Levitt, and Clifford Wilson have squarely faced the data at hand. As Weldon and Levitt put it:

> Extremely foul odors, like sulphur and ozone, are associated with both seance rooms and "badly haunted" locations. They are common as well to UFO landing sites. Contactees also note the odors in connection with extraterrestrial encounters.

Having bravely faced such unpleasant data and many other aspects of the UFO phenomenon repellant to believers and skeptics alike, this pair of Fundies reaches, with inexorable logic, the inescapable conclusion that UFOs and their occupants are demons. As Wilson and Weldon put it in their masterly study *Close Encounters: A* Better *Explanation* (1978): "Monsters, smells, and mini-men are frighteningly real. They come from Hell."

Others follow different biases and reach different conclusions. Fortean ufologist John Keel informs us that:

> Noxious gases play a role in many UFO reports. The objects, and sometimes the entities, are often surrounded by the smell of rotten eggs. Chemists identify this as being the smell of hydrogen sulfide.

And further:

> In earlier times the smell of brimstone (sulfur) was associated with the appearance of these strange airborne phantasms and the demons and gods who supposedly accompanied them. So the modern sightings—and smells—

are nothing new.

He goes on to argue that the chemicals which produce this smell must belong to the native atmosphere of the entities, and concludes:

> If sulfur and hydrogen-sulfide are important components of their atmosphere, where could they come from? Methane gas (good old "swamp gas") seems to be the main gas in the atmosphere of Jupiter. Perhaps the only place in our solar system rich in hydrogen-sulfide is—the center of the earth itself.

These unholy odors thus provide backing for the most "crackpot" of theories, the notion of the Hollow Earth populated with monstrous beings with supernormal powers.

Professor Alvin Lawson's Birth Memories Hypothesis, which explains abduction experiences as distorted memories of the abductee's birth, is also supported by the data at hand. Lawson notes the presence of "unpleasant tastes or odors" as an example of "perinatal" imagery present during such close encounters. Perhaps hospitals should begin airing out their delivery rooms, which apparently must reek of sulphur, ammonia, benzene, ozone, or other noxious gases.

For arch-skeptic and debunker Donald Menzel, the foul smells associated with UFOs unsurprisingly provide evidence for prosaic explanations. According to Professor Menzel, meteors are often accompanied by "a distinct odor"—"the smell of sulphur, onions, or cyanide." No doubt meteors account for many a close encounter. He further notes that luminous mushrooms abound in woods and swamps, and that "Decaying, they may produce an unearthly light and can give off a peculiarly foul odor." Thus, owls—which frequently come into contact with such malodorous mushrooms, or so the good Professor Menzel assures us—may shine with a phosphorescent gleam as they glide about in the night sky, stinking and causing UFO reports as their unsuspecting witnesses mistake them for flying saucers. There is no escaping such logic and rationality. It can only be accounted truly unfortunate that Professor Menzel did not live to see visions of owls accorded status as a common "screen memory" for abduction experiences—one can only guess the result such knowledge would have produced.

Other skeptics seem to disagree with Menzel, the doubters. They believe that the UFO experience is simply founded on cultural beliefs; since—according to them—UFO witnesses are thoroughly familiar with preceding cases, it should thus come as no surprise that such subtle details should be reproduced in case after case. This data thus proves these skeptics' belief that there is no novel phenomenon involved in the UFO experience.

By now it should not be surprising that these foul odors prove the extraterrestrial hypothesis as well. James McCampbell, in his study *Ufology*, notes that the sort of electrical discharge into the atmosphere that an alien craft ought to give off should resemble that from ball lightning; and detailed examination of the smells associated with UFOs supports his contention. He notes that such electrical discharge will create "activated" nitrogen and that:

> it will readily combine with many other elements whereas ordinary nitrogen will not. It combines with hydrogen to form ammonia (NH_3) and with oxygen to from nitric oxide (NO). This oxide is quite stable at high temperatures but below 150°C it reacts with oxygen to form nitrogen dioxide (NO_2). The dioxide can react with still other atmospheric gasses to form nitrobenzene ($C_6H_5NO_2$), an oily substance that is highly poisonous and has a strong odor

like oil of bitter almonds. Also produced by electrical discharges is a highly reactive form of oxygen known as ozone (O_3) whose odor one learns to recognize in association with sparking, electrical apparatus.

He further relates that:

The odor of ball lightning is "usually described as sharp and repugnant, resembling ozone, burning sulphur or nitric oxide." The reference to sulphur is readily understood as that element is a notorious air pollutant arising from automobile exhausts and smoke from industrial plants. Even in rural areas, the sulphur content of air may be quite high due to its production by bacteria in the mud of swamps and lake- and stream-bottoms.

The reader will have noticed that the odors mentioned are among the most common odors associated with UFOs. McCampbell continues to argue that all of these gases may be produced by irradiating the air with a pulsed discharge of microwaves.

Albert Budden makes a similar argument in favor of his own pet theory. Budden believes that UFOs are a phenomenon similar to ball lightning known as "earthlights," which are produced by tectonic stress, or a modern, man-made equivalent created by the electro-magnetic pollution of the environment. These earthlights may then affect the temporal lobe of human beings, causing them to hallucinate close encounters. The resultant full encounter story will then mix various objective and subjective experiences.

After noting a case from the "Welsh Triangle" in which, as a man investigated a strange humming noise in his house, "a peculiar smell reached his nostrils like that of burning rubber, but more sickening," Budden continues:

The smell like burning rubber can be created by, predictably, electrical discharges in the air. Such discharges change the energy states of various atoms, and numerous chemical compounds can be formed. It has been mentioned that nitrogen, making up 70 percent of the air, changes to a metastable state. This energized, or excited, nitrogen is called 'activated' because it readily combines with other atoms, whereas ordinary nitrogen does not: for example, it can combine with hydrogen to form ammonia, and with oxygen to form nitric oxide. It also reacts with other gases in the air to form nitrobenzene, which is an oily substance with a strong smell like bitter almonds. Ozone is also produced by electrical discharges (i.e., lightning). This can be smelt around electrical machinery to some extent and it is commonly reported in association with CE experiences.

Most notably, Budden continues: "These processes could account for the smell alone, but it could also have been produced as a hallucination by field stimulation of the brain." Yet another theory that is perfectly verified by the data at hand.

Remarkable as it may seem, then, scientific method demands that we accept that all of these theories are true. So, the next time you find yourself face to face with a flying saucer and notice the telltale smell of sulphur, ozone, ammonia, or benzene in the air, realize with astonishment that you are simultaneously witnessing a demon from hell, an inhabitant of the hollow earth, an extraterrestrial spacecraft, a meteor, a memory of your own birth trauma, an owl which had just collided with phosphorescent fungi, an earthlight and attendant hallucinations produced in the temporal lobe, and—most remarkable of all—a culturally conditioned expectation created by reading this essay.

The Lurker on the Threshold of Interpretation: Hoax *Necronomicons* and Paratextual Noise

If the *Necronomicon* legend continues to grow, people will end up believing it and accusing me of faking when I point out the true origin of the thing!
—H.P. Lovecraft (cited in Harms and Gonce, 47).

Tho-ag in Zhi-gyu slept seven Khorlo. Zodmanas zhiba. All Nyug bosom. Konch-hog not; Thyan-Kam not; Lha-Chohan not; Tenbrel Chugnyi not; Dharmakaya ceased; Tgenchang not become; Barnang and Ssa in Ngovonyidj; alone Tho-og Yinsin in night of Sun-chan and Yong-grub (Parinishpanna), &tc., &tc.
—*The Book of Dzyan*

There Is No Religion Higher Than Truth.
—Theosophical Society motto

Nothing is true. Everything is permitted.
—Last words of Hassan i Sabbah

The publication of hoax editions of the *Necronomicon*—a fictional work used as a prop in the weird fiction of Howard Phillips Lovecraft and other writers—may at first sight seem a simple matter. On closer examination this may no longer appear to be the case. It is not merely a question of the self-denying hoax—for the hoax versions are all either admitted spoofs, or readily indicate their nature as hoax by internal evidence—it is not merely that a hoax must not present itself as a hoax, in order for it to actually function as a hoax. Instead, the subject opens up onto a field that Gérard Genette has termed the *paratext*: roughly, the manner in which one text influences the interpretation of another text. The paratext may be a *peritext*, which appears alongside the text—examples include the title, author's name, preface, introduction, and so forth; or it may be an *epitext*, which appears in a physical location not directly connected to the text. Genette explains that "More than a boundary or a sealed border, the paratext is, rather, a *threshold*, or—a word Borges used apropos of a preface—a 'vestibule' that offers the world at large the possibility of either stepping inside or turning back" (2). Where the epitext is concerned, moreover, the paratext displays a "potential for indefinite diffusion" (346) as more and more texts become mutually relevant and interconnected. It is evidently this problematic which study of the hoax *Necronomicons* provides data for.

Before attempting to tackle the hoax editions of the *Necronomicon* themselves, it should be informative to observe how the subject is prefigured in Lovecraft's own work. Lovecraft saw the weird tale as itself necessarily similar to a hoax—in a letter to Clark Ashton Smith dated October 17, 1930, he says: "My own rule is that no weird story can truly produce terror unless it is devised with all the care & verisimilitude of an actual hoax. The author must forget all about 'short story technique,' & build up a stark, simple account, full of homely corroborative details, just as if he were actually trying to 'put across' a deception in real life—a deception clever enough to make adults believe it. My own attitude in writing is always that of the hoax-weaver. One part of my mind tries to concoct something realistic & coherent enough to fool the rest of my mind & make me swallow the marvel as the late Camille Flammarion used to swallow the ghost & revenant yarns unloaded on him by fakers & neurotics. For the time being I try to forget formal literature, & simply devise a lie as carefully as a crooked witness prepares a line of testimony with cross-examining lawyers in his mind. . . . This ideal became a conscious one with me about the 'Cthulhu' period . . ." (SL III, 193) In short, the weird tale is devised *as* a hoax but it is not presented as one, which effectively means that it is merely devised to be *like* a hoax. The difference comes from the concrete speech-act that sets the text adrift in the world. A hoax that is presented as a hoax, that presents itself as a hoax, is no longer a hoax, but while an actual hoax is not presented as a hoax, neither is a work of fiction presented as a hoax—but in the latter case this precondition for the hoax prevents it from functioning as a hoax. But then the "care & verisimilitude of an actual *hoax*" may create the suspicion in the reader that the tale is a fictionalized version of real events, and in effect an inverse hoax presenting reality as fiction rather than the other way around.

The possibility that such a fiction may be taken for reality is not all that remote, considering that even a seasoned "skeptic" like James Randi has included a pair of entries in his *Encyclopedia of Claims, Frauds, and Hoaxes of the Occult and Supernatural* which appear to take the historical existence of the *Necronomicon* as a mediaeval grimoire as uncontested fact (110-11, 159). He may, on the other hand, have intended these entries tongue-in-cheek, as the book does contain the occasional witticism, such as an entry on "Martinet Jardinier" which is actually a spoof based on Martin Gardner. If so, these arid attempts at humor are remarkably out of place in something apparently intended as a serious reference work. Likewise, it is interesting to note that the Cthulhu Mythos genre would later incorporate the idea that Lovecraft had disguised fact as fiction as one of its abiding clichés. An interesting example occurs in Robert Shea and Robert Anton Wilson's *Illuminatus!* Trilogy, in which a character inquires of Lovecraft "In 'The Case of Charles Dexter Ward' you quote a formula from Eliphas Levi's *History of Magic*. But you don't quote it in full. Why not?" and Lovecraft responds that "One doesn't have to believe in Santa Claus to recognize that people will exchange presents at Christmas time. One doesn't have to believe in Yog-Sothoth, the Eater of Souls, to realize how people will act who do hold that belief. It is not my intent, in any of my writings, to provide information that will lead even one unbalanced reader to try experiments that will result in the loss of human life" (331-32). In fact, Lovecraft employed even more caution than this passage implies, as he never published *The Case of Charles Dexter Ward* in any form. One can only wonder where his visitor had managed to acquire a copy. Elsewhere in the trilogy a scholar researching Lovecraft and other weird fiction writers explicitly states our theme:

> *The usual hoax: fiction presented as fact. This hoax described here opposite to this: fact presented as fiction* (296; italics in original).

To complete the cycle, all we need is a work of fiction that describes these prior works of fiction, which describe Lovecraft as presenting fact in the guise of fiction, as themselves presenting fact in the guise of fiction—by someone who believes that this is in fact true.

This ambivalent fiction-presented-as-fact vs. fact-presented-as-fiction status is put into play in "The Haunter in the Dark." The tale is told from the viewpoint of an anonymous narrator, who devotes the majority of the story to a paraphrase of the diary of Robert Blake, a young fantaisiste, and most of the rest to paraphrases of supplementary accounts from other witnesses and newspaper stories. The narrator, however, does not accept Blake's word for the events he describes. He begins with the assertion that "Cautious investigators will hesitate to challenge the common belief that Robert Blake was killed by lightning, or by some profound nervous shock derived from an electrical discharge" and that "the entries in his diary are clearly the result of a fantastic imagination aroused by certain local superstitions and by certain old matters he had uncovered" (DH 92). But "his death may have nipped in the bud some stupendous hoax destined to have a literary reflection" (DH 93)—note already the connection between the weird tale and the hoax. The narrator informs us that "the newspapers have given the tangible details from the sceptical angle"—which the narrator clearly accepts as the true account of events—"leaving for others the drawing of the picture as Robert Blake saw it—or thought he saw it—or pretended to see it" (DH 93). He therefore follows the latter course, despite his own rejection of the conclusion implied in it. The tale is thus constructed on ironic grounds: what the narrator presents as a hoax, the reader must assume to instead be true in the fictional world of the text, or the tale will not be an effective weird story. In short, Lovecraft has concocted a hoax (after his usual fashion) to present as fiction instead of an "actual" hoax, but then has the narrator argue that it is in fact a hoax destined for use in the construction of a work of fiction.

"The Haunter of the Dark," however, also opens up the field in another direction. In the story, the protagonist Robert Blake discovers a typical library of forbidden tomes: "He had himself read many of them—a Latin version of the abhorred *Necronomi- con*, the infamous *Cultes des Goules* of Comte d'Erlette, the sinister *Liber Ivonis*, the *Unaussprechlichen Kulten* of von Junzt, and old

Ludvig Prinn's hellish *De Vermis Mysteriis*. But there were others
he had known merely be reputation or not at all—the Pnakotic
Manuscripts, the *Book of Dzyan*, and a crumbling volume in
wholly identifiable characters yet with certain symbols and diagrams shudderingly recognizable to the occult student" (DH 100).
Now, most of these are the fictional inventions of members of the
Lovecraft circle, but the *Book of Dzyan* is another matter.

If Robert Blake had desired to read the *Book of Dzyan* (more
properly, the *Stanzas of Dzyan*), he needed to look no further
than H.P. Blavatsky's massive two-volume opus *The Secret Doctrine*, which contains both a translation of these Stanzas and select translations from the traditional commentaries on them, and
is itself comprised of Blavatsky's own lengthy commentaries.
Blavatsky describes the book: "An Archaic Manuscript—a collection of palm leaves made impermeable to water, fire, and air, by
some specific unknown process—is before the writer's eyes" (I 1)
written in a language known as Senzar, which ultimately derives
from "the inhabitants of lost Atlantis" (I xliii)—an unlikely story
that was not helped by wild tales of secret subterranean galleries
deep in Central Asian regions unvisited by Westerners, containing libraries left over from lost civilizations (some of the actual
libraries apparently described in these traditions have since been
discovered). The term *Dzyan* itself seems to have been invented
by Madame Blavatsky, and derives from a Sanskrit root that refers to meditation and by extension to the enlightenment that results from the practice of meditation. The same root gives the
Japanese term *Zen*.

Contemporary research has shown that Blavatsky did in fact
have contact with teachers of many different religious groups—
Rosicrucian, Sufi, Druze, Hindu, and both Hinayana and Mahayana
Buddhist. The books she refers to and sometimes presents transla-
tions of—the *Chaldean Book of Numbers*, the *Book of the Golden
Precepts*, and the *Book of Dzyan* itself—reveal genuine lore from

Sufi, Mahayana Buddhist, and other traditions, though the precise source texts cannot at present be identified. These traditional teachings have been recognized by such authorities as D.T. Suzuki, the famous exponent of Zen; Lama Kazi Dawa-Samdup, who translated the famous version of the Tibetan Book of the Dead edited by W.Y Evans-Wentz; and the ninth Panchen (or Tashi) Lama, who sponsored an edition of *The Voice of the Silence* in 1927. It seems that she was simultaneously charged with giving these groups' secrets to the world and at the same with time concealing her connection with them. In some cases, this may have been for mundane political reasons: a number of the figures she was involved with in India were actively fighting against British colonial rule and presumably would not wish to draw further attention to themselves from the authorities. The cover story referring to Tibetan Mahatmas—safely located in a country which was then closed to the West—provided the necessary blind to put authorities off the track. (Perhaps it is a significant coincidence in this connection to note that the first appearance of the *Necronomicon* in Lovecraft's fiction, which occurs in "The Hound," refers to its information on "the ghastly soul-symbol of the corpse-eating cult of inaccessible Leng, in Central Asia" (D 174)—where Leng is a fictional doublet of Tibet.)

Aleister Crowley provides yet another view of Blavatsky's work. In a commentary on *The Voice of the Silence*, Crowley—who was acquainted with Hinayana, but not Mahayana, Buddhism, and frequently takes issue with perfectly correct statements about Mahayana teachings—opines of the work that "it is better than 'genuine,' being, like *The Chymical Marriage of Christian Rosencreutz*, the forgery of a great adept" (236). In Crowley's view, then, a hoax may in fact be the genuine article. Crowley also described his own "Liber Trigrammaton" as "An account of the Cosmic process: corresponding to the stanzas of Dzyan in another system."

The most probable source for the *Book of Dzyan* itself has recently been identified. In an article Blavatsky said that the book "is the first volume of the Commentaries upon the seven secret folios of *Kiu-te*, and a Glossary of the public works of the same name" (cited in Pratt). This work, in its own turn, has created even more confusion, but the matter becomes settled when it is realized that *kiu-te* is a rough phonetic rendering for a Tibetan title correctly transliterated as *rGyud-sde*. This title refers to the Kanjur and the Tanjur, a massive set of some 325 volumes, copies of which were held by at least two of Blavatsky's contacts in the region. Indeed, Blavatsky herself refers to these works in the Introduction to *The Secret Doctrine* (xxvii) though she does not there claim them as her source for the *Book of Dzyan*. Nonetheless, the precise text in the Kanjur and Tanjur from which the *Book of Dzyan* derives has not been identified, and most likely has been withdrawn from public circulation.

An entire procession of cults and obscure religious sects has followed Blavatsky's lead, copying their doctrines from her and from one another while simultaneously denying their true sources and instead attributing their second- and third-hand revelations to further contact with the Hidden Masters of the Great White Brotherhood. This process has been called "genealogical dissociation" (Johnson 1995; 158) and has continued through groups more-or-less in the classical Theosophical mold, such as Guy Ballard's I AM or Elizabeth Clare Prophet's Church Universal and Triumphant, and also into more up-to-date models in the form of the flying saucer contactee cults that replace the Hidden Masters in their Himalayan hideaways with Space Brothers winging in their cosmic wisdom from Venus or the Pleiades. J. Gordon Melton has noted that the flying saucer is practically the only new element of the story—many of the older tales had the element of interplanetary travel already, such as Blavatsky's Hidden Masters originating in the distant past when the Lords of Flame traveled to earth from Venus—and that even this element is often absent from current contact accounts, leaving them almost indistinguishable from nineteenth-century accounts (7; cf. also Stupple).

But this is all by way of a digression.

While the construction of a weird tale *like* a hoax does not itself involve the construction of the tale as a hoax, there are two senses in which Lovecraft's fiction can be said to truly indulge in hoaxing. The first involves the use of the various paraphernalia of the Lovecraft Mythos—the invented gods and forbidden tomes shared by the contributors to the Mythos. It is perhaps significant that this technique seems to have first occurred to Lovecraft as the result of an interesting example of paratextual noise: a letter writer to *Weird Tales* named N.J O'Neail enquired whether there wasn't some connection between Lovecraft's Cthulhu and Kathulos, who had appeared in Robert E. Howard's novel *Skull-Face*; he also notices the presence of Cthulhu and Yog-Sothoth in a story by Adolphe de Castro, a Lovecraft revision client (cited by Mariconda, 35). Lovecraft writes to Howard, in a letter dated August 14, 1930, that "[Frank Belknap] Long has alluded to the *Necronomicon* in some things of his—in fact, I think it is rather good fun to have this artificial mythology given an air of verisimilitude by wide citation." (SL III, 166)

He explains the strategy further in a letter to William Anger, dated August 14, 1934: "For the fun of building up a convincing cycle of synthetic folklore, all of our gang frequently allude to the pet daemons of the others—thus Smith uses my Yog-Sothoth, while I use his Tsathoggua. Also, I sometimes insert a devil or two of my own in the tales I revise or ghost-write for professional clients. Thus our black pantheon acquires an extensive publicity & pseudo-authoritativeness it would not otherwise get. We never, however, try to put it across as an actual hoax; but always carefully explain to enquirers that it is 100% fiction. In order to avoid ambiguity in my references to the *Necronomicon* I have drawn up a brief synopsis of its 'history' . . . All this gives it a sort of air of verisimilitude." (SL V, 16) And in another letter, to Margaret Sylvester, dated January 13, 1934, he says: "Regarding the *Necronomicon*—I must confess that this monstrous & abhorred volume is merely a figment of my own imagination! Inventing horrible books is quite a pastime among devotees of the weird, & . . . many of the regular *W.T.* contributors have such things to their credit—or discredit. It rather amuses the different writers to use one another's synthetic demons & imaginary books in their stories—so that Clark Ashton Smith often speaks of my *Necronomicon* while I refer to his *Book of Eibon* .. & so on. This pooling of resources tends to build up quite a pseudo-convincing background of dark mythology, legendry, & bibliography—though of course none of us has the least wish actually to mislead readers" (SL IV, 346; ellipses as in original).

The reader will note Lovecraft's disingenuous disavowal of the intention of misleading readers, even though the strategy he outlines relies on doing precisely that. It should be noted that this strategy involves more than merely disseminating elements of the Mythos into multiple texts: in addition, many are altered in the process. In some cases this transformation reaches absurd heights, as in "The Mound," in which loathsome Cthulhu appears as "Great Tulu, a spirit of universal harmony anciently symbolised as the octopus-headed god who had brought all men down from the stars" (HM 136). This is intended to create the impression, amongst unwary readers, that author A and author B are not borrowing from each other—*or even from the same source*, but are instead borrowing from sources which had in turn borrowed from earlier sources, which in turn were ultimately derived from a single ur-source and which reveal the traces of evolution over time, much as the variant versions of real myths do. In short, the transformation of the elements of the Mythos not only does not detract from the air of verisimilitude through the creation of inconsistencies, but also adds to the air of verisimilitude by operating on another level. Since Lovecraft never codified his conceptions but instead continually added new ones while reconceptualizing the old (so that, for example, supernatural beings become extra-dimensional or ultra-terrestrial creatures more akin to the alien races of science fiction than to traditional supernatural monsters), this strategy provided greater room for his creativity.

It is noteworthy that one example of an earlier writer whose inventions were put to use by Lovecraft comes in Arthur Machen, for Lovecraft says, in the letter to Robert E. Howard cited above, that "[Frank Belknap] Long and I often debate about the real folklore basis of Machen's nightmare witch-cult hints—'Aklo letters,' 'Voorish domes,' 'Dols,' 'Green and Scarlet Ceremonies,' etc., etc." (167). In "The Haunter of the Dark," for example, Blake deciphers a text "in the dark Aklo language used by certain cults of evil antiquity, and known to him in a halting way through previous researches" (DH 106). Howard's Kathulos, which apparently first began the whole business, itself appears in a laundry-list of Mythos names derived from Lovecraft's own work, other members of the Lovecraft circle, Lovecraft revision clients, and precursor writers such as Ambrose Bierce and Robert W. Chambers, names which the narrator had "heard elsewhere in the most hideous of connections," in the form "L'mur-Kathulos," which likely adds a reference to the lost continent Lemuria (DH 223).

The second sense in which Lovecraft can be said to have truly indulged in hoaxing incorporates and intensifies the first. This refers to Lovecraft's revisions, which, as mentioned in the letters cited above, frequently include references to the Mythos elements created by Lovecraft and other members of his circle. It should be noted as well that to refer to these works as "revisions" is often a bit of an exaggeration: Lovecraft frequently discarded anything his revision clients had chanced to produce and simply wrote a new tale, almost purely of his own devising, to be sold as the client's work. The Lovecraft Mythos was not only disseminated through the work of many authors, but Lovecraft himself *was* many of those authors. The later publication of these stories under Lovecraft's own name—which he would be unlikely to approve of, both as a matter of professional courtesy to his revision clients and out of (quite frequently justified) concern over the aesthetic quality of these tales—destroys the paratextual effect intended by the author.

All of which brings us by a rather circuitous route to actual *Necronomicon* hoaxes. We will not deal here with such matters as the various spoof sale ads for whatever edition of the *Necronomicon*, nor with the card catalogue entries that a number of university libraries (Yale, UC Berkeley, etc.) have sported at various times, nor with the entries in assorted bibliographies, etc. etc. etc. Here we will deal only with actual editions of texts that purport to present the *Necronomicon* itself. Unfortunately, no Pierre Menard has arisen to re-write the mad Arab's text in the way that Menard re-produced that of Cid Hamete Benengeli. Instead, we have three main editions (there are others)—the DeCamp-Scithers, the Wilson-Hay-Langford-Turner, and the Simon *Necronomicons*. Of these, the first two are admitted spoofs. Each of the three presents within itself the denial of its own authenticity as the work of the mad Arab, as we shall see below. These hoax *Necronomicons* frequently display an utter lack of verisimilitude where a little research would have provided a much more convincing story: the Hay-Wilson-Langford-Turner *Necronomicon*, for example, spins a cock-and-bull story about Lovecraft's father obtaining the *Necronomicon* through his contacts in Egyptian Masonry and passing the book on to his son before going insane; in fact, while Lovecraft's father was not a Mason, his maternal grandfather, Whipple Phillips, not only belonged to the Masons but had himself founded a Masonic lodge. Clearly it was during little Howard's formative years, when grandfather Whipple took on the role of father to him after driving his real father insane, that the elderly gentleman introduced him to the Spell Book of Hell.

Lovecraft himself considered writing a hoax *Necronomicon.* In a letter to James Blish and William Miller dated May 13, 1936, he says, "If anyone were to try to *write* the *Necronomicon,* it would disappoint all those who have shuddered at cryptic references to it. The most one could do—and I may try that some time—is to 'translate' isolated chapters of the mad Arab's monstrous tome . . . A collected series of such extracts might later be offered as an 'abridged and expurgated *Necronomicon*'—although I am opposed to serious hoaxes, since they really confuse and retard the sincere student of folklore. I feel quite guilty every time I hear of someone's having spent valuable time looking up the *Necronomicon* at public libraries" (*Uncollected Letters,* 37-38). Perhaps it is unfortunate that Lovecraft himself did not close the field to further hoax editions; perhaps it is fortunate that the open-endedness of his enterprise remained unsullied.

Colin Wilson, in his "The *Necronomicon*: The Origin of a Spoof," regarding the Hay-Wilson-Langford-Turner *Necronomicon,* fulminates against Gerald Suster for daring to accuse the producers of the volume of "commercial opportunism," and he himself informs us that the book denies its own authenticity: "In fact, anyone with the slightest knowledge of Latin will instantly recognize it for a fake—it is subtitled 'The book of dead names'—when the word 'necronomicon' actually means the book of dead laws" (88). In fact, anyone with the slightest knowledge of Latin will instantly recognize that the word *necronomicon* is not Latin but Greek, and Wilson's translation is no more accurate than the (inaccurate) translation included as the spoof's subtitle.

He does, however, hit the nail on the head regarding the De-Camp-Scithers volume when he discusses the stories produced for the Wilson-Hay-Turner-Langford spoof before he had become involved in the project (the original idea was to present stories *about* the *Necronomicon*, not a hoax text of the *Necronomicon* itself): "It was awful. The writers all seemed to have the idea that all they had to do was to imitate the basic Lovecraft formula. And this formula, as we all know, is deceptively straightforward. The writer explains that he is cringing in a garret in Arkham—or Innsmouth—committing his awful story to paper by the light of a guttering candle. Six months ago, in the library of Miskatonic University, he came across an ancient manuscript written in mediaeval German. . . . He ignored the advice of the doddery old librarian, and proceeded to practise its magic spells in the hills behind Arkham. Even the violent death of the old librarian failed to deflect him from his foolishness. And now, too late, he realises that he has unleashed the Thing on the inhabitants of Massachusetts. . . . even as he writes, he can hear an ominous creaking on the stairs, as if an oversized elephant is trying to tiptoe on its hind feet. . . . But even as the door cracks open, he continues to write: 'I can hear its hoarse breathing, and smell its loathsome graveyard stench. . . . Aaaargh! . . . .'" (88; ellipses in original).

But this "basic Lovecraft formula" never appears in Lovecraft's work. It is in fact a cliché-plot that derives from the work of Lovecraft's less creative imitators—and those who in turn have imitated the imitators rather than the original, having found in them an example of "how to do it." In short, the imitation has eclipsed the original, becoming not only a model for the method of imitation but for the material to be imitated as well. While the elements described by Wilson do exist in many Lovecraft tales, the formula abstracts them from the novel conceptions at the heart of each tale, all of which contain some unique and innovative subject. Just such a story introduces the DeCamp-Scithers *Necronomicon*, explaining why the publishers have left the text in its original Arabic rather than provide a translation. It seems that the first translator that L. Sprague de Camp had hired disappeared without a trace; the second was heard screaming, whereupon his locked study was found empty; the third disappeared, spatters of his blood remaining on the walls, floor, and ceiling of his room (de Camp 125-126). In short, de Camp has done nothing with "the basic Lovecraft formula" except to apply triplification to it after the manner described by Vladimir Propp in his study of Russian folktales. The Simon *Necronomicon* provides us with a similarly suspicious tale of a mysterious appearing/disappearing manuscript, though it mercifully refrains from splattering its translators on the walls and ceiling.

There is yet another way in which the internal evidence of the texts presented as the *Necronomicon* denies that they are the *Necronomicon* that Lovecraft wrote of: they embody, not the Lovecraft Mythos, but the Derleth Mythos—for the authors themselves had fallen victim to hoaxing, conscious or otherwise.

The Simon *Necronomicon* describes Lovecraft's mythology as follows: "Lovecraft developed a kind of Christian Myth of the struggle between opposing forces of Light and Darkness, between God and Satan, in the *Cthulhu Mythos*. . . . Basically, there are two 'sets' of gods in the mythos: the Elder Gods, about whom not much is revealed, save that they are a stellar Race that occasionally comes to the rescue of man, and which corresponds to the Christian 'Light'; and the *Ancient Ones*, about which much is told, sometimes in great detail, who correspond to 'Darkness'. These latter are the Evil Gods who wish nothing but ill for the Race of Man, and who constantly strive to break into our world through a Gate or Door that leads from the Outside, In" (Simon xiv). In Robert Turner's commentary on the Hay-Wilson-Langford-Turner *Necronomicon* (Turner is the author of the actual text presented therein as an extract from the *Necronomicon*), he likewise accepts the Derleth Mythos of cosmic good guy Elder Gods vs. evil Old

Ones, although he uses this fact to argue that Lovecraft had borrowed his cosmology from the *Book of Dzyan* (!). But this whole scenario never appears in Lovecraft's work: it is the invention of August Derleth.

Derleth was able to insinuate his own concepts, which were frequently at great variance with those of Lovecraft, into common conceptions of Lovecraft's work in two ways. First, he was the publisher of Lovecraft's texts in book form, and provided them with introductions, giving his ideas greater influence on the reader's experience then they would otherwise have (he also spread these interpretations far and wide in magazine articles). Derleth tells us, for example, that "As Lovecraft conceived the deities or forces of his Mythos, there were, initially, the Elder Gods . . . these Elder Gods were benign deities, representing the forces of good, and existed peacefully at or near Betelgeuze in the constellation Orion, very rarely stirring forth to intervene in the unceasing struggle between the powers of evil and the races of Earth. These powers of evil were variously known as the Great Old Ones or the Ancient Ones" (Introduction to *Tales of the Cthulhu Mythos*, viii). This is all very unlike Lovecraft, in whose work the Elder Gods never appear (but perhaps this is merely a limit case showing how "rarely" they stir forth—never), and there is no unified pantheon of Great Old Ones. Indeed, the term "Ancient Ones" only appears in one story, "Through the Gates of the Silver Key," and this says of the protagonist: "He wondered at the vast conceit of those who had babbled of the *malignant* Ancient Ones, as if They could pause from their everlasting dreams to wreak a wrath upon mankind. As well, he thought, might a mammoth pause to visit frantic vengeance on an angleworm" (MM 433-34). Derleth's work, on the other hand, is filled with recaps of his basic cosmic good guys vs. bad guys scenario. Derleth further tells us that "To supplement this remarkable creation [the *Necronomicon*], Lovecraft added . . . the *R'lyeh Text*" (x). In fact,

Lovecraft never referred to the *R'lyeh Text*, as it was invented by August Derleth after Lovecraft's death.

In these paratexts to Lovecraft's work, Derleth provided not only summaries of these ideas, but support for them in the form of an alleged quotation from one of Lovecraft's letters. This, the infamous "black magic" quotation ("All my stories, unconnected as they may be, are based on the fundamental lore or legend that this world was inhabited at one time by another race who, in practicing black magic, lost their foothold and were expelled, yet live on outside ever ready to take possession of this earth again."), supports not only the expulsions and imprisonment of the Old Ones—a key element of Derleth's good vs. evil scenario, but also affirms that Lovecraft's stories are all based on a shared myth. In this case Derleth was the victim of yet another hoax, albeit both hoaxster and victim most likely believed in it in good faith. The actual author of the passage allegedly cited from a Lovecraft letter is one Harold Farnese, who gave the passage in a letter to August Derleth as a direct quotation from his correspondence with Lovecraft. Farnese, it appears, had little grasp of what Lovecraft was doing in his fiction, and simply projected his own concerns with black magic onto Lovecraft, and then presented a paraphrase from memory as a direct quotation—which Derleth then seized upon, as it fortuitously coincided with his own ideas about the Cthulhu Mythos, however much it might contradict Lovecraft's own words (Schultz 1990).

Second, Derleth presented many of his own works as "posthumous collaborations" with Lovecraft. Often based on a single sentence from Lovecraft's commonplace book (in which he kept notes of ideas for future stories), for practical purposes these can be considered the work of Derleth alone. Derleth was relatively forthcoming about the nature of this practice in, for example, his pamphlet *Some Notes on H.P. Lovecraft*, in which he describes the actual Lovecraftian material on which the stories were based, noting that only three of them "contain very much Lovecraft prose"—which itself is a bit of exaggeration, it would be more accurate to say that only three of them "contain any Lovecraft prose" (x)—and he gives the actual prose fragments he worked with. As he says "The rest of the stories grew out of jotting left by Lovecraft, insufficient in most cases to give any sure form to plot" (x)—which may in fact be viewed as a similar exaggeration. Nevertheless, the practice allowed Derleth to insinuate his own work in the minds of readers into the Lovecraft corpus, as the stories appeared under both of their names, implying genuine dual authorship, or even under Lovecraft's name alone. The most insidious example of this appears to be the current editions of *The Lurker at the Threshold* and *The Watchers out of Time* published by Carroll & Graf, which contain *only* Lovecraft's name on the front cover, spine, and title page, and on the back cover give "H.P. Lovecraft with August Derleth." (Thus the Carroll & Graf edition of *The Watchers out of Time* may cause some confusion amongst unwary readers, as it ends with the note that the title story was "Unfinished at the time of August Derleth's death, July 4, 1971".) The old hoaxster, who published his own work under the names of others in order to create singular paratextual effects through cross-comparison, now has another's work published under his own name, displacing the earlier paratextual effects with new ones, erasing and writing over his conceptions like a palimpsest. Taken together with the spurious "black magic" quotation, Lovecraft has been doubly erased and overwritten. The whole of this process has the effect of entirely inverting Lovecraft's open-ended, anti-systematic, ceaselessly productive practice into a celebration of him as the inventor and codifier of a closed Mythos that allows breathing room only in so far as newcomers may add additional creatures and entities to fill the slots left vacant by Lovecraft—such as, for example, Derleth's fire-elemental Cthugha: having arbitrarily decided that Lovecraft's creations corresponded to Aristotelian elementals, not even

Derleth could cram one into the "fire" slot, and so Cthugha's birth was mandated by the necessity of closing the system.

The title of *The Lurker at the Threshold* opens the field up onto yet another chain of association with similar fiction/reality paradoxes. The term appears to derive from the "Dweller on the Threshold" in Edward Bulwer-Lytton's novel *Zanoni: A Rosicrucian Tale*. Bulwer-Lytton belonged to a Rosicrucian group, and embodied a number of their ideas in his fictional works, not only *Zanoni*, but also *A Strange Story* and *The Coming Race* as well. Some of these ideas—such as the "Dweller on the Threshold" and Vril, a sexual energy force through which magick may be performed—were then incorporated into the theories of various later occultists—H.P. Blavatsky among them. The Rosicrucians themselves, it should be noted as well, had their origins in a seventeenth-century hoax and only came into existence as this hoax was imitated in real life (Washington, 36-40; Borges, 70).

While the hoax *Necronomicons* are quite evidently not the fictional work described by Lovecraft, a look at their actual contents may provide some clue as to what they, in fact, are. The Hay-Wilson-Langford-Turner *Necronomicon* contains a rather conventional set of rituals deriving from the common practice of ceremonial magick. As Wilson describes their goal: "the first thing to do was to find someone who really knew something about magic, and persuade him to concoct a book that could have been a perfectly genuine magical manuscript" (89), which they found in the person of Robert Turner. Turner's rituals tend to follow those actually used by ceremonial magickians rather slavishly, with some embellishment in the form of Mythos names and symbols. The Simon *Necronomicon* is likewise utterly conventional in its approach to magick: it mostly consists of ritual récipé texts transcribed from various Mesopotamian sources, Sumerian, Akkadian, Babylonian, and Assyrian, with assorted references to Lovecraftian (and Derlethian) deities tossed in at random. The inclusion of Mythos elements is not at all central to these works, since they could just as well have chosen any other myth-cycle, real or fictional, for the same use: it is yet another form of paratextual noise leading the reader onto a threshold—a threshold to the abyss of interpretation.

We now have the clue that we needed: the Hay-Wilson-Langford-Turner and Simon *Necronomicons* belong to the *grimoire* genre, the spellbook compilations used by mediaeval wizards. It is a commonplace in the grimoire genre to attribute authorship to the most unlikely sources—Moses, Solomon, Pope Honorius, Pope Leo III, Faust, or occasionally to more likely but nonetheless spurious sources—Cornelius Agrippa, Pietro de Abano. The texts furthermore tend to contain all sorts of anachronisms and otherwise improbable material. Viewed in this light, the misattributed authorship and other problems with the hoax *Necronomicons* mark them as authentic entries in their chosen genre.

And so, after a somewhat lengthy journey through a labyrinth of thresholds, thresholds which do not always lead one out or in as might have been expected at first glance, but instead twist and turn as if they comprised a labyrinth constructed according to some non-Euclidean geometry, we can conclude that the hoax *Necronomicons*—at least the Hay-Wilson-Langford-Turner and Simon versions—falsely claim to be the work of the mad Arab Abdul Alhazred, but in so falsely attributing themselves, they signal their genuine inclusion in the grimoire genre. The misattribution is the mark of their genre, and their very falsity is the condition of their genuineness. The hoax *Necronomicons* are every bit as "authentic" as the *Lesser Key of Solomon* or the *Sixth and Seventh Books of Moses*.

Works Cited or Consulted

Blavatsky, H.P. *The Secret Doctrine.* Pasadena: Theosophical University Press, 1977. Facsimile of original edition of 1888. In two volumes.

Borges, Jorge Luis. *Collected Fictions.* New York: Viking, 1998. Translated by Andrew Hurley.

Crowley, Aleister, with H.P. Blavatsky, J.F.C. Fuller, and Charles Stanfield Jones. *Commentaries on the Holy Books and Other Papers.* New York: Samuel Weiser, Inc., 1996. The Equinox Volume Four, Number One.

De Camp, L. Sprague. "Preface to the *Al Azif.*" In *The* Necronomicon: *Selected Stories and Essays Concerning the Blasphemous Tome of the Mad Arab,* ed. Robert M. Price. Oakland: Chaosium, 1996.

Derleth, August. *The Lurker at the Threshold.* First collected 1945. New York: Carroll & Graf, 1988. As by H.P. Lovecraft.

——. *Some Notes on H.P. Lovecraft.* 1959. West Warwick, RI: Necronomicon Press, 1982.

——, ed. 1969. *Tales of the Cthulhu Mythos.* New York: Beagle Books, 1971. Two volumes.

——. *The Watchers out of Time.* First collected 1974. New York: Carroll & Graf, 1991. As by H.P. Lovecraft.

Harms, Daniel, and John Wisdom Gonce, III. *The* Necronomicon *Files: The Truth Behind the Legend.* Mountain View, CA: Night Shade Books, 1998.

Genette, Gérard. *Paratexts: Thresholds of Interpretation.* 1987. Cambridge: Cambridge University Press, 1997. Translated by Jane E. Lewin. Foreword by Richard Macksey. Literature, Culture, Theory: 20.

Hay, George, ed. *The Necronomicon: The Book of Dead Names.* 1978. London: Skoob Books, 1992.

Joshi, S.T. *H.P. Lovecraft: A Life.* West Warwick, RI: Necronomicon Press, 1996.

K. Paul Johnson. *The Masters Revealed: Madame Blavatsky and the Myth of the Great White Lodge.* New York: State University of New York Press, 1994.

——. *Initiates of Theosophical Masters.* New York: State University of New York Press, 1995.

Lovecraft, H.P. *Dagon and Other Macabre Tales.* Sauk City, WI: Arkham House, 1984. Revised edition by S.T. Joshi.

——. *The Dunwich Horror and Others.* Sauk City, WI: Arkham House, 1984. Revised edition by S.T. Joshi.

——. *The Horror in the Museum and Other Revisions.* Sauk City, WI: Arkham House, 1989. Revised edition by S.T. Joshi.

——. *Selected Letters III.* Sauk City, WI: Arkham House, 1971.

——. *Selected Letters IV.* Sauk City, WI: Arkham House, 1976.

——. *Selected Letters V.* Sauk City, WI: Arkham House, 1976.

Mariconda, Steven J. "Toward a Reader-Response Approach to the Lovecraft Mythos." In Mariconda, *On the Emergence of "Cthulhu" & Other Observations.* West Warwick, RI: Necronomicon Press, 1995.

Melton, J. Gordon. "The Contactees: A Survey." In *The Gods Have Landed: New Religions from Other Worlds,* ed. James R. Lewis. New York: State University of New York Press, 1995.

Nethercot, Arthur. *The First Five Lives of Annie Besant.* Chicago: University of Chicago Press, 1960.

Price, Robert M. *H.P. Lovecraft and the Cthulhu Mythos.* Mercer Island, WA: Starmont House, 1990.

Pratt, David. "The Book of Dzyan." World Wide Web document: http://ourworld.compuserve.com/homepages/dp5/dzyan.htm

Propp, Vladimir. *Morphology of the Folktale.* 1928. Austin: University of Texas Press, 1968. Translated by Lawrence Scott. Revised second edition.

Randi, James. *An Encyclopedia of Claims, Frauds, and Hoaxes of the Occult and Supernatural: James Randi's Decidedly Skeptical Definitions of Alternate Realities.* New York: St. Martin's Press, 1995.

Schultz, David. "Notes Toward a History of the Cthulhu Mythos." *Crypt of Cthulhu,* No. 92 (Vol. 15, No. 2).

——. "The Origin of Lovecraft's 'Black Magic' Quote." In *The Horror of it All: Encrusted Gems from the "Crypt of Cthulhu,"* ed. Robert M. Price. Mercer Island, WA: Starmont House, 1990.

Shea, Robert, and Robert Anton Wilson. *The* Illuminatus! *Trilogy.* New York: Dell Publishing Co., 1975.

Simon. *The Necronomicon.* 1977. New York: Avon Books, 1980.

Stupple, David W. "Historical Links between the Occult and Flying Saucers." *Journal of UFO Studies,* New Series, Vol. 5.

Washington, Peter. *Madame Blavatsky's Baboon: A History of the Mystics, Mediums, and Misfits Who Brought Spiritualism to America.* New York: Schocken Books, 1993.

Wilson, Colin. "The *Necronomicon*: The Origin of a Spoof." In *Black Forbidden Things,* ed. Robert M. Price. Mercer Island, WA: Starmont House, 1992.

(Un)Dead Genres:
A Broadsheet

"Le Pique-Tête est sans doute un instrument ingénieux. . . ."
—Le Père Ubu.

Alternative History: But No Alternative to the Present.

Classic Horror: The Infernal Recurrence.

Conte Cruel: Sadistic Writers for Masochistic Readers.

CyberPunk: Heinlein with a Hairdo. Revenge Fantasies of the Computer Nerds.

Dark Fantasy: The Horror that Dare Not Speak its Name.

Disaster Story: Art Imitates Life.

Dystopia: Straight Realism. Future Present.

Erotic Horror: A Cold Shower of Lukewarm Blood. A Sexquisite Uncladaver.

Experimental Horror: DaDawn of the Dead. Flabberghastly Semi-Prose.

Extreme Horror: Mild Boredom. Over the Edge of a Knife.

FanFic: New Territories of Hell. Fandom is a Slice of Life.

Ghost Story: *Cliché*-Haunted Fiction. Flagging a Dead Hearse.

Hard Science Fiction: & Harder Reading—The Literary Techniques of a User's Manual.

High Fantasy: Low Yield. The Middle Ages for the Middle-Aged.

Heroic Fantasy: Hyborian Hyboredom. The Middle Ages for Teen-Agers.

Literary Science Fiction: Up-to-Date Packaging, Pulp Contents.

Magic Realism: Mundane Surrealism by Foreigners.

Military Science Fiction: Marinetti's Revenge—Fascist Futurists without the Art.

The New Gothic: The Old Mainstream.

The New Wave: Nostalgia for the Neo. The Retro-Avant-Garde.

Posthumous Collaboration: Two Writers Who Should Change Places.

Psychological Horror: Mass-Marketed Serial Killers.

Quiet Horror: & Usually—Inaudible.

Science Fantasy: The Sterility of Inbreeding between Hermaphroditic Hybrids.

Semi-Pro-Zines: Penny-a-Word Dreadfuls.

Series Fiction: The Commodification of Unoriginality.

Shared World: The Generosity of the Bankrupt. Chamberpotlatch.

Sociological Science Fiction: The Dystopiate of the Media Masses.

Space Opera: Banality on the Big Scale.

Speculative Fiction: The Surrealization & Suppression of Scientifiction.

SplatterPunk: Fart for Fart's Sake. The Revolution of Everyday Death.

SteamPunk: If Queen Victoria Invented the Debraining- Machine.

Sword-&-Sorcery: Violence for Vegetables. Clonan the Rhubarbarian.

Transrealism: Markings on a Continuous Roll of Toilet Paper.

Urban Fantasy: Back in the Gutter Where it Belongs.

Utopia: Dystopia (*q.v.*) through Rose-Colored Glasses. Hell as Heaven.

Vampyre Fiction: Beaten to a Bloodless Pulp.

The Weird Tale: The *Unheimlich* Manoeuver.

Zoïletic Genre Definition: A Dimwitticism. A Slow-Mot-d'Esprit. A Portmanteautal Disaster.

Printed in the United States
2302